RAVEN–FISH!
THE ASSISTANT

DAVID LISTER

RAVEN-FISH!
THE ASSISTANT

★★Corps du Chien Books ★★

First published in Great Britain in 2010 on Kindle by the Author
Second Edition published in 2016

Corps du Chien Books
36 Mandeville Road
Potters Bar
EN6 5LQ
UK

Main cover image from iStockPhoto.com
© Ershova_Veronika
Cover Design by Cover Creator

ISBN 978-0-9929045-7-9

Raven-Fish!
for
Michael David Lister
Primus inter pares.

The Assistant
for
Zak William Thomas
In amicitia autem nihil fictum.

Raz uncovers a skull.

Foreword

This book contains two stories, one (The Assistant) factual and one (Raven-Fish!) fictional ... apparently. One was written by my father just over a year ago, the other by a mysterious young gentleman in the mid 1930's. The latter chose to write in a combination of Old English and Latin and my father, with the help of his assistant, translated it. As for the two-stories-in-one format, you have only me to blame. I have also chosen to reproduce the esoteric, hand-written sentences just where they appear in the original work, and in my father's translation. Written in pencil, and almost definitely in the young gentleman's own hand, they are important and key to my father's discoveries.

When I read my father's account of certain archaeological discoveries made by him and his assistant, and then read the translated story, I noticed strong co-incidences that link the two in a most curious way. I have therefore arranged the chapters alternately – one of my father's chapters, followed by one from the translation and so on throughout the book in order to juxtapose the curious links. The books thus enmeshed, I have headed my father's chapters with standard numerals, and the translation with Roman ones. The format is not strictly adhered to, but almost so.

As to my reason for publishing, I am not at all sure. Of course, I would like to counter the tittle-tattle that has percolated throughout the world of the popular press, and I think his account goes some way to fulfilling that aim. As for the rumours that circulate in archaeological circles? Well, if a person opens up a new area of research so fundamental that it represents a shift in the paradigm of the discipline, it is bound to take some time for the dust to settle. Now Father has gone, I feel the weight of responsibility is mine to bear.

That aside, I found both stories interesting in their own right. They're hardly prize-winning material, but then Father was an archaeologist, not a writer. Nevertheless, I enjoyed them and it is reasonable to assume that others might too. After much consideration I have taken the advice of the first Duke of Wellington. I have published. It remains to be seen whether or not I shall be damned.

Rachel K.

.

I

~ The Year 793 ~
In which the fate of the Fish is discussed.

The cry of a man in abject agony assailed his ears. Dunstan Chase forced himself to grin. This dark chamber was no place to show weakness in front of his thegns. The two thegns flanked him, Brand Buckley with hand on sword showing enough fear for all three of them, and Frelaf Helton wearing an expression that Dunstan found, much to his own increased discomfort, manically elated.

The chamber, which was little more than part of a complex of caves accessible through a longhouse, had lost none of its otherworldliness and if anything, smelt far worse than on his last visit two years previously. Dunstan ground his teeth but maintained a grin. 'Godwin! That maggot-riddled barrel of rancid tallow.' Dunstan spoke under his breath, but Frelaf had the ears of an owl.

'Hold, my lord,' he hissed. 'Lest you cause us all to have our heads struck off.'

Dunstan seemed not to hear. 'That I should take my orders from a thegn,' he said, the grin finally replaced by a twisted look of fury.

'King's thegn, my lord. In theory, as an ealdorman you outrank him, but only in theory. Godwin is no common breed of the herd. None is closer to the king's ear.'

The cry of a poor tortured soul came again and Dunstan stopped in his tracks. Up ahead the cave narrowed and then opened into a second chamber. There the prisoners were kept, the place where they were tormented or left to rot. He felt no pride that he had brought prisoners to this place for Godwin to use as he saw fit. He remembered the two boys ...

Before the full revulsion of recalling his part in the grisly murder of innocents overwhelmed him, a bare-chested ceorl came from the next chamber and drew up

11

with a start. His muscular torso was slick with sweat and blood, the sweat his own, the blood not. Quickly recovering his composure he gave a slight bow of the head; a little too slight, thought Dunstan. Such impudence shrieked for just reward.

'Ealdorman Chase, is it?' the ceorl asked without due deference. 'My lord Godwin is impatient for your attendance.'

Ealdorman Dunstan Chase strode towards the next chamber, his thegns close at heel. Dunstan paused to land a firm back-hander across the ceorl's jaw.

The surly confidence fled from his eyes and he whimpered. He quickly recovered and scowled. 'Lord Godwin will –'

Dunstan struck him again, this time with balled fist. With loosened teeth and a split lip the ceorl landed heavily against the stone wall and before he could right himself Dunstan took him by the neck and slammed him once, twice into the rock. 'Your Lord Godwin will receive his full due from me. And be you his man or no, you will also receive what you deserve if your manners are lacking.'

Dunstan turned from the chastised man as of no further consequence. For his troubles, Frelaf gave him another slap in passing, and Brand delivered up his best but rather unconvincing look of contempt. The ceorl fell in step several yards behind, proper respect for his betters fully restored.

By his tonsured scalp, the prisoner was easily placed as a holy brother, but by no other mark or peculiarity of dress. He wore only his linen-clothes, and these were shredded and stained with blood. In his agonies he had soiled himself, and the stench was almost as unbearable as the sight of his broken body and the gobbets of unidentifiable flesh in which he knelt. His eyeballs had been burst with a spike and his face beaten until it was a bruised and bloody thing with little resemblance to any creature of this earth. The poor man was in that state just before death, when fully resigned to it and without hope of reprieve, the body begins to close down.

Dunstan stared and was caught between revulsion, pity and mounting anger. Anger won sway when he noticed the ceorl's cruel smile. The ceorl stood between him and the prisoner, who lay crumpled and chained to the irregular cave floor.

Dunstan drew his sword and strode towards the ceorl who yelped like a scolded pup and scurried out through the further tunnel. Dunstan knew it led to Godwin's chamber, and he became aware of the discomfort of his two thegns.

Dunstan held the hilt of his sword in both hands and with a quick downward thrust to the monk's neck close to the skull, he put the unfortunate man past all further torments, unless God had other's waiting for him.

'May the Lord have mercy upon his soul. And upon me,' Dunstan whispered. He fingered the silver cross at his neck.

'He would surely have had no mercy if you left His servant to suffer,' Frelaf said.

'Let us hope that Godwin is equally merciful,' Brand added.

The ceorl's excited jabbering came indistinctly from the last chamber.

'Busy telling tales,' Frelaf said.

Dunstan beckoned his retainers into a close huddle and spoke very low. 'Brand. Frelaf. I have made a decision and you must decide where you stand, for if Godwin has called me here to bring about my ruin, I shall not submit. If I die with that sluggard's guts wound round my blade, I shall die a happy man.'

'And the ceorl is mine,' Frelaf said gleefully.

Brand Buckley looked from Dunstan to Frelaf while his mind groped for a suitable answer.

'Have no fear, loyal Brand. I give you leave to walk back to the sunlight. You will lose neither my love nor your own honour.'

Brand smiled uncertainly. 'We ... we must all die sooner or later, so let's to it and die with our teeth at the enemy's throat.' Surprised, and rather pleased with his own brave words, Brand's smile became firm and grim.

13

Two of Godwin's thegns came from the chamber. Dunstan, Brand and Frelaf were dressed for the road with woollen tunics, close-woven hose and warm cloaks. And of course, no man would travel unarmed, but Godwin's thegns were equipped as if for war. Each wore a burnished byrnie of iron rings with interwoven yellow metal wire polished to look like gold. They wore identical helmets of polished iron with inlaid patterns of bronze and their tunics, of the best cloth, were uniform in colour and design, and each bore the same woven pattern. In any other setting either one of these men would be taken for an atheling. Here, they were no more than Godwin's lackeys.

One of them bowed low and passed on the compliments of his lord. Godwin would receive Dunstan in his chamber, but the thegns must wait outside.

Reluctant to leave his men behind but finding himself with little choice, Dunstan ducked his head to avoid the low natural ceiling and proceeded with one glittering thegn to the fore and the other following up behind. If ever he had been more vulnerable, he could not recall the time.

Dunstan Chase was of average height, but well set up, broad shouldered and without the slightest hint of a paunch. He wore his brown beard trimmed short and his hair to collar length. He considered himself well-proportioned for a fighting man. Frelaf was tall and wiry, surprisingly strong for one so light of limb, but the attributes of his body carried over to his features giving him a weasel-like face sprouting a straggly beard. Dunstan thought Brand too heavy in the gut, but even he was a sylphlike being when compared to the loathsome Godwin.

The king's thegn was taller than Dunstan, but also much bulkier. He usually strutted about either fully armed or in the most fine and colourful clothes, but this time he was dressed in a monk's habit and hooded cowl. That he had not taken holy orders was evident only from the axe he wore at his belt and a full head of hair.

King's thegn or not, Ealdorman Dunstan Chase was not about to show any deference. 'A gift from our unfortunate

14

brother?' Dunstan asked and waved a hand which encompassed Godwin's attire.

Godwin's round face was close-shaved, which exposed his cleft chin and full lips. It was most common for him to smile throughout any audience, but this time he was not smiling.

'The brother whom you have just slain? Shame on you Ealdorman to take such liberties in my house.'

'Shame on *me*? Godwin, if you had less of the king's ear I would happily skewer you as a heretic. To ill-use such as that poor brother, you are truly as odious as you appear.' And then Dunstan remembered the boys, who were more innocent still.

'It is no heresy to prosecute enemies of the king, and that wayward monk was Ethelred's enemy.' Godwin stoked his bald chin and smirked. 'Are you an enemy of the king, Dunstan Chase?'

A cold shiver passed through Dunstan. 'Indeed, I am his most loyal servant, as I have shown time and again. Now, I am here not to wait upon you, but to receive the king's command. So out with it, and I may be about the king's business.'

'I have other business to attend to, concerning your handling of my free man here.' Godwin laid a hand upon the ceorl's shoulder. 'Is it right for one born to nobility to chastise a man who has risen to his position by nothing but hard work and good service?'

'The man forgot his manners. I reminded him.'

'Perhaps the high and mighty should be reminded of their places from time to time,' Godwin said, and then turning to the ceorl, 'Go take the high and mighty ealdorman's sword.'

The ceorl needed no second telling and he closed the gap between himself and Dunstan and reached out for the hilt.

Dunstan slapped the man's hand away. 'You'll not disarm me, Godwin.'

Godwin's eyes narrowed and his face hardened. 'The king commands it!' he bellowed, the sound echoing back

15

from the next chamber. The house-thegns half-drew their own swords and came a step closer.

Dunstan's resolve to die fighting melted away. Such odds made the notion ridiculous. He drew his sword slowly and handed it to the ceorl who received it with unconcealed contempt.

'Now, my good man. You know what must be done?'

'I do, my lord. Chase must die, but is it your command that I should run him through, or rather must I strike off his head?'

Godwin feigned a look of shock and surprise. 'No, no, no, no! Whatever are you thinking? You are not to attack a man whom you should have greeted with humble compliments. Indeed not! What I had in mind is that you should fall upon the sword, as was once the fashion with patricians of Rome. A noble death for a lowly fellow.'

The ceorl went white with fear and his jaw flapped soundlessly.

'Come, come! We haven't all day to wait upon your compliance,' Godwin said as if he were hurrying a young novice to matins. 'Do it ... now!'

The ceorl looked from Godwin and then to Dunstan with pleading eyes.

'I tire of this,' Godwin said impatiently. 'You have the space of twenty heartbeats to end yourself in whatever fashion you find most acceptable, otherwise you will suffer an identical fate to our late and dearly missed brother-in-Christ.'

'No! Please,' the ceorl managed.

With a subtle signal from Godwin, his thegns advanced upon the ceorl, and knowing all too well the agonies he could expect, he squealed and then fell on the sword. It was a clumsy show and his screams filled the cavern, for the blade had failed to pierce his heart and only made a butchered mess of his intestines. Dunstan drew a small seax and for the second time in the half-hour sent a man to his maker.

He wiped the blades of seax and sword on the dead man's hose and sheathed them, though he would as soon have plunged either into Godwin's bulk. 'Sometimes it seems to me I've seen more bloodshed in this place than on the field of battle.'

'And yet, by my actions I have curtailed the need for many battles and saved the lives of hundreds,' Godwin said.

'If that's how you choose to see it.'

'It is, and now to the reason for your presence.' Godwin bade Dunstan sit at the oaken table that occupied the centre of the small cavern. The cave was lit by oil lamps in niches about the wall and a ring of candles set in an iron band and suspended from a chain directly above the table.

Dunstan made himself as comfortable as possible on a stool while Godwin sat on a throne of a wooden chair with fleeces for cushions.

'It seems, dear Dunstan, that there is another little elf to put out of harm's way.'

Another boy? Dunstan hoped not. 'The late King Elfwald has a third surviving son?'

'He has, and as you were so efficient in ending the last two ...'

'It was you who slew Elf and Elfwine. Don't put their blood on my hands, Godwin.'

Godwin spread his palms sideways and assumed a look of innocence. 'And you brought them to me because you thought I intended to feast them upon ale and pies?'

If another man in the wide world was more the devil on earth than Godwin, Dunstan hoped they would never meet. 'Listen! I know full well that in time lads grow broad shoulders fit to match the measure of royal mantles, but there are means, and there are means.'

Godwin nodded sagely as if weighing Dunstan's words. Dunstan knew better than to be taken in.

'I should have banished them? A lad can travel the world over and return, perhaps with a fyrd under his banner. Imprison him then? But no, prisoners by their mere presence call out for daring rescue and ruinous restoration.'

Dunstan sighed. 'You could have dealt them a merciful death, and yet you humiliated them and drew out their agonies. Tell me Godwin, was it King Ethelred's command that they be tortured to death?'

'The King cares nothing for detail. It was by my command and occasionally by my hand that the elf boys suffered. We all hope for a swift death, but a slow and painful one sends out such a powerful message, don't you think?'

'There are those who deserve to die in agony,' Dunstan said while thinking that one such was close at hand. 'Those innocent lads did not.'

'Not so innocent! They were bloodied in battle. They'd both had women. Each of them was more man than lad and warming right quickly to the pleasures and intrigues of court. And then there is the little matter of their First Born status.'

'They were just fifteen and seventeen years old, and innocent of any treachery. As to being First Born, it is but a childish nonsense.'

'Perhaps, but they *were* the sons of our king's enemy. Let us be content that they suffered for the sins of their father, no matter that they had yet to achieve a man's full bulk or make much use of the shaving blade. Why so squeamish, Dunstan?'

'Level no womanly ways at me, Godwin. I would gladly have slain them myself, but I find no pleasure, neither any necessity in torture.'

'Then it will please you to learn I want only the head of Elf and Elfwine's little brother. You are free to kill him as swiftly and as painlessly as you may, but you *will* bring me his head.'

Dunstan nodded. 'And where might I find his head?'

'Why, still upon his shoulders, good fellow!' Godwin laughed at his own jest until he noticed that Dunstan found no amusement in his wit. His laughter trailed off and he told Dunstan that the lad whose life was to be taken was called Elfgar. He gave him a none-too-recent description and told him of his last known whereabouts, although that was several years ago. Then he acquainted Dunstan with the last curious detail.

'Now Dunstan, this may be to your advantage. The last of the little elf lads has no reason to fear the knife in the dark. You see, he is ignorant of the fact that he is an atheling. He has no idea at all that he is a son of Elfwald the pious, Elfwald the good, Elfwald the once and never to be again king.

'Then why …?'

'Why kill him? *He* may not know who he is, but others may come to know, as I have, and there are those who would seek to make use of him against the interests of King Ethelred. So, you have my command, which is by way of saying, you have the command of Ethelred, King of Northumbria.'

Once Godwin was certain that Ealdorman Dunstan Chase had committed his instructions to memory, he made it known that failure to kill the boy and make a trophy of his head would make it very likely that Dunstan's own head would be forfeit.

Then the audience was over. Dunstan found himself being ushered back towards the cave mouth with his thegns and thence to the longhouse which acted as an antechamber to the natural caverns.

'I see you admire the arms of my thegns,' Godwin said.

Dunstan was keen to be gone, and did not feel inclined to inform Godwin that far from admiring their garish equipment, he thought it unfit for battle and rather unmanly.

'A gift from King Charles of the Franks,' Godwin boasted with a wide grin. 'A *personal* gift you understand, and not by way of our king.'

'Godwin, you never cease to impress me. You are plainly the equal of kings and emperors, entirely wasted in your present position.'

Godwin pretended to preen at the compliment, although Dunstan's sarcasm was far from lost on him. Godwin always knew that one day Dunstan would go too far, and now he had. He smiled at his cleverness, for he had already sent out a party of his own men to track down the atheling boy, and if they caught him first, he would have the

19

excuse he needed to destroy Chase. As usual, everything was proceeding quite according to plan.

Wulfhere, son of Penda, became king of Mercia upon the death of his brother, Peada, who was killed.

Once out of the longhouse Dunstan and his thegns mounted sturdy, shaggy-legged ponies and rode out of Godwin's burgh. The ealdorman remained silent in his saddle until the wooden walls of the fortified town were out of sight, and then Frelaf could control his curiosity no more.

'If it pleases your lordship, might we know our commands?'

Dunstan held his reply until Frelaf became worried that he had spoken out of turn.

'It's another young atheling,' Dunstan said at length. 'Just when I should be taking note of the Mercian king and looking to our coastal defences, I am commanded to seek out and slay another little boy.'

'What coastal defences?' Brand asked.

'Precisely! We have none, and it is King Offa's belief that the Northmen spoil for adventure. Spies tell us their lands are full and they seek new ones.'

Frelaf chuckled. 'Do you mean those long-bearded heathen fellows who trade in trinkets and furs? Do they really believe they are the equal of the king's fyrd? Or yours for that matter?'

'A thief can come in the night if the door is left unbarred and unguarded. Such is Northumbria's coast; little but an open door with not so much as a brush to put across the frame. But the thief must come and do as he will, for we are commissioned to hunt for the blood of a royal whelp.'

'A canker on the Northmen,' Brand said. 'Tell us of the boy. Where must we go, and is he as devoid of defences as our rugged coast?'

Brand's answer had to wait until the ponies had negotiated a steep bank and a shallow stream. They clambered up the opposite bank and joined a woodland path. Sunlight slanted through the broadleaved trees. It was still warm, but the chill of evening would soon be upon them.

Before Dunstan could make answer, they came upon a brace of ceorls who were about despoiling a dead man's marker. Before Dunstan could challenge them, he noticed the inscription.

'Elf-Latin,' Brand spat as if the sight of it has soured his spittle, and then crossed himself with the sign of Christ.

'Not so,' Dunstan said. 'The letters are liken to elf-Latin but see, it is the common tongue.'

The ceorls had broken the stone into three and had loaded two parts upon a cart, but the cart was not sturdy enough to take all three parts, and in any case, the base was still buried in the ground and showed no sign of yielding. Dunstan challenged them. Their reply did not surprise him.

'Our lord Godwin will not suffer such stones to be upon his King's lands, and so we are charged with their removal.'

'Very good,' Dunstan said. 'Be about your business.' He turned his pony to continue but not before he had read the inscription. So this is where the murdered boys had been put to earth. Was Godwin so cruel that he denied them even their resting place? Dunstan needed no answer and kicked his mount's flank.

Dunstan told his men what he knew of their new quarry; his name, his lineage and that the boy was ignorant of his royal blood.

'And how should we find him, my lord,' Frelaf asked.

'Well, as to his looks, he has red hair, straight legs and is likely of uncommon elevation. When he was thirteen it is said he had the face of an angel, but like as not the passing years have left him pock-marked and hunger-pinched. As to his whereabouts, when he was young he was taken under the tutelage of Alcuin of York in the court of King Charles. But now he is seventeen and probably a bawdy-house tap-boy in a burgh somewhere between the Forth and the Humber, selling stale beer and giving his arse freely when all the whores are all taken. In short, nothing is known about him these last four years except he came back to Northumbria and that he yet lives and gives our noble lord and king many sleepless nights.'

Brand's pony stumbled and he let out a squeal. Regaining his seat, he reined in close to Dunstan. 'If he was taught by Alcuin, it is possible he is now a holy brother.'

'Very good, Brand. Your thoughts and mine are one, and so tomorrow we begin a long ride to York, a veritable warren of little brothers.'

'Not just an atheling, but also a holy brother,' Frelaf said. 'This commission is rapidly losing its appeal.'

'We'll do as we are commanded, and then have Higbald or another bishop shrive us. We have our duty, and it was never written that duty must be pleasurable.'

Brand looked very unhappy. 'Can we be compelled to murder by such as the likes of Godwin, or even the king himself?'

Dunstan grinned mirthlessly. 'When it's do murder or be the victim of it, the niceties of law become a little blurred.'

Brand let out a long sigh. 'So we set out to find and slay a lad by nothing more than the colour of his hair and the chance that he may be a monk.'

'Not quite,' Dunstan said. 'There is something about him that time cannot erase. Under his throat about the place where the collar bone meets above the breast, he has a small needled wode-mark like unto the symbol of our Lord Jesus Christ.'

'A cross pricked under the skin?' Frelaf said. 'I think that most apt for a brother, if he is to be marked at all.'

'Not the cross,' Dunstan said. 'I talk of the earlier symbol.'

'The fish?' asked Brand.

'Yes Brand. The young atheling is marked with the fish sign of Christ's earliest followers, and by that mark we shall know him.'

2

~ 2008 ~
Bone and Stone

This was not going to be my Sutton Hoo. I looked into the compacted soil that filled the skull's eye sockets, and they looked back at me above the grinning, mocking jaws. Where was my Arthur? This wasn't him; here did not lie the once and future king. For the sake of my assistant, I tried to show some enthusiasm.

The earth absorbed the dead meat from these bones and then spewed them out again a thousand years later. The skeleton was still more than half buried: the ribs were emerging and the legs were spread like something from the Halloween edition of a top shelf magazine's centrefold; I was tempted to cover the pelvis to preserve our subject's long gone modesty. The pelvis was narrow so I was fairly certain this scaffolding once shored up the body of a man. We couldn't be sure until the sacrum was fully exposed because the skull showed a brow line halfway between male and female, but my assistant obviously shared my assumption.

'Looks like this chap was just thrown in the hole lay as he may,' Raz said.

He had my grandfather's turn of phrase, which I found odd coming from a man in his early twenties. But he was right: the skeleton we plied over that chilly October afternoon had been interred without ceremony. Whether by nature covering a peasant who starved and died alone, unseen and unmissed in the forest, or by murderous hands guided by a will to be rid of incriminating evidence, or any of a number of other possibilities, it was my job to find out.

'They say you're getting old when policemen start looking young,' I said. Raz cocked an ear, no doubt wondering what gemstone of philosophy his master was about to impart. 'But to archaeologists such as us, I think the passing of years might be measured by some sort of inverse ratio to how long the police keep a potential crime scene active.'

Not long ago a find like this would have been buzzing with plod for days. Our bony friend excited the local CID for a little over an hour. The fact that the skeleton was revealed in the hollow left by a falling oak, itself at least four hundred years old, convinced them that if any crime was involved in this death, the perpetrators were centuries beyond the reach of law's long arm. There was also the matter of the artefact, a thimble-sized vessel made of yellow metal; dare I hope to say 'gold'?

The perfect murder, I thought. *When you bury the corpse, throw in an ancient-looking trinket, a bronze buckle or flint arrowhead and the police won't give it a second look.*

'Perhaps I'll concede I'm in the clutches of old age when a scene such as this no longer excites me,' Raz said after a little thought.

Oh Raz, very good! Bravo, you little bastard. Raz's serious face broke into a momentary wide grin. He'd got me again, good and proper. Having kindled a smile that never quite reached my lips, Raz's bright countenance faded to seriousness once again. The sun had peeped out from the clouds for a brief moment, and now he had returned to his usual, rather too serious and perhaps a little troubled self.

Raz moved in close to get a view from another angle. I looked from the soil encrusted skull to the young living face. My eyes traced the line that marked Raz's eye socket and mentally, I stripped the skin from his skull and compare the two, wondering if his bones would ever be the centre of attention for some archaeologist of the future. It was a chilling thought and I tried to put it aside. I experienced a brief but strong emotion of loss: for the man in the grave, for Raz and for me; so little time we are allowed to wear our flesh; how little the remaining armature tells of our lives.

Raz brushed off a little more soil from the jaw and paid close attention to our friend's teeth. It is almost a habit with him and I'd often wondered if he held a secret wish to be a dentist. 'What do you make of that, Professor?' he said pointing with his bodkin-like stick. It was his little trade mark, that stick; he used it as a pointer on power-point presentations when briefing field technicians while the rest of us had moved on to laser-pointers. It reminded me of the archetypical magic wand.

Raz and his wand, me and my trusty old WHS trowel: I'd had it since student days and it was once saved from theft because I had engraved it with the rune for the letter K.

As he pointed, the wand appeared to conjure a little wad of black material with a silvery-grey sheen into the back of one of the skull's lower molars. At first I thought it was an indication of decay, but no, it was most definitely a man-made addition to the tooth.

'Bugger me cross-eyed!' I said as that almost forgotten twinge of excitement thrilled through me. I apologise, but I am not known for eloquent and well thought out epithets, especially when faced with an anachronism. 'He's got a filling!' I got in closer and shone my torch at the infernal enamel encased imposter. I could almost hear my next paper forming itself in my head: *Seriation of Amalgam & Dental Techniques – Ancient Civilisations to Present Day.*

'That's very remiss of the constabulary,' Raz said. 'Shall I recall them to finish the job properly?'

Has this boy no faith in his skills? I wondered. 'It's *not* a contemporary body, Raz. Didn't you prove that to me with your observations of the stratigraphy?'

'Well, nothing's certain until the C 14 tests come back.'

'Bugger all that radiocarbon bollocks,' I said. A character flaw, I know, but back then I was still trying to affect the down to earth man of the world façade by the use of salty language. I'd been doing it for so long that it came naturally. I was the Gordon Ramsey of archaeology. 'It's a wonderful tool for validation, but it doesn't replace the need good, basic, old-fashioned field craft. I concur with your original assessment. The last time this fellow saw the light of day the Romans were still here … or at the latest, Alfred was getting ready to re-sit his GCSE in cookery.'

My attempt at humour failed on Raz as he leaned in close to the jaw, like an archaeological dentition. 'Not a murder scene then, despite the filling?'

I was sure he peered over in time to catch my grin. He'd seen it before, but not very often. 'Aha! The professor has that look on his face. Is he intrigued?'

'He is,' I said of myself. 'And he doesn't think he has enough time to finish the preliminaries before the daylight fails.'

Raz really was a cracking assistant. Many a time he knew what I wanted before I articulated the need.

'I'll head off and secure the services of a local bed and breakfast.'

'Good lad! As local as may be had.'

'And shall I call Mrs Professor and tell her hubby won't be home tonight?'

'Strangely enough, this deep corner of the forest is good for a signal, so leave me to speak to Jenny,' I said, flipping open my mobile.

I heard Raz slam the Land Rover door as I dialled home, the sound deadened by the intervening thirty metres of woodland. The engine turning over coincided with Jenny answering the phone.

Raz needed to get out more and leave the fusty archives for a while. Let the reference books and Society papers gather a little 21st century dust while he sank a few jars at the club with his mates. Instead of getting down and dirty with old bones, he should be encouraging young ladies to get down and dirty with his. It was all too late for me, but I'd be damned if I allowed another young life to be sucked into dusty graves and old potsherds.

I saw my younger self in Raz and all those wasted opportunities were still before him. There was still a chance. But as had I thirty-odd years ago, Raz was settling into a persona far too old to suit him.

I'd been eighteen and nervously awaiting my first term at university when I ambled along Broad Street. Blackwell's had just relieved me of several pounds in exchange for my copy of Clark Hall and Meritt's *Anglo-Saxon Dictionary*, fourth edition – and one or two other tomes I would need – and the Bodleian soaked up the sun in circular majesty on the opposite side of the road. What a magnificent edifice. Better still, what treasures within. I wanted to feel a part of it all, so I took my new dictionary from its paper bag and held it in the crook of my arm, title turned outwards for the world – well, Oxford at any rate – to see and it was at that very point that I began to act the absent-minded professor. I assumed an air of bemused awe, quite false you understand, and bumbled around the colleges hoping I'd be mistaken for a don.

I wore a Norfolk shooting jacket that I'd purchased mail order from an ad in *Horse and Hounds*, a remnant from my days as the young country gentleman – fishin' and shootin' doncha know – complete with scuffed shoulder pad from continual raising of my over-and-under 12-bore. Took me an age to get that scuff mark just right, but with the head of a broom; that jacket was never within half a mile of a shotgun.

Now, I shrink with embarrassment to recall it all. Efforts of a lonely boy trying to fit in – somewhere.

I soaked up the atmosphere of Oxford while carrying a book published by the Cambridge University Press, and yet I was destined for neither of these great centres of academia. I was to complete my studies in a university far to the north, but unfortunately, not quite so far as Edinburgh which had been my first choice.

I dropped the absent-minded act pretty quickly. There were too many of the real deal at university, and I found it hard enough to cope at all without trying to maintain an image. While enjoying the atmosphere in the Mens Bar (that's 'Mens' as in Latin for 'thought' and does not indicate that sexism was alive and well in my Alma Mata) I began to find a skin that felt quite snug.

Perhaps I'm still not past squeezing myself into a convenient skin. When I came to the world of popular TV archaeology, the absent-minded professor spot was already taken. So too was the eccentric with the bush hat and lamb-chop whiskers, and the well-presented hot-stud slot was also

27

filled, not that I could have taken that place even had it been vacant for a hundred years. The amateur but keen celebrity type had several representatives and the former Army officer come dapper presenter needed no applicant. Not so unnatural then, that I should become the irascible old duffer who swears a lot. Maybe it is in nature itself that we adapt to the role that needs filling.

And having lived a life of adopted images, compromise, and following anybody's star but mine, what could be more understandable then my desire to fortify Raz against the pitfalls and sirens that blur a man's true path. Was I so stupid that I thought youth would listen to reason? Was I so vain that I imagined Raz would have sufficient respect for me that anything I said would be more than stale air? No to both questions: Raz would ultimately go his own way whether the path be truly his or not. I would do no more than regale him with the odd tale or two of my own youth. So it would not be a case of 'Do what I say, not what I did,' so much as 'See what I did, and see the result.'

That ought to do the trick, I thought. But I was wrong again and was about to discover that I had more to learn from Raz than ever I could teach him.

Raz came up trumps with the accommodation. Not only a stone's throw away – a five minute drive and just outside the perimeter of the Estate – but almost a find in archaeological terms. What a place! As soon as we turned off the country road, the grey stone house allowed us a glimpse through the surrounding trees like a demure but formidable matron lifting her petticoat. It screamed 'Bastle' at me and I knew at once it was several hundred years old. It had all the signs of once having been fortified against incursion by those thirteenth to seventeenth century desperadoes known collectively as the Border Reivers. Bastles were typically half-house and half-castle keep, and I thought I'd seen them all.

'I thought you'd like it,' Raz said.

I was being obvious again.

'But there's a downside.'

28

'No dinner?' Christ, I hoped there would be dinner. It was always forefront in my list of requirement and I didn't feel like trawling round for pub grub.

'We're okay for dinner, but there's only one room. I'm afraid we have to share.'

'That's not a problem, unless you snore. I don't.' Jenny says I do but it's a lie.

'And worse still, it's a double bed.'

I was quite proud at the speed of my response. 'In that case, pick whatever part of the floor upon which you wish to sleep. I'm sure I can spare you a pillow.' Even as I spoke my mind ran through the options whereby we might both get a comfortable night. A makeshift bolster might do the trick, or top and tail, perhaps. Or let's just be adult about the issue and not let homophobia lead to one of us freezing.

Raz chuckled.

Damn! He'd got me again. And just as always, his levity was quickly shrouded in seriousness. Not for the first time I wondered what sadness lay at the core of this young man.

The room was actually quite spacious and had twin beds decently separated by a central and shared bedside cabinet of old, dark oak. Our room was at the end of a long corridor, windows on one side doors to other rooms on the other, and down some steps off a kink to the right. It was next to one of two bathrooms and its position lent it degree of privacy. The whole place was low beams and very thick stone walls and I estimated the probable period of build as mid sixteenth century. Unusually for a b & b the room had its own open fireplace and neat little store of logs. There was a health and safety warning on a small enamel plate attached to the hearth that if a fire was set the fire guard must always be in place.

The décor was bright and somewhat Laura Ashley, and there were two easy chairs, a comfort provided to compensate for the lack of a decent guest room downstairs. Apart from the fireplace the room was different from any other I had experienced in one way only: the paintings on the walls were not the usual selection of bland flowers, birds or country scenes but of old cars. Every wall had its share of

1920's flivvers and pre-War jalopies, all in a style very reminiscent of Jack Vettriano.

'Different floor level, solid stone walls all round,' Raz said, caressing the stone window sill like a long missed lover. 'I guess we're on the top floor of a medieval extension.'

'It's more probable that we're in part of the original building, and the rest of the house is the extension.'

We returned to unpacking our things, or rather, I put my spare shirt, socks, underwear and wash-kit in a drawer and Raz dropped a Morrison's plastic carrier-bag in the corner of the wardrobe. A good archaeologist is never without a change of clothes, but there are no rules concerning what constitutes acceptable luggage. Mine was an old webbing haversack that I'd bought for fifty pence from an Army surplus store back in the seventies on the occasion of my first field trip. It had accompanied me on every trip since and was rather worn and frayed at the edges. Just like its owner, I suppose.

Raz decided to take a shower before dinner. I said I'd rather wait and have mine in the morning; a wash at the sink would do me. Raz undressed and I turned away to give him a little privacy. But I caught a glimpse of him reflected in the over-sink mirror demurely dropping his drawers, and all at once, I wanted his body.

Fear not: I had already passed through my mid-life crisis; it involved a rather large and powerful motor cycle (that was much too heavy for me), so there was no chance of repressed sexuality jumping out and grabbing my assistant. But it couldn't be denied: I wanted his body … instead of mine. He stood at six-one – maybe a tad more – slim and lightly muscled, dark auburn collar-length hair and pleasing features – good looking without being material for a Jean-Paul Gaultier advert. I thought about inhabiting that body for a moment and began to list the growing defects I'd not miss: creaky knees from too many digs; back, neck and shoulders that often gave me pain, for the same reason. I dare say every trade or profession attacks the body in its own peculiar fashion.

And while on the subject of fashion, if I was somehow magically transferred into a youthful body like Raz's, I would certainly adorn it with more care. I'd never seen Raz dressed otherwise than scruffily – not including his initial interview – and he wore no jewellery, not even a watch. There was the bronze 'Viking' cloak-pin he always sported on his shirt pocket, a reproduction no doubt, that he said was a mark of his profession, but other than that, nothing.

As he left for the bathroom next door it struck me. Raz was a bit of an enigma, funny sometimes and quick-witted, but often with a veneer of sadness – or rather the lighter side of his nature seemed to be the veneer, and sadness the dark core. I knew nothing about his family beyond the fact that he was orphaned at a young age. From nowhere, I was immediately convinced that Raz inclined in another direction. He was unattached and never spoke of girlfriends. Of course! That was it, the deep and ever abiding pain that seemed to be part of him. I had always put him down as fey, when in actual fact he was ...

Now you see why I'm better with relics, for with real people I am far too inclined to jump to conclusions. I *get* relics, people less so.

In that moment with the hot water gurgling away down the plug-hole I felt dreadfully sorry for Raz, and a strong desire to let him know it was alright. Whilst never being my cup of tea, homosexuality did not bother me. I considered myself quite modern and I could never understand what all the fuss was about. I remember when Rachel, my daughter, was eight and a member of a popular boy band came out. What was 'gay', she asked me at breakfast just after the Radio 2 news had reported the revelation, and 'Is Stephen going to be alright?'

'Of course he is,' I assured her.

Yes but what was 'gay', she persisted.

I thought about it for a moment. Jenny and I had decided always to answer direct questions from our children as honestly as we possibly could. Much to the horror of her grandparents, Rachel knew the facts of life before she was seven. 'Well, some boys fall in love with blond girls,' I said.

'Some fall in love with brunettes, and others fall in love with other boys. So Stephen will be perfectly alright, as long as he chooses a nice, kind boy.'

I was off the hook; my daughter appeared perfectly satisfied and accepting of my answer, and that pretty well sums up my feeling on the subject.

Now here was Raz, isolated and lonely in his sexuality, and I knew I needed to help.

By the time Raz returned from the shower I was quite proud of the fact that I had a healthy little blaze going in the hearth.

'This'll help you get nice and dry,' I said, and then left his damp, towel-wrapped form in search of the dining room.

I've said it before, but it bears repetition: Raz really was a cracking assistant; when he joined me and the other guests at the dining room table, he brought a nice brace of reds with him, a Shiraz and a robust and fruity Turkish number. And thanks be to the gods, the other guests, an elderly couple who were doing their own version of Wainwright's coast-to-coast, were teetotal.

'Father and son?' asked the kindly looking old lady. It was a misconception with which I could happily live although I was beginning to think of us more as friends. Raz smiled guilelessly while I explained our true relationship.

'Master and *padewan*,' Raz added to my total bemusement. The elderly couple were more worldly wise than I for they appeared to understand and I have since come to learn the term derived from a popular series of science fiction films.

Back up one paragraph and delete. It appears I am now re-assuming my teenage-cum-octogenarian persona, and this after *promising* myself to be true to my reader. I was not in the least confused by the term '*padewan*'. I knew perfectly well it came from the *Star Wars* saga and that it referred to a kind of apprentice. Once again I apologise, but it is difficult the slough the habits of a lifetime.

Dinner was a three-course meal of simple fare, but beautifully prepared and fully satisfying. After a glass of the Shiraz I began to relax, and share the usual small talk.

'Ooh! You're archaeologists?' Mrs Taylor, the landlady said on overhearing a snippet of our conversation. 'Jack *will* be glad to hear that as he's into old things. Castles, museums ... and cars!' She waved a hand that encompassed the flivver-adorned walls. 'My Jack loves his cars.'

'I couldn't help but notice the paintings,' I said. 'Are they by Jack Vettriano?'

'Lord no!' she said with a high pitched, loud peel of laughter. 'Jack *Taylor* is what they are. He's a bit of an artist is my Jack.'

A suitable murmur made up of 'Oh reallys,' and 'How wonderfuls,' passed from the guests, self included. Mrs. Taylor accepted the praise on behalf of her husband with a mixture of grace and diffidence, and then pudding was served: chocolate steam sponge with rich chocolate sauce; one of my favourites.

The professor was having a good day, and if later on I could convey my support and total acceptance to Raz, it would end on a high note. Of course, my powers of deduction were soon to prove well below par when it came to living breathing human beings. 'Stick to bones and stones,' Jenny might say. Raz was no gayer than the rest of us, and here I should add, I am one of those people who believe that very few of us are entirely K1 or K6 on the Kinsey Scale of sexuality.

Later, up in our room, Raz and I drew the easy chairs close to the now blazing fire. Nicely mellowed by alcohol and lifted to a state close to ethereal by the fire's warmth, I looked for an opening onto more personal matters while we discussed the recently uncovered skeleton.

Raz pointed out that in the almost two years he'd been with me, he had rarely seen me excited by a find. He even asked me if I liked archaeology at all.

'For instance,' he said. 'You seemed positively bored with today's skeleton until we noticed the filling. Just the find itself was enough to make my heart race.'

'I've been in this game a very long time,' I said. 'One becomes … jaded, personally if not professionally. Do you think a fireman wets his pants every time he is in a fire engine with the bells and blue lights going? No, but I'm willing to be the first time was the most exciting thing in the world. It's the same with me. Each new find is a professional challenge, and there is curiosity and interest, but no longer excitement.' I didn't tell the entire truth, which was that years of experience had predisposed me to disappointment. And if you are determined to be disappointed, you will be.

'Anyway, I feel a new paper coming on,' I told Raz as I shimmied into the yielding comfort of the chair. I recalled my thoughts from earlier in the day. 'Shall I write one on the development of dental techniques through the ages?'

Raz contemplated the suggestion, unsure I was being serious. 'I can't see the publication proceeding without a few broadsides from the Doctor.'

Oh Raz you insensitive youth, why ruin the moment? I had been perfectly happy up until then, but he had to go and spoil it. The Doctor and I were … well, to say 'rivals' would be putting it mildly. You will hear more of him later – unfortunately. I made no comment to Raz's mention of the odious man. No matter; the wine modified what otherwise might have turned into a sour mood.

'When *did* dental fillings come into use?' Raz asked.

I wasn't at all sure. 'I think there's evidence for the use of a kind of ground silver paste as far back as the seventh century, but I'm talking ancient China, not Europe. I have to admit it's not within my area of expertise. Not my thing, really.'

Nor were skeletons come to that. Fair enough, I held a qualification in osteoarchaeology and I was sufficiently versed in forensic anthropology that I was on the books of several constabularies in case of grisly finds on their part, but at heart I was a stones man. And more specifically, those inscribed standing stones known as Class 1, 2 or 3 according to their age. I had written papers on them, but nothing very original except for one that was never widely

34

accepted. My best provided a little evidence to support the findings of Dr Howlett whose work I admire, but for whom I must admit a little jealousy for publishing before me. Oh and do not think Dr Howlett is *the* Doctor, whose name I will not mention.

Why do I love these old stones? It is important for me to answer that question at this point in the story, for it will allow the reader to feel a glimmer of what was to come for me on the following morning.

The stones, with their irregular lines of 'lower case' Latin are almost my very reason for being an archaeologist. Legend pointed to the existence of a stone of this sort which bore a mythical inscription, only … and here I open myself up to ridicule … I harboured the small and timid hope that one day it might be found not to be so mythical as most believed. One day it would be found, and one day a man such as me – or a woman – would brush away the dust and soil of centuries and read the line: *Hic Jacet Arthurus Rex Quondam Rexque Futurus.* I came into Archaeology as a young man who hoped beyond hope that these words, *Here lies Arthur, the Once and Future King,* were more than just an invention of a medieval poet.

Was that belief still with me when I sat before the dancing fire drinking wine with Raz? No, but by that time the stones had a different but no less strong significance for me. To me they proved that Rome didn't leave these shores and turn out all the lights, never to be properly rekindled until the coming of the Normans. The land was not plunged into mindless savagery once Rome fell, for the stones gave the lie to that theory.

I had written papers, as I have said, but one of them went too far. Why is there such a dark spot in the history of these lands? Why are the centuries clouded between the fall of Rome and the coming of the Normans? We have such a wealth of archaeological evidence before and after, and such a dearth in between. It did not seem natural to me, unless …

And here I must bite back gall at the memory of the slating I received at the hands of the good Doctor who shall

35

not be named. I should have bided my time. I should have accumulated a little more evidence before publishing. I should have, but I didn't, and the Doctor saw to it that my reputation was virtually sunk.

You see, it was my contention that there must have been some concerted effort to hide the realities of the so called Dark Ages from future generations. In short, the darkness of the Dark Ages was quite deliberate. The Doctor made me a laughing stock and almost ended my very modest TV career. That the media thrives on controversy is the sole reason that I managed to hold on. They'd wheel me out whenever they ran short of anyone else to put in the lime-lit stocks and the Doctor would be there with a full supply of rotting vegetables.

That night I absorbed the warmth and the alcohol and the company of a young man who restored my faith in the younger generation, and though I had no way of knowing it, I sat of the very precipice of discovery. Had I known what the morning would bring, I would not have slept a wink.

We discussed dental fillings, and the position and situation of the skeleton. Were we looking at an inhumation, or the remains of one whom nature had covered where he fell in death? And we pored over Raz's draft *Skeleton Record Sheet* and wondered which box to tick, because the body was not 'supine-and-extended', 'flexed' or 'in a crouch' but rather tipped or dumped limbs akimbo, and there wasn't a box for that. We acknowledged how lucky we were that the find was on a private estate, so we didn't have to worry too much about the integrity or security of the find, and we discussed how we might progress on the following day. Raz suggested I might contact the producer who fielded the series of TV programs in which I sometimes appeared as third fiddle, but I countered it was a little early to press the popular launch button on the find, just yet. How wrong I was.

We decided to turn in for the night, and then an opportunity presented itself to move on to more personal matters. Raz brushed his teeth as I dampened down the fire, and then he stripped down to his very faded and washed out boxers.

'You won't attract the ladies in tatty old drawers like that,' I said. 'Or the boys, if they're more your thing.' Had the wine not eased me into a false sense of closeness with my assistant, I would never have said such a thing for fear of an industrial tribunal for sexual harassment. Maybe we were moving towards friendship, but in the eyes of the world we were work colleagues. No, not even that: I was the boss and Raz was on my staff.

Raz had bagged the bed by the door and slipped under the duvet as I undressed for bed. He'd rolled his eyes at my last comment, but he smiled at the same time and didn't appear to have taken offence. He must have been considering the answer carefully, for I was flicking my book open to the mark by the time he replied.

'By the time my girlfriend saw me in my boxers, she was sufficiently past initial attraction to be put off by my poverty.'

I closed my book with a clap and chuckled. 'That's the sneakiest attempt of asking for a raise I've ever heard. Don't I pay you enough?' The mention of a girlfriend, so maybe I had jumped to the wrong conclusion, or maybe he was putting up a smokescreen.

'If I was motivated by money, I wouldn't be an archaeologist. As for the pay, it's adequate so long as you don't expect me to start shelling out for designer knickers.' He flashed his grin at me and I chuckled some more.

Well, I'd given him an opening and I think I had shown quite subtly that I had no problems when it came to sexual orientation. He could be gayer than a May morning for all I cared, so long as he continued to do his job well.

He snuggled under the duvet and obviously had no intention to read. I asked him if he minded the light while I finished my current chapter. He did not, and so I continued with my book. A couple of pages later I happened to glance over. Raz was looking at me – or perhaps through me to something beyond. I had come to know him for his serious look, but his frown was quite noticeable and he looked troubled.

'Everything okay, Raz?'

He snapped out of his private revelry. 'Sorry, I was miles away.'

I returned to my book, but only for a sentence.

'I'm just wondering,' Raz said. 'Why did you mention "boys" earlier on, when you were talking about whom I might attract?'

I shrugged. 'No reason at all really, it's just that I've learned it pays not to assume anything,' I said, leaving out the part about convincing myself he was gay on the flimsiest of evidence. 'It would be wrong, and perhaps even hurtful, for me to make the wrong assumption for a feature of a man's personality as basic as sexuality.'

He looked a little relieved. 'Oh, I see. Only, I sometimes wonder if anything rubbed off on me from … something that once happened.'

My mind quickly mustered appropriate ammunition for my mouth, centred round 'going through phases' and 'juvenile experimentation' but thankfully I had no time to launch because Raz then went on to shock me with the awful revelation that as a 17-year-old he had been subjected to the most awful assault. 'Gang-rape' sums it up well enough without having to go into details. I felt at the same time honoured that he should trust me with such intimate information, and revolted and saddened by what he had endured.

'You are not a cruel, selfish or lustful swine, so I don't believe anything at all rubbed off on you. And quite frankly I do not consider what you went through as a sexual experience so much as a brutal and violent attack.'

Raz went quiet and did not answer, whether through contemplating my words or embarrassment I couldn't tell.

'Did they catch the bastards?'

Raz shook his head. 'No, but they all paid, one way or another.'

Now I was spooked. Had Raz tracked down his attackers, one by one, and slit their evil throats? Couldn't say the thought didn't have a certain appeal. Just desserts, I'd say, and serve them bloody well right. It was that I was seeing Raz in a new light that felt odd and disconcerting.

'I shouldn't have mentioned it really. It was a long time ago, but it's not really something I like to discuss.'

Seven years wasn't such a long time, but I got his drift and asked no more questions while assuring him that if he ever felt like talking, I'd be happy to listen. I hated the thought that such a loathsome experience had soured him to the joys of intimacy.

We were up early next morning and reversed our choices of the previous evening: I showered and Raz washed at the sink. Although I felt closer to Raz, there was also a little awkwardness, and we both moved swiftly into professional mode.

If anything breakfast was even more delicious and sustaining than dinner. Fruit juice and cereal – Raz chose porridge – followed by the most full and generous of English breakfasts with toast and homemade conserves and lashings of fresh farm butter. The inimitable and talented Jack was on serving duty that morning, and as the elderly couple had eaten even earlier and were no doubt several miles closer to the east coast, we had his undivided attention.

I congratulated him on his artwork; his round red face blushed a little redder as he waved the complement away with a spatula. 'Just a bit of fun really,' he said. 'But Sallie tells me you're a pair of bone-kickers.'

That particular term sent my blood pressure to a couple of points below cardiovascular accident, but I hid it well. The BBC has a lot to answer for. I affirmed that we were indeed 'archaeologists' (said a little too forcefully) and that the BBC drama *Bone-kickers* was good for a laugh but bore no resemblance whatsoever to the real job. Roman hand-grenades indeed! Were I to have a premonition just a little way into the future, I think the idea of Roman hand-grenades would have been easy to accept, by comparison.

Jack told us that there was something in the pigsty we might like to see. 'There was a young feller like you who came to visit when my Dad was young, or so the story goes, and he was blown away by it.' Young fellow? He must have been addressing his remarks to Raz.

'Really,' I said trying to sound interested. 'I look forward to seeing … whatever it might be.' I returned my full attention to a succulent rasher of bacon and hoped I could silently convey my disinterest in whatever the pigsty had to offer unless it was more bacon.

Jack went off to refill our teapot and I rolled my eyes at Raz. He smiled and shrugged. Just as I suspect every profession brings its associated ailments, so too does it bring the standard set of misconceptions and expectations. I doubt if there is a policeman in the land who has not walked into a pub only to find one bright wit throw his wrists together as if handcuffed and say 'Okay Guv, I'll come quietly.' Is there a single Traffic Warden who has not heard the joke about why he has a yellow band around his hat – to stop people parking on his head – or a doctor who has not been regaled with a list of ailments from someone he has just met at a social function? And so it is, just as the mere presence of a publisher or TV director brings out every moth-eaten manuscript that ever was written, in a like manner the archaeologist attracts an awful lot of dusty old tat.

I've been shown a rusty butcher's knife that the proud owner had convinced himself must be a Roman gladius, a skull that turned out to be made of bone-coloured resin, a piece of 'medieval' glass that had 'R. Whites' written on the bottom and a 'caveman's axe head' that was no more than an natural oval of poor quality weather-worn stone. Admittedly I was once handed a spadroon complete with leather scabbard (minus the brass parts and stitching) that had turned up under the floorboards of a seventeenth century Scottish farm house, no doubt from where it was hidden by a highlander trying to escape 'Stinking Billie's' mopping up operations following 'the '45', but such gems are by far the exception that prove the rule.

'Maybe he'll forget,' I said to Raz. 'I for one don't relish the prospect of grubbing round a pigsty.'

Oh that every pigsty should house such glory. When breakfast was done Jack had *not* forgotten, and led us into a small pitched-roof extension to the main house that hadn't seen a pig in a hundred years. Now its main function was to shelter Jack's quad-bike and seconded as a tool shed. It smelled of petrol rather than pig-slurry and I was immensely relieved.

'Can you see it?' Jack said with a beaming smile splitting his face. He was like an expectant and excited schoolboy, which was nothing compared to what I would be like within a few minutes.

I couldn't see a thing. Well, of course I could see the workbench and tools. And yes I could see the old besom in the corner and … oh God, is that *really* it? In the other corner was an old sharpening wheel – a circular whetstone in an iron frame that bore the steam-hammered likeness of General Kitchener. Now, out of politeness, I would have to pretend to be impressed by a Victorian relic that was of hardly any interest to the archaeologist, if not the collector. That was going to be my let-out: I'd tell him it wasn't of much archaeological value, but a collector would love it.

And then I noticed Raz. He was staring, slack-jawed, high into the dark corner of the building. I followed his gaze and saw it: right there, built into the wall and forming part of the gable end, was a stone, or rather part of a stone. It was triangular in shape and on its side, but the lettering was clear.

'Class 1?' Raz said in little over a whisper.

'Yes, yes – or perhaps Class 2. See there is part of a cross. And the lettering is consistent with those found in the south-west, but it's not Latin.'

'Looks like Old English,' Raz said.

My chest was tight and my vision popped at the periphery with little stars until I remembered to breathe. I could hardly believe it. It was just a stone, but now you know, these very stones were my speciality, and what was more, I thought I knew where the other part of this fragment was displayed.

These stones are usually found in the south. Only one has ever been found this far north, excluding the Pictish examples, and I was virtually certain that I was looking at another piece of that same stone. To say my excitement knew no bounds couldn't even begin to describe how I felt. Industrial tribunals be buggered! I grabbed Raz and hugged him, and then for good measure I hugged Jack too.

III

~ 793 ~
In which we find the Raven at his roost and the Fish sporting in his home pool.

Two longships were moored at the wharf. *Thought* and *Memory* they were named; Odin's Ravens, and as fine a sight as they were in the late afternoon sunshine, bobbing gently in a sea of sparkling gems, it was not the pair of sleek raiders that held Finn's attention, but a flesh and blood couple of ravens that circled and sky-danced high above the fjord.

Finn waited outside his father's longhouse where judgement would soon be passed on him, so he was glad of the distraction and tried to imagine the view from the birds' perspective.

They would see the smoke rising from the longhouse and from the little huts of the slaves who had scraped together enough fuel. The forest would appear like a field of cabbages from so high up, and Finn himself would be no more than a curious looking insect dressed in a blue tunic and red hooded cowl. Would the ravens be able to tell how nervous he was?

The paths connecting the longhouse to all the other buildings in the farm-village called Gradigheim, would appear as yellow-brown threads strewn on a bolt of green linen, and even Odin's Ravens would seem no more than a pair of floating twigs.

Finn became so absorbed in the intricate flight of the ravens – now soaring, spiralling high, now drawing in a wing to tumble and then to recover – that he didn't hear his cousin's approach. Tosti's greeting brought him back down to earth where cold reality slapped him hard.

'Why the long face, Finn?' Tosti said. 'You killed a slave. So what? Who's going to miss him?'

'Father for one. He was one of father's favourites. A shield bearer.'

43

'There'll be others who can be taught to do a battle-slave's duties. Uncle Bjorn will break your nose and box your ears and that will be the end to it. And he'll be doing you a favour into the bargain. Why, if you went into battle as you look now, unscarred and pretty as a girl, the enemy would have a hard time deciding whether to fight you or tup you.'

Somehow, Finn didn't feel at all reassured. 'He scarred my brother for less *and* that was when my mother was still alive. A slave trained to be a shield bearer is a valuable possession.'

There was no more time for speculation. Gudric opened the door and called Finn through. Finn took a deep breath, put on a mask of grim resolve and walked in, striding purposefully past the byre and towards his father who sat at the far end of the long hall. If there was one certainty, it was this: showing the slightest hint of fear would multiply his punishment threefold.

Finn noticed his mother's father sitting close to the hearth: a waste of good warmth, and far past the time when the useless old bag of bones should have left this world. It couldn't be long before someone helped him along the way.

A few more steps, past the two sleeping cubicles, one his father's and the other his father's sister's, and then he arrived, standing before his father, his aunt and Gudric who took his place at father's left hand.

Bjorn wore his dark-auburn beard long and bifurcated. His shoulder length hair flowed out from under a blue, woollen cap with embroidered edges and he was adorned with amber beads and silver trinkets suspended from leather strings. His heavy woollen tunic was dark blue and even his trousers were not left plain. Dressed in such finery, he could be mistaken for a jarl although he had no noble connections, nor did he seek them. He was a common chieftain, happy to be absolute ruler of his tiny kingdom. That it was by consent of his people lent him an additional sense of pride and achievement.

'So boy, you think sixteen is young to achieve your first man-slaying?'

Finn was not sure how he should reply. 'He was only a slave Father. Perhaps it does not count.'

Bjorn appeared not to hear. 'Well, it is not. I was but fourteen when I first killed a man.'

Finn had heard the story many times, but felt it unwise to mention the fact.

'And the man I killed was a warrior. He was a Dane, one among many who thought to raid my father's lands for plunder and slaves. They took neither for none returned to their own lands in the south. They left us a fine ship and though it had no mast or sail we adapted it, and in the following spring we went a-raiding ourselves, and I slew many times and still I was not as old as you.'

Finn tried to look impressed, as if he'd never heard the story before.

'Take off your tunic boy, and your shirt.'

Finn obeyed at once. Perhaps he was to receive a flogging. He could bear that.

'Now, over to the hearth with you.'

A flogging was one thing, but the fire implied more painful punishments. As he came closer to the hearth Finn was sickened to notice an iron brand, its tip nestling deep in the red hot centre of the fire.

'Now, out with it, Finn. I've heard your tale once. I wish to hear it again. How came you to destroy my shield bearer?'

Finn swallowed hard. He recalled the time he had been made to watch his brother while he recounted the details of a misdemeanour, and at the end of each sentence, father punched him to the ground. Finn expected no less, and possibly a great deal more.

'Speak I say!' his father bellowed.

Finn drew himself up, determined to weather whatever punishment was meted out. 'I called the slave to the glade up in the forest where the incline first levels out,' he began.

'Which slave?' Bjorn asked, although having heard the tale once before he knew perfectly well.

'Your shield bearer. The thrall I killed.'

'Yes, but what was his name? Gudric is recording this, and I'll have things done properly.'

45

Finn realised he had no idea what the man's name was. He was a slave and he came when he was called; that was good enough. Finn had never thought to enquire of his name. Did slaves have names other than Fetch-Pot, Hearth-Boy or Washer-Girl?

'I don't know his name, Father.'

'Then tell me, how did you call him to you when there were chores to assign?'

Finn thought for a moment. 'I called, "Hey, you!" and he came.'

Bjorn shook his head and clucked his tongue in pretence of disbelief. 'You kill a boy who has been part of the household since you were a babe, and you don't know his name?'

'No, Father.'

'Do you know the name of his sister?'

'His … sister?' Finn had never really thought of the relationships between slaves.

'Yes, his sister. The girl you were rutting with three times a week until you got her with child. You know she died in childbirth?'

Finn had no idea. Slaves often died, and then you went raiding for new ones. He assumed the girl who he'd often chosen to warm his bed had died, but he never thought to wonder how or why. There were other girls, and prettier. He had not missed her.

'I see you have yet to learn the value of things, boy. Now, on with your tale.'

'He came to the glade as usual. He is … was a skilled spearman and good with the axe –'

'He was my shield bearer. What did you expect?'

'Nothing less, Father. That's why we sparred together. Every day we would spar with spear hafts, wooden swords or shield and blunt axe. But this time when we began, he came at me with a live spear, sharpened head knocked on and pinned tight, while I still had only the haft.'

'And what to that? Did you wonder why he should so weigh the odds in his favour?'

'I had no time to wonder. He came at me and it was clear he had forgotten ours was a mock battle. He lay on so hard and fierce it was plain he was after my life.'

'Can you think why that might have been? A slave boy who hasn't seen so many as twenty summers comes at his master's son for blood, knowing full well that even victory would mean his own death. What could he have been thinking?'

Finn knew his father's questions were rhetorical. With his newfound knowledge concerning the relationship between his attacker and the girl he'd used for pleasure, there was but one obvious answer, and that saved him from voicing anything but the reason he knew most likely.

'Perhaps he thought me responsible for his sister's death and meant to avenge her, no matter what might befall him after the act.'

'Aha!' Bjorn said as if the light of knowledge had just shone down on him. 'Very like. Very like indeed. And so you have killed twice. The boy died by the spear, which you control like a true warrior. And his sister died by the spear between your legs, over which, it seems, you have no control at all.'

Sweat poured down Finn's torso, whether it was due to proximity of the fire or fear of the pains to come, he did not know. Nor did he know why his father appeared so concerned for the lives of slaves. Slaves were often killed, and as for the girl, well nearly all the boys who had outgrown rough-sporting with each other rutted with the slave girls, so it was far from certain that he was responsible for getting her with child.

'Wake up, boy! Do the flames draw you in?'

That is exactly what they were doing, just like the ravens earlier. Finn stood straight and took his eyes from the hearth.

'Now you will hear my judgement,' Bjorn said. Gudric sat poised with a quill newly dipped in ink. The tools for writing had been plundered a year ago, and since then Bjorn had become fascinated by the process and took a passion for recording everything. Gudric wrote runes on the paper although he had gained a rudimentary knowledge of the Roman letters in his travels.

'A slave girl dead of a child in her belly is of no consequence. I hope you found pleasure with her before she began to swell. A slave who attacks his master's son is a dead man, whatever his reasons. He deserved death, but not such a quick one as you dealt him. No matter. The scoundrel is dead and deserves to be so. But you have deprived me of my shield bearer, and for that you must make recompense. Face me, boy.'

Finn turned to face his father and screamed inwardly when he noticed the glowing brand. Before he could react he had been seized by a pair of carls who appeared one at each arm and Bjorn pressed the brand onto the centre of Finn's chest.

It was held there for no more than a moment, but Finn's sweat and flesh sizzled as herald to the white hot pain that spread like lightning through his body. He would have cried out, but a ladle of cold water was doused over his chest and took away the intensity of the agony. He bit down hard and held his eyes tight shut until he was certain no tears would fall.

'And so I brand you with the sign of the raven, which has ever been the mark of warriors in our clan, and I assign you as my shield bearer. Though you are two years younger than I had intended for your first raid you will accompany me when next we go a-Viking, and that will be after the passing of four weeks.'

Through the pain Finn could hardly believe his luck. Why, this was no punishment at all. Since he was a small boy all he had longed for was the day when he could take to the sea on a sleek raider. His killing of the slave counted as a man-slaying after all, for he had been marked as a warrior and would soon join the crew of a raiding party. This time he could not prevent the flow of his tears, for tears of joy were harder to contain than those of pain.

Here is wisdom. Let him that hath understanding count the number of the beast.

Brother Sebastian spied on two young men as they clambered about the rocks. He kept close to an outcrop so as to stay hidden. Secretly, so secretly that he dare not admit it to himself, he hoped Elmo would fall into the sea. He didn't want him to drown, but the humiliation of a thorough soaking would do him good.

Scandalously, both boys were sporting around in nothing but their shirts and drawers. Father Paul would hear of this behaviour. Eric was just a slave and knew no better, but Elmo had no such excuse, even if he was only a novice. Sebastian was unconscious of the spiteful grin that marred his otherwise fine features. He relished the thought that he would be assigned to supervise Elmo's penance.

It was then that Brother Sebastian saw an opportunity to increase Elmo's impending discomfort. Hitching up his habit at either hip he hurried to where Eric had left his cloak, tunic, hose and shoes, and Elmo his habit, hose and sandals. Gathering them all up in an untidy bundle he gained extra pleasure from the thought that the slave's lice would infest Elmo's habit, and then he stole away formulating a story as he went. He would tell the other brothers he found the clothes on the beach and decided to bring them to the safety of the monastery. As to the boys, he would say there had been no sign of them and he'd sew the seed that they were up to no good.

Then it happened that all through England such a sign in the heavens was seen and some called it the long haired star.

'Don't overreach yourself,' Eric said. 'If you fall now those rocks will shred you to pieces.'

Elmo looked down and swallowed hard. He wasn't very high up, but the rocks looked sharp and spiteful. 'Nearly there. If I can just ...' Elmo stopped talking and concentrated on maintaining his balance as he reached for his prize while ignoring the frantic swoops and dives of the soon to be dispossessed bird. 'Got it! Now we shall each have an egg for our supper.'

He handed the egg to Eric and then eased himself along the ledge and back onto the grassy turf that covered most of the tiny island he called home.

It was a beautifully warm and sunny day and the boys sat on the ground without fear of getting their linen underwear damp. If Elmo had worn his outer clothing while climbing rocks, it would have made the egg-gathering expedition next to impossible.

'Perhaps we should stick to the eggs of Cuthie Ducks. They can be gathered with ease,' Eric said.

'I doubt we'd find any this late.'

Eric spread the eggs on the rough grass and counted them. 'Eleven in all, so that's one for each of the monks and four left over.'

'You take those. One for you, one for your good wife, one for your little one, and the last for mother.'

Eric smiled at the thought of mother's face when he brought the eggs home, but his smile didn't last. 'Hey! Where're our things? Surely we left them on that rock.' He stood, ran to the rock and cast round looking for the clothes, hoping the wind might have moved them along a little way.

'Look no further Eric. There go our clothes, safe in the arms of Brother Sebastian.'

Eric looked to where Elmo was pointing, and there in the distance, Sebastian rapidly closed upon the monastery door, with his stolen bundle clenched to his chest.

Eric ground his teeth and pounded a fist into his open palm. 'That man! Were he anything but a holy brother, I should knock him on his arse and never grow tired of kicking him.'

Elmo chuckled. 'Let your anger go, brother. Nobody is more aware of Sebastian's short-comings than Sebastian himself. He will surely set himself some painful penance for this act – worse than any beating you could deliver.'

'Aye, perhaps. But not before he has made sure you have a penance to face. Is there a monastic rule against collecting eggs?'

Elmo frowned while he tried to recall any rules that might apply to ducks or auks. 'None, as far as I can remember. A hundred years ago Saint Cuthbert blessed the ducks hereabouts, but Sebastian will brew evil from the fact that we were both out of our top clothes. He'll probably imply the two of us were flouting an edict or two of Theodore of Tarsus.'

Eric began to laugh. 'I hope that doesn't mean what I think it does.'

'Oh, it does brother. It does. Now, come sit down again and mind the eggs. I've no rush to return to the monastery in nought but my drawers, so let's put the evil moment off a while and talk.'

With one last look towards the monastery, just in time to see Brother Sebastian disappearing inside, Eric sat down on the warm grass. 'Everyone has a cross to bear, and surely that man is yours.'

Elmo let his eye trail past the two storey stone-built monastery with its little beacon tower, and away on to the sea. There were few places he could stand on the island where the sea was not visible in all directions, and on wintry days the only comfort to be had was by the refectory hearth, but on days when the sun shone brightly there were fewer locations more peaceful and restful to the spirit. Elmo thought of the time he had said goodbye to his family and sat back while a slave rowed him out to his new home. He had only been back to the mainland with specific chores and even then chaperoned so that he would not be tempted to sample the pleasures of secular life.

Looking towards land he could see those building in the little town of Annebelle which stood close to the harbour, and if he looked up to the right, the neighbouring village of

51

Warkworth rambled on up towards the high ground. The heat haze hid the far Cheviots, just as they masked the horizon.

'How's mother?'

'She's well, but misses her son.'

'She still has you and your family around her.'

'True, but a mother wants all her sons safe by the hearth while at the same time knowing it can never be so.'

Elmo picked a tiny sea shell off the sole of his foot. 'Even adopted ones?'

Eric plucked a blade of grass and chewed at one end. 'You know as well as I she loves us equally.' He drew the blade between his thumbs and blew a raucous note which scared a pair of puffins to flight.

'Did you ever resent your cuckoo-brother, that he should be dropped into the nest and receive equal shares?'

Eric stopped trying to make tunes with the grass and stared sideways at Elmo. He rolled his eyes and gave no more answer than that, for no more was needed. Elmo felt suitably admonished.

'And how of my sister-in-law, and my beautiful little niece?'

Eric smiled again, radiantly with thoughts of his wife and little Maud. They had been wed for almost two years, both bride and groom fifteen years old when they made their vows, and little Maud had recently taken her first faltering steps.

'Emma is well, and Maud more beautiful every day, though you have yet to set eyes on her. I think it exceedingly cruel that we live so close, and yet you are not allowed to visit.'

Elmo set his eyes to the horizon. 'For the time being I must be content with the news you bring.'

Eric stared out to sea for a long moment. 'You know, we can see Coquet Island from all along the coast, and from Annebelle's harbour mouth a dot that we imagine is your window. On clear days we can see the monastery door and mother fancies that one of the tiny figures she claims to spy upon, no larger than an emmet, is you, and that you are on the beach thinking of us.'

Elmo felt pricking at the back of his eyes and swallowed hard. This talk of family threatened to release emotions he would rather stay hid. 'Then you must tell her she is right, for I often come to the little beach and gaze towards home, and my thoughts are always with family.'

Eric looked out to sea where the horizon was lost in a thick haze. Elmo thought he too might be feeling vulnerable.

'Well, Brother brother,' Eric said stripping off his shirt. 'Have you lost the fighting skills you once had? Or is wrestling just another sport that's against the rules?'

Elmo stood grinning widely. 'Everything is against the rules, Eric. So lay on, if you have the nerve. As for me, I might as well do all my penances in one go.' He threw his shirt down and flew at his brother, taking him low and tackling him to the ground.

They wrestled, ever mindful of the position of the eggs, until they were exhausted and with no clear winner they fell away from one another and sprawled on the grass. The exertion had drained away all emotion. There was a time when Elmo could easily best his slightly younger brother, but no longer. He wondered if Eric could best him with the blade, but he thought not. Though he would never touch a sword again, he felt sure the years of training had left their indelible mark.

'Does Theodore have an edict against lying under the sun with your brother?'

Elmo chuckled. 'I should be surprised if he doesn't. It costs me a penance if I glimpse anything below my belly button when I dress in the morning – should I choose to confess it.'

Both boys shared laughter until Eric broke off abruptly and sat up.

'What is it, Eric?'

'I've just remembered. I brought a gift for you. It's from mother, but I had it in my belt-pouch. When I retrieve it from wherever Brother Sebastian has taken it, I doubt I'll be allowed to give it to you.'

'Mother remembered that it is Saint Elmo's day tomorrow?'

'No brother. She remembered it is the seventeenth anniversary of the day she took you in while I was but the roundness of her belly.'

'The events coincide. When I became a postulate I was given the name Elmo because my arrival fell upon his feast day.'

'We'll keep his feast right enough, but we will think of you. And forgive us if we think of you as Elfgar, just for one day of the year.'

It was another life. So long ago, but Elmo still loved the sound of his old name: Elfgar, son of Thomas Gerefa and brother to Eric.

'I have an idea, Elmo. I'll put the gift under that old Cuthie Duck nest – the one we found in the tall grass near the well.'

Elmo was about to remind Eric of his vows of poverty, and that perhaps he should take the gift home, but he knew for all the vows in the world, he would not hurt his mother. And then also, something of the little boy remained in him, and he looked forward to claiming his gift. He would volunteer to venture out early to draw water from the well, and then he would retrieve it.

Elmo nodded and winked. 'Tell mother thank you for me. Now, there's no more putting it off. I'll be late for Vespers at this rate. Let's hasten our embarrassment to an end.'

Elmo led the way feeling strangely free to be out of his habit and he enjoyed the feel of the warm grass under his bare feet. It contrasted so completely with that of the cold stone monastery floor. Inside drear shadows cut off the sunlight and there was a brooding air of menace.

'Brother Elmo! There you are,' Sebastian said his voice dripping with false concern. 'We have been worried about you and thought you might have drowned.' His voice then changed and took on a harsh, spiteful tone. 'But I see you have been … at play.' He made the last word sound like the worst sin under the sun.

'We brought eggs for supper, Brother Sebastian.' Elmo held out his shirt and Sebastian peered down at them as if they had an evil smell to them.

'Take them to the refectory, and then wait until I call you to Father Paul. He wants to see you.'

'And … my clothes?'

'Go as you are. If you are so careless with your habit, perhaps you do not deserve one. And you boy,' Sebastian said, turning to Eric. 'Your chores here are done. Go back to your little boat and be off with you.'

'I'll not leave without my clothes.'

'Yours are in your boat. Now go!'

Eric made an aggressive move towards Sebastian, but Elmo shook his head. So, Sebastian would escape a beating but Eric was not going to let him off entirely. He was of the firm belief that rudeness should never go unchecked.

'Did *you* put my clothes in the boat? If so, then *you* had better go fetch them, and be quick about it.'

There was a definite tone of command in Eric's voice and Sebastian knew instantly that he had made a mistake. Despite the ragged look of his garb, this lad was no slave. He hesitated for a moment before his resolve dissipated like steam from the pot on a hot day.

'I'll bring them to the porch for you. My apologies,' Sebastian offered, then scuttled out and away to the beach.

'I'm sorry, brother,' Eric said. 'I suppose he'll be all the harder on you now.'

Elmo grinned. 'No doubt at all, but it was worth it.'

Sebastian returned with Eric's clothes and hurried away to hide his embarrassment. When he'd dressed Eric took Elmo in a brief embrace, an action which in itself would have brought more penances if seen, and said goodbye.

'Give Emma and Mother my love, and a little kiss for Maud.'

Eric's demeanour changed.

'What is it, Eric?'

Eric shook his head. 'It's nothing. I just … I felt that I should never see you again, that we would never again exchange words. But it's just silliness. Parting always makes me feel thus.'

With a last wave, Eric left. Elmo suddenly felt very alone and was overcome by a sense of foreboding that had nothing to do with his impending meeting with the Abbot. A sickening chill passed through him and he felt that his brother's premonition would surely come to pass.

He'd shaken off the feeling by the time he reached the refectory and endured the varied looks of his brothers. Some were silently scornful, some amused, and others pretended not to notice that the youngest brother was parading in his small-clothes. Elmo decided the wrestling had been a bad idea, for his drawers were streaked with bright green grass stains, which could go a long way to support any lies Brother Sebastian chose to spread.

Brother Mundwyn, who was a visitor from another monastery, was baking bread and the smell was mouth-watering. He was a cheerful man in middle years, unnaturally tall and thin with a face that spoke of many adventures. He had a deep scar across his cheekbone and Elmo often wondered if he had been a soldier before becoming a monk, although others thought him a former stonemason from his practice of marking the dough with a species of pointing tool. His threadbare habit was dark grey and over this he wore a deep blue scapula which carried the mark of his Order – a tiny embroidered emblem which appeared as a circle within a square, and Elmo believed the silver and black ring he wore, inscribed with numerals, was also a symbol of his Order.

The oak table at which Mundwyn worked had a generous dusting of flour, and flour flecked his clothing with white, just as age flecked his hair. He bent over a large mass of dough and kneaded it without mercy, as if it had affronted him by its very existence. He looked up from his work, down again and then up quickly as if noticing for the first time that Elmo was inappropriately dressed. Standing up straight, he threw the dough ball down, sending up a puff of cloud which made him flap his hands about to ward it off. When the flour had settled he leaned forward and peered at Elmo from under thick eyebrows. He cocked his head, by way of asking the obvious question.

'I am to wait here until Brother Sebastian calls for me, Brother Mundwyn. And then I am to attend Father Paul.'

'Dressed in your drawers and shirt? Yes, I've heard.' Mundwyn looked over his shoulder towards the stone stairs, and then over his other shoulder before fixing Elmo with a stare and beckoning him closer with a turn of his head.

Elmo moved in close, eager to partake of a little bit of conspiracy. Maybe Mundwyn was going to say exactly what he thought of Sebastian.

'The bread basket,' Mundwyn said in a forced whisper. 'The tall one with the lid on.' And then he gave Elmo a fat wink before returning to his kneading. He paid no further attention to the boy nor did he appear in the mood for more conversation. In reality, no more was needed and Elmo hoped he knew what was in the bread basket. Lifting the lid he was relieved to see his un-dyed novice's habit and other clothes and he was back inside them in hardly any time at all. As he latched his last sandal Brother Andrew, a slight, black haired little bird of a man came into the refectory and with a face carrying all the woes of the world, he told Elmo that Brother Sebastian awaited his attendance outside the Abbot's room.

Elmo nodded a goodbye to Mundwyn, who was completely absorbed in his dough, and followed Brother Andrew up the stairs that led to the common room and then along the central corridor with its tiny cells branching off at either side and finally to Brother Sebastian who faced Father Paul's door with his back to the corridor.

Brother Andrew bobbed apologetically and retreated back the way he'd just come.

'You are such a disappointment to us, Brother Elmo. You —' His words stuck in his throat when he condescended to allow his eyes to fall on Elmo. Surprise was quickly consumed by anger. 'Where did you ...? Who ...?'

For a moment Elmo thought Sebastian would order him to strip again or rip his clothes off by his own hand. It was clear he was extremely put out that his spiteful plan had been thwarted.

'Brother Mundwyn,' he said venomously as the scene unrolled in his head. '*He* told you where to find them, didn't he?'

Elmo was spared having to answer, because the door opened and the Abbot, Father Paul, filled the frame with sunlight behind him. The corpulent Abbot looked like a well fed angel with an effulgence of heavenly light bursting from him. Of course, the illusion was spoilt once they entered his room and the source of the light was seen to be no more than sunlight pouring in at the window. Father Paul's window had panes of the best glass set in a wooden frame and it was a gift from the bishop for his long years of loyal service.

Elmo had been in this room often, for it was his task to fill the Abbot's bath tub every Saturday after Vespers. Father Paul lived with much the same austerity as his brothers, but for two exceptions: his weekly bath and his large, soft bed with its eider feather quilt and pillows. Of course, the size of the room could be considered another luxury; it was three times the size of the cells in which the brothers slept and found privacy, and it was the only room in the monastery that boasted a glass window.

Apart from the bed and the tub, the only furnishings were a small table and plain chair, a strongbox, a small bookcase and a giant armoire big enough for a man to step inside.

'Thank you, Brother Sebastian,' Father Paul said as he sat at the table. 'You may go.'

Sebastian's gaze shifted nervously between Elmo and the seated Abbot. 'But Father ...'

Father Paul held up a hand to cut off any further argument. 'I have your account, and I'm grateful. Now, please leave us, so I may interrogate our wayward novice.'

'Of course,' Sebastian said with a smile as honest as the sirens' song. He backed out of the room as if the Abbot were a species of royalty and closed the door making as little sound as possible.

'I'm glad you found the wits and wherewithal to dress yourself, Brother Elmo. I would have found it disconcerting and embarrassing should Brother Sebastian have had it his way.'

Elmo smiled weakly.

'So, out with it, young man! I know Sebastian's intimations of debauchery and lewd horseplay are greatly manifestations of a suspicious mind, but I am curious to learn how you came to be out of your habit in broad daylight. I hope you didn't go bathing, for the tides about this island are notorious and can be wicked cruel. Should I lose you to silly and unreasoned play, the good Bishop Higbald would make me his errand boy and the rest of my days would be spent shuttling between Lindisfarne and Rome.'

Elmo opened his mouth to speak, but got no further.

'And I will fill your days with penances if you were messing about in our boat. If it is ever broken up on the rocks, we shall not easily get another. And who was this other lad with whom you were sporting?'

'Eric Gerefa, Father. He is the son of Thomas, sometime reeve of the Parish of Warkworth.'

'Ah yes. Thomas. Very sad. So unfortunate. I think I am beginning to understand. You were playing boyish games with your adoptive brother.'

'Yes, Father. Well, collecting eggs so that we might all have one for supper, and …' Elmo fixed the Abbot with a stare, uncertain that he had heard correctly as the old man's words registered in his mind.

'Oh, I forgot,' said the Abbot. 'I'm not supposed to know you have family in Annebelle, am I?' He began to chuckle. 'Abbots have their sources of information, you know. I have better sight than a bowl of pottage and keener hearing than an ear of barley. By all the jugglers of Jarrow, give me a little credit, boy!'

Elmo felt a deep blush rise from his collar and cover his entire face. The Abbot found this amusing.

'Well then, you collected eggs – I must say I'm rather partial to collops so tonight we dine well – and what else?'

'What else, Father?'

'Yes, you gathered eggs, and then what did you do?'

'We – erm – we …'

'Yes, yes, come on! You what?'

'We wrestled.'

Father Paul lost his cheerful look and his eyes turned stony. Elmo felt his insides knot. 'You … wrestled?'

Elmo gulped and nodded.

'And did you win?'

Elmo shook his head. 'No Father. It was a draw.'

'Hmph,' came the Abbot's nasal repost. 'When I was a lad, I frequently wrestled and more often than not I was the victor. But I am no longer a lad and neither are you, so we must have done with the pastimes of rude boys. You should know better! What tales of our behaviour do you think your brother will take home to the town? How do you think we will be thought of, that our novices practice such rough and common behaviour?'

Elmo felt very ashamed. Father Paul was a kind man, and he felt utterly wretched for disappointing him. 'I am sorry Father.'

'And so you should be. Now, how are you with your Antiphons?'

'I have learnt them almost by heart. There are a few responses that I have yet to master.'

'Then you shall master them by Matins on Monday and then you shall lead, and woe-betide you if you are not perfect. Bede had them under his belt when he was a tiny boy of six or seven, so it should not be past your capabilities.'

'Yes Father. I mean, no Father.'

'And as further penance, you shall collect our daily water requirements every morning at first light, for a month. Let the other brothers benefit from your nonsense.'

'Thank you, Father,' Elmo said. He could not let it show, but this was no penance at all and would facilitate in the recovery of his gift from the old nest by the well.

Father Paul dismissed his youthful and recalcitrant monk, and the door was shut before he lost his stern countenance and smiled again. 'Ah, to be young again,' he said to himself. He allowed his thoughts to wander back down the road of long years until he came to a village that was his own boyhood. 'Ah, to be young again,' he whispered once more as tears sprung to his eyes. Abruptly he gathered himself into the aged body and mean room that was his present condition and blinked hard. 'Christ before all,' he muttered and returned to his duties.

Next morning, Brother Elmo dressed in the dark and rushed through dawn prayers. He planned to fetch the water – and his gift – between Matins and Prime. It would be a rush, for it took seven journeys back and forth from the well to fill the cistern with the day's water needs. It was a task with which he was quite familiar, and he padded the cross-yoke of the two-bucket contraption with his spare hose to save his shoulders from excessive bruising, but he had only completed one trip when he heard voices from the beach.

Setting down the buckets and yoke he hitched his habit and scurried to the gap in the rocks that led to the beach, and pulled up sharp, sand in sandals, when he saw two slaves dragging a small rowing boat away from the lapping tide. Three other men stood by and watched. They were clearly fine gentlemen, dressed in rich warm clothing cut in the Frankish style. Cloaked and proof against the biting chill of early morning, they were armed with swords slung from baldrics. One of the three also carried an axe and he appeared grander than the other two, who Elmo took for thegns, and he wondered what on earth they were doing so early in the morning. The island rarely had visitors, and never so early or so unexpected.

Calling out, he asked if they needed any help with the boat. They did not, but they beckoned him over so they could converse without having to raise their voices to be heard over the voice of the sea.

'Welcome to Coquet Island, sirs, and to our humble monastery. We have no fine food but there is bread to share, and ale.'

'Most gracious. We will gladly partake,' the leader said in an accent with which Elmo was unfamiliar. And then turning to his retainers, he said 'Red hair! The lad has red hair.'

Elmo unconsciously lifted a hand to the hair above his ear.

'May I ask, good Brother? Are you the novice who goes by the name Elmo?'

'I am sir, and at your service.'

The two thegns exchanged glances and looked very pleased with themselves, and their leader spoke again. 'Then, Brother Elmo, we have business, you and I,' he said, and his hand lifted to rest lightly upon the pommel of his sword.

4

~ 2008 ~
Two's a Crowd

As intriguing as the apparently anachronistic dental filling might have been, I don't think there are many, knowing my interests and history, who would berate me for leaving the skeleton to Raz while I stayed behind to examine the stone. That is exactly what I did, though not without a pang of guilt.

I was leaving Raz in charge of the dig. I was confident of his skills in both field technique and leadership, but there was one problem. Now, if you are a person who just happened to stray across this book, my revelation about Raz may not seem worthy of comment, but if you are a fellow archaeologist you may well take me for a bigger fool than I am. If you are the Doctor or one of his cohorts who has obtained a copy only so you may visit Amazon to award it one star, I could care less about your opinions, but not a lot.

Raz has no degree. He did not go to university. He may well be the only assistant to an archaeologist at my level of the profession so devoid of formal qualification and so loaded with natural ability. Since meeting Raz I have come to the opinion that it is unfortunate that a person's qualities may be passed over if they haven't got that piece of paper to flap in a prospective employer's face. And before you credit me with an innate feeling for an applicant's qualities, hold back for you will soon see that Raz came before my panel for less than noble reasons on my part.

It was just over two years ago as I write, and I was in need of a new assistant. Mandy was leaving to have a baby, and try as I might I could not persuade her to take maternity leave and come back to me. I don't like change, and Mandy was a very good assistant. But there was nothing to be done but advertise for a new one. Applications were in and I had enrolled the help of a colleague to help me with the paper sift.

Most of the applicants were, if anything, overqualified. One was older than me and held a doctorate. I felt flattered, and rather intimidated, that such a calibre of chap should wish to be my assistant. It was while I was reading and re-reading his CV that my colleague, Hazel, began to chuckle.

'There's a lad here who's a total no-hoper,' she said. 'No degree, just a handful of certificates and diplomas from Birkbeck, but he says he is fluent in Old English and Latin.'

I chuckled. 'Brazen little man! Let me see.' I held out my hand for the application papers. '"Raz Reeves"? Interesting name. What do you think Raz is short for? Ralph? Raphael?'

Hazel shrugged. 'Ramone?'

'Ye gods, spare me,' and I chuckled some more. But the lie – for who can be fluent in a language that has not been fully drawn out from the mists of time – had hooked me and I began to read a CV that I would otherwise have filed in the 'round-topped filing cabinet' without a glance past the qualifications box. Suddenly a petty and cruel little plan took seed.

'Do you feel like teaching him a lesson, Hazel? How about we call him in for an interview? We'll put him to the test. I'll handle the Anglo-Saxon and you take the Latin. Just like a language oral, we won't speak a word of modern English with him from the moment he enters to ten seconds later when he shuffles out, red-faced and penitent.' I know it's pretty much standard these days, but I hate CV's that are more faerie-tale that fact.

Hazel removed her back designer glasses so they would not diminish the flash from her eyes. 'Professor, I'm surprised at you. That is downright cruel.' Her disapproving look morphed into something more conspiratorial and almost lascivious. 'But don't you just hate it when people lie on their CVs?'

A day spent interviewing people can be very tedious, and in my case quite stressful as well. I wonder how many interviewees realise the interviewers are often at least as nervous as they are? So, to break up the day with some light relief, I schedule Raz's interview for the early afternoon:

64

drive away the accumulated cobwebs with a bit of mirth, and freshen up for the rest of the day.

Only, it did not quite work out that way. First his appearance: he did not wear a suit or tie, and yet his smart casual clothes set well on him and blurred the edges in much the same way as his easy manner. He was confident without being brash, quiet without being timid and the moment he walked in the door I began to feel very disappointed in myself. There was no way in the world this young man was going to get the job, and I had dragged him all the way up here for nothing more than a spiteful joke. I exchanged a remorseful look with Hazel and I could see she was thinking the same.

I opened with an Anglo-Saxon greeting and without the slightest hint of surprise, he replied perfectly and with an accent I can only describe as west-country-cum-German. It sounded so right, and made me wonder if my pronunciation, after all these years, was entirely faulty. Hazel then introduced herself in Latin and bid Raz sit down. He thanked her, again without appearing at all phased, and I realised our joke had just fallen very flat.

We moved through the interview, and Raz moved back and forward between Old English and Latin with apparent ease. And where I sometimes struggled to find the right way to ask a question, Raz always answered fluently and even used words I had never heard before.

Having proved his point, I called a halt to the bilingual interview and I was very relieved to continue in English. Despite his lack of qualifications, his hold on the basics of archaeology in general was more than sound, and he was very conversant with my period of special interest. When he left the room, both Hazel and I were silent for several minutes.

'Well,' Hazel said; an exposition rather than a question.

'Well, indeed! What do you think of that?'

Hazel looked stunned, tinged at the edges with mild euphoria, like a person who has just made an exciting discovery they can't quite believe. 'What an extraordinary young man.'

'Agreed, and I want him as my assistant.'

Of course, the board wouldn't hear of it: paying all that money (hah!) to an unqualified man. I took him on anyway; invented a post for him, so I did. He became something between a general factotum cum field tech cum anything else I could think of, and with several shows of petulance to the purse-keepers and numerous promises to trim my budget in other areas I managed to secure a meagre salary for him. To make it one upon which he could live, I topped it up from my own funds and all I can say is I hope Jenny never reads this. (Unlikely, as she has no interest in my work whatsoever). To my great relief, he accepted the post and with as much apparently genuine pleasure as if he had secured the advertised post.

By the time my official new assistant left for a top-job of his own, Raz had proved himself, and so six months ago I had no difficulty in persuading the board he was up to the job, degree or no. Raz became my official assistant, and I have every faith in him. Why then, my concern as he drove the Land Rover away from the house that morning? Well, he was going to be in charge and there were those under him who were better qualified, at least in recognised terms, and though he was the gold to their guinea-stamp, I hoped the situation would not lead to unpleasantness.

Please don't think that my misgivings lasted longer than the receding sound of his engine. As soon as Raz was gone, I hurried back to the pigsty. While Raz had a list of duties that including contacting the local coroner's officer and other legal niceties, I was up a ladder enthusiastically supplied by Jack Taylor, with my head held at ninety degrees to my neck, making the best I could of the thousand-year-old inscription.

I hadn't the slightest doubt that the fragment of stone that had sat in a cabinet in the British Museum since it was found sixty-odd years ago, was part of the one used to build the wall of this pigsty. I had studied it and knew the inscription. Well, it wasn't hard to remember. Triangular and smaller than its pigsty brother, the first line was part of the word that preceded the broken edge and comprised the partial word 'rend'. There followed the two extremities of a Celtic cross followed by the Old English word for 'below'. The next line had only the word 'the' followed a line down by 'when all'. And that was it! '...*rend below the when all*'. Not a lot to play with really.

So try to imagine my excitement. All the aches and pains ensuing from my awkward posture halfway up a ladder were as nothing compared to the work at hand. Here before me, quite literally, was another piece of the puzzle, and it was the piece that fit *directly* to the left of the one in the Museum.

'I shield ...' was the first term I deciphered followed by 'aerostber', a word I could not translate. Desperately trying to recall the exact position of the words on the Museum stone I performed mental gymnastics trying to align the letters I had in my memory with the hard cold ones before me. Of course I had telephoned one of my staff at the university to e-mail me a copy of the photo I kept of the Museum stone, but I was just too impatient to wait for it. I had completely forgotten that the stone featured as part of the cover illustration of my published book, so all I had to do was call up Amazon.co.uk and the image could have been with me in seconds. However, memory would have to suffice.

It was like completing an IQ puzzle designed to test spatial awareness, and it was soon solved. I assumed 'aerostber' was the incomplete word preceding 'rend' on the Museum stone. Placing them together I found myself contemplating another Old English word with which I was unfamiliar: 'aerostberend'.

Just as in German, which derived from Old English almost as much as modern English did, Old English words were often made up from pre-existing words which were run together. Where an Englishman says 'submarine', a German will say 'unterwasserboot'; literally 'under water boat'. So it was that I was able to split my new word into 'aerost' or 'early' and 'berend' or 'carrier'. Early-carrier? It still didn't mean a great deal, and I wondered if I should have kept Raz here with me on this job rather than dispatch him off to Old Bony.

So the words didn't immediately lend themselves to a lot of meaning. Was I any less excited? Was I buggery! I now had a most intriguing phrase to contemplate, for when I put it all together in my head, the solid and the remembered, I had this: *"I shield early-carriers' blood below until the time when all ..."* You may be assured I was as frustrated as Hell that there was at least one more part of the stone that was *never* likely to be found, but even to find so much as this was hugely significant. This is often the archaeologist's lot: wonderful and uplifting finds, but finds that are rarely complete. A long pondered question is answered but in the long run, provides nothing but a bigger question. What on *all* of God's earth was an early-carrier? The HMS Ark Royal made out of reeds? The ancestral source of the Aids virus?

Early-carrier? It had the ring of oppression about it, as if early-carriers were a kind of servant, but that could not be. Stones were not inscribed for slaves or servants, but for those of high status. After flying about on the wind for a while, like a fly-fisherman's line, my mind hooked into an idea. Maybe, just maybe, the term early-carrier referred to an ancestor who carried an important name – the first of a dynasty or noble family. Yes! That *had* to be it.

No, dear Professor, it didn't.

Jack, God love him, brought me a mug of tea and asked me what I'd discovered so far. I didn't mention the translation I carried in my head nor even the existence of the matching fragment in the British Museum, but I certainly conveyed my enthusiasm for the find.

'There was another piece, you know,' Jack said.

'Really?' I replied, wide eyed and innocent.

'Aye. The story goes it was fetched off by that lad years ago, when my Grandfather held the lease on this place.'

'Did you ever hear who he was - his name, or anything at all?' I recalled there was no record of who found stone fragment or indeed, the location of the find. The Museum had absorbed a small private collection just before the

Second World War. The collection included the fragment but it came without provenance.

Jack stroked his double chins while he searched his memory. 'Can't say as I ever heard his name, but I do have a photo of him. See, I got my love of old cars from Dad. He took photos of them whenever the chance arose. And yon chap was happy to pose by his motor in exchange for that bit of old stone.'

I asked if I could see the photo and Jack said he'd dig it out once he'd finished his chores. I was about to offer my assistance when my mobile sang out.

'You'd better zip over here Professor,' Raz's voice said from the other end. 'There's been a development.'

Usually when we uncover human bones, the process is slow and painstaking. The earth is often compacted so tightly that the resulting material can be harder than the bones it surrounds. So with the utmost care we debride particle after tiny particle. The skeleton starts off as a trace of varying colour in the ground and slowly begins to stand out in three-dimensions, almost reluctant to stir from its slumber of centuries.

I was surprised then to find Old Bony almost ready to break away from the cloying earth altogether and make a run for it. Already miffed at having to walk from our digs to the dig – Raz had taken the Land Rover earlier if you remember – I almost blew my top when I saw how much of the skeleton had been exposed as it hinted at sloppy technique and short cuts. Maybe Raz had been watching *Bone-kickers* after all.

Very intuitive and sensitive to words as yet unspoken, I am sure Raz knew what I was thinking for he looked hurt and ill-judged and his words carried a hint of indignation when he explained that, far from compacted, much of the earth had been loosened when the tree had fallen.

'Of course, yes the roots,' I mumbled. 'I see you have made good time, but what is it that draws me from my stone, Raz?'

Raz flashed his teeth in one of his all too rare smiles that were so infectious. I felt the grumpiness in me quaver like a coward before the enemy. It made one attempt at holding firm, and then fled for the hills.

'What is it?' I said chuckling.

'I shan't tell you. See if you can spot it.'

I won't bother to regale you with the response such a comment from any previous assistant would have drawn from me. My editor would cut it out anyway. Without any repost at all I looked down into the grave.

'Definitely a male then,' I said.

'Yes. Very narrow sacrum.'

I carefully stepped into the hole. My knees clicked and a nasty pain shot through my hip. 'Ooh nasty! Cut marks on the bones. Looks like the busy little osteoclasts have tried to repair some of them. Tortured then, over a period of time.' That was one explanation at any rate.

'Very likely, but that's not it. Look around more carefully.'

Careful boy, there is a limit you know! I looked more carefully. More specifically I looked to the foot where the metatarsal bones lay splayed and disconnected by time … and yes! I had it. 'Too many toe bones! There's another body lying below the first.'

'All very true, but keep going.'

My goodness, were there more than two? I could see no sign, so I stooped to look more closely at the bones clearly visible. The epiphyses of the long bones told a sad tale, admittedly one that would have to be confirmed at the lab, but clear enough for me to express my thoughts. 'Oh dear, he was just a boy.'

Raz nodded sadly. How strange that we should feel such empathy for one so long dead. 'I'd put him at between fifteen and twenty at the time of death,' he said.

Well, it was all very interesting, but nothing that couldn't have waited. My grumpiness was rallying and returning from the high ground, but I didn't want it to make its presence known to Raz, who was after all, leading his first important dig.

'Thanks, Raz. I look forward to seeing your report. Meanwhile, back to the stone with me. Give us a hand …'

We clasped one another palm-to-wrist in the manner of the Romans and Raz heaved me out of the hole.

'Not so fast, Professor. You've spotted a good deal, but I wouldn't have called you over for any of that.'

Raz's grin was becoming rather annoying. *Just tell me for crying out loud.* 'What then?' I looked back into the grave, checked everything three times. The solution evaded me until I caught Raz's gaze and he chucked my eyes into the desired direction with a flick of his. The tangled roots of the old oak, torn up and on display, were caked with great clods of earth. And there was something else. As I concentrated on the something else, my universe contracted into that one impossible spot. Maybe this *was* my Sutton Hoo after all.

Held in the hoary old roots was a large slab of stone, and I knew immediately that it was the last missing part and that it would fit with the other two, one back in the pigsty and one in the British Museum.

I didn't hug Raz. This time my excitement was bounded in steel. It was bounded by the impossibility of the situation and I could already hear the hoots and shouts of derision. There wasn't a fellow archaeologist in the land who would believe I hadn't somehow pulled off the most cynical of hoaxes. Even before I went to check for signs of an inscription I could hear the derisive calls in my mind. *Here comes Professor Piltdown with his fake stones.*

Consider: a man whose speciality is inscribed stones merrily happens across a missing part of the stone he has studied for years, shoring up the walls of a pigsty, and then lo and behold, abracadabra, the very next day he finds the rest. And yes, I knew the stone well enough to know in my heart that this root-bound shard was the last of the missing pieces. I knew the very instant my eyes fell upon it despite the clinging clods and ravelling roots.

The steel bounds burst and I stumbled. Raz caught and steadied me, then asked if I was alright. His words were little more than a faraway echo to me. I moved closer to the root mass all the time considering how best to validate this amazing discovery. Perhaps we'd start with a dendrochronologist who could tell us the age of the tree. A botanist to look at the roots and give an opinion as to how old the roots were and how long it would take them to extend their hold over the fragment. We'd need someone to give independent confirmation to our stratigraphic findings – the age of the various layers from now all the way back to the time of burial: a hard job in light of the disturbance caused by the ripping of the roots as the tree fell.

I reached out and manoeuvring my hand through the thick roots I touched the stone and to this day I swear my fingers tingled with electricity – self-generated by excitement, no doubt, but no less tangible. I remember hoping that on the other side of the stone there was some legible inscription that had survived the centuries and then I began to wonder how best to dislodge the thing from the tight grip of the roots. With that, a large clod of earth dislodged itself and fell away, and then the now loosened stone slipped straight out of the tangle and fell face up, next to the smiling skull.

'Damn! I hope you got a photo of the stone in situ,' I said. It is hard to stress how important it is to record every stage of every discovery.

'Several dozen, and from every conceivable angle,' Raz assured me. 'Digital and good old fashioned film.'

I jumped down and if my knees creaked this time I have no recollection of it. With the gentlest of brushing, letters were revealed and the inscription was clearer than on the other two pieces.

I read the inscription, translating as I went along. 'It says "*shall know from lesser men they took the blow*".' I took a moment for me to recall the partial inscriptions on the other stones and then put them all together. I recited it out loud for the benefit of Raz.

I shield early-carrier
Blood below
Until the
Time when all
Shall know from
Lesser men

72

Here I should explain something about the rhyme encompassed within the inscription. Poetry from the relevant period did not rhyme at all but was based on alliteration. The Old English version of the inscription did not rhyme … nor did it alliterate, so the rhyme apparent in the translation is purely coincidental. Admittedly, where a choice of words existed, I plumped for the rhyming one. Example; the last word could be 'blow' or 'strike'. So we may call the presence of rhyme, 'assisted coincidence'.

We looked at the skeleton reaching out to us from the long years past.

'So he was an early-carrier, whatever the blazes that means.'

Raz asked me what I meant and I told him about my translation of the phrase spanning the other two pieces of the grave marker. He asked me to spell out the original Old English word.

'Aerostberend.' Raz spoke in a whisper, mulling the word over and over so the light might shine on another angle and cast new meaning. '"Early-carrier" doesn't ring true to me.' He knelt close to the stone and cocked an ear as if listening for a still small word, a coherent vibration from the stone that spoke to his bones. I can tell you exactly when the penny dropped, for it shone on his face.

'Professor! Translate "gastberend" for me please.'

It was an easy one. 'It means "human",' I said.

'And yet the literal translation is "hero-carrier" or "hero-born", so might not "aerostberend" mean –'

'First-born!' I shouted the answer that was always lurking in the shade, now forced out by Raz's bright illumination. 'My God, you're right. It means "first born".' The inscription now bore repetition and so I repeated it in full with the newly deduced meaning in place of the old one.

I shield first-born
Blood below
Until the

Time when all
Shall know from
Lesser men
They took the blow

The Celtic cross separated the words 'blood' and 'below' in the second line and similarly the two words in the third. There was another set of symbols between the two words in the last line but one: a simple bird shape followed by a geometric symbol made up of a circle within a square and to the right of this, an icthus or to put it crudely, a Jesus-fish symbol.

'Nobles, perhaps, killed by commoners,' I said. 'We need to work on this excavation. There may be an entire family down here.' I was about to start issuing instruction when I noticed that Raz stood quietly with dipped head. 'No,' he said. 'There're only the two of them.' He looked up at me and his eyes were moist. 'Brothers, I think.'

It is strange how we can be affected by deaths from long ago, but when youth and injustice are involved, time is no barrier to emotion. I cite the two princes in the Tower; young Prince Arthur, first blinded and then put away by his Uncle John and even Caesarion who was never heard of again once Octavius was on the road to becoming Augustus. But empathy has little place in determining the facts, no matter how much TV producer may love it. You have to be a pretty strong character not to let a director put words or emotions into your 'talking head'. They want drama, but they forget that the viewing public are quite able to perceive massive leaps in logic. It is one of my pet hates in popular archaeology that a possibility in one scene becomes a theory in the next and an accepted fact by the end of the program.

'Brothers, you say? Well, perhaps but let's not jump to conclusions,' I said, conveniently forgetting my earlier 'nobles killed by commoners' comment, although in fairness to me the inscription did lend itself to my off-the-cuff deduction.

For a few moments we returned to the event with my attention firmly and almost disbelievingly fixed upon the stone, and Raz's, I am willing to bet, on the still emerging skeletons. I am further willing to bet that the same disturbing thought lurked at the back of each of our minds.

'We should report this,' I said, bringing that thought to the fore.

Raz nodded slowly. 'You want me to make a start on the form? Only, it's not as if we've got much to report at the moment.'

Raz was dissembling by proxy: of course we had something to report, but Raz had seen into my soul and was making the excuses I wanted to hear. This was *my* find – *my* precious, as Gollum would say – and I didn't want anybody moving in and taking it away from me. I could picture a scene where the Doctor, curse his boots, made great play of my premature paper and persuaded the board that I was not to be trusted. I could see his gloating face as he took away my project. The boys in the grave called out to me for rescue, bony hand held in supplication as the Doctor hid the story they wanted me to reveal.

But of course, to keep the find to myself would be professional suicide. As much as I wanted to continue there was the matter of resources, my time away from the day job and other practical considerations.

'We have to stick to the required process,' I said, flicking my eyes towards the two field techs who were sitting astride a limb of the fallen oak eating their lunch. I moved close to Raz and lowered my voice. 'So let's get cracking with the paperwork, but there is no reason, just yet, to mention the find in the pigsty.'

I thought I saw a movement below and as I looked, a trick of the light made it look as if the skeleton had winked at me. Certainly the smile seemed wider.

Raz's smile revealed an awfully similar set of teeth. 'Are we being ever so slightly naughty?'

'I think perhaps we are, but I have the distinct feeling we are doing the right thing.'

Raz was serious again and he nodded thoughtfully, that frown once again knitting his eyebrows. 'Me too,' he said. 'I'll see if I can get us the room again for tonight.'

I phoned Jenny and told her of the find. It was pointless trying to enthuse her with anything to do with my job; it bored her rigid. I knew from past experience that any excitement I showed would be blown away by her thinly veiled indifference, so I just reported the facts and told her I'd be away for one more night. I then listened while Jenny told me what a terrible inconvenience it was that she should have to walk the dog for the second morning in a row.

As it transpired, I left Raz with the dig and returned to the pigsty. Luckily there were no guests due at the house that night, so I was able to secure separate rooms for Raz and me.

While I studied the embedded stone and its setting in thorough detail, I looked forward to dinner and a fireside debrief of the day's events. How was I to know that before bedtime, we would have another piece of the ever expanding jigsaw?

V

~ 793 ~
In which the Raven Spreads His Wings and the Fish Faces his Fate

With the oars dripping copiously from the rack, a sudden gust of wind filled the sail and the *Thought* surged forward. Finn stood at his post, both hands gripping the steer-board. Gradigheim receded into the morning mist as the raider picked up speed along the fjord, but Finn kept his eyes forward and his mind on the open sea.

It was not what he had expected, neither the departure nor the first leg of the long journey. Yes, people had come to see them off, but he had expected more excitement. Instead all except the children had said their goodbyes quietly. There was dignity, pride and forbearance in the eyes of the women, guilt in the demeanour of the warriors who stayed behind despite the fact that they were only obeying the chieftain's command, and shame in the old men who had outlived their usefulness. All this Finn saw, but no excitement. He remembered previous departures differently and couldn't wait to be on the ship instead of left back on the shore. He wondered if he was remembering those earlier times from a child's point of view. Now he was a man, and the reality was more ordered, more efficient.

Bjorn stood up at the bow, cloak billowing and one hand grasping the stem-post. The crew went about their tasks quietly, adjusting a shroud-pin here, testing a sheet there; Tosti tightened the strap that held all the spears secure to the aft-post and Gudric swore under his breath when he hit his ankle on the upturned gunwale of the faering.

Bjorn had insisted on bringing the faering instead of the usual, much smaller ship's boat, and its extra length and beam, and the protruding, folded mast took some getting used to. The crew knew every inch of their ship and could move about the deck in the dark, but the fifteen-foot faering was like a dead hog on a narrow path: it got in the way. But Bjorn's word was law, and no amount of bruised shins or stubbed toes would change that.

Finn breathed deeply of the fresh, tangy air. The late spring sky was clear and it promised to be a sunny day, but the wind over open water brought a chill with it and Finn was glad of his woollen layers and hooded cowl. Come night and he would open his wooden chest – it also served as a seat when his turn came to row – and draw out his cloak.

'*Memory* means to overhaul us!' Bjorn called from the stem. 'Are we going to let that happen?'

Even as the ragged call of 'No!' rose from the ship, Finn caught sight of the *Memory* pulling ahead on the land-board side.

Excitement at last! Finn kept a close eye on his father for directional commands although he couldn't understand why the chieftain ordered the sail trimmed in such a way that the *Thought* slowed a little. Just like the rest of the crew, Finn had learned never to question his father's commands and was used to the fact that they were not often accompanied by explanations. Nobody raised a question even when the *Thought* fell a length behind the *Memory*. Finn suspected the additional weight of the faering was hampering their progress, but then Bjorn ordered him to push the steer-board. The ship veered to the land-board side with the stem of the *Thought* just yards from the stern of the *Memory*, and then the *Thought* stole her sister-ship's wind. Now *Thought* leapt forward and *Memory* wallowed for a moment. As the *Thought* swept past the *Memory*, Finn's crewmates derided the opposing crew and called out insults. The other crew gave as good as they got and one of them dropped his trousers and waggled his bare arse in such a comically insulting fashion that Finn wished he had brought his sling-shot on board.

Something passed between the respective captains and with no more than a look, frivolity was at an end. The two longships completed their race to the sea shoulder-to-shoulder.

When night fell, the crews of both ships made camp on a small narrow stretch of sandy beach. The cove gave shelter to the ships and the beach made for a convenient stopping place, but there was no easy way up to the land beyond. This suited Bjorn well, for it meant that equally, there was no easy way down to the beach for any opportunists who might see a chance to ambush the his men.

They could have taken the hospitality of Bjorn's cousin whose settlement was less than an hour's easy rowing along the next inlet, but Bjorn preferred seclusion in the days leading to a raid. Hospitality meant mead and ale. Mead and ale meant horseplay and that often led to fighting. Bjorn did not want to lose any of his warriors to drunken brawls when he needed them all for the raid ahead. There was another reason: Bjorn never spoke of his plans until he was about to cross the open sea.

The camp fires were kept small and voices low. Gudric told Finn that he should join Tosti and the brothers Aki and Abi by his fire because Bjorn wished to instruct them separately as to their duties come raiding time. They had time to settle to a meal of stew before Bjorn joined them, rolling out of the seaward shadow like silent doom.

'So you are here, all five,' Bjorn said. His hood flapped in the light breeze as strands of hair flew around under his woollen cap. Like the other warriors, he wore a sword hanging from his baldric but was otherwise not dressed for battle. War gear was heavy and cumbersome and only served to drown a man at sea.

'Five should be enough,' Bjorn said musing to himself. 'Now dish me some of that stew, and I will tell you my plan.'

This was no raid for slaves and plunder, although any plunder to be had would not be left begging. No, the main objective for this raid was to kill monks and any other followers of the White Christ who happened to get in the way. The king had made it known that he tired of the missionaries who plagued his shores and stuck their long noses and beardless chins into his fjords, but they were never ending: deal with one and then along came another to replace him. One or two villages had even shown signs of converting to their lily-livered religion, and the king would not have it.

'Now, I shall lead *Thought* and *Memory* to the large island they call Lindisfarne whereupon there is a monk-house of good size. We will kill all the mewling spawn that infests the isle and take whatever gold there is to be had.'

Finn liked the idea of killing, but had rather wished he could try out his battle-skills. There was little honour in killing one of these monks, but at least he would be doing the king's will.'

'But you five will not be coming with me.'

Finn was about to protest, but held his tongue.

'Instead you, Finn, will command the faering and sail it a little further south, to a place wherein the mouth of a river lays a dog's turd of an island with its own burden of worms.'

'Me ... lead? Thank you, Father.'

Bjorn ran a finger under his nose and sniffed loudly. 'I know what you're thinking. Will five warriors be enough? And I tell you it will be plenty. You will be facing no more than ten White Christ monks who cannot fight to save their lives because they are as weak as baby girls and even those with brawn are not allowed to fight as it is against the laws of their religion.'

'Can there be a religion that does not honour the skills of a warrior?' Finn said.

Bjorn leaned close. 'Ask Gudric. He knows a thing or two about the White Christ and all his cowardly saints.'

'That I do,' Gudric confirmed. 'And it gives me a mind to sport.'

Bjorn laughed, clapped his son on the back and took his leave, and his bowl of stew. Finn watched until his father was a silhouette crouching by the next fire.

'So, tell me Gudric, what of these cowards, and what of your sport?'

Gudric scraped the cooking pot for any remaining dregs of food and then sat close to Finn before beckoning the other three close. 'See, these White Christ monks are wont

80

to take the names of saints when they join their order, and it is the mark of their saints to die a curious and painful death. It gave me the idea that instead of dealing death quickly to the monks, we should cause them to die in a manner befitting their chosen name.'

Aki and Abi laughed and nodded their approval and Tosti grinned too.

'Are there many White Christ saints, and have you memorised so many manners of death?' Finn asked.

'Many and many,' Gudric said. 'And I have made it my pleasure to know them all.'

Gudric and the four younger men laughed softly.

'And shall my sword or my spear be the bloodier?' Finn said.

'Blood aplenty for all and more besides,' Gudric said. 'And those that don't bleed out shall shrivel upon fires like their fallen saint. I feel this will be a raid to remember.'

'Indeed it will, come what may,' Finn said. 'For I hear that no man forgets his first raid, and of us five only you, Gudric, have gone raiding before.'

At Tosti's request, Gudric began to relive his first raid, and the young men listened in awe, and all were glad of the dark.

A cursed day upon this earth, when Bloody Mary had her birth.

Elmo feared he was about to lose his head. The nobleman before him drew his sword and Elmo wanted to run from the beach and call out a warning to his brother monks, but he knew there would be no outrunning the arrow of the thegn armed with a bow.

'Here, sir, your father's blade,' the nobleman said dipping his head respectfully and holding out the sword, hilt foremost. 'I am Eovan Tucarus of Skol-Jerrag, once in his service and now in yours.'

Elmo did not wish to touch the tool of death, but his reluctance was overcome by the strong desire not to insult such a noble gentleman. He took the blade and made a show of examining it while in reality trying to make sense of the stranger's words. The heft, the balance and the magnificent workmanship: it was without doubt the finest sword he had ever held.

'Sir, this is indeed the work of craftsmen and the owner must be the equal of kings, but there has been a mistake. My father favoured the axe and was but a poor reeve. His year's salary could not have commissioned the likes of this – and please sir, cease your bowing. You do me great but entirely undeserved honour and you owe me no service.' Curiously for grown men who were not in holy orders, their faces were clean-shaven, a fact that Elmo had only just absorbed.

The nobleman withdrew the finely crafted scabbard and held it out for Elmo to take. 'I speak not of Thomas Gerefa, he that took you in as an orphan, but of your true father and my liege until his disposition and murder these four years past.'

Elmo took the scabbard quite unconsciously and slid the blade into its silver-chaped home. 'Nobody knows who my true parents were,' he said trying the grasp and hold down thoughts that flew about his head like loose threads in the wind. 'I was left in a basket at the causeway to the Holy Island at low tide. If I hadn't been found by a party of monks returning to the monastery from York, the tide would have turned and I would have floated out to sea and drowned.'

'There was never the chance you would be lost,' Eovan said. 'Call your apparent abandonment an expedient against evil eventualities that have now come to pass.'

'I was *meant* to be found by the holy brothers?'

'Aye, and there was never a doubt of it and if I sound certain it is because it was I who placed the basket on the wet sand as the brothers' drew close to the crossing, and I who waited unseen until they took you up and across the causeway to safety.'

Elmo gripped the sword close to his chest as he tried to grapple with many tumbling thoughts. Eovan was a young man and if he truly had placed the basket almost seventeen years before, he could not have been more than a boy himself. Elmo's thoughts became solid and took the form of numerous questions, but there on the little sandy beach he had no time to ask them.

'Now, was there not mention of bread and ale? Must we stand with the wind blowing into our nether-clothes when I suspect there is a warm fire within a spit's range?'

Elmo remembered his manners. 'Of course, sir. Please go up and into the monastery. Brother Andrew will greet you, and I will join you as soon as I may. I have chores to attend.'

'Fetching the water?' the nobleman said spying the yoke. 'A fine job for an atheling, but no doubt good for the spirit.' He turned and with no more than a flick of the eyes he instructed one of the thegns to attend to the water.

'No please sir, you mustn't. I am a novice and the lowliest of my order. It is not meet that such gentleman should relieve me of my penance.'

The nobleman and both thegns laughed. 'Penance, is it?' said the thegn who had been chosen to fetch the water. 'I cannot image what evil deed has earned you such stripes, but rest! If you will not own that you are atheling and I but a poor knight, then you must concede that I, as a man of war, have a duty to serve the man of peace. Lead me to your buckets sir, point me well-wards and then take my lord to your abbot.'

Elmo led Eovan and one thegn to the monastery while the other saw to the task of fetching water, and he thought it ill fortune that instead of Brother Andrew, it was Brother Sebastian who was there to greet them. Ill-fortune there was, but it soon attached itself to Sebastian when he began to chide Elmo in the strongest and most derisive terms available to a holy brother. He was cut short by a fierce interjection by Eovan of Skol-Jerrag that had Sebastian almost grovelling in abject apology.

'Please forgive me sire, but I saw only a novice carrying an implement he has foresworn and it blinded me to your noble presence.'

'No matter, for truly my light is dim when I stand next to the radiance of the atheling.'

Brother Sebastian tried to see the joke, but did not wish to commit to feigned laughter until he understood it.

'Do you not see it, man?' Eovan said impatiently. 'The light that shines about him?'

Sebastian regarded Elmo with a bemused look. 'Well … erm … I see Brother Elmo … but –'

'Our noble guest jests with you, Brother Sebastian.' Father Paul stood half-way up the stone staircase. He came down two more steps before addressing Eovan. 'So, it has come to pass.'

Eovan bowed. 'My Lord Abbot, regretfully it has.'

'Then we have no time to waste. Will you take food and wine in my humble cell, and there shall we discuss what is to be done?'

'Most gratefully.'

'Then come.' Father Paul turned to go back up. 'Gentlemen, Elmo. Follow me. And Brother Sebastian, please arrange the refreshments.'

Brother Sebastian scuttled off to the refectory.

'Perhaps Brother Elmo has matters that require his attention,' Eovan said. 'For I hope we may speak a moment in private, Father Paul.'

'So be it. Elmo, go and ….' The abbot appeared to cast about for a suitable chore. 'Hide that sword somewhere safe, and then when it is ready fetch the food that Sebastian is preparing.'

Father Paul dragged his bulk up the steep stairs with some difficulty and the visitors followed.

There was only one place to hide anything in the tiny monastery, so Father Paul might just as well have said 'Take that sword and put it in Saint Cuthbert's cell'. Cuthbert had lived there a hundred years earlier when the building was even smaller and was little more than Cuthbert's stone-walled and earthen-floored cell. The rest of the building had

84

grown round it and over it, so that it was now accessible only by lifting a section of floor boarding. Previous abbots had deemed the place the equivalent of a holy relic, but Father Paul was far more practical and found it a convenient storage space.

Elmo was lowering the trapdoor when Brother Sebastian grabbed him from behind and spun him round. 'Who are those … those *brutes,* and what have you to do with them?' His eyes were full of malice and he was like a coiled snake, ready to strike.

Elmo was not afraid of Sebastian, in fact he rather pitied him. Pity would fly out of the window though, if he attempted to strike him, and Sebastian would fly backwards onto his arse. Elmo filtered the anger from his reply and spoke in a measured tone. 'Those gentlemen are far from brutes, Brother Sebastian, and though their mission may be known to Father Paul, I am not privy.' He thought it prudent not to remind Sebastian that the nobleman had called him atheling; Sebastian mocked him more than sufficiently as the son of a warrior, so there was no telling how he would deal with news that he was son of a king.

Sebastian grasped Elmo's arm and pulled him along towards the refectory.

Elmo jerked his arm out of the senior brother's grasp and Sebastian turned to stare as if at a worm coming up between the flagstones. 'You *dare* to –'

'You may lead and I will follow, Brother Sebastian, but I will *not* be dragged.' In that instant the warrior's way, long ago taught but never forgotten entirely, returned to Elmo and he allowed his body to relax and his senses sharpen. He would not allow a single slap to land upon him. Never again! He was past accepting such rude handling from Brother Sebastian.

Brother Sebastian must have sensed something of the change in the young novice, for his face dropped an instant and then he turned, muttering, to lead the way.

Sebastian threw several hunks of bread and some cheese onto a serving platter. 'There! Take that up to the Abbot, and when they're done come back here and wash the plate … and the spoons and knives and prickers.' Having given his instructions, Sebastian left the building dragging a train of ill-tempered malice with him.

'Gone to cool his nerves,' Brother Mundwyn said from a corner. Elmo had not seen him sitting in the shadow by the pantry. 'So hot his blood that it's best he jumps into the waves and there to sit a while.' The white-haired monk chuckled and chewed upon a twig.

'Surely I am a disappointment to him, Brother Mundwyn.'

'Be you the youthful Bede himself Sebastian would find fault in you. So fearful, he is, that his own shortcomings may stray into the light that he makes much of the faults in others. Now, the pot has boiled. Take it up while the water is yet hot lest our visitors take their mead steaming.'

Elmo picked up the tray of food and drink and paused at the doorway. 'I fear I am to learn more of myself than I think I may bear.'

'How exciting,' Mundwyn said. 'For I believe the wriggling grub is about to split out of his leathery coat. Come back to me when all is done and show me your many-hued wings.'

Elmo tapped Father Paul's cell door with the toe of his shoe by way of a knock and when bid enter called that he could not work the latch, for his hands were not free.

Eovan opened the door and stood aside, bidding the boy enter with a deference that embarrassed him.

'Come in, come in Brother,' the abbot called with an avuncular tone. Lay the feast upon the table and we will sit and eat.'

The others all sat round the table and when Elmo was invited to join them he made a conscious decision to ignore the feelings that screamed against the inappropriateness of being treated as an equal by the abbot and these visitors.

'Break yourself some bread, Brother Elmo,' Father Paul said and at the same time Eovan poured him a cup of wine.

Elmo thinned it with hot water and drank.

'There must be no skulking in the shadows,' Father Paul said. 'We must dare to tread out in the full sunlight and tell you everything, for your life is in danger and to hide the fact would serve you ill.'

Elmo had already guessed as much. If he was truly atheling and son to a deposed and murdered king, that king had to be Elfwald and it was common gossip, spoken in whispers and with hand held to mouth, that Elfwald and his two young sons had been murdered. A third son could *hope* for a kinder fate, but expect nothing better. Elmo voiced his suspicion and Eovan confirmed it.

Elmo nodded slowly while he imagined deep dungeons and a dark, secret death. 'They do say King Elfwald was slain because he carried First Born blood. If, as you say sir, I am his son, then that blood runs in my veins and I am doubly cursed.'

'Doubly blessed, some might say,' the thegn said.

'There can be few, if any, of mankind's younger children who do not carry a little First Born blood, but there are few left indeed in whose veins in runs undiluted. My lord Elfwald and his lady were two such, and so in you the blood also runs pure. And yes, it was almost the greatest reason for his murder, second only to the fact he was king. Those taking on the golden circlet are very prone to die by the envy-driven blade.'

In me the blood runs pure? Elmo thought of the many myths and legends that surrounded the First Born and he tried to imagine which of them carried a grain of truth. But of one thing he was sure: to both state and church, the First Born were anathema, and both institutions meant to end them. No trace or reference of them was allowed to survive.

'Am I to deliver myself up?' Elmo tried to keep the fear from his voice. 'Did you come hither with a warrant for my death?'

Father Paul coughed in horror of the very thought while Eovan was left to speak. 'The very opposite! I would die before I allowed you to be taken.'

'And I too,' Father Paul said, 'although Rome would flay me alive for harbouring the thought.'

Elmo thanked the abbot. 'But how is it Father, that you serve the Lord and yet would defy His word to protect the wicked?'

'Although some might call it blasphemy, I say there is much difference between the word of the Lord and the word of the church. They are *not* the same and there is a small band of us within the church who seek to give succour to the First Born wherever we should find them.'

'The edict to strike all references of the First Born from our manuscripts was one measure deemed necessary for our protection,' Eovan said. 'Though it suits Rome, and indeed, the church claims authorship to the edict.'

'You ...?'

'Yes, Elfgar. I am First Born as are my retainers, though there be but few of us left upon all the lands of the world – and fewer still with each day that passes.'

Elmo had discarded his old name. Elfgar did not fit him anymore. He was Elmo the novice, not Elfgar the atheling, and yet he knew he had little choice in the matter. 'Fewer by each day passing? You ... we are being killed?'

'We are leaving, and so must you. That is our quest. We must gather all together and leave. A brother and acquaintance of ours who knows the truth about you was taken by Godwin and word is that he was put to torture. If Godwin of all people knows about you, then we haven't a moment to waste.'

'We flee? But where to, for there is no place we may go that does not feel the touch of the church.' Elmo had heard of lands far, far to the east of the kingdoms of Charles the Great, but could a civilised man live in such places?

Eovan smiled. 'There is a place we may and must go, to which the church and all its hosts are barred. There are gates that only we may pass, and to those secret ways we must hasten.'

'But Alcuin's quest,' Father Paul said. 'His letter.'

'Hold, sir!' Eovan said. It sounded more like a command.

'Alcuin!' Elmo's face shone from the shadow of recent disclosures at the mention of his beloved tutor's name. 'You have news of Alcuin?'

'Better yet, I have news *from* Alcuin,' Father Paul said. 'He has sent me a letter, and one to you also.'

A letter from Alcuin! In spite of so much dark news, the thought of a letter from Alcuin made Elmo's spirits soar.

'Alcuinus scribbles letters by the wagon-load,' Eovan said. 'And although we have been spared much by his interventions, we cannot endorse all he says.'

'He has a quest for you, Brother Elmo.'

Eovan furrowed his brows and gave Father Paul a withering look. 'His quest and ours do not make easy bedfellows. We must take Elfgar to safety as soon as we may. There is no time for quests that delay us.'

Quest! Quest? 'And yet I may see the letter?'

At the same instant Eovan voiced in the negative while Father Paul said yes.

'I *shall* see the letter, sir!' Elmo said rising.

Father Paul and Lord Eovan of Skol-Jerrag both looked at Elmo as if seeing a new man.

'Of course you shall see the letter,' Father Paul said. 'Whether you shall act upon it is another matter, but I will countenance no interception of a message between men. To interrupt such discourse is ill-mannered in the extreme, if not a veritable sin.'

'Thank you, Father.'

Eovan gestured for Elmo to be seated once again. 'Very well, you shall see the letter. But first, let us discuss your lineage.'

Elmo knew his lineage very well. The monks of Lindisfarne had given him into the loving care of the household of Thomas Gerefa. He had grown knowing the love of a mother, a father and a brother. He had been taught to read, and skill at arms when he was old enough. At twelve years of age he had travelled across the sea to the court of King Charles where Alcuin of York took him as a student. Alcuin chose not to teach him as a holy brother but as the secular son of a friend, and so his martial skills were not neglected. Elmo became friends with Pepin and Louis, the Emperor's sons, and studied with them until he was fifteen. It was only at fifteen that he foreswore the warrior's life and a year later that he went to begin his life as a monk on Coquet Island. What more was there to know? He did not wish to be so doused by his First Blood that it washed away all that was dear to him.

It wasn't until after Sext, the midday prayers, that Elmo had time to be alone. He walked to the far side of the island and sat with his feet dangling over the low cliff edge, scanning the mainland hills as the afternoon sun shone through thickening mist.

First Born! How to separate the myth from the truth? Was he to live forever, or until a blade or some other misfortune steal away his life? Could he work magic? Was there really a light within him? They said that a heavenly light shone about the place where Elfwald – his father – was slain. Was Elfwald truly his father? Why not? Nothing to the contrary was known of his life before he was abandoned to the mercies of the good monks.

A chill breeze moved in with a thick bank of sea mist and Elmo wrapped himself about with his own arms. For all his questions and uncertainties, he was none the less the son of Thomas and brother of Eric. What did blood matter when compared to love and nurture? And with that thought Elmo rose, feeling comforted. He could not be sure, but he thought he saw a boat out to the seaward side of the isle, and then it was gone again. He squinted to peer through the mist but saw nothing. Perhaps it was just another seal.

At length resolved to assert the watery ball,
He in himself did whole Armadas bring;
Him aged seamen might their master call,
And choose for general, were he not their king.

'I think the White Christ has sent this mist to hide his worshippers from us,' Tosti said.

'Shut up!' Finn hissed. 'The White Christ wouldn't have the guts. You've heard Gudric's stories about meekness and turning the other cheek. Do you think he would stand a chance against Thor?'

Alrik's twins snickered and Finn grinned at the thought of a battle between such ill-matched gods.

Once again four pairs of eyes concentrated, trying to peer through the mist, leaving only Gudric leaning over the prow on the look-out for rocks.

Finn wondered how *Thought* and *Memory* were faring. They would not attack the larger island of Lindisfarne in a mist such as this, but there was no turning back for Finn. Bank upon bank of damp mist had rolled in less than a half hour after the faering had been set loose from *Thought,* so the raiders would not have had time to reach their objective. In such mist they would have trouble finding it and they dare not sail too close to such a rocky coat.

'They'll heave-to out at sea.' Finn spoke his thoughts aloud.

Tosti asked what he was talking about.

'Father's ships won't raid while the clouds are kissing the waves. He'll have *Thought* and *Memory* safe out to sea and away from the biting rocks. We'll meet when this muck lifts.'

'The monks will wait for us. We'll just have to come back another time and spoil their fireside feasts.'

Finn thought he saw the tiny island but it was gone again at the whim of the shifting veils. 'There'll be but little waiting for the monks of dog-turd island. I can almost smell it, and we can do our work under cloud or sunlight with just as much ease.'

'No need to smell it,' Gudric called softly from the prow. 'There it is!'

A thrill passed through Finn as the island solidified from the mist ahead. This time they had a fix upon it, although it was hard to determine size or distance. Was it a rock or the whole of England? 'Reef the sail and break out

91

the oars. There are many rocks about this island, so we must have a care.'

Gudric twisted the prow-end shroud-pin and they all helped to fold the mast back along the length of the faering. In the next instant, the twins and Tosti began to row. Gudric called his steering instructions from the prow and Finn manned the steer-board. There were many semi-submerged rocks but the mist had thinned a little and Gudric was able to give ample warning. They picked their way carefully around the island making for the landward side where Bjorn had said there was a small sandy beach – the only part of the island suitable for a landing.

'Put up those oars Tosti, and string your bow,' Finn said as if there wasn't the fainted possibility of his command being questioned. 'And nock an arrow as soon as you may. If this was my island I'd have a watchman posted.'

As the faering rounded the southern point of the island the lighter colour of the sandy beach came into view, and two figures could be seen sitting by a small rowing boat. One of the two never rose again, for Tosti's arrow took him in the heart as he sat. By the time the second had rallied his mind to action, Tosti had nocked his second arrow. The man on the beach made a dash for higher ground and the sanctuary of the monastery but he fell, shot through the neck. The arrow had entered just below the skull and his dead body fell like a sack of grain.

There was no time for Finn to congratulate his cousin before there was a sickening crunch as the faering came down hard upon a jagged rock. The clicker smashed like eggshells and the sea gushed in. Silently the men jumped overboard. The water came to their waists so they were able to drag their boat to the shore before it went under with their war gear.

'Stand ready with your bow while we arm,' Finn said. 'Shoot anybody who shows themselves in the gap.'

Tosti pulled the arrow from the dead man next to the boat and deemed it still fit for use. The other warriors immediately began to arm, helping each other on with the heavy byrnies and latching helmet straps under their chins.

A figure appeared in the gap between the rocks that gave access to the beach. A monk! He paused, as if trying to see through the mist, and saw the danger too late. Tosti bloodied his arrow for a second time, but struck low, piercing the monk's belly. The man looked down and screamed. Another arrow hit a little higher but still the man did not fall. Muffled cries of alarm could be heard from higher on the island and the twice-shot monk still stood and screamed until Gudric, now fully armed, ran forward and thrust a spear under his ribs and up into his heart.

Gudric looked over his shoulder and chuckled. 'I hope this one was called Sebastian,' he said tapping the embedded arrows with his bloody spear.

'Let's be at them then, like wolves among the sheep!' Finn growled and ran up past Gudric. The others followed and each let rip with a cry that would only be satisfied by blood.

'Don't kill them right away,' Gudric yelled. 'Remember, they are to die according to their saint-names.'

Finn led the raid and charged towards the little monastery. He doubted Gudric would have his way. From what he had heard about these monks, they would drop dead at the sight of him. He prepared to drop his spear and take a flying kick at the flimsy-looking door but when he was half-a-ship's length away, the door opened – and warriors streamed out.

One dropped instantly, another victim to Tosti's skills. But the others charged. Finn smiled: there appeared to be only two of them and they were not armed for war. They had swords only, not even shields.

One was upon Finn and hacked off the end of his spear. Through Finn's defence, this had suddenly become a real battle. The warrior thrust with his sword. Finn dodged the thrust, shield-barged the attacking warrior and planted a fist square in the middle of his face. He fell back, blood and snot bursting from his nose. Finn had time to draw his sword but he did not have time to strike. The warrior was taken by two spears at the same time, one thrust by Abi from the left, and from the right by Aki. The other warrior lay with an axe-cloven skull and Gudric ran forward and kicked open the door. Cries of terror from within stopped abruptly as Gudric looked in. He then seized the door knob and slammed it shut.

'No more warriors,' Gudric said with a leering grin. 'Just a gaggle of monks who long to provide us good sport.'

'Then let's not keep them waiting,' Tosti said.

Finn looked into the eyes of the fallen warrior, and lusted for more killing. This one yet lived, but with two such spear-wounds he would bleed out within moments.

'There!' Tosti shouted while he fumbled to nock an arrow.

A monk had run to the corner of the beach and was shouldering a small boat into the waves.

'Leave him to me!' Finn yelled. He sprinted towards his next victim, chain armour beating out a rhythmic, dull clash in time with his footfalls.

Meanwhile Gudric nodded and booted the door in for a second time. He entered followed closely by Tosti and the twins, and the screaming began again.

6

~ 2008 ~
The Mysterious Mr Bennett

Jack gave me free access to the pigsty and I got busy with my digital camera; close-ups of the stone fragment, wider angles to show its setting, and numerous shots to back up a very interesting theory I was beginning to formulate concerning the building. I took some measurements and began to prepare some notes on the surrounding land for one of our geophys people, and time flew by. It was early afternoon when Jack, with poorly concealed excitement, invited me into his kitchen for a coffee. As I suspected, coffee was no more than the putative reason for Jack's hospitality.

The kitchen had a rustic feel to it, completely in accordance with expectation. There was an Ager neatly filling the width of a recessed fireplace that could almost be described as an inglenook, ancient oak furniture and an old butler sink that made up for lack of modernity by sheer practicality. Mrs Taylor must have shot off to town or something, for I noticed the Range Rover was not in its usual place.

No sooner had Jack poured hot water onto the granules than out came an old album. I guessed it was part of Jack's father's collection from the monochrome photographs of pre-War motor cars. Turning the pages with care, Jack stopped at a roughly A4 sized print near the back.

I knew at once I had to have a copy. The photo represented an excellent piece of continuity and provenance for the Museum Stone, because there it was, clear enough to make out the engraving, being held up by a man in a floppy cloth cap kneeling by its side. Jack began to describe the car in the background in terms of engine type and performance, until I asked about the man.

'Can't really say much,' Jack said. He went on to tell me that the man's name was Bennett and he was estate manager for whoever owned the land back in the thirties.

'He was doing the rounds, which included this place. See, Grandfather was a tenant-farmer and he got Dad, who was just a lad at the time, to show Mr Bennett round and that's when he saw that old bit of stone propped up in the pigsty and the other one forming part of the wall. He took the freestanding piece away, and that's all I know.'

A name, a job and a traceable employer: it might not sound much but I felt certain it was all I'd need to find out more about the mysterious Mr Bennett.

'Do you happen to recall Mr Bennett's Christian name?'

Jack shook his head. 'I don't suppose Dad, or Granddad for that matter, ever knew it. The family wasn't exactly on first name terms with either the gentry or their agents.'

I was about to ask him about the land owner when Raz stuck his head round the door.

'Must've smelt the coffee,' Jack said cheerfully. 'Come in, there's more in the pot.'

Raz just wanted to tell me how well the dig was going and that there were just the two skeletons in the grave. Jack prepared a coffee for Raz while Raz and I studied the photograph. Raz pointed out a row of three metal badges screwed to the grill of the old car. One was an RAC badge and one was an armorial bearing, the blazon clear enough to trace through a copy of *Burke's General Armoury*, but it was the third that sent a shiver down my back. It was a simple geometric design of a circle within a square. The look of blank disbelief on Raz's face must have mirrored my own, but we had no time to discuss the matter before Raz surprised me with another aspect of his knowledge.

'Name the car, and you can have dinner on the house,' Jack said, the challenge shining out of his eyes, the certainty of winning framing his mouth in a mischievous smile.

'Looks like a 1936 Crossley Regis,' Raz said.

'Spot on,' Jack said, somewhat crestfallen. His look of confusion and disappointment in losing the implied bet was quickly replaced by one of tentative hope that here was a fellow veteran car buff. Raz quickly disabused him of the idea and explained that the Crossley was just about the only old car he could recognise.

'Oh,' Jack said with downcast eyes. 'Just don't let on to Mrs T that you're getting dinner free. She'd skin me alive.'

'We wouldn't dream of calling in a bet we hadn't shaken on,' Raz said.

Not so free and easy with department expenses I thought. Luckily for the bursar it was the wrong tack; Jack had his pride and a bet was a bet.

'Perhaps instead of a free dinner,' Raz said, 'you might let us have a copy of the photo.'

Honour restored Jack perked up and assured us he would run us off as many copies as we liked just as soon as he'd scanned the image into his computer. Hang the expense; Raz had shown his worth, once again.

Raz and I went to the nearby pub for some lunch and the conversation was about the coincidences that abounded. Nature blows down a tree and throws open a grave and a new dig; we find a piece of Class 2 stone in a pigsty that fits the Museum Stone I have studied for years; the next day we find the last lost piece and upon its base, among other patterns, is a circle-in-square design. And today we are shown a photo wherein a car sports a badge bearing the self-same design.

'It's all incredibly Dan Brown, if you ask me,' I said spluttering breadcrumbs in my soup. This was too exciting to let my mouth off talking just because it was already employed eating. 'It's as if some hidden hand is moving all the pieces into place.'

'I don't really see it like that myself,' Raz said. 'The only real coincidence is that you found the fragment in the pigsty.'

'But the recurring emblem,' I protested. 'And another fragment turning up within twenty-four hours of the first. It's all ...'

'Easily explained!' Raz said, interrupting my excited blither. 'The three pieces of stone where never very far away from each other, until Mr Bennett took his piece, the piece that eventually became the Museum Stone. And the base bore the emblem of the local land owner perhaps, an emblem that changed little over the centuries and still had associations with the area in the nineteen-thirties.'

I remember shaking my head emphatically. 'No Raz, I don't buy that. Heraldry isn't so persistent. It doesn't much pre-date Norman times. It certainly doesn't stretch back into the dark ages proper.'

'Well, it patently does, unless you have another explanation.'

When he put it like that … What other explanation could there be?

'I'll ask a few question back at the estate.' Raz drained the last of his bitter-shandy. 'Maybe they have records of who owned the land before they did.'

After lunch Raz dropped me off at the pigsty and he returned to the dig, but not before I had him check the pigsty. I wanted to see if he supported my theory.

Raz stood *contrapposto*, one hand on his hip and the other outstretched to touch the brickwork of the sty, totally absorbed, oblivious to his modern-day surroundings and looking like the model for many a marble statue of Alexander the Great. 'Definitely Roman proportions,' he said remembering where he was. 'The bricks could easily come from an earlier building. And the general architecture is in keeping with the period.' Ripping his eyes from the old stone at last, he fixed them onto an old fossil and treated me to one of his smiles. 'I think you're right!'

As the Land Rover rounded the drive and was swallowed up by the trees, I was left feeling very pleased with myself. Raz agreed that the pigsty was the oldest part of the building and that it could easily date to the eighth or ninth century. In other words, the fragment of Class 2 stone could easily have been built into the wall shortly after it was dislodged from its original location – from grave marker to pigsty in anything from a matter of days to a hundred or so years. I began to feel that building the stone into the wall of a pigsty may have even been a deliberate insult on the part of the builders. They were mocking those whose grave it should have marked by making it mark a place of pigs and filth.

I must have spent another hour or so examining the walls and making notes; where the brickwork ended and the stonework began, the positioning of lintels and the design of the gable. I was enjoying another hot drink in the kitchen with Jack when, true to his nose, Raz smelt the tea again and returned from the dig having secured it for the night.

The evening unfolded much the same as the previous one and concluded with Raz visiting my room for wine before the fireside. We had already discussed the day's discoveries, or so I believed, and there was time to plan the next phase before bedtime. Since the previous evening's intimate revelations, I was careful to listen for any signs that Raz may wish to discuss them further. Part of me wished he had never mentioned those awful events in his past, because it made me see him differently and I am quite certain he did not wish to be perceived as a victim.

As to our discoveries, they led us in two directions. The bones and stones would follow well-trodden paths to further illuminations, whereas hunting down the provenance of the pigsty stone called for a different kind of detective work. I wanted to know more about Mr Bennett. What had he done with the Museum Stone? Had he written any papers? Who was he and what became of him? I supposed it what just possible that he was still alive, although he would have to be in his late nineties by now. We discussed the leads we had and how we might follow them.

It was while I listed the possibilities – trace the family coat of arms shown on the grill of the old car; see if Mr Bennett was mentioned in their archives; check the old land registers – that I noticed Raz playing with something between his fingers. I had forgotten all about the artefact, despite the fact that it might be made of gold.

'Steady with that Raz,' I said as he chucked it from hand to hand. 'We don't want to lose any evidence by careless handling.' I noticed that Raz sported that smile again and he leaned in close and worked a conjuring trick on me so when he opened his hand the little vessel had apparently vanished.

'Very clever,' I said deadpan. I wanted to call him an idiot and tell him the object should by now be in protective find-bag and secured in the strongbox screwed to the Land Rover floor. 'Now magic the damn thing back again and put it away properly.'

Undeterred Raz flourished his empty hand, put it to my ear and then like the chap and kiddies parties who brings forth silver coins from six-year-olds ears, he brought out the vessel. It hadn't happened yet, but one day Raz would catch me at a bad moment and I'll let him have an earful of his own. Strangely, Raz's presence always dampened my irascibility. He leaned in again, other hand to other ear, and drew forth a second vessel and then held them both up for me to see.

'Two! My god, where did you ...?'

'It was below the upper skeleton and above the other ... a little above L-4.'

'The fourth Lumbar vertebrae? Wasn't that roughly where the first one was found in relation to the upper skeleton? Let me see.'

Raz nodded enthusiastically and handed me the vessel. 'As far as I can tell from the police report, yes the objects were found in the same relative positions.' He positioned a hand in front of his stomach to illustrate the point. 'My guess is they were swallowed. Nobody would toss a pair of naked and tortured bodies into a grave and leave the gold.'

'It *is* gold then?' I had been certain it would be. The objects had the buttery yellow look of ancient gold. 'And the bodies were put in naked? Are you certain?'

'Pretty much. There're no fibres, no soil staining or discolouration that might show the presence of cloth or leather, except it looks pretty likely the bodies were tied together at the ankles, wrists and hips.'

My fertile mind conjured up a view of two bloody corpses being carried on a pole like a pair of slaughtered deer.

100

'Why would they swallow little golden goblets?' I wondered aloud.

'Why would the boys each be given a dental filling which isn't really a filling?' Raz went on to explain that the deeper skeleton had an apparent filling on the same tooth as the first, but on closer examination the fillings proved to be something more like markers, not drilled into the teeth but secured by a sliver of a tang wedged between the teeth and held in place by pressure.

'It's almost as if someone knew the boys were to be killed and disposed of ignominiously – anonymously even – and wished to mark the bodies for posterity.'

'For *us*, Professor - someone wished to mark the bodies for us!'

Raz still smiled, but the underlying emotion shifted and gave him an almost desperate look. I felt he needed me to agree with his bizarre and somewhat eerie assessment. 'In that *we* are posterity, then yes. Someone marked the bodies for us … and I am now quite certain that this find is of immense importance.'

As I write it occurs to me that I opened this tale staring not so lovingly into the muddy eye-sockets of the top skeleton and that I failed to even skim over the preliminaries. These first examinations of the site included a good look at the tiny golden object.

'Celtic markings, I believe,' said the police forensic medical examiner as he handed over the scene and the object. With one glance I dismissed his assessment but nodded nonetheless. As soon as the police packed up and left I asked Raz for his opinion.

'It looks like a child's thimble or a little bell, with a little plug of clay or dried soil in the opening,' he said.

'And the markings?'

He took out a jeweller's loupe and stuck it in his eye before bringing the vessel close. 'Reminds me of the markings found on beakers.' He looked up and grinned, the loupe still in and making him look part human part robot. 'Come to think of it, same shape as well, just a lot smaller.'

'And of course, it's made of metal instead of pottery. Do you think we're looking at a grave very much older than we first suspected?' The Beaker Folk, if they ever existed, were prehistoric.

Raz took out his loupe and pocketed it, and then kneeled and ran his fingers gently over the bony face. 'You think these might actually be Beaker Folk?'

'What do you think?' I said, never one to provide my students with answers or my assistant with cause to doubt me.

'It doesn't fit the facts,' he said encompassing the grave with a wave of his hand. 'Let's get this site gridded, and then we'll see what we find.'

'I concur,' I said, by which it was understood I was giving the go-ahead.'

The miniature vessel may well have taken up more of my time were it not for the discovery of the pigsty and then the stone.in the root. Now, sitting by a wonderfully roasting log fire with a nice wine in one hand and the mini-beaker in the other, I peered hard at the little golden object and try to fathom a way for it to fit in with all the other facts and speculations.

'Don't you think it a little too considerate of someone to think of future archaeologists and give us all these clues – faux-fillings and swallowed trinkets? It sounds a little far-fetched to me.'

'Perhaps,' Raz said before taking a long sip of his wine. He swirled the remaining liquid and looked into it as if trying to scry the answer. An answer of sorts came, for he smiled to himself. 'We look at a cloud and see a camel or a whale ... or a weasel. Faces spring at us from the patterns on wallpaper. Humans were ever thus. We take the little we have and try and make the full story.' He fixed me with a look of certainty. 'I think that's why I love this job. From two or three parts of the jigsaw we try to see the whole picture, and so long as we are open to adapt and reassess and admit our errors in light of new discoveries, speculation must be an essential part of our work.'

102

I felt an old man's joy in a young man's bright spark of intuition. Wine-mellowed, my heart smiled. As usual I kept my heart disconnected from any trait of appearance that might show my feelings. '"Humans were ever thus."?' You speak as if you were a species of alien reporting on an inferior race. Who on earth taught you how to speak?'

We chuckled a little, but as always, a vein of melancholy and seriousness lay under the surface of my young assistant ... my *padewan*.

'They say fatherless boys seek out fathers everywhere,' he said. 'Maybe I found my father in old books and dead languages.' His eyes caught mine and held for a moment. 'And ...'

After a moment he returned his gaze to the last of his wine and did not finish the sentence. It left me hoping I could guess the rest and feeling that, if indeed I had become a kind of father-figure to him, I would not let him down.

Fathers: how very much they ... we ... have to answer for. Unlike Raz I was not an orphan, but I had grown up fatherless nonetheless, so I saw the truth in his words and if I could provide him with something I had never experienced, perhaps we would both be enriched.

Shall I tell you who my father-figure was? I think perhaps I might, although it will do nothing for my reputation. My father was Mr Spock. There! What did I say? You think me an idiot. But I am not about to slap a paternity suit on the actor Leonard Nimoy, for it was the character he crated and not the man himself who became my father-figure. I was thirteen or fourteen when *Star Trek* first beamed down to England's TV shores, and I immediately identified with the character, an alien living in a human world; a man with a huge store of knowledge but who didn't quite get it; a great store of humanity without knowing how to be human. Like Spock I had no problem sticking to the rules. Like Spock I was left confused when the rule-breakers got the results. Most illogical.

I lived and live in a world where the same society that sets the rules promotes the rule-breakers. Think of your average cop-show. Is the hero the hard working guy who works by the book, or the maverick who throws the rule-book away and follows his gut-instincts? I rest my case, and life often follows art in this respect. It is almost as if rules were written for the worker-ants so the rarefied super-beings can achieve their aims and soar into the sky while lesser mortals do the work.

Excuse this poor worker-ant and help me down from my soapbox.

I grew to realise that rules were written for the strict adherence of fools and the guidance of wise men, but that is a conclusion that came late in life. Sometimes the rule-book is too slim a volume to hold inspiration and ingenuity. Still, I never break a rule without carefully considering my motivation.

Sometimes, in a meeting or when sitting in my study in front of the computer contemplating my next paragraph, I will find myself steepling my fingers as an aid to concentration. Thanks, Spock; one of your sons turned out right ... eventually.

I never could raise one eyebrow though.

I topped up our glasses, finishing the bottle, and we talked about how we'd proceed. The excavation of the skeletons neared completion. The find had been extensively recorded, photographically and by use of standard archaeological methods. There was not a lot else to be done with regard to the Pigsty Stone, which was just as well because I was due to deliver a lecture the next day. We sketched a plan and then discussed the reports we would each have to write.

I wanted to keep the finds as close to my chest as possible and consequently the only outsiders I had spoken to were Jenny and my daughter Rachel. It dawned upon me that Raz may have been freer with his lips than I, and so I asked him. Who exactly had he told about the find?

'Only Jacqueline Watson,' he answered. 'She's a post grad doing a D.Phil. We met at a dig last August.'

I was a little disappointed. 'You know her well?'

'Well enough to have given her some of my genetic material.'

Ye Gods! I had heard some euphemisms for it but that took the biscuit.

Raz threw his head back and laughed. Once again he had read my thoughts. I can only imagine the look on my face, but I concede it was probably comical.

'She's working in genetic archaeology,' he said hardly able to contain himself. 'I let her pluck out one of my hairs so she can practice her PCR techniques.'

'Of course,' I said. 'What's so funny?'

'Never mind, Prof,' he said rising to take back the golden vessel. 'I've lots to do in the morning, so I should get to bed.'

'Me too,' I said, and the joviality of the moment led me to make the offer that had been on my mind all night. 'Oh and … I hope you will consider me friend enough that … should you wish to discuss that personal matter that came up yesterday, you would feel comfortable to do so.'

Raz smiled and slapped my shoulder. Absurdly I felt our roles reversed and that he was the experienced, middle-aged man and I the boy. 'Of course I think of you as a friend, Prof. And thanks, but it was all a long time ago and am past worrying about it.'

For once, I could not suppress a smile. 'Well, I'm glad we're friends, although many might not approve. Our relative positions, you understand, not to mention the generation gap.' Here I was again, about to kill the moment for the sake of appearances.

Raz beamed away my confused and muddled attempts at furthering the conversation. 'To quote the well-known motto of Edward III's renowned order of chivalry, "They who don't like it can fuck off!"'.

I slapped my forehead and shook my head. I had never before heard Raz cuss. I hoped it was not my bad influence. 'Mr Reeves, I think you need to work on your translations of Old French.' *Honi soit qui mal y pense* would never sound quite the same to me again, although I felt the Knights of the Garter had probably intended the same translation as Raz's … and I like to think His Royal Highness the Duke of Edinburgh would be with me on that one.

Raz took his leave chuckling his way along the hall. Maybe he wasn't used to alcohol. As for me, the alcohol and Raz's words left me with an ethereal glow. I think it is fair to say I went to bed happy that night.

7

~ 2008 ~
Colonel Mustard in the Library with a Dagger

I have a theory: generally speaking our luck and emotions even out over the course of our lives. Good luck, bad luck; happy, sad: we pretty much all get equal shares. You can't be a top sportsman without having gone through a lot of hard work. Oscar winning actors, for the most part, have had their share of waiting at table or wearing the banana-man suit on the way up, and many will feel the pain of loss and rejection on the way down. Peaks and troughs. For me though, no peaks or troughs, no jam or bitter pills; just an even spread of bland margarine over white bread. Sufficient to sustain but not to excite, so the finding of the stones was the cherry on the icing on a cake full of jam. But success was not an animal I was used to and I wondered when it would bite. Of course it bit, and those sharp fangs came to me from the most unexpected quarter.

There were lectures to deliver and meeting to attend; a hundred and one minor but necessary nuisances that all served to keep me giving my full attention to the dig and the stones. In the end Raz and I decided to report all our finds, except one. We included every detail about the dig and most of what we knew about the stones, but I thought it expedient not to mention our curious predecessor, Mr Bennett. Tracking him down had become our secret objective, but such was my conscience and scruples when it came to rules, that I would have had to mention him but for one fact. Mr Bennett was not an archaeological find. He might provide a lead in determining the importance or otherwise of the circle-in-square symbol that seemed to be a theme linking our recent finds – the stone and the photo of Mr Bennett's old automobile – but I could easily justify keeping him out of my report if I had to.

It was a Tuesday evening about a week after the skeletons had been fully excavated and taken to the lab. I'd left Raz in charge of all aspects of research into the grave and the bones while I concentrated on the stone and the illusive Mr Bennett. Truth be told, there was not much more I could find out from the stone and Bennett was proving to be like the Scarlet Pimpernel. I'd had no luck tracing the grill-mounted shield badge through *Burke's General Armoury* or any other tome of heraldry and the relevant land records were ambiguous as to the past ownership of Jack Taylor's bastle. The records had been lodged with solicitors in London and lost in the blitz – a direct hit in 1941. The circle-in-stone symbol was equally undocumented. I was in my study when I tried to apply some lateral thinking: if I can't trace the man, perhaps I can find a lead on his car. Within quarter of an hour I had found a number of websites dealing with old cars and a couple specialising in Crossleys. I sent off an email and prepared myself for the disappointment of not receiving a reply. The reply arrived while I was making a cup of tea for Jenny and myself, and it was the first stage in getting a grip on Bennett.

I could hardly believe my luck that the very car in the old faded photo was still alive and the proud possession of a Crossley enthusiast. Over the next few days and several exchanges of emails between myself, the owners' club and the gentleman who owned the actual car, I had an address!

The elderly owner of the Crossley Regis had taken particular care to preserve everything that had come with the vehicle when he purchased it back in 1967 including an old wicker picnic basket, a box of matches and a packet of Senior Service cigarettes. The cigarette packet contained five cigarettes, a picture card of a man on ice skates labelled 'Skating – C.W. Horn' and tucked between the cardboard and the lining paper, three calling cards, all in the name of 'Mr Jason Bennett, Estate Manager …' and you will have to forgive me for not mentioning the house, as I rather expect its present owners would curse me if my literary indiscretion led to trespassers. On the other hand, the grand house is now open to the public during the summer, so maybe they would bless me. Either way, I think it best to keep certain locations unpublished for the time being.

I ran down the stairs two at a time, incurred Jenny's wrath for frightening the dog, and then told her of my good luck. As usual, Mrs Professor was hugely underwhelmed and asked me to remind her if this had to do with my work or was it one of my other 'little projects', the latter said in such a way to make it sound like an utter waste of time. Well, another time I might have bitten, but on this occasion my excitement was blunted at the edges but not subdued, and give Jenny her due, once I explained the importance of this new clue she at least attempted to show some interest.

It was a long time since Jenny had shown any interest in anything that was of interest to me, but by eleven the next morning, I realised it had been a shard of sunlight through the gathering storm-clouds.

I had a noon meeting to attend and a late evening lecture, so there was no need to leave home early. I caught up with the latest on the skeletons from Raz, and then just as I cradled the telephone receiver, the postman knocked. There was a small package for Jenny from a clothing catalogue purchase, my latest copy of *British Archaeology*, the usual annoying sheaf of junk mail, and an impressively sturdy and high quality white envelope addressed to me using my full title, including my academic qualifications. My ego was massaged as my curiosity peaked.

The letter was from a solicitor. The solicitor purported to represent Jenny. He was a divorce solicitor.

I do not intend to be diverted from the story in hand, and I merely mention this by way of explaining the added pressures that were suddenly thrust upon me. Apparently I had been remiss in certain husbandly duties. We never went out. We hardly visited anywhere or anyone. I was completely self-absorbed. To say that I was side-shunted would be to put it mildly, but I did not allow myself to become derailed. Of course I was stunned as I tried to assimilate the contents of the letter. I have few recollections of the stilted conversation that followed and I find it hard to record anything about my emotions. The one memory that comes through clearly, is of me wondering how I would get my shirts ironed. We had been together for over twenty

109

years, and all I could dwell upon was the practicality of buying a new ironing board and wondering if it would fit in my office at work.

So come the peak, so come the trough.

But let's move on. We have discoveries to make, and my domestic situation will not stand in the way.

Three days later Raz and I were standing in the grand hall of a modestly proportioned stately home an hour-and-a-half before it opened to the public. A friendly factor, we'll call her Elizabeth as it fits her sensible kilted and twin-set appearance, had left us in the presence of a red-marble version of the Dying Gaul and several fine oil paintings while she went to notify her boss, who we will call Lord James, third Viscount of … ah, that would give it away now, wouldn't it?

My preconceptions of Lord James were shot down as soon as the young man – mid-thirties at most – dressed in jeans and a sloppy sweater stepped lightly down the grand staircase, his tan canvas espadrilles making hardly a noise. I had mildly chided Raz about his informal attire, but now it was I that was out of place. Raz had also gently mocked my trousers, shirt and tie combination in country colours as making me look like a Kosovan general or a scout leader. Cheek!

Lord James greeted us with a genuinely friendly smile and we completed the informal formalities before being shown to the drawing room. He appeared fascinated by our discoveries and took the copy of Mr Bennett and the Crossley Regis – not to mention the Museum Stone – with careful enthusiasm, and he recognised our Mr Bennett immediately.

'Why, this is young Jason,' James said at once. 'Daddy talks of him often, and Grandfather – he's the one who used to refer to him as "young Jason" and the name stuck – held him up as a paragon of virtue.'

'And he was the estate manager?'

James poured us coffee from a bone china pot. 'He was more a friend of the family really, although he did take on some of the factor's functions. As I understand it, he was

110

somewhat into your line of work as well, but more a sort of talented amateur.'

It was all so exciting. I contained myself while I explained about the Museum Stone and the Pigsty Stone and expressed my hope that we may learn something about Jason Bennett that connected with these archaeological finds.

'There may well be,' James said. 'I don't suppose you're aware, he wrote a book in Latin.'

A gaping jaw was all the answer I could muster. It was Raz that asked if there were any known copies of the work.

'I'm not so sure there are any copies at all, but I can lead you to the original without a moment's delay. It lives in the music room.'

The next few moments were a blur. James led us out of the drawing room and up the sweeping staircase, along a hall and into the music room. He explained that he maintained some old family traditions, and that is why he had never thought it necessary to move the book to the library.

'He we go,' James said pulling a dusty and well-worn violin case from a high shelf. He accidentally dislodged a stack of sheet music which engendered its very own cloud and made James sneeze. He apologised for the dust and added that it was virtually impossible to do much about it with the number of staff he could afford to retain. So much background noise to me as James took the case over to a coffee table by the casement.

'*Et voila!*' James said as he opened the lid and positioned the case for me to see the contents. 'Father took it to some publishers once, but they weren't interested. Their attitude was pretty much "Who would read a novel written in Latin?" Have to say they had a point. I've barely looked at it myself.'

'May I?' I said as my fingers itched to take the small leather-bound volume.

James assented with a flourish of his hand and a dip of the head.

111

And then our story took on a new dimension. Embossed on the front of the book was the title of the book, *Raven-Fish!* And there, below the name of the author was … and I am sure you have guessed … another representation of that circle-within-square symbol. Raz and I exchanged glances, a signal that we had both taken note of the symbol.

'Raz, look!' I said as I opened the book.

'Some Latin, some Old English,' he replied. And then, generously 'Our combined skills shall come to the fore when we translate … if we're allowed.' He looked enquiringly at Lord James.

'Why of course!' James said. 'I'd love to know what it's all about. Neither Father nor Grandfather read more Latin than they had to. I gather both pretty much hated it at school and I took modern languages.'

'Latin is a language as dead as dead can be …' Raz said.

And James hit the ball that Raz had placed in the air: 'It killed off all the Romans, and now it's killing me.' They both chuckled and then James went on as he leaned in and turned a few pages. 'If you'll allow me … ah yes, here! You see, there are several hand-written interludes done in pencil. Jason's own handwriting I shouldn't wonder, and in plain English, though Lord knows what they mean.'

A quick scan of the early pages and I was able to say the opening of the novel, if that's what it was, concerned one Ealdorman Dunstan Chase and his visit to an odious official named Godwin. Opening the pages at random, I came to a passage in Latin about some monks on an island, and another about Vikings. The words were ancient, but the style was that of a modern novel and in a typical printing font for the 1930's. Why on Earth had Jason Bennett decided to write a novel in two such ancient tongues? He may well have been nothing more than an eccentric, but a little voice inside my head was telling me there could be only one reason and that was that the story held clues as to his archaeological discoveries.

I handed *Raven-Fish!* to Raz while I negotiated a deal with Lord James. In fact, such was the young aristocrat's trust and generosity that it did not call for much negotiation at all. He allowed us to take the book into our keeping for as long as it took to complete the translation and all he wanted in exchange was a copy of the transcript.

Raz appeared uncommunicative after James led us to the library. James left us alone with permission to search the shelves for any other works by Bennett. I was about to ask Raz if he'd seen a ghost when he caught me with such a look I wondered if I was the one having a supernatural experience.

'There's something in the first chapter ...' he said before trailing off most ominously.

'What? Raz what are you talking about, man?'

'There's a piece about the grave of some murdered boys, and the deliberate smashing of their grave marker.'

Cue, discordant violins; spotlight on the lead actor's face slack with disbelief, fade to black all around. I felt a sudden chill and I forgot to breathe for several moments. And I almost had to feel for the strings attached to key places about my body for I felt sure I was being deliberately jerked around. My mind groped for an explanation, any explanation. I quickly concluded that the murdered boys in the book and those in our recently discovered grave where not the same, for how could they be? How could Jason Bennett know anything about the grave, which had lain undisturbed for at least a thousand years?

If I thought that was going to be the most surprising revelation *Raven-Fish!* had to offer, I was soon to learn differently.

VIII

~ 793 ~
In which the Raven inflicts grave hurt upon the Fish

The monk rowed for dear life assisted greatly by the strong side-current. Finn swore and hurled a stone at him. In that it was aimed for his head it was a poor shot, but it drew a yelp from the monk as the stone hit solidly between his shoulder-blades. Then he was swallowed up by the mist and safe from further attack. A head shot would surely have brained him.

There was nothing more to be done about it, although it was just possible the monk might fear the sea, and sneak a return. Finn sat on the sand and listened to the death-screams that pierced the monastery walls. When all was silent, after perhaps half an hour, he ran up the beach to join the others. He was about to charge in through the gaping doorway when he heard a noise from the far side of the small building, a sound midway between chiming bells and a shattering pot. He reached the far wall in time to see a very fat and elderly monk bounce off the turf, having descended by a fall from a broken window. Finn ignored the monk for a moment as his interest was taken by the window itself. He had heard of glass windows but never seen one before.

Gudric's head thrust through. 'Hah! He was hiding in a big cupboard trying to protect a lad. The fat old fool thought he'd escape did he? That one's called Paul, so if the fall didn't kill him, strike off his head and he'll have the death of his namesake.'

The elderly monk drew himself up upon hands and knees and Finn smiled: he couldn't have offered himself up in a better position. Finn lifted his blade and brought it down in an arc of lightning, the polished iron catching a sunbeam that escaped the mist. It was a perfect strike and the monk's head leapt off in a spray of bright blood.

Gudric whooped with glee as the head rolled down an incline and came to rest several feet from the twitching body.

'Come join us Finn. Just the lad left alive now and he's called Elmo. His death will be almost as sweet as the Blood Eagle once we've done sporting with him.'

Finn's own blood surged with lust for more killing and he ran back to the door. Bursting through into the dark interior he gagged at the smell of loosened bladders and bowels; several of the monks had disgraced themselves before they died. One half-skinned was still alive – just.

With dead, dying and mutilated monks all around him and the flagstones slick with gore, the slaying had done nothing to cool Finn's own surging blood, and indeed had merely fired another kind of desire. Finn wanted a woman, and clenched his teeth in anger because he knew there were none on this island. It was then that he heard a cry and a chorus of raucous laughter coming from the floor above.

Running to investigate, up the stairs and along a narrow hall to a room at the end, Finn was assailed by the sight of Tosti's white arse pumping back and forth made all the more dazzling by a ray of sunlight pouring through the broken glass window. He was thrusting furiously into a monk who had been bent over a heavy oak table and was being held in place by Alrik's twin sons. He'd been stripped of draws and hose, which lay tattered on the stone floor, and his habit was hitched up over his shoulders obscuring most of his flame-red hair.

'His name's Elmo,' Gudric said, almost dancing with manic glee. 'And *have* I got a death for him!'

It was difficult to see the monk's face but he had the body of a youth, and Finn guessed he could not be much older than himself.

Aki chortled. 'Soft as a woman, Finn. Want a go, before Gudric slits his belly and winds his guts out on the roasting spit?'

Finn smiled and felt himself quicken still more.

115

'Shame there's no real women, but we've all tenderised this one for you. It'll be like sliding into warm liver,' Abi said.

The brothers laughed and then cheered as Tosti bucked convulsively while letting out a wordless cry of release. He collapsed over his whimpering victim for a moment before pulling out and adjusting his dress.

'Come on, come on. Take him quickly. I can't wait all day,' Gudric nagged while dragging a small roasting spit from the hearth.

'I'll take him in one of the other chambers,' Finn said pointing to the hallway. 'I don't care for an audience.'

Tosti tied his trousers and scratched his balls. He was smiling his teasing smile and Finn knew this signalled a dose of friendly derision.

'Frightened we'll see your spear, even when battle-ready, is little more than a wifey's bodkin-spike?'

Finn was now the centre of attention and Gudric, the twins and Tosti roared. The abused monk slid to the floor, his vulnerability firing Finn still more. He loosened the drawstring and lowered his trousers just enough for the men to be assured of the potency and satisfactory dimensions of his equipment. They made approving noises and now Finn laughed too.

Sheathing his sword Finn strode over to the monk and with one hand holding up his trousers he grabbed a handful of the young man's hair and dragged him to the chamber followed by a wind of laughter and insults. Gudric told him not to be too long.

Once in the chamber Finn threw the monk to the ground and began to shed his war gear and lower clothing. Bending double the heavy byrnie slid off easily and clashed to the stone floor. Baldric, belt and trousers he flung into the corner of the tiny, empty cell. He cast an eye round quickly and noted a small golden goblet. He threw it to the ground, stomped it flat and kicked it towards his discarded clothes. There was nothing else here to take, just bare walls and an old stone seat.

The monk lay in a heap at his feet and Finn looked down at the shaved circle of scalp surrounded by hair so red that it could easily have been that of a kinsman.

He looked round again and up to the ceiling where an iron candle-holder dangled from a chain. When he looked down again the monk had risen to his knees and his hands were raised as if in prayer.

Finn pulled back then slammed his fist into the side of the monk's face sending him down, once again, onto the floor.

Finn hit him twice more, and then in a frenzy of rending, stripped him of his habit and shirt, threw him face down over the stone seat and then took him, hard and violently, just as he had seen Tosti do. The monk's subdued cries of pain only served to make him thrust deeper, and the approving laughter coming from outside, still more violently.

With the final shudder and the last thrust, Finn pulled out and wiped himself on a piece of rag that had once been the monk's habit.

He was getting dressed when Gudric's head appeared round the stone portal. 'Finished?'

'No! Get you goblin-face out of here before I trim its ugly beard!' Finn shouted. 'I'll come out when I'm ready!'

Gudric looked suitably admonished by the hersirs's son and withdrew quickly.

The monk still lay doubled over the stone; unconscious, perhaps. He looked like a sacrifice to the gods and Finn decided he would give him a quick death. Call it a reward for the pleasures rendered. Let Gudric find another to disembowel.

Finn finished dressing and strapped on his belt. The baldric back in place he drew his sword and rolled the monk off the makeshift altar. He hit the floor with the slap of flesh on cold stone. The moment had come to send the lad to his gods.

Finn drew back his sword arm. *Not gods, but one god only*, he remembered. No matter, gods or god; now was the time. He was about to strike when he became conscious of the noises of the sea, and with that sound came the memory of a story Gudric had told about the Christian god. He strode over and peered out of the window. It seemed a storm was brewing and the sea was beginning to boil.

That story: it was about the White-Christ calming the storm and about a man-god walking on water.

'Hey you,' Finn said in the English tongue, which he had learnt as a boy from his slave-nurse. The young monk did not stir until Finn slapped his thigh with the flat of his sword.

He drew himself up onto his knees, and although naked and in pain, assumed an air of dignity which somehow impressed Finn.

'Kill me quickly,' Elmo said wearily and resignedly. 'And I ask God for forgiveness. In the face of death I was weak …'

'Shut up! Never mind all that,' Finn said. 'Tell me, can your White-Christ god calm the storms and walk on water?'

Elmo dragged himself up to full kneeling height, his eyes screwed up tight as he brought a hand to his lower belly. 'God can do anything,' he strained to say through the pain.

'Good. Then I might have a use for him. You're coming with me.' Finn bent forward and was about to grab a handful of the monk's hair. Instead he held his hand out and after a moment Elmo took it. Finn snatched up a tattered remnant of clothing and told the monk to clean himself with it, and then seizing his upper arm Finn escorted the naked monk into the main chamber. Before Gudric or the twins could protest he announced that he was keeping the monk as a slave. Gudric flapped his jaw a little, but knew better than to argue.

Abi began to voice dissent but quickly stopped when Finn fingered the hilt of his sword.

'I said, Abi Alrik's son, that this man is my property. Now, I am sure you know what you must do to take another man's property, don't you?'

Abi shook his head and held up both hands. 'No, no, no. He's yours. I meant no …'

118

Finn laughed and dug deep into his pouch. 'Here! Have this instead.' He threw the crushed golden goblet in a shallow arc, and Abi caught it with glee. For Gudric he had only an evil look. Gudric smiled sheepishly and went off to find Tosti. It was unlikely they would be off this dog-turd of an island before the next day, Finn thought, what with the building storm.

Victorious York did first with famed success,

To his known valour make the Dutch give place;

Thus Heaven our monarch's fortune did confess,

Beginning conquest from his royal race.

Elmo struggled through the longest night of his life. Despite the luxurious comfort of poor Father Paul's bed Elmo could not sleep. His guts drew at him and griped with the pain of recent assaults. The raider, who called himself Finn, lay naked under the quilt and snored beside him like a wild boar. The noise of the storm raged enough to drown out all other sound, or so Elmo reasoned, but twice when he had tried to creep out of bed, Finn had stirred, both times cutting any hope of escape short with a knife held to the throat, each time the herald for more acts of debauchery.

That the brute had used him in a variety of obscene ways made Elmo feel filthy and sick with shame. That Finn's unwanted attentions kept him from being torn apart by the other raiders led to his resigned acquiescence and thereby more shame. Better he should give himself up to death.

A sudden gust of wind brought a few raindrops in, splashing Elmo's face. Finn had rammed his circular battle-shield into the stone window and stuffed all round with garments torn from the dead, but there were a few gaps to let in a water-laden draft, and a little moonlight from time to time.

119

The wind blew again and with it more raindrops. Finn stopped snoring and Elmo prayed that he would not awaken. This night was not a one for answered prayers; Finn slipped out of bed, his bare feet slapping on the stone floor as he crossed to the fire where he busied himself with a taper, prodding it among glowing embers until it took to flame. With this he lit a lamp. He came back and sat on the edge of the bed. To Elmo's horror, but not surprise, the raider was aroused yet again and he steeled himself for yet more indignities.

'You monk! Awake?' Finn kicked him through the bedclothes.

Elmo knew he could take no more. 'I'll have no more of you, sir,' he said under his breath. 'My time is here. You must finish me.'

'Is life so empty that you would prefer death over a little sport?'

'You will kill me anyway, once you tire of me, once the seas calm and you are ready to sail away. I have no illusion that you shall let me live.'

Finn stroked his wispy beard. 'No, you'll die only if your god fails to calm the waters for us. But that isn't until tomorrow. So, if you wish to live until tomorrow ...'

Elmo drifted off into sleep sometime after the act he knew would always be remembered as his great sin ... if he were allowed to live. He was received into sleep's healing arms in the belief that nothing would shrive him of such wantonness despite the fact a knife was held to his throat. His body had responded wickedly and he was unworthy. But the thoughts did not rob him of a deep, oblivious sleep.

He awoke to the harsh scraping sound of Finn pulling his shield free of the surrounding stone work. Bright sunlight poured it and Elmo was dazzled. Finn was bare-chested but had already pulled on his trousers and boots. Elmo sat up, remembering that he had no clothing to put on.

'Say one word about me lying under you and it will be your last,' Finn said like a throwaway remark of little importance.

'And yet lying *over* me is an act of which to boast?' Whatever else last night had done, it had rid him of the fear of death. He was already dead, and the dead do not fear death.

'You see no difference?' Finn said staring down at Elmo as if he were a complete dolt. 'Then there is nothing left of the warrior within you at all. You are a worthless man, and well suited to dress in your white frock. Find yourself a new frock and get dressed, woman!' Finn threw his tunic over his arm and strode out of the abbot's bedroom to a raucous round of cheering from his fellow warriors.

Elmo swung out of bed and strode out after him, naked but curiously no longer ashamed; nudity was little enough compared to the shames that would be a long time fading. He ignored the derisive laughter and foul comments of the raiders and when one of them slapped his bottom with a loud clap as he passed, Elmo turned and pushed the offender onto to his own ample arse. If the act brought death, then so be it. Instead it brought more laughter and a strange species of approval. Even the fallen raider leapt back onto his feet laughing, and he clapped Elmo upon the back.

He hurried down the stairs and tried to look neither at the raider who skulked there nor the piles of carnage that had lately been his brothers. Stepping over them and avoiding the concealing pools of blood, he made for the corner of the refectory that had been used to launder clothes.

'Is this one ripe for slaying, Finn, or is he still your bed-pet?' the older raider called up the stairs while drawing his sword in anticipation of the answer he craved.

Finn's voice stabbed back from above. 'He is still my *slave*, Gudric, so leave him be … but don't let him stray.'

'But he is such a pretty little thing, and I never had him yesterday, so may I …'

'No! I said leave him!'

Gudric pushed his sword fully home with an angry snap of metal on metal and treated Elmo to a spiteful sneer while he muttered under his breath something about sharing the spoils of battle.

121

Elmo pulled on some drawers and a pair of hose from the knot of clean clothing. He soon found a shirt and Brother Andrew's spare habit, so taking a kitchen knife he cut a little off the hem and then dressed, the habit now a tunic coming just past his knees. If he was to be taken aboard with the raiders, he would be hindered by a habit of proper length.

He stepped over a body that had been stripped and partially flayed and felt sickened by the death that poor Brother Bartholomew had suffered. The screams still rang in his ears. Next to him Brother Benjamin had been impaled with a spear but not before the raiders had driven him through with splinters of wood in his eyes, through his nose and lips, under his fingernails and elsewhere in places with all intent to cause maximum pain. These raiders were not men, but foul beasts from the deepest pits of Hell. With a huge exertion of will power, Elmo did not allow his eyes to fall upon the other corpses. It crossed his mind that he may soon suffer a similar fate, but it was as if the ignominy and agony would be played out upon his body, and his body was something other than himself – somehow detached.

Elmo was hit by a hank of bread when he reached the top stair. One of the raiders told him the seas were too heavy for them to risk leaving until later and then instructed him to drag all the dead outside.

Elmo exceeded his instruction and spent the rest of the morning washing the corpses as best he could and then burying them. So lately dressed he stripped to his drawers again to deal with such bloody work, and once he had dealt with those inside he began work on those who had fallen under the sky.

Here was little Brother Andrew with two arrows in him. And the two slaves who had rowed Eovan Tucarus and his thegns over from the mainland harbour had fallen, arrow-pierced and close to the sea. The thegns were dead within a few strides of the monastery door and Father Paul whose body and head lay yards apart was round the back. While he attended to the gory duty he detached himself from reality and moved like a creature of instinct. The only thought he

122

later recalled was that a head was much heavier than he had imagined.

He said prayers over the shallow graves and dug an extra grave, for the part of himself that had died: he needed to acknowledge the passing. Then, when the sun was high, his work was done and he turned to leave the little plot and found his way blocked by Finn. How long had he been watching?

'Where is the noble warrior?' Finn called out over the unrelenting noise of the wind and crashing waves.

Elmo knew immediately that he was referring to Eovan Tucarus of Skol-Jerrag and for the first time he realised that he had not come across Eovan's body, such was his complete detachment. Nor had he seen the bodies of either Brother Sebastian or Brother Mundwyn from the Order of Blue Friars.

'Answer me! Where is the warrior laid?'

To protect Eovan lest he should be somewhere sore hurt, Elmo lied; he pointed to the empty grave. 'There lies Eovan Tucarus, a First Born prince of Skol-Jerrag.' Surely a pagan would not recognise the heresy of speaking the name 'First Born'.

'First Born?' Finn said, clearly surprised. He circled the grave looking down and the mound with awe. 'I, Finn son of Bjorn of Gradigheim, bested a First Born warrior-prince?' He knelt, touched the newly dug soil and fingered a small hammer-shaped trinket he wore from a leather thong about his neck. 'He would have made a worthy opponent had he not been outnumbered and unarmed.' Standing, he drew a sword from his belt. 'Bury this with him,' he said hefting the warrior's sword through the air.

Elmo caught it by the hilt and it immediately fell comfortably into his hand. Elmo wondered if Finn had any idea of the error he had just made. He made a feint and then sliced the blade through the air in a figure-of-eight before assuming a relaxed fighting stance.

Finn's eyes widened slowly as he reassessed his position. Both young men knew that Elmo could strike him down before he had time to draw his dagger. But Elmo also knew that to kill a man was one of the greatest of sins, greater even than the sins he had endured and perpetrated. He put up the sword, and then kneeled by the empty grave that would not remain empty for much longer.

Elmo buried the sword under six inches of soil and patted it down interring his last chance of escape.

'You are a strange one,' Finn said when the task was done. 'And all my gold says that you walked the warrior's path before you threw away your manhood.'

'My father was a warrior, and a son will learn his father's trade until he grows a mind of his own.'

Finn smiled grimly and nodded. 'When your time comes to die, I'll not use you as a dinner-goat. You'll have the loan of a good sword and you can die in battle against me.'

It was clear Finn believed he was extending a boon to him, so Elmo thanked him. They returned to the monastery via a rock pool where Elmo washed away the blood and the mud. He half-expected to see Eovan, but it was not to be.

Elmo dressed and returned to the refectory where he found the raiders all drunk.

'We must put to sea,' Gudric said through a slurring leer. 'For it has come to me … not only did the White-Christ calm the storm, but Elmo, his saint, is the patron to all seamen. We'll not sink!'

'Unless greater gods wish it,' countered Finn. 'And all gods are greater than the White-Christ, even Loki!'

This drew laughter from all the drunken raiders. They pressed still for an early launch, for one of them had found the monks' boat and deemed it fit and strong enough to bear them all, but Finn told them that good omens or not, they would wait a while and see the storm abate.

It did not abate, and Elmo prepared himself for death because he was resolved not to suffer the pains of the previous night.

Finn bolted the door to Father Paul's room and undressed until he stood in naught but the necklace with the hammer-shaped pendant. This he took off, turned it around and put it back on the other way. He must have noticed Elmo's puzzlement.

'Come here! See, it has open eyes on one side, and closed on the other.'

The little silver trinket was shaped like a war hammer and true enough, it bore the semblance of a face with open eyes on the obverse and another with closed eyes on the reverse.

'Under the sun I have my own eyes open and all that befalls me is of my own making. But when I sleep I turn the eyes to face outward, and Thor protects me until morning.'

Unconsciously Elmo fingered the fish tattoo at his throat.

'So, now to bed and sport,' Finn said getting under the covers.

'To bed, aye,' Elmo said. 'For I should freeze else, but to sleep or to death. I am in your hands, and the Lord's.'

'I shall be easy on you. I shall make it pleasing for us both.'

'You shall leave me be, or slay me. I'll not submit to anything else.'

Finn showed an icy countenance for a moment, and Elmo believed his end was close, but then Finn beat a hollow in the pillow and settled to sleep. 'Anyway, I want no more of you,' Finn said sulkily. 'You are not sufficiently woman-like for my interest in you to survive the boiling blood that follows battle and slaying. Why, I would lay a knot-hole in the ship's planking when my blood is up so.'

Elmo slept deeply, undisturbed by either Finn or troublesome dreams.

The raiders rose early next morning and feasted on stale bread. The boat was dragged down the beach from its place among the sand and tough grass, and despite the heaving sea, they were resolved to launch.

'The temper of the sea is much improved since yesterday,' Gudric said. 'But still, call upon your god and your namesake.'

'I am no necromancer,' Elmo said. 'And the Lord Jesus Christ does not descend from on high to perform tricks.'

Another raider, Aki, the one who had slapped his rear the day before, took his shoulder in a friendly grip. 'Say a

125

prayer is all we ask, brave monk,' he said in a voice too low for any but Elmo to hear.

Elmo did as he was asked, and called for the blessing of his Lord to protect the small boat and all who sailed in it.

They put out to sea and raised the little sail. Elmo was made to stand at the mast while Gudric took the steer-board and the other's stood by with oars.

At first the going was good, but as soon as the little boat cleared the protective limbs of the island, the side-current took hold and they were swept to the south. Gudric soon had a feel for the prevailing wind and shouted instructions which the others obeyed without question.

Elmo was soaked by the spray from a wave that broke over a jagged rock, far too close for comfort, and Gudric fought to beat to the seaward side of the isle. He eventually succeeded but then the sea became fiercer without the sheltering influence of the small island. The boat was tossed about and a tall wave hit athwart, spilling over the gunwales and all but scuttling them.

Finn directed the oars to be shipped and had all but Gudric bailing out water. Another wave hit and carried them into a black decaying tooth of a rock which warped a clinker board.

'Back to the island!' Finn called. 'We're taking on water.'

'Your gods are useless, boy,' Gudric yelled.

Gudric adjusted the steer-board but another wave hit and another rock bit.

'Time to die, monk, and more the pity this boat is without a windlass.' Gudric abandoned the steer-board as a hopeless job and had drawn his sword, his arm already drawn back to run Elmo through, but before he made the killing thrust, he fell, head split by Aki's thrown axe. The next few moments were a confusion of splintering wood and cries of terror. Then the boat keeled over tipping everyone into the sea and for the next few seconds, moments that seemed an eternity, Elmo did no more than try to keep his head above the black, icy waves.

He trod water and tried to get his bearings, but the waves were too high for him to see the island, although the

126

mainland was there, tantalisingly solid but so distant. Then he was hit by a soft piece of flotsam. It was a body, and it was Finn's, a large bloody gash across his forehead, and Finn either dead or unconscious. Something in Elmo rejoiced and he reached out to pull the body under, but the feeling was short lived, and furthermore, shocked him. If he could turn the other cheek, just as the Lord Jesus had done, if he could save this man who had so ill-used him, then perhaps his own sins would be forgiven.

He took the limp Finn under the chin and swam on his back towards the mainland being careful to keep Finn's mouth and nose clear of the water. Then, rising upon a wave he saw Coquet Island and adjusted his direction. He had to beat to the landward side of the isle, for to attempt a landing anywhere else would mean landing either not at all or as bloody rock-shredded pulp.

He kicked with both legs and made deep strokes with his free arm, expending all effort so that his lungs ached just as if he were running a long-distance sprint. Twice he came close to being dashed by semi-submerged rocks and then, at last, the rip than ran south between the isle and the mainland took him. He was able to rest for a while, treading water until the little beach came into view, and then once again he thrashed for all he was worth.

He dragged himself and Finn up the wet sand where they laid like two soggy rag dolls. Elmo collapsed and made no effort to move until he regained his breath and then he half-carried half-dragged the still unconscious raider into the shelter of the monastery.

He manhandled Finn up the stairs, stripped him of his wet clothes, washed and bandaged his head-wound and put him into Father Paul's bed. Then he stoked up the fire, for they were both frozen half to death. Elmo was certain that Finn would die anyway – and good riddance, but at least he had done his duty as a Christian – and that he was like to be taken by a chill himself. But then again, could the First Born die of such commonplace ills?

Recalling something from the previous evening, Elmo went to the sleeping raider and lifting his head he slipped off the hammer necklace and then put it back on again with the eyes facing the world. Elmo would pray for Finn's recovery out of a spirit of duty and charity, but it wouldn't hurt for the man's own gods to watch out for him as well.

~ 2008 ~
The Translation of Raven-Fish!

The next four weeks was a period of personal highs and lows for me. The lows are not directly germane to this story, so suffice to say they had to do with my domestic situation. Jenny was divorcing me, straight out of the blue, and I just didn't get it. I had never been unfaithful. I think I was a good father to Rachel; I really didn't know, and if I began to dwell on the whys and wherefores I started to sink into a suffocating mire of self-pity, so I did my best not to dwell on it. The exciting developments concerning our discoveries could only help in the circumstances, or at least that is what I believed at the time. Perhaps with no such excitements to keep me diverted, I may have made more of an effort to get to the bottom of Jenny's motives. As it was, I accepted the fact that Jenny had made a decision, and tried to think about the practicalities of separation.

I threw myself into the translation of Jason Bennett's book and much of myself is to be seen there in the English version, because I embellished direct and often dry translations of the narrative and sometimes the dialogue, so that it read as more of a story than a dull account. I daresay it started life as a rather exciting story and lost some of its own verve because the Old English is just not there anymore. Much of it has been lost and back in the 30's when Jason Bennett wrote the story there was still some work to be done.

I found the story about a novice monk and a Viking thrown together in violent circumstances compelling but it quickly became clear there was another dimension to it. The story walked hand in hand with our discoveries and appeared, quite eerily, to flesh out the dry bones of the dig and even the stones. It was as if Bennett had some considerable foreknowledge of what we would one day dig up. Bennett was, after all, an archaeologist and I soon became convinced that he had access to material since lost or hidden. Yes he had seen the Pigsty Stone and taken into his care what was to become the Museum Stone, and placing them together it would be easy to conjecture that there was one more part missing. But how on earth could he have known that the stone once marked the grave of two murdered boys? Coincidence was far from ruled out, but I never liked coincidence.

Raz was a great help in translating both the Old English and Latin passages and would often work with me in my office until late at night when the security man would nose in to see if everything was alright, probably hoping to find the old professor in a compromising position with a third year girl endeavouring to elicit a good pass mark in her finals.

Raven-Fish! was not a very long book and we soon had a first draft, at least in note form. There was one scene in the story that made me uncomfortable as it involved the violent sexual attack of the monk by the Viking, and it was Sod's Law that Raz was with me when I translated it. It couldn't help but dredge up a best-forgotten part of his past.

The scene was quite detailed and I wondered how much I should translate. In the end I translated it all but spent much time making it less graphic and more 'fade-to-black'. It was Raz who advised me that some of it should remain, for how was anyone to feel the horror of it otherwise? So if you should ever read my translation of *Raven-Fish!* and find your sensibilities under attack by that chapter, blame the boy! It was certainly a section that could never have been published in the 30's, and I wondered if that's why Bennett had written his story in esoteric tongues.

At last the first draft notes were complete. I closed my notebook at past midnight one Friday evening feeling satisfied and excited by the import of the story. Our friend Bennett obviously felt as I did about the darkening of the Dark Ages, because his story, which I suppose we must call an Old English fantasy, gave fictional support to my long held theory.

Now it often happens that fiction is rooted in a rich subsoil of fact and my mind was full of hope that we may, through Bennett, come to facts that were open to him and sadly closed to us. And it wasn't beyond possibility, for he had left clues in the book in the form of pencilled-in phrases where one might normally find breaks in the story.

These passages were quotes, sometimes from the *Anglo-Saxon Chronicles*, one from the Bible, and one or two from sources I could not discover. Apart from the last two insertions they did not appear to pertain to the story in any way and so they represented an immediate enigma. Raz and I concluded simultaneously that Bennett was leaving us a series of clues. We had to crack these clues and we were not helped in that we had no objective. To what was he giving us clues?

We were discussing the apparent clues when Mr Holding, the security man popped his head in, which we knew was his polite way of telling us to sling our hooks so he could lock up and partake of whatever nocturnal pastimes he favoured.

'Good Heavens,' I said checking my watch. 'I sincerely hope I haven't robbed you of an entertaining Friday night with your friends.'

Raz chuckled and shook his head. 'That time again,' he said. 'I hope Mrs Professor doesn't make free with the rolling-pin.'

He caught me by surprise. I was tired and must have let slip some facial clue that not all was well in that department. I gave him the brief details of the situation as we made our way to the car park, and Raz made suitable noises of commiseration. I made light of the potpourri of hurt, guilt and confusion, and instead voiced much of where I was to store my vast collection of books.

I felt quite desolate on my drive home, a place that no longer felt like home and soon would be no longer, and I believe I shed a few tears before I pulled myself together and applied my mind to Jason Bennett's hidden messages.

Before preparing for bed, which was now a fold-down in the spare bedroom, I took up Bennett's book once again and opened it to the title page with its illustration: a reproduction of an original pen-and-ink drawing of a big, gnarled out-of-leaf oak with crows – ravens I suppose – sitting in the branches, some with fish in their beaks some without. In an ornately penned scroll below the erased tree roots were the numbers "6 – 3 – 9 – 1". I wondered if Jason Bennett had drawn the original; it was not signed.

I was restless but being too cosy to plod down to the study to fire up my main computer, I used my laptop to check my e-mails. I wonder if anybody ever responded to, or even opened, those spam messages about Viagra or penis enlargements. There was no proper mail but I still didn't feel sleepy. I decided to drop a line to Lord James and let him know of the progress we were making, and thank him once again for allowing us free and unlimited loan of the book. I used my official e-mail address not thinking that the system administrator had access to it. It was an error that would lead to problems a few weeks down the line. I should have stuck to just the letter, in which I went into more detail.

The letter written, printed off and the envelope sealed down and stamped, it was now well past midnight and I opened up my Facebook profile for lack of anything else to do. There were no entries I felt like commenting upon and I was about to close down when the instant messenger pinged up with a serious looking default photo of Raz.

'Hi, Prof!' it read. Well, I was pleased to see Raz's words but it took me a moment to reply having never used this aspect of the site before nor any other form of instant messenger.

'Hello, Raz.' I eventually managed, wondering if I had pressed the right buttons to send my reply across the cold expanses of cyberspace.

'Please may you swing by and pick me up here tomorrow?' came the next line followed by an address, one that I was fairly certain related to Raz's home. Morpeth wasn't hugely out of the way so I sent my agreement. I was more than happy to pick him up, guessing that he had problems with his dilapidated old motor, and furthermore at

Morpeth there be archaeologists. One of the county's repositories for archaeological information was based there and I thought it wouldn't hurt to see if there was anything about Coquet Island in the records, this being the location of the monk's monastic home in *Raven-Fish!*

Yes, Coquet Island exists, as do other locations mentioned in the story albeit their names have changed. One 'Annebelle', for example, is now known as 'Amble', and there are other such places where Jason Bennett has used a name from antiquity rather than the modern equivalent. It makes sense of course, as he was writing of those times.

I am happy to mention Coquet Island by name because, unlike Lord James's grand pile, there is no chance of unwanted visitors, the island being a bird sanctuary these days and completely out of bounds to members of the public. Any reader curious to see the place may stand on the sands of the mainland beach and gaze out across the sea, or perhaps take a trip around the island in a little boat that does excursions in the summer months. You will see seals and depending on the time of year, puffins, and if you look at the buildings through binoculars, you may even notice the stonework of an ancient monastery incorporated into the fabric of the nineteenth century structures that were built to serve those who looked after the lighthouse.

With plans to pick up Raz next day and visit the local archaeologists, I went to bed at last: a squeaky and uncomfortable fold-away. It wasn't entirely necessary as Jenny had not banished me from the bedroom. In fact, it was my choice to vacate, and probably done, I'll admit, from some childish feeling of spite, but like the house, the marriage bed no longer felt welcoming. Nevertheless, I went to bed more cheerful than I might have were it not for Raz's message.

Raz had given me the address of a large, late Victorian detached house of red brick that lay in the shadows of overgrown boundary shrubs. The house was hardly visible from the road through the tall privet, and the sides were bordered thick with yew. The lack of light gave the whole plot a somewhat gothic appearance, and having parked on the gritted front drive I knocked on the door almost expecting it to be answered by a wizened, cobweb-covered butler, or perhaps a Frank N Furter impressionist complete with fishnet stockings. I chuckled as the image reminded me of Freshers' Week when I was a lad at college.

The door opened, complete with requisite creaks, and there stood ... Raz. But he was in jeans and an un-tucked shirt with bare feet and no coat, whereas I had expected he would be ready to go.

'Time for a coffee?'

'Yes, of course. No rush,' I mumbled, meaning the exact opposite.

I had also expected, on seeing the size of the house, that Raz would be ensconced in an attic room or something on the first floor and that the whole place would be divided into bedsits, but not so.

The house was carpeted throughout but otherwise had a very pre-War feel to it. Despite the gloomy exterior it was cosy inside and warmed by enormous iron radiators that must have been close to a hundred years old. Where was the potted aspidistra, I wondered.

'The kettle's on but first a quick tour. Through here,' Raz said swinging into a room on the right.

Total Heaven! A house with a library.

'Not many books left, but I only inherited the house. The contents went to various other relatives and although they kindly left most of the moth-eaten furniture, they had most of the books, all of the silver and anything that looked remotely valuable.'

The room was large and there were floor-to-ceiling banks of built-in shelves. There were old leather-bound and brass-studded easy chairs, a writing desk and a drinks trolley of polished hardwood and the most wonderful marble fireplace, complete with a roaring fire. I wasn't sure what that would do for the humidity in a library, but it was certainly good for the soul on a cold November day.

'You inherited the house? I thought you were an orphan.'

'As in no mother or father. Quite correct, but I have a smattering of other relatives scattered about the globe. Anyway, onward and upward.'

We visited every room in the house except Raz's bedroom and the tour concluded with a large, airy bedroom and modest *en suite* that he described as the lodger's room. The last lodger, a post-grad zoology student from our own university, had moved out at the end of the summer term and Raz hadn't got round to re-letting.

'Which is a bit of luck in the circumstances, as I thought you might like to move in. And plenty of room in the library for all your books.'

I was quite speechless.

'Of course, it would only have to be temporary, until you can settle somewhere on a more permanent basis, but at least you won't have to move your books into storage.'

It suddenly seemed like the best of solutions; I accepted with barely disguised alacrity.

But time was moving on. We had our coffee while we discussed the moving arrangements: timeframe, financial considerations and general associated domestics, but then it was time for work. We went via the Morpeth archaeology venue I mentioned earlier and although we did not find anything relevant in the short time we had, one of the staff was very helpful and promised to dig round for anything that might be of interest.

With feelings of nothing but growing friendship and gratitude towards Raz, it came as quite a shock later that day when I ran into Gwen McCreedy, my colleague in genetic archaeology.

'That assistant of yours need his arse kicking!' she said after collaring me and dragging me into a side office. She then proceeded to interrogate me as to Raz's professionalism, especially as pertaining to field work.

'Impeccable,' I assured her and then went on to evidence my opinion. 'Why? What's he done?'

She sucked a molar and looked at me as if assessing my sanity for employing the likes of Raz and not believing a word of my favourable judgement of him.

'I've just spent weeks sucking the DNA out of those bones you dug up,' she said. It hadn't been nearly that long. She was exaggerating. '... only to find out that Mister Smarty-Pants-Without-A-Degree Raz Reeves has ballsed-up the samples.'

'What do you mean?'

'What I mean is, soon as I had the results I knew I'd seen the chain before. Reeves took part in one of my student's projects and his DNA is ... a little unique, shall we say. So when I saw the same sequences in the sample I knew the oaf had been less than a hundred percent with his sterile techniques. The stuff we got from the bones is that close to him I'm beginning to wonder if the little sod wanked over the bones. I fully intend to chew his ears off next time I see him, so be warned.'

It's my own fault. My salty-mouthed TV persona has led many to believe I speak like that all the time, and they descend to my perceived level.

'*Bled* over them perhaps, but the fluids you so crudely mention are ...'

'Yes, yes, I know. Just a figure of speech, but either way I am going to make him wish he'd never been born.'

Hadn't she heard of industrial tribunals, or bullying in the workplace?

'You'll do no such thing!' I replied, probably a little too forcefully. Gwen was shocked to see a side of me that she had not previously experience. Something territorial, I suppose. 'He's on *my* staff and if he needs a bollocking, *I'm* the one to deliver it.'

'Um ... sure. Of course,' she mumbled. 'See to it that you do, if it wouldn't be too much trouble. Meanwhile I have to start from scratch with new samples.'

Later that afternoon I was due to meet with Raz at osteoarchaeology where a report on the skeletons was due to be delivered. I'd find time to have a quiet word with him about his DNA *faux pas*.

We had some time to spare before the meeting was due to begin, so over a coffee in the canteen I went over Gwen's concerns, very diplomatically.

136

Raz frowned for some moment. 'I can't say I'm overly impressed with Dr McCreedy's scientific methodology,' he said.

'Meaning?'

'When one receives unexpected results, it's pretty bad form to grab the first explanation you see flapping about and run it up the flag pole.'

'Sorry Raz, but I don't see that she has a lot of choice.'

'No? Well who's to say my DNA isn't similar to the bones?' I'd imagined Raz would accept his error and offer the necessary apologies. It never occurred to me he'd make a stand, shoulder to shoulder, with such a ridiculous theory. Would I always be at the mercy of his sense of humour? He'd got me again.

He broke into that Raz grin and put both hands up in surrender. 'I *suppose* there's a chance I *may* have contaminated the sample. I remember grazing my knuckles on a flint, so perhaps. I'll seek out the good Dr McCreedy and throw myself upon her mercy.'

'Fair enough, but wait until after the meeting. It's time to get a move on.'

Most of our conjectures were confirmed. The skeletons were both of young men, the youngest of whom was barely out of puberty. There was evidence that they had died bloody and painful deaths, and each had a little silver marker in the lower left jaw, held in place by a tang jammed between the last two molars. They showed us a close-up photo on the overhead, and I do not suppose you will be very surprised to hear that under magnification an engraved symbol could be seen and that symbol was the ever more common circle-within-square that had become an intriguing theme of our research.

The eldest of the two boys had apparently met his eventual death by a deep stab through the upper midriff, a *coup de grace* that most probably punctured his dorsal aorta. This conclusion came about because the tip of a blade was found embedded in the corresponding thoracic vertebra. Damage to the cervical vertebrae suggested the younger boy probably suffered trauma to the neck, sufficient to sever the spinal cord and thereby cause death.

Now here is the value of careful cataloguing and cross referencing. One bright technician had studied this tiny shard of corroded metal in great detail, and matched it to the missing tip of a blade found in a grave dig in the late nineteen-fifties. It is clear from the newspaper reports one reads that cold-case investigations are beginning to show incredible results, with perpetrators of grisly crimes being brought to book after ten, twenty – sometimes thirty – years, but who could beat our record? Everyone at that meeting sat back to take in the implications, that a skeleton found fifty years ago looked favourite as the killer of one unearthed a few weeks back, and that a thousand-year-old crime was that much closer to being solved.

Raz and I exchanged looks, and the looks said 'Let's keep quiet about Lord Godwin, at least for the time being'. What was the alternative? Build a theory on a work of fiction? I think not. Of course, should we solve the clues and come to Jason Bennett's sources, events may take a different course.

There was one very unfortunate consequence to the amazing discovery of the iron dagger-tip and its connection to the rest of the blade. It was an exciting discovery, and the sort one cannot help talking about. And the Doctor, God bless him (even if I can't), always kept his ears close to the ground, especially in any research involving my team. The Doctor – let's call him Dr Smith, shall we? – heard about the discovery and began to show a lot of interest.

Here I should emphasise that should there be a real Dr Smith within my profession, than I apologise but rest assured, you are not my nemesis. I have chosen the name to protect the wicked and make it just that little bit harder for the actual incumbent to litigate against me.

Never mind the Doctor for now, because I have left the most intriguing find until last. I was pleased when the isotope report tended to confirm our belief, corroborated by the revelations in *Raven-Fish!*, that the boys were high born. The isotope data was strangely bland and inconclusive, except with regard to traces of lead. These showed a high exposure to metal and suggested that the boys had been of sufficient station to dine off silver plate. A pleasing result, but once again Raz and I remained silent concerning the source of our pleasure. Interesting, and now to the intriguing: the skeletons were identical in terms of isotope results, just as they were in respect of their unique dentition. Although it is known as a rare phenomenon, we seldom encounter a skull with an entire third set of teeth, so the fact that both had, as it were, a second set of permanent teeth lying deep in the jaw underneath the main set was cause for much comment. The conclusion: the bodies must be those of very close relatives who shared a dental mutation. I knew in my bones Gwen McCreedy would confirm this once the new DNA tests were complete.

Later in the week we also had a report on the geophys in the vicinity of Jack Taylor's B & B bastle. There was a chance that ground a little to the south-west may have once been the site of a pagan – most probably Roman – temple. The resulting map from the geophys survey showed the typical if somewhat diffuse shape of such a structure, which is – and I hope you are not becoming bored – a circle within a square, the whole structure being some six metres across, wall to wall. We are, of course, talking nothing more than sub-surface compaction of stones that may or may not have indicated the early presence of a building. If we were lucky, the square represented the foundations of the external walls, and the circle, the inner sanctum, if you will, which typically rose like a short tower. There would have to be a dig to confirm the speculative findings. And this is where Dr Smith stuck his big nose in: he wanted to be part of it. Professional etiquette did not allow me to say 'Piss off, you nosey bugger!'

Despite the Doctor's unwelcome interest, it was all very exciting. Raz and I felt we had a handle on the research, aided as we were by the revelations within *Raven-Fish!* We decided to go over our plans but not wishing to be overheard, we discussed the matter while we walked round the grounds. We spoke in hushed tones and changed the

139

subject when anybody drew too close. With apologies to John Le Carré, *Tinker, Tailor, Soldier ... Archaeologist.*

Among our early excursions, we'd set up a trip to Coquet Island so we could get a feel for the place and look at the archaeology.

Don't even think about it! Professionals within the same region may well extend certain courtesies towards one another, and the warden of the bird sanctuary had been most friendly and accommodating, but to reiterate, the island is strictly off limits and anyone trying to land without permission will be blasted out of the water by a sea-skua launched by a Royal Navy frigate. Well, we can but hope. It was a trip we were looking forward to, and we hoped there might be some small indication of the veracity of the information given in *Raven-Fish!*

Meanwhile, I was close to completion of the polished version of the translation and there were certain leads suggested in the book that I will mention later. Suffice to say we concluded that, at this stage, we should concentrate on the clues. There wasn't a lot of point in flying off on what might prove to be pursuits after feral water fowl until we had exhausted all efforts to turn the key in Jason Bennett's curious locks. Time and again his book, fantasy though it may be, proved beyond a doubt that he had information we did not and his hand-written inserts were the closest we had to a key.

Back home Jenny hit me with another bombshell, although in truth I should have been ready for it. She had already stopped cooking meals for me, but at least she left me the makings in the fridge or freezer. When I got home that night, she told me that she was going away for Christmas.

'I've been invited to my sister's,' she said. 'Rachel will join me there straight from her rooms. So I'll be away from the Friday before Christmas until the Saturday after new year.'

That was closer to a fortnight than a simple 'away for Christmas', and I said so.

'Well I'm going, so get used to it. Do you want me to order anything in or will you make your own arrangements?'

I mumbled something about making my own arrangements.

As things turned out, Christmas wasn't half bad. After speaking with Raz, I hired a van for the day after Jenny's departure, loaded up my books, clothes, professional tools and other bits and pieces and moved in to my new accommodation. I left her a note informing her that should she have the need, she could contact me at the office.

Though Christmas was surprisingly pleasant, and I shall speak of it later, 2009 was to bring its own wagonloads of strife, personal and professional. Nevertheless, it is easier to brave the worst storms when the lighthouse beacon shines brightly, and *Raven-Fish!* was indeed to prove the brightest of beacons. And if I needed still more light to bring me through the darkness, it was provided by Raz Reeves, despite the ill fortune that was to fall at his own feet.

X

In which the Raven is at the Mercy of the Fish

Elmo dragged the straw-stuffed pallet from his cell and laid it at the hearth. He needed to stay in Father Paul's room to keep watch over Finn, but at least he was free from sharing the same bed. He brought his blanket and gathered others from the cells of his brothers who would no longer need them and set about constructing himself a cosy nest. He kept on the dry shirt and drawers he had taken from the dwindling store in the laundry and settled to sleep, though he found it difficult to relax his frozen limbs.

Finn slept as quiet as the grave. Elmo wondered if had slipped from this life to the mysterious hereafter since the last time he checked for breathing; he was past caring and decided to wait until morning before venturing out of his blankets to find out. By peeping from his nest, Elmo could make out the slight mound Finn made under the covers in Father Paul's bed. Slight as a boy and yet cruel as a ravening beast from Hell; not for the first time Elmo contemplated drawing a knife across the raider's neck. Would it really be such a sin? Only duty and the obvious answer to his unspoken question stayed his hand.

Elmo slept deeply and without dreams. He woke to dawn light and the sound of Finn's fretting. Throwing off the covers he was surprised to notice the fire still burning well, and then he realised it was not dawn, but late evening, the early summer sun in no hurry to bid the day farewell. He had slept but a few short hours, nevertheless the chill was out of him and he felt refreshed.

Finn on the other hand was on the borders of death, that place where the mind wanders and the body thrashes. His eyes, half open, were sunken in a pool of pale flesh, and his body ran with sweat. He had the sheen of the glazed piglet the brothers had shared last Christmas, and his body gave off at least as much heat.

Once, when he was yet to take his vows and lived in the court of King Charles of the Franks, Elmo's friend and fellow student, Louis, who also happened to be King Charles's son, had taken such a fever. The physicians had assured Charles that fever was the body's way of casting out demons, and to assist in the process the patient should be brought near to the fire and swathed in many blankets. Alcuin said 'Pish!' and told them a fire needed to be put out not stoked up. Louis was stripped and laid over with wet cloth, and on the second day his fever broke and he recovered to full strength.

Thoughts of Alcuin always made Elmo smile in his heart, and he would take Alcuin's advice over anybody's.

Elmo filled Father Paul's bathtub with two hands of cold sea water, drawn from a rock pool, and lowered Finn into it. Using a cloth he squeezed water over his head and upper body and kept on bathing in this fashion despite the delirious protestations emanating from Finn. Soon his body no longer felt like coals to the touch, and as a bonus to Elmo's senses, his polecat stench was also washed away.

Dragging Finn's wet body from the tub and onto the warm stone floor in front of the hearth, Elmo dried him and put him back to bed drawing a thin sheet up no further than his navel. Folding a soaking wash-cloth he placed it on Finn's forehead and tried to trickle some fresh well water past his lips.

Elmo felt pleased with his work, and he found he could feel no hatred for Finn while he was caring for him. Not once, while he bathed or dried or put him to bed, did he think evil thoughts or contemplate the ways in which he may bring death to the heathen wretch. And nor had he thought of Finn as a heathen, only as a man who might be saved.

When next Elmo woke, it was past dawn. Finn still slept but easily, his mind no longer oppressed, his body free from the taunting of demons. The storm had passed, from Finn and from the world, for the sky was clear and the sea calm.

While Finn slept on, Elmo prepared dough and then set five loaves to bake. Later he would cut some strips of cured meat and set them to boil so they might enjoy a broth for dinner. It might pay to search out more eggs too. When that was done he set to darning the clothes of those who were slain and had been buried. He had already washed them, as best he could, and the blood stains mostly gone.

Outside a sea breeze blew cool and auks skimmed the waves. Little brothers, they were called, with their black feathers, white-bibbed like certain orders of monk, although Elmo was yet to meet a monk with such a large and colourful beak.

Smoke rose lazily from somewhere in Annebelle; too much for a bonfire and Elmo wondered if a roof had caught fire. That might explain the smell of burning he had noticed earlier although he was surprised it could reach so far. He breathed deeply and looked at his hands, amazed that he alone still lived while all his brothers slept in their graves. The bodily pain from his ordeal had subsided. It only hurt when he needed to squat. Suddenly he thought of the sword he had been given by Eovan Tucarus. Perhaps he should retrieve it from Saint Cuthbert's cell and arm himself before Finn regained full strength. It was a stray and unbidden thought and he soon put it aside, but it led to other thoughts of those hours before the raiders came.

His mother's gift and Alcuin's letter: Elmo was torn between the two but as he was already outside, he thought to seek out the gift first.

Just as Eric had said, the gift was set under the Cuthie Duck's nest by the well. Unwinding the waxed cloth he pulled out a small brushed-leather pouch held shut with a draw-string. Inside were several metal items and a tiny roll of parchment. There was a belt-buckle and a ring marked with old runes. Next, a small trinket of gold rolled into his hand and he wondered at it, for it resembled a miniature drinking vessel and it looked to be made of gold. Inside the faerie-cup was a fillet of the softest gold rolled into a tiny scroll. He picked it out and so soft was the metal that his fingernail left a mark.

He looked about him as if he might be caught by Father Paul's ghost at some pagan practice, for he knew that of old prayers were written in such scrolls of metal.

Carefully unrolling the yellow, buttery metal, he read the words graven thereon and they said simply *I am Elfgar, First Born prince.*

Perhaps there may be answers in the parchment, but he dare not unroll it here for fear the wind might snatch it. He took his little collection of treasures back into the monastery and laid them upon the refectory table. And then, he read the scroll, a note from his mother, penned by another for she could neither read nor write.

Ah! It was his brother's hand. Eric had been taught to read and write even though he had no intentions to become a scribe or a monk. In this respect he was probably unique among the men of his own age and station, if not in the whole of Northumbria, at least in his own small town.

Elmo's mother opened with a formal greeting but moved on to brief salutations of a more intimate nature. How he was missed. How often he was prayed for. And then to the import of the various items: the golden beaker was a gift from his father, not Thomas Gerefa, but his real father whom, Mother said, had been a great man. She would leave the details to the deacon Alcuin, she said, for she was certain he would soon be made privy to the secrets of his origin.

The beaker had been brought to her by a holy brother who travelled as if the devil were at his heels. She was to get it to her adopted son as soon as may be, and instruct him that should he feel his fate and doom were upon him, that he should swallow the small ornament so that thereafter his remains might be recognised as those of his father's son.

Elmo took up the beaker and turned it in his fingers. Small though it may be, it would be no easy feat to swallow it.

He returned to the note. The ring had belonged to his grandfather, Oswald. That is, his adoptive father's father. Mother thought it fitting that he should have something, a family treasure, from the family who raised and loved him.

145

The buckle had also been his grandfather's and Elmo considered replacing his own plain buckle with this ornate one. But no, Father Paul would not have approved of such finery.

And then came a heartfelt valediction and a cross in saltire, no doubt by his mother's own hand. He held the note to his cheek that he might absorb something of the love that was put into it, and then read it once, twice more. Not for the first time Elmo felt the magic of writing, that feelings and meaning could be conveyed across vast distances in space and time. The man who could spell could indeed cast a kind of magic. To write something down was to make it into a species of reality. To cast the name of the beast into words was to throw a rope around its neck.

Elmo turned his thoughts to that other letter, the one to him from his beloved tutor and friend in Christ Jesus, Alcuin. But after secreting the golden beaker in a pocket in his drawers, he went back outside and buried the ring and the buckle in the vegetable garden. He measured the position of the interment by counting the bricks in the south wall and in the east and drawing an imaginary line from the two; where the lines met he buried his treasures to keep the safe from raiders and over-zealous monks who may see sin where none existed. The stones of the wall, some of them, had letters scratched upon them for it was the wont of an early novice to practice his letters while he was at his gardening chores.

The south-wall stone bore a graven letter N in the Roman style and the east wall a T. Thereafter the Fish penned upon a piece of scroll these two letters and put down six numbers, which were measure of the hand, the better to find his treasures in some unimaginable hereafter.

146

Elmo washed the soil from his hands in a salty puddle and hoped that he had seen an end to burials for many a year to come. Waving his hands in the warm air to dry, and then completing the task by wiping them upon his habit, he enjoyed fond memories of Alcuin.

Since Alcuin had taken Elmo to King Charles's court, he had been father to him, and brother and best friend. The many years between their ages and experiences mattering not a whit, Alcuin had often said that their friendship was equal, for what the older man paid in experience and wisdom, Elmo compensated for in full with enthusiasm and freshness of life. When he was just a small boy, Alcuin had even been mother to him and treated the boyish wounds of his flesh and spirit with tender care. Alcuin delivered firm guidance with confidence but never cruelty. He admonished, when it was necessary, with words that supported rather than scourged and he had never in all their years together been spiteful or mean-spirited.

When Elmo broke free from the shackles of childhood and became a young man, his friendship with Alcuin blossomed and they would spend hours in discussion of matters philosophical, the older man never playing the card of age or station to support an argument he might be losing.

While there was Alcuin in the world, Elmo knew he would never truly be alone. It was time to find that letter.

To my Dearest Little Brother, from Albinus ...

Elmo smiled; Alcuin had hailed him 'Little Brother', but had written it in the form that referred to the comical little auks that lived on the Island. Alcuin, often playful in his missives, was calling Elmo a puffin. It had not been difficult to find the letter. It was in Father Paul's great chest, crumpled but otherwise undamaged from the raiders' rude scrutiny. With a quick glance over towards the still sleeping Finn, Elmo read on.

Can it really be that more than a year has passed since I delivered you unto the captain who would sail you away to Northumbria? But of course it is, for not a day has passed when

I do not think fondly of you and miss you like a loving father misses his little son and do not those days stretch behind me like a long road receding into the unfathomable distance? I trust you are devout in those practices of cleanliness and exercises of the mind and body which I imparted to you and which may help see you into an age when I am long to my eternal sleep.

Alcuin went on briefly to enquire about his progress and to express hopes that Father Paul and the other monks were kindly towards him, and then to the nub of the matter. Alcuin spoke of King Elfwald and of his three sons, of whom Elmo, sometime known as Elfgar, was the youngest. So it was true. Now he had it from Alcuin, he knew it to be so and all doubt was dispelled.

I hope you will forgive me, Little Brother, for keeping this from you. Know that you were hid amidst the vipers that would bite you, and so ignorance was a shield to keep you safe. Do I call your playmates and fellow students vipers, and thereby intimate that their sire was chief among the serpent-kind? Rather I say they are misguided and that they hold Heresy a great sin.

What of Heresy? There are many kinds, but did the word ever fall from the lips of Our Lord? I doubt it very much, for it is a word of the Church and it covers many arguments that cannot be won by reason. Those who choose to read the excluded gospels are Heretics because the Church says so. Those who doubt the Trinity are Heretics and others too for a myriad of reason, but of all the Heresies none stands higher than the Heresy of the First Born. We say First Born, for even to form their true name with our silent lips is to invite censure, imprisonment and death. Is any other Heresy so damning that it cannot be written down, but passed from mouth to ear and then only in a whisper?

So complete is the task of wiping the First Born from our records and memories, that most forget them or remember them falsely as gnarly beings who inhabit tree stumps or flitting, smoky folk who bring us dreams or night mares.

But there were those, and are those, who love Truth second only to Our Lord, and your loving brother in Christ is such a one and so was that venerable monk who some time lived at Jarrow and who secreted away those passages that he was meant to destroy. I too have some time been set to pare away words that speak of the First Born and rewrite great scrolls without certain passages that formerly existed. I am a guardian of that Truth concerning the First Born that the world is soon to forget, but I will that they remember. But the time is not now, and unto you I commend a quest.

That word again. Elmo sat heavily on the edge of the bed and Finn stirred a little. Who was Elmo to complete a quest?

Who is Elmo to complete a quest?

Elmo blinked and looked again at the line that spoke his unspoken question. Did Alcuin know him that well?

Elmo is a noble heart, and brave. And Elmo is also Elfgar, First Born prince, so in whose hands would this quest lay easier? None, I should say, for into your hands I commend the posterity of your Race. There are other First Born yet in the World, but they are persecuted whether of low station or high, and a day may soon come when all have passed from this World to that place where only they and you, being of them, can go. You too must go there soon and Eovan Tucarus, the bearer of this letter, will tell you the road you must take. But first, the quest.

Alcuin wanted Elmo to take a book, which he said was entitled *The Truth of the First Born*, and in its special vessel, bury it within the foundations of Skol-Jerrag, the last stronghold of the First Born, and then he could take leave of the world or remain, according to the promptings of his heart.

There was one final request put so forcefully that it was indeed a command, and that was for Elmo to destroy the letter once committed to memory. And then followed Alcuin's farewell.

If there is a perfect love, it is love without want of anything in return. To love without desire or the intercession of base wants or needs, to delight in another's company for that company alone and not what it might yield in worldly favour, to have a heartfelt

149

wish for that beloved to fare well in the world and to know happiness and weather adversity with fortitude. A love like unto the love Our Lord has in his heart for his flock. In that I know this kind of love I am blessed and I think there is no need to set a name to my beloved.

I am old and the World and its schemes move apace. Perhaps these will be the last words you shall have from me. If I pass to my reward with time to spare for a last thought before I go, you, Little Brother, will be there smiling and bidding me a fond farewell, and I ask that you think of me, from time to time, in that place where you might walk and I cannot. As I live in you I cannot die.

Your most loving brother in Christ.

Alcuin.

Elmo wanted to read parts of the letter again, but found he could not see well through the water in his eyes. He fisted both eyes and sniffed deeply before beginning his search for Alcuin's book, *The Truth of the First Born.*

It proved more elusive than his mother's gifts or Alcuin's letter and it was nowhere to be found in Father Paul's room. Perhaps such a dangerous document needed to be kept in the safest of places, and on Coquet Island the safest and most secret of sites was Saint Cuthbert's cell.

Whereas the refectory had a floor of stone flags, the small antechamber was of wooden planks. In one corner the planks formed a trap door. As Elmo lifted the door he remembered the last time he came here was to hide his true father's fine sword. But thoughts of the weapon fled as the glow of fire lit the interior of the cell, and then Elmo remembered that the cell did indeed have a fireplace. A shadow moved within and Elmo hardly dared to hope that after all, he was not the sole survivor of the raiders' barbarous cruelty.

'Brother Sebastian?'

'Not he, I'm afraid,' came an irascible reply. 'Say Brother Mundwyn instead.'

'Brother Mundwyn!' Elmo leapt down to the stone floor, ignoring steps and a more seemly descent.

'Hold up there, lad!' Mundwyn fought off Elmo's hug. 'Are you hurt?'

'Not as yet, but keep up that bear's grip and I may yet suffer a cracked rib or two.'

'Is Sebastian in here with you, or Eovan, the noble knight?'

'Neither. Sebastian made good his escape to the mainland in Eovan's boat, and … I took Eovan, who was sore wounded, to another place.'

There was something in the way Brother Mundwyn spoke, something in the look of his eyes. Another place?

'Do you mean the place where only the First Born may go? You are First Born too, Brother Mundwyn?'

'Indeed I am not.' He straightened his habit, crumpled from Elmo's embrace. 'There are occasions when such as I might touch the borders of that land. But pish! What of the raiders?'

'Dead, all but one.'

'And the one?'

'Near death, or has been. I think it certain he shall live now. He rests in Father Paul's bed.'

'You nursed him,' Mundwyn asked, shuffling his elderly frame closer to the little fire.

Elmo felt ashamed. He helped a heathen to live.

'Good lad,' Mundwyn said. 'You're the man I hoped you'd be. But more on that later. It seems an age since I saw the light of day, and you must tell me what befell our brothers, although by the screams that came to me, I think I know well enough.' He made for the steps.

'First I must look for a book,' Elmo said casting about the small room.

'There it's, if you search for Alcuin's book.' He pointed, not to a book, but to a stone the size of a man's head but somewhat flattened and with a seam running around the middle.

'The book is inside? May I look?'

151

'To that, yes and no. The book *is* inside but you mayn't look for I have already sealed it with a run of hot lead about the join.' He gestured towards the hearth where a silver-stained pot and an iron ladle rested. 'I know what is to become of the book and I thought it expedient to hurry it along the way.'

This Brother Mundwyn was entirely more than he seemed, and come to think of it, Elmo had seen the emblem of his order elsewhere and very recently. Lifting his habit he fumbled inside his drawers and drew forth the little golden beaker. The side of it bore the same shape and that was a circle inside a square.

'That furrowed brow holds back many questions, lad, I'll be bound. And I shall make you answers, but for now I will tell you that I came to this place at the bidding of a friend who knows of the First Born and what is to be done.'

'Alcuin!'

Mundwyn smiled. 'Alcuin fretted over your good health and worried that the monks might ill use you as many in other places are wont to do with their novices. I am happy to say my initial report was that the monks of Coquet Island were far above such ignoble actions.'

'And should they not have been I would have reminded them I was once a warrior's son with many warrior's skills, such as the ability to deliver a bloody nose.'

Mundwyn laughed. 'And so I assured Alcuin, but he sent me anyway. Now please hold off until I can drag myself out of this abode of mowdy-warps and breathe the good air.'

Elmo took the stone and was surprised that it was so light for such a heavy looking piece. He followed Mundwyn out of the cell and closed the trap behind him. The fire would soon burn itself out and was quite safe to leave in its stone hearth.

'Take that upstairs,' Brother Mundwyn said, pointing to the stone. 'I must walk under the sky for a while, lest I forget the look of a cloud.'

When Elmo came to the door of Father Paul's room he was confronted by a naked Finn standing on a chair by the window.

'What are you doing?' he demanded, half-afraid that the young raider was about to hurl himself out.

Finn was unsteady on his feet but had regained much of his strength. He stepped down from the chair with a slight stumble. 'I needed to shit and I thought you would like it little if I did it in the bed.'

Yes, the raider had gained much of his strength and all of his former baseness of manner.

'You … out of the window?'

'Where else?'

'There is a pot under the bed.'

Finn looked under the bed and laughed. 'You shit in pots?' He stumbled again and fell. Elmo helped him back under the covers.

'Stay here and I'll bring you a strong broth.'

Finn mumbled and chuckled at the same time. 'Don't bring it in a pot you shat in.'

Elmo pulled the cover over Finn and turned to leave for the refectory when he noticed something, or rather, the absence of something. 'Where's my letter?' he said forcefully.

Finn peeped out from the covers. 'That ball of paper? I used it as an arse-wipe.'

Elmo was horrified. He ran out and down the stairs and left the monastery, doubling round to the back. There was Finn's splattered mess under the window and a single, besmeared strip of paper, but most of the letter had already been taken by the wind.

Elmo walked slowly back to the monastery and sat on the bottom step, desolate. He had intended to read Alcuin's letter again and again until the ink wore away by the persistence of his gaze, but in the event he had only been allowed to read it once. He tried to tell himself that at least Finn had saved him the trouble of destroying it, but he felt no better. His shoulders hunched, he saved his muscles the effort of keeping him erect and he was on the verge of

153

giving in to tears when Brother Mundwyn made a creaky-limbed ascent from the beach.

'It appears something is afoot in Annebelle. The citizens are set to arms.'

'You can see that far?' Elmo said without enthusiasm.

'Not in any great detail, and I may be wrong, but best we are ready to leave at a moment's notice. How's that sick raider?'

Elmo ground his teeth unconsciously. 'Almost restored, thanks to the Lord.'

'Your words say one thing and your face another. Would you rather he died?'

Elmo looked over his shoulder into the cool interior of the monastery. 'I'll say only that if God had willed it so, I would not have railed against fate.' He stood and walked to the top of the beach and strained to see across the water. 'Do you think a larger body of raiders harries the townsfolk?'

'Unlikely. I think it more probably that fear has called the fyrd to arms. Brother Sebastian made good his escape so the alarm must be raised.'

'And yet nobody hurries to our rescue.'

'They must believe nobody lives to be rescued, which is close to the truth. If you had drowned trying to rescue the raider, I would not have tarried.'

For the rest of the long morning Christian duty fought with personal desire within the young monk. While he mixed a poultice of bog-mosses, goose grease and herbs with which to treat Finn's head wound, he imagined he was pounding belladonna and yew seeds into a potent poison. As he applied the medication with gentle care, he stayed his hands from throttling the patient. When he held a spoonful of thick broth to the raider's lips, he restrained the urge to upend the hot liquid over his lap thus scalding that instrument of humiliation he wielded with such evil alacrity. This thing, this man, this beast whose pleasure was murder and rapine, who had killed his brothers and First Born kinsmen, and used him as a vessel in which to expend his base lusts. Elmo's calm and relaxed face was flesh over grinding jaws.

'Give me the spoon,' Finn snapped. 'I can manage it well enough.'

'And right glad I am to be relieved of the task. Here!'

Finn shuffled up in the bed to sit more comfortably and took the spoon with a snatch, and the bowl of broth with a measure more civility. He said thank you, as if it were an alien phrase, and began to feed himself, looking sidelong at Elmo as if expecting an attack at any moment.

Elmo went to the hearth and began to sweep out the cool ashes. The day was warm and there was no need of a fire, so he merely set the logs ready for the evening. His father's sword rested to the side of the nook and he ran the backs of his fingers up the finely tooled scabbard.

'You had me in your power,' Finn said. 'Why did you let me live? Why did you pull me from the sea that took my comrades?'

'The way of a beast is not the way of a man, or so I believe. It is natural that we may be moved by base needs and lusts, but a man has free will and may rule himself with but a little effort.'

'Mealy-mouthed riddle-talker!' Finn spat. 'You mean you wish to kill me but you don't have the balls, so unmanned are you by your White-Christ man-god.'

'I mean I wish very much to kill you, and that I have the means, but that a man alive is a being full of life that may yet see the light, and a man dead is worm-fodder.'

Finn laughed and fingered his hammer-trinket. 'You think you will convert me to your woman's religion.' He looked at the trinket, and again he looked trying hard to focus upon the engraving. 'Did you turn the eyes towards the world?'

'I did,' Elmo said. 'So good it may do you.'

'It *has* done me good. I am hale and gaining strength, so I thank you.' This time his gratitude appeared genuine. He took off the necklace and reversed it once more. 'Now we are even, all blood-debts paid. I saved you from Gudric's windlass and you saved me from the greedy waves.' He put the bowl to his lips and drained the rest of the broth. Wiping his mouth on the back of his hand he threw the bowl towards Elmo who snatched it from the air before it could glance off his skull.

'Now I shall sleep a little more,' Finn said. 'And give you a last chance to slit my throat, for when I wake to full strength I will make you mine again, or kill you. For certain I will not stay in your power.'

Elmo took up his father's sword and withdrew six inches of polished iron blade. 'Then that is the hour we shall fight, for I will not submit to you.'

Finn smiled widely. 'You will fight me, and you a lily-livered monk? I've never heard the like.'

Elmo snapped the blade home again. 'It appears I am an odd species, part monk and part First Born atheling.' Elmo spoke the heresy out loud and felt the skin and the back of his neck tingle.

The smile immediately passed from the raider's face. 'First Born ...?'

'And well enough trained in the arts of war. If you oppress me I have no doubt the warrior in me will come to the fore.'

'Then I have much to look forward to. But first, sleep.' Finn slid under the covers and closed his eyes. Within five minutes he was snoring.

The hours passed. 'Do you think the Viking lad a danger?' Mundwyn said as he drew a stool close to the refectory fire. It was past noon; Finn still slept upstairs while the elderly monk and Elmo shared a light meal of bread and salted fish.

'What word is this, "Viking", for I have never heard it? Is it the Northmen's name for foul spawn of Hell?'

Mundwyn considered while he chewed. 'No, although the enemies of the Northmen often consider it so. But to my question, if you please.'

'Do I think him a danger? Well, he says he means to use me again or battle me to the death, but I think he talks in excess of his intentions. For the things he has done, I hate him and I am constantly moved to finish him while he sleeps. And yet I shall not. I hold mercy dear, and …'

The unspoken words hung in the air, diffused into the stone walls and filled the shadows. They reverberated until Mundwyn could stand it no longer. 'And what?' he said irascibly. 'Finish what you were going to say, man.'

'I must acknowledge that because of Finn, I yet breathe and live. I hate him for what he has taken away, and yet I feel there is a bond for what he has bestowed.'

Mundwyn nodded and took a draft of ale. Both men then settled to a contemplation of the flames in the hearth. It was warm outside, but it took a long time for heat to penetrate the thick stone walls so the fire in the refectory was rarely allowed to die down.

Elmo stared deep and was drawn in to a fiery land of flames wherein danced beings from stories, fictitious folk who had populated his mother's bedtime tales. His heart was warmed and he smiled, but then it was as if his mother and his brother's wife and little Maud were all in the flames and being consumed alive. The daydream turned into a nightmare and he pulled his mind back into the refectory with its flickering shadows, stacks of plates and breadbaskets, the field mouse scurrying across the stone floor, Mundwyn drifting over the boundaries of sleep …

'Mundwyn,' Elmo called sharply.

Mundwyn jumped back to full wakefulness and asked grumpily what it was that necessitated such a rude awakening.

'I had a letter from Alcuin,' Elmo said.

'I know of it, and of its import. As I said, I know what is to become of his book, although not the route of its journey, and I know the good deacon has commended a quest into your hands. In that there is any help in this feeble old frame of mine, it is yours.'

'And right glad I will be to have it, but first you promised to answer my questions concerning my heritage. All I know of the First Born is that it is heresy to say they ever existed. Alcuin's letter eased my mind a little on that matter, although I need to know why some might consider me a walking heresy. I must have knowledge of who I am and where I come from.'

'And no doubt, what is your purpose in life, too.' Mundwyn stretched his back and rubbed his hands together cracking the knuckles. 'Let Brother Mundwyn tell you the answer to all the world's questions and save you the bother of having to live, for we live to find our way in this world, and who we are, and what cause moves our blood to make a stand.'

Elmo felt foolish and gently admonished, although in the same way that his dear Alcuin may have admonished. There was no spite in Mundwyn. 'Then save the world for another day, but now shall we talk of the First Born?'

Mundwyn stood and shuffled to the fire, his stiff knees creaking. He lifted the back of his habit so the warmth of the fire could ease the chill from his bottom.

'Where to start?' Mundwyn said. 'At the beginning or at the end? It is far from an easy decision as far as the First Born are concerned, for they, you, are alpha and omega. They were there at the beginning of our history and they shall be there when time runs out and the doom of all things is at hand.'

Elmo felt a chill that had nothing to do with the temperature. 'The Lord God is alpha and omega. It discomforts me that you should lay those titles before others.'

'The Lord God is a mystery beyond all telling, beyond all reasoning. Better we should think of Him as all existence and all the secrets contained therein and leave it at that. Hard enough it is for me to talk of the First Born, so don't ask me questions that have no answers that words can form or ears may hear.'

'Agreed,' Elmo said drawing his stool closer to Mundwyn and the ethereal flames. 'Let's to the First Born then.'

Mundwyn walked in a little circle, shuffling and wearing an expression that was rooted in a mind that searched for a beginning without success. He came back to his place before the fire and lifted the back of his habit once again.

'I still struggle to find a beginning. Rather, ask me simple questions, and I shall respond as best I may.'

'Very well,' Elmo said. 'You say my kind is alpha and omega. Speak to me of the alpha.'

Mundwyn nodded and smiled. 'The fathers of our father's fathers and back, father and father and father an hundred fold, we were but naked and unknowing of art or the skills of the artisan, of husbandry or philosophy, when the First Born came to us from our shared omega and they watched over us while we grew to knowledge. They gave us pots and beakers of baked clay and showed us how to make them. They eased us from the rude caves and muddy holes and little by little they lent a supporting shoulder while we learned to build.'

'And their omega?'

'At the end of all time the children of our children's children and child and child and child an hundred fold, *we* shall be the First Born when all things come to an end, and some of us shall go to that place where only the First Born may go, and others will return to our alpha, and so the cycle is complete, a never ending circle within the four corners of existence.' Brother Mundwyn lifted a hand to rest upon the emblem of his order.

Elmo rose and stood eye to eye with the older man. 'And is it true the First Born never die? Shall I live to see that omega and become part of the circle?'

Mundwyn's eyes fell for a moment. 'Nothing that carries life may live in this world forever. As First Born you shall carry life until your body is so damaged it may carry it no longer, but no harm will come to you by illness and age shall not weary you.'

'I might be killed by assault and die in battle, and yet not be taken by a fever?'

'Tell me Brother Elmo, how many times did you ail as a child? How may fevers? How often the bloody flux?'

'Never so much as a fever, though many times a cold. Mother always said that being left upon the causeway to Lindisfarne and being brought to the Holy Island by the monks infused my little body with goodness that did scare away all ailments.'

'As First Born you could lay with lepers and never take on their burden. Now tell me, have you ever lost a tooth?'

'Louis struck me a savage but accidental blow with a practice-sword once and a tooth was indeed knocked loose. But another grew in its place. Alcuin said I was most fortunate, but that it was not unknown for people to have another tooth that might descend to take the place of one lost.'

'Lucky indeed, Elmo, but rather than luck it is a mark of your kind. First Born are known by their straight legs, comely looks and good teeth.'

'And so I would indeed live forever if I avoided battle and the footpad at night?'

'One day, if you tarry in this world, you will meet your doom. If a man walks a path an hundred times and does not meet with a bear, he shall live. On the one hundredth and first time he will meet the bear and die. You might walk the path a thousand times, a score of thousands or you might meet with the bear on the morrow. Even if not open to disease or the ravages of time, you cannot hope to walk this earth and always avoid the bear. Nothing that carries life may hope to carry it forever, and as First Born the bear is likely to take the form of a dagger in the night.'

Elmo circled the room, paused to look out of the small window, his eyes saw the white, fluffy clouds but his mind did not.

'Then it is irony that my body carries all this life, and yet because I am a living heresy, I will be unlikely to see more summers than my brother Eric.' He stopped by the bread basket and lifted the lid. Peered in, replaced the lid. 'And what of the other stories? May I work magic? Perhaps turn these few loaves into many?'

'You are not Our Lord Christ, and you may not make magic, except in one respect. You're innately capable of crossing to that place where the First Born may walk, and others may not. As to transfiguring folk into animals, bringing down storms and becoming invisible, these are all fancies and the stuff of romances and beggars' tales. As to how you may make the crossing, I know not. It is for you to learn.'

'But you told me you could alight upon that road, if only at its borders.'

'That is different, and it is a skill that surpasses all description, so don't ask.'

The two men spoke long into the afternoon and Mundwyn revealed all he knew about the history of the First Born: their secrecy, the wish to remain a quiet but rarely seen influence, and then the jealousy that their differences began to engender, especially after the coming of the Church. They were a power that the Church could not countenance, so they could not be suffered to live. Now few remained and most were slain or gone into that other place.

As the afternoon became early evening, Elmo and Mundwyn returned to the chores and duties of monks, the spiritual and the secular, and Elmo tried to concentrate on the tasks at hand leaving his unconscious mind to make order of all he had heard on this extraordinary day of revelation.

That evening Finn sat by the hearth in Father Paul's room to take a light supper, and then once again to bed. Elmo slept in his nest by the fire.

The next morning after a breakfast of fresh bread and honey, Finn dressed. Elmo kept a wary eye on him lest he should launch a sneak attack, but he did not appear to have the appetite for combat. He looked like a man ill at ease inside his head, battling with choices, leaning towards one while wanting the other. Elmo left him to it while he returned the refectory. There were chores to be done.

He was checking on the dwindling food supply when Brother Mundwyn flew in at the monastery door.

'We must away!' he cried. 'Gather enough for a short journey of two or three days and don't tarry.'

Elmo jumped to his feet. 'What has happened?'

'A boat comes, and by the gaudy armour of the occupants I'll wager they're Godwin's men.'

'Godwin? I've never heard of the fellow.'

161

'No, perhaps you have not. But he's heard of you and he means to have your head. Your friend aloft he'll use to satisfy his lust for blood. Now to it! There's no time to lose.'

'We haven't a boat?'

'Stop gabbing and gather your things. Leave the means of escape to me.'

'Surely we could hide, and the warriors will believe we were slain by the raiders.'

'No, we must leave. They'll not rest until they have your head. They'll dig up the graves and when they see you do not number among the slain they will turn this island over. Every stone, every bird's nest – nothing will remain until they have you.'

'How many are they?'

'Five, not including the boatmen, and all armed for war. We are three and not all with a sword, let alone armour.'

'Finn and I have good war blades and I know where there is another.'

Mundwyn started to protest, but Elmo was out of the door and running to the burial place. Eovan's blade had not been in the soil long enough to take on more than the first rosy bloom of rust. And Elmo had the feeling that Mundwyn knew how to wield a sword.

11

~ 2009 ~
Balancing the Books

Early February 2009, a Monday morning, snow everywhere, the country at a virtual standstill; I should have known it was going to be a bad day when I slipped on the ice and stuffed my face straight into a granite kerbstone. All the time I was waiting in casualty, every stitch the doctor put in, all I could think about was being late for an important meeting with the board. It was a three-line whip and nothing short of death was about to be an excuse for not being there. The way things were I am sure my death would have been quite a convenience. But I'm ahead of myself. Christmas was a surprisingly pleasant affair.

I had several reservations about moving in with Raz. What would people think? Was it appropriate given our professional relationship? Would sharing accommodation lead to difficulties in the workplace? All these and a half-dozen more were all pretty obvious and tended towards the practical but none of them were uppermost in my mind. My main concern was that I was moving into young man's territory, and that was a land I had never before visited. Oh my body had been there, but emotionally I'd moved from 14 to 40 completely bypassing all the years in between. The other way of looking at it, I never got past 14. Here I was, rapidly heading towards 60, and in many respects I was Peter Pan. At 20 I didn't get what it meant to be a young man. Nearing 60, I got it, but it was far too late and yet there was a place inside that was always empty for want of those missed years.

I was determined not to impose myself into Raz's private life. I would not even attempt to fill that missing place at his expense. It was going to be a case of sharing living space and nothing more and even then, only on a temporary basis. As it turned out, I had not accounted for

Raz's wishes and it quickly became evidence that he wanted me as part of his private life.

Or was it that he wished to extend his professional life into his home? Like me, he was not the kind to leave his work at the office and we spent many hours discussing *Operation Raven-Fish*, as we called it. All the research concerning the skeletons, the stones, and the two books; we lumped it all together under that heading *Operation Raven-Fish*.

There was absolutely no denying that in 1936 Jason Bennett had access to archaeological information that he wove into his Dark Age fantasy. The mention of the tiny gold beaker-charm, the extra teeth and the description of that circle-within-square symbol that kept cropping up – he *had* to know about them, and as we had but recently come to discover these things ourselves through uncovering the skeletons and additional pieces of the stone, the question remained: how, and what was his source?

As to his source, Raz and I hit upon the idea at the same time. *Raven-Fish!* was an entertaining fantasy, but again and again we found facts that fit into it, such as mentioned above, the beakers and the extra teeth, so it wasn't too much to hope that Elmo's quest revolved around another existing source, and that was Alcuin of York's book *The Truth of the First Born*. Elmo's quest was ours too, but whereas Elmo was charged with burying it, ours was to unearth it and bring it back into the light of day. And Bennett's clues, well they must unlock the way we were to achieve our quest.

Maybe that was to be my Sutton Hoo after all, and Elmo was my Arthur. To uncover new texts by that inveterate writer of letters, Alcuin of York, would be a find of immense importance standing all on its own. That they might throw light onto the age of darkness, now *that* was too much to hope for. An archaeologist trains himself not to hope for too much and then he won't be disappointed. Well, this one has, at any rate, in life as in profession.

We considered that the term 'First Born' was a metaphor for the prehistoric Beaker Folk, but not one of

164

Jason Bennett's making. *I shield first-born blood below*, proclaimed the first line of the stone inscription, a cry from more than a thousand years ago, so the sobriquet was no fiction of Bennett's, but perhaps the Beaker Folk styled themselves First Born, or others referred to them thus.

Why, you may be wondering, should Raz and I be so convinced that Alcuin's book existed? Let me tell you about the small golden vessels that Raz found in the grave. In *Raven-Fish!* Elmo receives one as a gift from his mother, and inside he finds a tiny scroll of soft gold that he unrolls to find the words *I am Elfgar, First-Born prince*. After translating that line, how long do you suppose it was that Raz and I could keep from checking out the other two tiny vessels, the ones we found with the skeletons? If I stretched it to an hour I would be exaggerating. We were back at the collection as fast as we could make it. We had booked out the finds as quickly as decorum allowed and unpicked the tiny stoppers of compacted clay that sealed the open end of each vessel with more haste than care.

In archaeology we call such rolled up strips of metal 'cursors'. They are never common, but not at all unknown in the vicinity of pagan temples, and they are almost exclusively made of lead rather than gold, to the extent that only two are known to be of gold and they were the two found in our grave dig. Cursors usually bear inscribed short prayers, calls for the intercession of the gods, requests for the relief of pain, the finding of wealth, the death of an enemy. The ones Raz and I found in the little beakers bore no prayers or requests. *I am Elf, First-Born Prince*, said one and *I am Elfwine, First-Born prince* said the other. The names were spelt Aelf and Aelfwine and the script and language was Old English but apart from that they were perfect counterparts of the example mentioned in our translation of *Raven-Fish!*

This put to bed any lingering notion that Bennett wrote without hidden knowledge. This explains with crystal clear clarity why Raz and I were on a mission. From the day I moved in with Raz, less than a week before Christmas, we worked together on *Operation Raven-Fish* during office hours, and we discussed our research and leads at home.

It had been my plan to spend time in my room, but as I moved in Raz gave me the old *casa mea, casa tua*. Our bedrooms were our own, the rest of the house was '... just as much yours as it is mine,' Raz said. 'Kick back, slum it, walk round in your designer underwear ... just feel at home. Only don't sell the ornaments or sublet.'

'I think I can manage that, thanks Raz. Just tip me the wink if you ever need me out of the way and I'll make myself scarce.'

'That won't happen.'

'I just thought you might want to bring a young lady back or ...'

'There is a girl I see from time to time. But when Jacqueline comes to visit, we'll go upstairs if we want to be alone. I wouldn't dream of shooing you out of your own living room.'

'Jacqueline Watson?'

'The very same,' Raz beamed and winked.

It appeared he was giving her his genetic material after all. The point was, Raz made me feel at home right from the start.

'Well, tip me the wink anyway, and if I am waltzing the halls in my CKs, it'll give me time to pull on a pair of trousers.'

My large collection of books barely took up half the available shelf space, but at least they made the library look a little more fit-for-purpose. There was also a large desk in a nice corner where I could plug in my computer and set up a study. I was going to arrange things in my bedroom but Raz suggested the library as being less cramped and more comfortable with easy access to all my works of reference. Couldn't be better.

'I was wondering,' Raz said with his denim-clad legs and white-socked feet sticking out from under the large Victorian desk as he plugged a Wi-Fi aerial lead into the back of my Dell. 'If you wanted to pay a little less rent, maybe you'd like to go fifty-fifty on the household chores.'

'*Tu trabajo, mi trabajo*,' I said. 'And I wouldn't dream of paying you a penny less. It's already peppercorn.'

Raz's head popped out to where I could see it. He was wearing his lop-sided smile. 'You speak Spanish!'

'Not so any Spaniard would notice. Just add it to the long list of languages I've had a half-hearted go at.'

And then, blow me down, he went into a long Spanish dialogue, of which I recognised about two words. Every day, another surprise. Later, when he went into town for a haircut and I was nosing through his CD collection in the living room, I wondered just how many languages he could speak. His collection was eclectic to say the least, but not just in the diversity of musical styles. There were German CDs, *Rosenstolz, Tokyo Hotel, Revolverheld*; Japanese albums, *Hikawa Kiyoshi, Shinji Takeda, Beautiful Green*; there was even a Norwegian album by a group called *Glittertind*. I sneaked a quick listen *(¿su música, mi música?)* and categorised it as Viking Rock.

From day one then, we divvied out the jobs equally, or rather we divvied out the work equally. Any job that needed doing we'd both have at it together until it was done. I even learnt to iron, and I wondered if Jenny might not consider it about twenty years too late.

And while we prepared meals, or cleaned or saw to the laundry, we either concentrated on the work in silence or bounced ideas off one another concerning *Operation Raven-Fish*. Sometimes we talk of current affairs, rarely office gossip but never anything about Raz's past. Nothing sinister, and I'm sure if I asked he'd tell me, but I didn't want to impose.

'I was wondering,' Raz said on the Monday before Christmas. He would often open a conversation with that line. We'd just had prawn pasta; I was washing the dishes, Raz drying. 'In a war, or at least a protracted one, it's invariably the nation with the strongest economy that wins, at least in the short run.'

'I'll go along with that. It's certainly a statement that history backs up.'

'Well, what if you cut out the "war" bit and went straight for the economy? Slowly you gain positions of strength over the nation's economic infrastructure, and when the moment is right, you sabotage it. Deliberately over-extend. Borrow too much knowing what the consequences will be. Draw the whole population in with the philosophy of have-now-pay-later. You could bring a nation to its knees without a shot being fired.'

I stuck the wok on the gas hob to dry it thoroughly. Once I'd left one out overnight; it wasn't a hundred percent dry so I spent half the next morning wire-woolling the rust off while Jenny tutted her disapproval and muttered under her breath.

'Economic war? I suppose it might be possible.'

'And do you suppose that's what's happening to our economy at the moment?' The serious look; the furrowed brow: I spotted the warning signs; Raz was about to get me once again. In the next moment he would be grinning and I would be questioning my ability *ever* to see through his japes.

'Of course it is,' I said. 'They've already sighted nuclear subs in the Thames Estuary. Soon we'll have the gold-starred red banner stuck slap-bang in the middle if the Medway and we'll be paying Dane geld all over again.'

Raz swatted me with the tea-towel. Something in his lop-sided smile leapt from him to me and right about then, everything was right with the world and God was in his Heaven. I flicked Fairy Liquid suds at him and we were suddenly both twelve-year-olds.

I have this theory that everything evens out. In just over a month I would start the day by cracking my face open on a kerb stone, and end it on my knees … all because of the economy … and the fact that the fucking council hadn't salted the fucking road.

That evening we made a serious effort to crack Jason Bennett's coded, hand-written inserts. I'd typed up a page with the text of all the inserts, one after the other, as they appear in *Raven-Fish!* and had it on my desk in the library. I drew up another chair for Raz but instead he took the sheet and sat on the floor in front of the roaring log fire. I joined him, every informal action making me feel more at home – part of the furniture – well in.

We had already concluded that the clues referred to dates but couldn't work out their relationship to one another, to *Raven-Fish!* or how they might be put together to give us some answers.

'*Wulfhere, son of Penda …*' I said. 'An entry from the *Anglo-saxon Chronicles*, the year 656.'

'The number of the devil,' Raz said. 'Six-six-six.'

'*Then it happened that all through England such a sign in the Heavens was seen and some called it the long-haired star.* The comet that 'foretold' the Battle of Hasting, 1066. And then the line about bloody Mary. She was born in 1516.'

Raz looked up, brow furrowed, head cocked. 'They all end in a six,' he said. 'Do you think that's significant?'

'Perhaps,' I said taking the paper from the floor. 'It holds true for these two verses from John Dryden's poem *Annus Mirabilis* – the year of miracles, 1666.'

'And then there's the last two clues that mention Elmo and Finn by their nick-names, and once again the number six crops up. See, just here!'

I read, '*The south-wall stone bore a graven letter N in the Roman style and the east wall a T. Thereafter the Fish penned upon a piece of scroll these two letters and put down … six … numbers …* I see what you mean. Six does appear to have certain significance, but for the life of me …'

'As I suspect, do the letters N and T.'

Raz had that look in his eyes, mischievous and on the cusp of spilling the beans. He knew something more. I prompted him to continue with no question but the eager look on my face.

'See here, back to Dryden's poem. Why two verses? That only indicates the same year twice, so what's the point? And why did Bennett choose these particular, apparently random verses from a very long poem?'

'I think you have an inkling and I hope you're going to tell me before I am forced to wring it out of you.'

'The first verse used as a clue is verse fourteen. The second is verse twenty. N is the fourteenth letter of the alphabet and ...'

'T is the twentieth! Raz you're onto something!'

'Yes. Shame I don't know what though. The number six and the letters N and T are significant, but I haven't a single idea as to why.'

N, T and 6. N ... T ... 6. NT6. NT6NT6NT6 – That night I had bloody nightmares about those two letters and one number. Round and round they spun, and come morning they were still no more connected than they had been at bedtime.

The pair of us had frazzled our brains silly trying to fit those random letters and number into a framework of meaning. We also added the sum of all the numbers given in the clues, divided them by some God forsaken value we'd come up with by converting N and T back into numbers. We even considered visiting all the places associated with the events mentioned in the clues. Both of us were stumped when it came to naming a place the Four Horsemen of the Apocalypse might call home, so we gave up over a bottle of St Emilio removing to the living room where there was another log fire.

I sank into a hugely comfortable leather chair and toasted my toes, enjoying the glow. Raz sat on a fleece rug and lost himself in the dancing flames.

'What are you doing for Christmas, Prof?'

With all the hustle and bustle of moving in, not to mention the ongoing wrestling matches with Jason Bennett's clues, Christmas had gone completely out of my mind. I'd sent Jenny and Rachel Christmas cards, Rachel's with a cheque inside, and that was about the extent of it.

'I'll probably just have a quiet and reflective day. What about you?'

'We've got people coming for Christmas dinner,' he said sitting up straight as if he'd just remembered something.

'I'll be out of the way. Stick to my room and ...'

'Nonsense, Prof! I said *we've* got people coming. Not *I've* got people coming. When is the penny going to drop?

You're not just Roger the Lodger. You live here, and you're a friend of mine. So you can jolly well meet some of my other friends.

'It's a bit late I suppose, but is there anyone you'd like to invite?'

Sad old git that I am, I couldn't think of a single one. 'I can only think of one person I'd like to invite, and as it appears he is co-host, the invite isn't necessary.'

The old Raz grin. 'More splodge, Prof?'

I held out my glass. 'If this is what you call splodge, I can't wait to taste the good stuff.'

'Christmas is but four days away. You won't have to wait long. What are you doing tomorrow?'

'Nothing much, why?'

'Come help me choose a goose, then. And we'd better knock together some mince pies and stuff.'

'And put up a tree?'

'Why not?!'

Christmas morning there was a ring at the doorbell. We'd had an early warning of an imminent guest appearance by the popping of shingles under tyres.

'I'll get it,' Raz said. A moment later he was back. 'It's a young lady.'

'Ah,' I said. 'Right, I'll go upstairs.' I thought Raz was tipping me that wink.

'It's not Jacqueline. It's someone for you.'

He'd got me again: Rachel's face popped up from behind Raz's shoulder and that was the beginning of my best Christmas, bar none.

I'm reminded of the Patrick Stewart film version of *A Christmas Carol* – near the end where at long last, Scrooge let's his hair down and has fun. That Christmas I was the Scrooge who let his hair down, and I am pleased to say I had considerably more to let down than Patrick Stewart, even if it was all grey.

Raz's friends were a mixed bunch. I learnt that he played in a band, *Granite Harp Strings*, and I met his band mates. There were friends from abroad, others from college – and I wasn't even the oldest. Eleven of us in all. We pulled

171

crackers, wore silly hats, ate too much, drank a little more than we should, played games, laughed incessantly and listened to the Queen's Speech. *Granite Harp Strings* entertained us for an hour or so. Raz was lead in an unusual ensemble where he played viola in place of a guitar. I showed my ignorance the first time I saw it by calling it a violin. It had been a couple of days earlier when Raz came into the living room with it.

'Ah! You play the violin, unless there's a Tommy-gun in that case.'

'It's neither a violin not a machine-gun,' Raz said. He sat on the floor, his bare feet crossed like some sort of a Buddha, and placed the case on his lap. He flipped the catches and opened the lid, then slipped a velvet cover off the top and presented it for my inspection. 'It's a viola, just a little bit bigger than a violin, with a deeper tone.' He was like a little boy showing off his favourite toy, and he touched the instrument so delicately that it was clear he loved it.

He went on to tell me about his band as he tuned the strings.

'The case looks new compared to the viola,' I said.

Raz told me the instrument was pretty old and that he's had it from a friend – Andrew Garner, or something similar.

And then he played, and I learned something more about Raz. He stroked out a tune so sweet and sad, and so captivating that an age might have passed. It was a piece called the *Ashokan Farewell* which he explained was a modern take on a style played circa the American Civil War.

With the band, he played in a different style altogether, full of verve, lively and catchy.

Towards late evening when there were only four of us left, Raz and Jacqueline excused themselves after a little canoodling on the couch and went upstairs giggling, their intentions very hard to misinterpret. This left Rachel and I by the fire.

Like the other rooms in the house the living room had a high ceiling with a plaster outline of a star, in the centre of which sat the electric light rose. The flex was of the old kind with a fabric sheath and the lamp was a mock chandelier. Light shafted off the silver glass balls and the other bright decorations that swathed the six-foot Christmas tree. It also glanced golden, natural highlights from Rachel's long, brown hair.

'There's an open bottle of that Chateau Potensac '79, just begging to be finished,' Rachel said. 'Do you think we dare, Dad?'

'I think it would be a crime not to. Don't want the air to spoil it.'

Rachel poured. There was enough for a good-sized glass each.

'Mmmm.' Rachel stuck her nose into the large wine glass. 'I'm getting black cherries, and dark chocolate ... and ...' She dissolved into giggles that set me off too. This was by no means our first glass of the afternoon.

'It's been so lovely to see you,' I said. 'Such a wonderful surprise. I'd quite thought you'd spend Christmas with Mum.'

'Mum's got her sister and the rest of the family. I didn't like the thought of you being on your own, so when I got the call from Raz ...'

'Very thoughtful of him. Quite restores my faith in the younger generation ... as do you,' I quickly added.

Rachel swept her hair from one shoulder and over the other, then lifted her knees and snuggled up, leaning into me. Nearly twenty, and still liked a cuddle from her old dad.

'You know,' she began, 'I was almost surprised when Raz and Jacqui went up for a spot of early evening nookie. I was almost certain you and he were ... an item.'

'I beg your pardon! What on earth ...? How ... what made you think ...?

Rachel giggled. 'Oh Dad, do keep your wig on!'

'How can I ...' Much too loud. 'How can I keep my wig on when you've just come out with something as outrageous as that? What made you think it in the first place? We're only sharing a house, not beds, for Heaven's sake!'

173

'First of all, there's nothing outrageous about it. You and Mummy have fallen out of love – a long time ago as far as I can tell – and you fell for a handsome young guy. It wouldn't be the first time in the history of the world.'

'For the last time, I have *not* fallen for Raz. For Heaven's sake, woman!'

'But you like him a lot. I can see it in your eyes when you look at him.'

I took a big gulp of Chateau Potensac – might just as well have been house plonk from the *Dog and Duck* – and nearly choked. 'There is a whole world of difference between "like" and what you're suggesting.'

'Love then. You love Raz, don't you, even if we're not talking in *that* kind of a way?'

Another hit at the wine, a sip this time. A shrug. I felt the burning red of my ears and neck subsiding. 'There is … an emotional element in my feelings towards Raz, yes. In many ways we're on the same wavelength. And he gives me an insight …' *into the missing years* '… into something I can't quite place.

'Whatever it is Dad, it's mutual, because he looks at you in the same way. And whatever you like to call it, I find it quite sweet. It restores my faith in the male species.'

In the silence that followed, the sound of squeaky bed springs from the spare bedroom and Jacqueline's sighs of passion penetrated softly, down through the floorboards and ceiling.

'Very Meg Ryan,' Rachel said.

'I'll have what she's having … No! I mean … I'm quoting from the movie and …' My ears and neck were as hot and red as ever they had been, and Rachel couldn't hold it in.

'Oh Dad! Can't you ever just relax and give up worrying what anybody thinks.' This managed through laughter so prolonged it brought tears to her eyes. '"I'll have what she's having". Bloody priceless!'

My options were, spoil the whole evening, or see the funny side. I saw the funny side and I don't remember if I'd ever laughed so long or so hard with my daughter as on that

174

Christmas evening in 2008. When Raz's short but triumphant cry pierced the floorboards signalling that he had indeed donated his genetic material, we were off again, but now *sotto voce* so as not to embarrass the two little lovebirds up in their nest.

Rachel began to talk of events in her childhood and then, not surprisingly, the conversation moved on to the situation between Jenny and me. I acknowledge I may not have been the best of husbands and bit back the urge to build up all Jenny's faults into a wall of defence. But this book is going to be called *The Assistant*, and not *The Soon to Be Ex-Wife*, so I'll move on to when the conversation dipped, and I was again troubled in my thoughts. Silence has a way of doing that.

'I still find it hard to believe that you thought I had any interest in *Raz*, in *that* way.'

Rachel had made us coffee and we managed to make room for another mince pie each. 'It's just that you seem so much more alive, more open, when Raz is around. It's like when I brought home boyfriends. Most of my friends' dads were total pigs with their boyfriends, but you seemed to open up. It was as if you were a house with shuttered windows, and when I brought a boy home the windows were all flung open and the light poured out.'

What a perspicacious daughter I had. The windows were open so the empty room might be filled. These were young men who were living the years I missed.

'The old warhorse is rejuvenated when there are colts about, and anyway, you always had such a good taste in young men, even Harry the Goth, once you get past his eyeliner and black nail varnish.'

'And that's another thing!' Rachel said. 'The weirder they were the more you liked them.'

'Nonsense! I merely find it an admirable trait in people to have the courage to look just as they wish, and to be themselves. I like that about Harry, his ability to be unique and just the way he wants to be. So if you suspect I'm a closet-case, you're correct. I'm a closet-non-conformist!'

Rachel shook her head. There was obviously no hope for me. 'Dad, Harry doesn't weave his own spider-web t-shirts. He buys his stuff from Kinky Angel or Goth Shop. His Converses are from Next for Heaven's sake. I love Harry to pieces but he's whack, not Wittgenstein … and he isn't being unique, just conforming in a slightly different way. And then there's his self-confidence; like a mouse living in Cat Alley. I mean, the first time we had sex …'

I put my fingers in my ears and started saying laa-laa-laa. I didn't want to think of my sweet little girl all grown up and in adult situations. Rachel laughed, threw a cushion at me, and called me whack, so perhaps I did have something in common with Harry the Goth after all.

Whack? Never mind … moving swiftly on.

Nor is this book going to be called *The Professor Does Self-Psychology for Dummies*, and I think I have revealed quite enough to enlighten the dark empty space within me, the one I'd hardly noticed since moving in with my assistant.

The rest of the year and most of January was taken up with lectures, meetings, and fulfilling the more mundane duties of my contract. There was little time for *Operation Raven-Fish* except what we could fit in at home, and that had mainly to do with deciphering the Bennett texts.

And then came that last morning in January: frantic e-mails, messages on the answer-phone, texts on the mobile, and all amounting to the same thing. *Meeting on Monday. Be there!*

I made it on time, just, but had I been a little late I am sure the bandaged cheekbone with the little pink blush where blood was trying to leak through, would have bought me a late-pass.

'Oh, sore looking,' said Chair as he waved me to a seat. 'Slip on the ice?'

'Got it in one.'

'What's the damage?'

'Nothing broken, but they reckon I'll have a nice Action Man scar … permanently.'

'A young German would kill for such a mark.'

'Maybe in 1936,' I said and then wondered why my mind had hit upon such a date. Bennett! You were invading my mind with your blitzkrieg tactics and your flaming code. Bennett, if you have something to say why not just say it? Why wrap a stupid mystery in a bloody enigma and serve it up with esoteric custard?

The rest of the board assembled and then, we were off: it was a specs-off-wipe-the-brow, long sighs and specs-back-on routine from Chair. He appeared incapable of coming to the point, so the dirty deed was left to Vice-Chancellor. The economic situation; how archaeology depended greatly upon building companies for sponsorship and funding and of course we all knew how much the building trade was in a slump and something has to give and we're sorry Professor but it is your department.

They wanted me to drop Raz. My assistant was an expensive, not to mention under-qualified luxury the department could ill afford. Expensive? Had anyone drawn his file and actually *looked* at his salary? I had the pick of any number of students, they went on, and I could have them for free. Raz who hadn't even got a degree, after all, and luckily hadn't been with us long enough to attract a redundancy settlement, would have to go. And you Professor, should be the one to tell him.

I told the board a few things first and not in any way that might be termed elegant. I drew heavily on my TV persona forgetting that there was a time and a place.

And then Chair floored me with an insinuating question. 'Is it true your *living* with the young man?'

His mouth formed a twisted little smile when he saw how he'd stopped me in my tracks.

'I share accommodation, which means that you get even more value from him because a lot of the time we're discussing work and furthering our research.'

'A *lot* of the time? Perhaps, but I don't think the board thinks it is very seemly that senior staff should share accommodation with junior. Still, the problem is solved, and discipline won't have to be considered as he's to go.'

Discipline? There wasn't a single rule that Raz or I were breaking. Bullying bastards!

I tried to come back at them again, but they would not be swayed. Raz was to be gone by the middle of February – just over two weeks' notice with pay in lieu of the other two to which he was entitled.

After the meeting Chair caught up with me in the corridor and tried to placate me with a few words of sympathy. 'Sorry the new year is already turning out to be such an *annus horribilis*,' he said. 'But we'll weather the storm, I feel sure.'

And right then and there, in the midst of my misery and defeat, I had an answer. *Annus horribilis* – the awful year – made me think of John Dryden's poem, *Annus Mirabilis* – the year of miracles. Now why did the poet believe that 1666 might be such a momentous year? It was because in Roman numerals, it was the one year, the *one* year possible, that used all the Roman numerals once and each in the correct order. 1666 was MDCLXVI in Roman numerals and such a year could never come again. It was a one-off for all eternity.

I knew with certainty that this was a break-through as far as the Bennett code went. *Bennett – we're right on your tail!*

XII

~ 793 ~
In which the Raven and the Fish adopt a new Battle-Cry

Finn wondered what all the shouting was about. Who was shouting in the first place, for it did not sound like Elmo? There was little doubt from the tone though, that it was a call of alarm. Finn quickly armed himself as best he could and threw his baldric across his shoulder. He had just slapped his helmet on when an old monk burst into the room.

'Come Finn, the enemy is upon us and we are outnumbered. Follow me!'

There was a time to wonder and a time to take action. Finn would save his wondering for later. Who was this old man that allied himself to Finn against unknown enemies? From where had he come? Where was Elmo? These questions, though they clamoured for an answer, would have to wait. Fighting dizziness and nausea, Finn snatched up his cloak and ran after the old man who was descending the stone stairs three at a time.

Out through the door they flew and there met with Elmo who carried two blades and was dressed in the clothes of one of the First Born thegns. One of the swords Finn recognised as the recently interred blade of the noble First Born warrior, and the other was a weapon of such magnificence that for a moment he forgot the urgency of the situation.

'Come!' shouted the old man who appeared burdened with many bags and satchels. 'They are at the beach. We must fly!'

Finn followed the old man who ran towards the north of the island and Elmo tarried to lend Finn an arm, for in his weakened state he found he needed it and was glad that

179

he was not encumbered by heavy armour, his byrnie being lost at sea.

'Unless this old man knows of a secret bridge then it is by flying that we shall have to escape. Better we had turned to fight than to corner ourselves.'

Finn followed Elmo's frightened eyes and felt some of that fear when he saw how close the warriors were, all with drawn swords and armed to the full.

'Don't dawdle!' shouted the old monk whom Elmo called Mundwyn. 'We must to the ragged rocks as fast as we may.'

'Yes!' thought Finn. 'And there, light-footed, to make a stand against armoured men whose cumbersome gear might make them slip and drown.' Finn now understood the tactic.

They ran on over the tussocky grass putting up many a noisy flock. On past the well they flew, with the angry voices of the warriors close behind, until they came to a low cliff and there beyond, the sea boiling around black teeth that were the spiteful rocks. There would be no dancing between these jagged islets. Here was no place to make a stand.

There was nothing for it but to stand, back to the drop, and hope to drag an enemy or two into Hell after him. He turned, drew his sword and stood. He did not stand alone, for Elmo was there, his own magnificent blade gleaming like the very sun above, and standing shoulder to shoulder with nothing of the lily-livered monk about him.

Finn took his eye off the rapidly approaching enemies, barely a hundred paces away, and grinned grimly at his battle-brother. 'To Hell then! Together and with many an enemy to hold our hands.' Finn reached out with his left hand and touched Elmo at the throat where there was an icthus tattooed, and then he brought his hand to his chest whereon was the seared mark of the raven.

'And our battle cry shall be Raven-Fish. Let Hell hear it and tremble, for this day two mighty warriors will join the ranks of the underworld!'

The thegns were now close enough to smell their sweat.

'RAVEN-FISH!' Finn screamed with such force that it tore the very air.

'RAVEN-FISH!' Elmo shouted, causing the leading enemy to falter in his advance.

Again, and together, the new battle cry split the air, and then Finn felt a thick hoary arm take him about the neck, and he knew he was betrayed.

'No Hell for little brothers-in-arms today,' Mundwyn said close to his ear as his grip tightened and Finn struggled for air.

And then the world made no sense. The gleam on the leading enemy's gilded helm, now as close as a double arm-span, flashed bright to fill the whole sky. Everything was golden-bright and dazzling to the eye. At the same instant there came a tremendous rush of air as if at the bow of a raider when a storm blew, followed by an impact that forced all the wind from Finn's body.

Finn found himself in a heap of tangled limbs and his face was buried in thick grass. He struggled to right himself knowing that his deathblow must surely be upon him, but when he stood, there was no enemy close, nor even within sight. The scene before him was so different he put a hand to his head, wondering if his brain had been addled.

The sea was now far, far away. He was high up and the land all round bowed to this place and humbled itself, being more lowly and in awe of height.

The old man, Mundwyn, was stretched out in a stand of broken bracken and did not move. Elmo picked himself up slowly and pulled tussocks from his hair and off his clothes. Behind was a huge pile of wood, a beacon ready to light and a little down on the landward side of the hill, a rude cottage with a thatch of grasses for a roof through which smoke drifted.

'I know this place,' Elmo said. 'I came here once with my father one year, when he took to beating the bounds. This is Ros's Beacon, and look there out to sea, the tiny sliver of black like unto the size of a thumbnail.'

181

Finn looked out over the distant waters. 'I see it, separated from the mainland by no more than a hair's breadth of silver sea.'

'That thumbnail is Coquet Island, whereupon we stood until scant moments ago, yet Annebelle is a good day's ride away. And there, in the other direction, lies the King's seat at Bamburgh.'

Finn wasn't listening. Instead he was looking at his hands, which he then brought in to feel his legs and then his head, as if checking that he was still hale. A feeling of warmth spread through his body and his grinned widely.

'Can it be that I have crossed a Faerie bridge, and lived to walk the Hidden Path of the First Born?'

Elmo did not answer. When Finn looked he was hurrying to the body of the old man.

'Brother Mundwyn! Hey Finn, help me sit him up.'

Finn got an arm about the old man's back and helped to raise him. His head lolled and his eyes rolled inside his skull. He tried to speak but the effort was too much.

A spindly figure sprang from the bracken. 'Go away, or I shall call for the King's men!'

Finn turned to see a stick thin, frail old man dressed in a raggedy knee-length tunic of a green so dark it was almost black, and wearing a battered leather hat like an oversized Phrygian cap. The spear he carried looked sharp enough, but it would not be a fair battle.

'Hold off, old man,' Finn said. 'We mean you no harm. Help us get our sick friend close to a fire.'

'Be gone, or I shall do you harm.' He shook the spear menacingly. 'I am the keeper of the King's beacon, and none may walk here without my leave.'

Finn decided he would have to end the grumpy old bag of bones and take what he needed, be it fire or that halfway decent-looking spear.

'We have bread to share,' Elmo said. 'Freshly baked.'

The beacon-keeper's head stuck out from his tunic on a thin turtle-like neck. 'Bread? Hard that it needs a soaking?'

'Still soft, only hours off being warm from the oven, and with a golden crust.'

The old man licked his lips and his eyes widened. 'What ails your friend?'

'He is weary to the bone from the long road. That is all. He carries no fever and is free from all but the common breeds of flea. See here, a whole loaf to yourself for a spot by your hearth.'

The old man put up his spear. 'Done! Bring him hither,' he said and shuffled down towards the hut.

Finn shook his head. Elmo was back to being a monk, bartering for what he could take with ease. He spat then helped Elmo raise Mundwyn to his feet.

The hut was cramped and smoky inside and the beacon-keeper's wife was as toothless, dishevelled and filthy as her husband and sported a very large wart to the left of her hooked nose – a veritable hag. She was called Amberjill – a sweet name for such a sour face – and the beacon-keeper was named Bray.

Over the course of the next hour Mundwyn recovered sufficiently to talk. Apparently it cost the body much to traverse the hidden ways of the First Born. For a mile covered in the world of men, it cost the effort of ten along the hidden path, and from Coquet Island to the top of the hill called Ros's Beacon it was more than ten miles of crow's flight and therefore Mundwyn suffered the rigours of a journey of a hundred miles.

'And with a lad under each arm, the strength drawn from me was that much more. I am as weak as a new-born kitten.'

'Yet we covered the distance in the blinking of an eye,' Finn said. 'Is it always so?'

'It is. Needs you must be able to spy your destination with your own two eyes. A man cannot use the path to reach a place that is hidden to his sight, and he must hope that he does not see so far that the journey will kill him. I at least shall recover.'

They spoke in hushed tones, but the hut was small and the owners were definitely eavesdropping.

'Can you teach me this thing, to move where the First Born trod and to arrive at the instant I set out to journey?' Finn was excited by the prospect of such travel.

'It cannot be taught by such as me. I can only walk there myself because I was once led under the water by one of the First Born, and thus had my eyes opened to the pathways.'

Amberjill lent forward and gabbled. 'Your friend has addled his wits,' she cackled with witchlike laughter. 'Opened his eyes under the water indeed! Is he a fish, or a frog?'

'Hold still, Jill, lest these fine gentlemen takes back what's left of the bread.' Bray was discomforted by his wife's manners. 'Pay no heed to her, good sirs. It is her wits what's lacking. Fourteen babbies and but one that lived and he as addled in the head as she. It's done for her, so it has.'

Amberjill reached out to the half-loaf remaining, tore off another chunk and stuffed it into her mouth. 'My good boy brings me coney by the brace and game-cock. Brom is quite the man with sling-and-shot, but today we make do with bread alone.'

'And very fine bread too, if you don't mind me saying,' Bray said before swatting Amberjill with his cap. Perhaps embarrassed, or maybe sensing the need of his guests to speak privately he withdrew from the hut and took his wife with him.

'We are an odd band, lately enemies and now cast together,' Finn said. 'What are we to do now?'

'I think we must return to the island for there is a quest I have been given, and it depends on an artefact which is still there.'

'No Elmo, the book is here, in that sack,' Mundwyn said. 'See how overburdened I was with rocks and boys? It is a wonder I still breathe.'

Elmo took the stone-encased book from the heavy cloth bag and held it up. 'I was entrusted with a quest, and must bury this stone at a place where once stood a town of the First Born. And yet, I do not know the way.'

A quest! The term stirred Finn's blood. Where there was a quest, there was battle and adventure and sport with many maidens. 'A quest indeed,' Finn said. 'Count me pledged!'

But alas, Finn did not know the way either and had never heard of Skol-Jerrag though it reminded him of a drinking song he father was fond of singing.

'May we come to this place of which you speak by the Hidden Paths?' Finn asked of old Mundwyn.

'It is a journey of many days and even if I could stand upon the world's shoulders and see as far, the leap would surely kill me. No, we must have ponies and a wain and supplies to keep us for a week.'

'I hate ponies,' Finn said. 'Last time I sat astride one I bruised my balls so badly I couldn't fuck for a week.'

'A *whole* week?' Elmo asked. 'I'm surprised you didn't curl up and die, poisoned by a surfeit of your own seed.'

Finn nodded in enthusiastic agreement before wondering if Elmo was making fun of him. He doubted the monk had fucked once in his entire life, except for the time … and that didn't count. For a moment his thoughts shamed him, and then they turned to that slave-girl whose name he could not remember; the one who had died with his child in her belly.

'Anyhow, where might we get ponies?' Finn asked, dismissing images that were making him uncomfortable.

'Not at Chatton,' Elmo said pointing to the west. 'They need every nag they can have nearing harvest-time.'

'Go to Lindisfarne,' Mundwyn said. 'Seek out the prior at the Holy Island and say who sent you and what you require. He will see to it that you are well furnished. Then come back here, by which time I will be recovered. I shall be your guide to Skol-Jerag.'

They set out early next morning. Bray had persuaded Finn to put his tunic on back-to-front because no Englishman, or Frank for that matter, walked about with his neck so exposed. He also advised Finn to keep his mouth shut as his words were coloured with such an unfamiliar sound he would immediately be marked as a foreigner.

Elmo gave Bray two more loaves and a small pot of honey that they might tend to Mundwyn. The old couple waved as the two young men descended the sandstone hill and all the while Amberjill performed a little jig and sang, 'Honey, honey, honey,' until they could hear her old voice no longer.

***

In Annebelle the town wore a mood of chilled expectation. Those who had not been gathered outside under the threat of violence hid in their houses and hoped they would not be torched, their home to be a funeral pyre, as had happened to the poor widow of the late reeve.

The cold, bare hut with its compacted soil floor contained three naked people and three fully clothed. Of those naked, the young woman and the tiny little girl were dead, lying in spreading pools of their own blood, throats slit and other wounds speaking of torture before death. There was evidence that the woman had been raped. The young man, the widow's son, was bound to a chair with loops of rough hemp but still alive, and this signalled by his gut-wrenching sobs. He bore no sign of injury, other than chafing where the ropes touched, and he looked to be healthy of body, although indisposed by means of his captivity.

Of those clothed, there was the King's thegn Godwin, a lesser thegn in rich, Frankish armour and Bledwyn, the master-torturer.

'I have glad tidings for you, Eric Gerefa,' Godwin said, his tone happy as if greeting an old friend. 'Your cuckoo-brother Elmo, sometime known as Elfgar, is dead, swept out from his island refuge by a wave which took him to be drowned in the sea. I have the news this minute and from one of my loyal captains who saw it happen and all before his very eyes.'

The corpulent thegn reached down and took the child's body by the ankle. 'And so you see, your bravery was all for naught, and none of this was necessary.' He held the little

186

body up high and then let it go so that it hit the ground head first with a sickening crunch, a once living child, now so much dead meat.

Eric leant forward as much as his binding would allow and a pitiful sound left his lips that might have been intended to say 'Maud'.

'Ah yes, poor little Maud, and all her suffering upon your head because you chose to protect a heretic.'

'I *told* you *all* you asked, may the Lord forgive me, before you laid a single mark upon either my wife or little daughter. I betrayed my brother and you still tortured and killed them.'

'But surely you can see that was too late. I asked you before and you lied. And I knew that I may put all the tortures of the world upon you and still you would not speak, so why waste my time? But every man has a weakness, and yours was family.'

'But I *told* you what you wanted to know. I *told* you. There wasn't any need to burn my mother in her house or to …' Eric's head fell and once again he was wracked through with sobs.

'Their suffering was your punishment for your earlier dissemblance. But if you cannot see that, your eyes are a wasted gift from God.' Godwin crossed the floor and dipped his palms into the woman's congealing blood then returned to his victim.

'Look here!' Godwin ordered. He held his palms close to Eric's face. 'See the blood of your wife, and on your head be it.'

Eric cried in horror and tried to look away, but Godwin had the master-torturer hold his head.

'Look again, and look long, for it shall be the last thing you see.'

Eric screams vied with Godwin's laughter as he gouged out both the young man's eyes with his thumbs.

When it was done, Eric slumped against the ropes, blood trickling from empty sockets and Godwin studied the plucked and burst eyeballs, turning them over in his hands. He squeezed the thick liquid from them as if squashing a

187

pair of fat, ripe cherries and then casually discarded the resulting mess by dropping it onto the floor.

'Has he suffered enough?' Godwin asked of Bledwyn.

The big, stout necked fellow shrugged.

'I think not,' mused Godwin. 'For lying to the King's thegn the boy is nothing but a filthy turd and he shall be treated as one. You're to be thrown on the midden like the rest of the town's shit and there to end your worthless life maggot-ridden. But the maggots shall have an inroad.'

Godwin hurried to the master-torturer's bag and took out a pair of nipping-tongs, long handled and useful in the clipping of horses' hooves.

'Spread his legs,' Godwin said. 'I mean to deprive him of his privy parts.'

Bledwyn did as he was ordered, and the other thegn averted his gaze. Godwin advanced with the implement of torture and positioned the jaws so a mere snip would achieve his aim. But then he pulled back.

'On second thoughts, I wish to walk him to the midden so he may feel the mockery and derision of all the town, and I'll be hard pressed to have him walk if I've just relieved him of his pizzle. No, I have a better place for the maggots to take hold. You spoke lies, Eric Gerefa, and those lies were shaped by your tongue.'

Godwin snipped out Eric's tongue. The master-torturer watched and learned, and the villagers were chilled by the gurgling screams.

Eric Gerefa was led to the town midden, empty eye-sockets leaking pink-stained tears and blood coursing down his chin and chest. The townsfolk were not at all forthcoming with laughter or derision and had to be bullied to the task and then only joined in half-heartedly. There were looks of hatred, but they were all for Godwin.

Eric was hurled into the midden and the folk were ordered to pelt him with filth until he be buried alive. It was surprising how very few of the town's men or boys were accurate with their noisome missiles and one, a clod of straw and dung obviously thrown very wide of the intended target, landed on Godwin's boot. He ordered the offending lad be whipped for his negligence. Later, the same lad was handed a silver coin by the town reeve and given leave to miss archery practice the following morn, as he had proved his aim was sound.

A runner then came, and Godwin and his retinue were forced to quit and attend swiftly to a matter in the north. He proclaimed that he had urgent business upon the hill where Ros's Beacon now blazed, but that he would return within two or three days and expected to find the body of Eric Gerefa still on the midden, dead and maggot-ridden. He warned that any who gave him aid would suffer the same fate.

As soon as Godwin and his soldiers left, the townsfolk let drop their clods of filth and sadly went home, but none was so brave as to help Eric in this, his most dire time of need. They were ashamed to leave him to die, but they were also afraid, and fear held the day.

***

At the foot of the hill called Ros's Beacon, Elmo and Finn picked up a shepherd's track that ran east and followed it through a stretch of what Finn called *fjall* and then into a wood. They rested for a while and Elmo adjusted Finn's dress so that it looked less foreign and made him turn his baldric strap so the tooling would not show.

'Bray gave you good advice. If we encounter folk on our journey, keep your lips sealed and let me conduct the conversation.'

'I think I can imitate your flat and dull tone,' Finn said, doing just that.

'A fair effort, but to be on the safe side ...'

A yaffle flew by and gave its high, clear piping note when it saw the young men sitting on a fallen tree.

'There!' Elmo said. 'Your speech is like the yaffle's flight. Up and down, up and down, and never holding to a straight line. You sing your words whereas I speak mine.' He took a sip of water from a skin. 'If it were only our speaking that was so different.'

'Agreed, for if you were more of a man and less of a cowardly woman, I think I could grow to like you. Why, when we stood shoulder to shoulder with swords in hand, I almost felt you to be a brother.'

'I felt that too, and if I could rid my mind of the images of murderous evil you did on my brothers in Christ, perhaps I could like you too.'

'Murder you say? It was not murder but battle, only your brothers were too cowardly to defend themselves. The way of the world is be strong and take what you want, or be weak and lose it.'

'Who is the stronger, he who is master of himself, or the man who gives in to all his animal lusts?'

Finn sniffed and drew a sleeve across his nose. 'Ah, that. Well then I shall admit it. If I have a single regret it is for the way I used you. My blood was up and you were there and the nearest thing to a woman. How was I to know we would later face battle together? And so, for that alone, I am sorry.'

Elmo was far from comforted by the meagre, almost grudging apology. Finn was sorry, not for the despicable acts, but for the fact that because he and Finn had later stood together in battle, those acts were somehow tainted.

'So, am I forgiven?' Finn said, an arrogant demand for an answer rather than a humble request.

'No,' Elmo said. 'Not for the way you used me or forced me to use you. And not for the murder of my peaceful brethren, nor yet of the warriors who were my kin … or of the boat-slaves.'

'Then how shall I atone? By blood, is that it? Then let's have at it before we take a step further.' He leapt up from the fallen tree and drew his sword.

In an instant all the hurt and misery boiled up and Elmo too was up with sword in hand, and for the first time since late boyhood, he called unto himself his warrior-skills.

The forest clashed with the sharp ring of iron upon iron.

Immediately Elmo had the upper hand. He had forgotten nothing of his former skills and the First Born

190

blade was light and perfectly balanced. He rained slicing blows and Roman thrusts upon Finn who fell back expending all his skill and effort just to deflect the attack. Elmo rightly assumed that Finn's martial prowess was severely hampered by his lack of a shield, whereas Elmo had learned to fight with or without one. It was also true to say that Finn was not yet back to his full strength after his near-drowning and head-wound.

Battles only last half a morning in romances. This one was over in half a minute and ended with Finn on his back, tripped over the log, with a First Born blade cool at the skin under his Adam's apple.

'Finn grinned, laughed grimly. 'I *knew* there was a real warrior under that woman's garb. Thrust then, and send me to the Halls of Hell where I shall feast with my ancestors.'

Elmo put up his sword. 'Don't be absurd. I shall not take the blood of one who has promised me help in my quest. What help would you be as a mouldering pile of worm-fodder? Your ancestors must needs dine without you this day.' He reached out his hand and Finn took it.

'You're a strange one,' Finn said. He bent to retrieve his sword, sheathed it and then brushed the leaves and soil from his clothing. 'But I owe you a blood debt still.'

'Perhaps in the days ahead you may find a way to pay it.'

Elmo looked at his sword-hilt and wondered if by some magic it had drawn forth his old skills.

'Do you still hate me?' Finn said. 'Am I forgiven in that man-Christ way that is yours?'

'I will separate in my mind Finn the man from the actions of Finn. I will ever hate and despise what you wrought, but I find I can no longer hate you.'

Finn shook his head. 'Your words make me cross-eyed. Let's away and come to your Holy Island before my head sets solid like a boiled egg.'

Later, they came to a crossing of the paths where there was a vacant gibbet. Below and some way to the side there was a whetstone, the finding of which they thought most propitious.

Finn set about grinding the nicks of their recent battle from his blade, and Elmo found that his blade was in no need of repair, its edge as keen as the day Eovan Tucarus gave it to him.

'First Born blades and elven maids ...' Finn chanted and fell to laughter.

'What of them?' Elmo re-sheathed his sword while Finn worked on.

'Of the blades you have just learnt. Of the maids I'd blush your virgin ears by the telling, so I'll keep it to myself and say only that no blade, be it of iron or flesh, may endure the First Born but all are left worn and soft.' He laughed again and grabbed his crotch obscenely.

'Is your every thought and action ordered by your balls?' Elmo said shaking his head.

'Are you so removed from yours that you forget you are a man? If I hadn't seen them for myself and just now felt the wrath of your sword-arm, I would swear you were a eunuch.'

Elmo took a long suffering breath, rolled his eyes, and then set off on the road to Bamburgh and the Holy Island, but he hadn't gone a yard before Finn called for him to hold up.

'See here,' Finn said stooping a short way along the path that led south. 'Pony muck, just short of steaming and enough to spread an entire field. An army has recently come this way.'

'Hush! For it seems the rear-guard has yet to pass.' Elmo heard raised voices and the pounding of hooves. 'Take up your pack and remember, keep your mouth shut.'

'Shall we hide? Surely there is time.'

Elmo gave Finn a sideways glance. 'You don't strike me as the hiding kind, and anyway, they are almost upon us.'

Elmo and Finn walked side by side, north along the main road towards the sound of horses, keeping to the edge so as to avoid the hoof-churned mud, and soon a pair of riders were upon them, both lads hardly older, perhaps even younger, than Elmo and Finn. They were armed lightly but ready for war.

'Cheerful greetings!' called the leading lad as he reined in.

Elmo returned the compliments, Finn waved and smiled.

'Are you come from the west to relieve the good brothers of Holy Island?'

'We have business there, yes,' Elmo said.

'Then it pains me to say, you are too late, for Lindisfarne has been raided by grim warriors who came in two long boats. They have despoiled and laid waste to all the holy places of the island and plundered all treasures. The monks have been cruelly slain or driven out, robbed naked. The novice-boys were either killed or taken, to be slaves I should say.'

Elmo seethed and it took all his strength not to draw his sword and lop off Finn's head as he stood.

'Did you not run into the main fyrd?' the mounted youth asked. 'My Lord Dunstan Chase must have passed here not a quarter-hour past, riding at its head. He has gone on to Annebelle for word has come that the little island close by was also raided.'

'What of the raiders?' Finn said.

Elmo stared daggers at him, although he had spoken with very little accent.

'They are cowards, for as soon as their devilish work was done, they returned to their boats dragging treasure and captives with them. A number of the boys must have been deemed too weak to give good service, for they were thrown into the sea as the boats drew away, and all were drowned.'

'My brother among them,' the other warrior said. He had remained silent until then. 'And he was just twelve years old. How I long for the day when I may stand face-to-face with a dog-cur Northman!'

'It strikes me as didn't before,' the first said. 'And excuse me for being so bold, but you are both well and finely armed with noble blades, and yet un-horsed and dressed in little more than travelling clothes. How so, and who are you?'

Elmo saw by the look of uncertainty in the young warrior's eyes that his suspicion had been roused and that the situation had once again come to rest at the very edge of danger.

'It is true, sir, that our family, once respectable, has come upon hard times. Our fathers' blades will be the last of our treasures to leave us, and please forgive me if I choose to protect my family name by refusing to name it.'

For a moment, the boy was on the brink, but he responded to Elmo's honest countenance. 'Then farewell, and may you come to restore all that was yours. We must attend to our duties.' He dug in his heels and the pony half-reared before moving to a swift canter along the road to the south closely followed by the other knight who managed a cheery wave through the pain that must have been in his heart.

'You dissemble almost as well as you fight,' Finn said from the side of his mouth.

Elmo watched until the warriors and their mounts were swallowed up along the forest trail.

'What of the boys?' Elmo asked. 'The ones who were taken.'

'What else?' Finn said dismissively 'They'll become slaves. The strongest and prettiest might be taken east and sold for good silver. The rest, those that survive the crossing, will probably be working my father's fields within a week. Those that show weakness will be cast into the sea.'

'Your father's fields ...?'

'There's little doubt my father led that raid with his ships *Thought* and *Memory* – Odin's Ravens.' He smiled with pride.

Elmo wanted to fight Finn all over again, and this time, finish him. But the quest and the promises made: he shook his head trying to hide the disgust he felt, and began to walk south.

'We follow those babies in armour? I thought our way was to the north.'

'It appears there is nothing left for us in the north, so we will go to Annebelle and there hope to find friends and avoid foes, unless you have a better idea.'

Fish made a good point, and Raven made a dash for it.

Finn ran the few steps until he caught up with Elmo. For the next hour they walked in silence. Elmo's head was full of the imagined cries of the brothers and novices at Holy Island as they suffered humiliation and death at the hands of Finn's kin.

Elmo stopped suddenly and turned on Finn. 'Tell me! Will the boys, the slaves, be well-treated?'

Finn looked bemused. 'They're slaves. How should they treated but as slaves? If they work as they are told all will be fine. If they are lazy or disobedient they will have their ears boxed.'

'What if they run away ... try to escape?'

'Why then, they will be killed, or hobbled.' Finn grinned as if sharing a joke. 'It is hard to run away if your toes have been hacked off.'

Elmo struggled to contain his anger.

'What would happen to an English slave who ran away?'

At once, Elmo's anger cooled. 'Much the same, I suppose. Unless he is a slave to the Church or a monastery, and then the biggest punishment would be to be sold on to a less generous master.'

They resumed their journey, silent once more. They came to a road that ran by the coast and so high that their sight reached the far horizon over the silvery sea and then as the sun shifted the sea became blue and the skies clear. At noon they hurried off the road and hid in a stand of bracken to avoid a body of horsemen who galloped north.

'Dandy fellows,' Finn said when they had passed. 'If they fight as well as they look, they would make good battle-sport, all but for their fat captain.'

'Frankish armour, I think, just like the knights who tried to take us on Coquet Island. Hiding from them was the right thing to do.'

Several hours later they spied Coquet Island from their coastal path and then went inland a little and so through the village of Workworth. Not wishing the risk the ferryman, they went west and south until they came to a river crossing and then doubled back on the other side and thence on towards Annebelle.

'So there's how you use your slaves,' Finn said as they approached a noisome midden by the road.

Elmo looked and saw a human foot sticking out of the filth, part of a naked thigh and enough of the chest to know the body was that of a young man. The flesh, where it showed through the massed companies of bluebottles, wore the pallor of death.

'We would never use a slave thus, Elmo, so I'll have no more of you haughty words. Look here at our feet, great clods of dung. I'll wager he was pelted until he became as he is now, and that's half buried in shit. Give me the Blood Eagle any day!'

'I'm appalled. Believe me, it is not at all our usual habit to show such disrespect, even towards a slave.'

'A criminal then? Stole a loaf. Farted in front of the King mayhap? Still, it is unseemly. He could have been thrown off a cliff for the sea to take with no more effort.'

'I can only imagine his sin was so great that he deserved the most ignoble of disposals. And yet his body appears unbroken when the gravest of crimes would see him mutilated and torn apart. Indeed, great his sin must have been.'

Finn chuckled. 'I think I would have liked him.' When Elmo did not answer or react in any way, Finn added that he had spoken in jest and that Elmo was a dullard for not laughing.

Elmo was troubled as they passed by and he feared for his family and neighbours lest this rudely discarded fellow had done some hideous evil upon them. Hang a felon on the gibbet, perhaps, but throw him into the midden?

Annebelle was unusually quiet. There was no sign of Lord Chase's fyrd, nor were there people about their chores or children playing. The wooden houses with their thatched roofs were mostly shuttered up, each with a broom across the threshold. At last Elmo and Finn came to the longhouse that always had an open door and unbarred by the broom, so that travellers might pass in and take refreshments in exchange for coin. Inside it was warm and inviting, that is until several of the guests hurried to leave as soon as they had observed who entered.

'Is it our weapons?' Elmo asked the innkeeper.

'No, young sir,' the innkeeper's wife said. 'It is your face, for they recognise you as Elfgar son of Thomas, one time reeve of this town, and they do not wish to be here when you learn of the cruel doom that has befallen your kin.'

Elmo's heart sank and he felt faint. 'Mother?'

'Gone to her rest and by no natural cause.'

'Eric?'

'Gone, and also his wife and little Maudie.'

Elmo stumbled and was only saved from falling because Finn steadied him about the shoulders.

'Hush woman!' the innkeeper ordered. 'Brush off any more visitors and close the door. You sir,' he said addressing Finn. 'Bring your friend and our former neighbour in to my private room so that he may have the whole story.'

'I think he has had as much of the story as he needs,' Finn said forgetting to modify his accent. 'His family is dead, what more is there?'

'It is a tale as grim as may be, but it is not without a glimmer of hope. Come sir, bring him now. Wifey! Fetch some bread and ale. '

~ 2009 ~
Cipher Master

It was a grim journey home from that meeting. The weather hadn't improved, the roads were awful and I was the harbinger of bad news. How would I break it to Raz that he was out of a job? Was there any way round it? But bobbing up from the cold grey waves that flooded my mind was a survivor, waving his arms for attention, and that survivor was the exciting breakthrough concerning Bennett's clues.

'It's the old cliché,' I said as Raz opened the door for me and ushered me into the warm hall. I was so late he'd been worrying that I'd had an accident and seeing my patched-up face his worries were confirmed. 'There's good news and there's bad news,' I continued after assuring him I'd live. 'And the bad news has nothing to do with this little bump on the face.'

'Will it wait until you've had a large mug of hot chocolate? You look half-frozen to death.' Raz took my damp coat and hung it over the radiator in the hall.

'If you can stand the wait, Raz, I'd love a cup, and a hot shower.'

'Sorted,' Raz said. 'Have a shower and the chocolate will be waiting for you in the library. The fire's warmer in there.'

'Will do, and if you're having a mug yourself, you might like to spike it was a brandy. The bad news is very bad.'

Twenty minutes later I was showered and changed and cradling a steaming mug of comfort as I looked out of the library window into the white blanket that was the garden.

'The snow's getting heavier,' I said trying to put off the inevitable.

'The south had it pretty bad last night. They reckon it's our turn next.'

We swapped diversionary small talk about gritters and snow ploughs and the whole damned country coming to a standstill and then Raz couldn't stand it anymore. He demanded the news without further prevarication, and I told him.

He looked into the fire, and nodded slowly, brows furrowed – and then, almost as expected, the old Raz grin. It made him look younger, especially with his shorter haircut.

'No problem, Prof. I'll work for nothing. Just pay me a little more rent so I can make ends meet, and it's business as usual. I can't dip out of *Operation Raven-Fish* at this stage.'

'I couldn't possibly … could I?'

'If you *want* to let me go, then fine, but …'

'Of course I don't want you to go. This is an appalling situation, and I told them so.'

'Then I'll stay, and what's more, if I'm no longer employed by the department I can concentrate all my efforts on our project.'

I agreed and suddenly the bad news didn't appear quite so bad after all. We'd sort out the financial details and we would carry on, trying to get to the bottom of the mystery concerning skeletons and stones and Bennett's book.

It sounded pretty good in theory, but in the next few days came to realise this was only the first hurdle. It was as if our work together was being deliberately hampered by forces unknown, forces I suspected were being mustered and controlled by my old friend, Dr Smith.

'So Prof, what's the good news?'

I'd almost forgotten there was any. That drowning man had bobbed down for the third time and had probably given up all hope of rescue. I grabbed him by the hair and yanked him to the surface.

Raz was as excited as I and we rushed to spread the desk with our notebooks and relevant papers.

'Prof, you're definitely on to something. Every single one of the years alluded to in the clues follows a pattern. 656 is D-C-L-V-I in Roman numbers, 666 is D-C-L-V-X-I and so on. Each year uses the numerals only once, and in the correct order, leading up to 1666 when each of the possible numerals is used once. I think 1666 is the key.'

199

'But where does it get us? The pencil-written inserts give us a year, and the year gives us Roman numerals in a set pattern, but how does a neat arrangement of Roman numerals lead us to a location where we might find Alcuin's book?'

Raz shuffled through the papers and then seized up a notebook and thumbed through the pages. 'We need to find a converter-clue. Maybe the two inserts that don't refer to dates are clues of how to use the numerals.'

'Possibly. Or should we look for locations associated with the given years?'

'1666 – Great Fire of London, the Monument in the middle of London. But no, I doubt if there's a big enough nook in the monument to hide a book, if we're looking for a book at all.'

I pulled out the chair, sat and pulled it back so that my knees were under the desk. I slid the clue-sheet to the centre and ran my finger over the word of the last clue. *Fish made a good point, but raven made a dash for it.* And then I began to chuckle.

'Oh God, Raz, we're on a roll!'

Raz leaned over to read the clue for himself, casually draping an arm over my shoulder.

'Let's see Prof. What've you got?'

'"Fish made a good *point*, but Raven made a *dash* for it." Points and dashes, dots and dashes. It's so bloody obvious. Bennett's talking Morse Code for crying out loud.'

We were like two little boys who've been given the afternoon off school. I leapt up punching the air and then we hugged and danced around the library. I ignored my protesting knees.

We calmed down long enough for me to go online and print out the Morse code and then we were faced with the archaeologist's dilemma: more information, but never quite enough. Okay, so Morse code was involved somehow, but for the lives of us, we could not figure out how.

We turned numerals into Morse, Morse into numeral, tried to follow the narrative of Elmo and Finn's journey to see if that gave us any viable clues. We even considered bringing in help in case there was a mathematical element to the cipher, in which case neither of us was qualified to do more than grub around in the dark.

It was early hours before we went to our respective beds, and we were no further along the road to discovery. My head buzzed so much I didn't drift off until about four.

The next morning we were pretty much snowed-in and so we decided to take the advice of the local police. Our journey to work did not seem particularly essential given the risks we'd have to take, and even less so when the secretary phoned to say that the department would be shut for the day. It gave us all the more time to lay our minds upon the altar of fruitless effort. It was a frustrating day at the outset, and we could not make any progress with our cipher-cracking mission, going round and round the houses and never finding the right door to open. We were firmly shut out, and it was almost a relief when noon came and we could apply ourselves to the practicalities of preparing lunch.

If the morning was frustrating, then the afternoon was annoying and I have to say, made me more than a little paranoid. At two-thirty the phone calls began.

The first call was from Chair. He commented on the weather and made mention of clouds and silver linings in respect to our unexpected day off. Then he asked if I had passed on the news of imminent dismissal to Raz. He was sorry and all, but the admin had to be prepared. I told him that I had and mentioned our arrangement, that is, the one about Raz working for me for free. Chair went quiet. He said he wasn't sure about that. I told him not to concern himself and that the matter was settled.

The second call came from Lord James, the third Viscount of Wherever. He wanted *Raven-Fish!* back as, after all, we'd had had it for several weeks, and of course we'd be allowed to look at it whenever we wanted. That is, when Dr Smith had finished looking it over. James did not seem as friendly as he had been, and although the change in him was subtle, it made the hair on the back of my neck stand up.

Why wasn't I surprised Smith's name had cropped up, I wonder? How had Smith even got to hear about the book?

The third call was from Chair again. He had spoken with other members of the board and they were all in agreement. Raz could not work for me for nothing. My heart lifted for a moment; they must have changed their minds. I felt sure they were going to let him stay, perhaps on a smaller salary. Some hope! No, what Chair was telling me was that Raz would not be allowed to work for me at all. There was health and safety to consider as, no longer being employed by the department, he would not be covered by insurance. And access had to be considered; it would not be appropriate for a non-employee to be allowed the level of access an assistant would need. And I would also be depriving some poor student of a valuable learning experience. Finally he was sure I could see the trouble it might brew with the various unions.

I passed this all on to Raz, and I began to wonder if someone was deliberately making waves. If not Smith himself then Gwen McCreedy, or perhaps Chair himself who didn't like the fact Raz and I shared accommodation because his nasty little mind equated sharing accommodation to sharing bodily fluids.

'So what if we were?' Raz said when I railed against the old fart. 'We still wouldn't be breaking any rules.'

All very annoying, but it was the last call that really made me paranoid.

The call came through, not like the others on my mobile, but on Raz's landline. He took the call in the library while I shuffled papers for the umpteenth time. I noticed Raz appeared surprised and a little subdued, and then appreciative but not interested: 'Thank you, but I don't think so.' When he hung up I was dying to ask who it was, but I resisted. I didn't have to resist for long because Raz volunteered the information. The call had come from Dr Smith.

'Smith!' I said. 'What the Hell does he want?'

'He wants me,' Raz said. He explained that the good Doctor had offered him a position. It was a good one: not

202

only would it represent a promotion but he'd be on a much hirer salary.

I swallowed down gall and kept my emotions under perfect control. Mr Spock would have been proud of his adoptive son. 'In view of the situation Raz, perhaps you should consider taking the job. It's the logical thing to do.'

Raz looked at me from under smouldering eyebrows and spoke through a mouth set for battle. 'In view of the situation Prof, don't you think his offer is more than a coincidence? Don't you smell a rat and a fucking big one at that?'

It was only the second time I'd heard Raz use that particular cuss-word. Notwithstanding, I had to agree, and this was before Raz told me the Doctor intimated he would still be able to work on our project if he took up the job offer.

It was all getting away from me. My Sutton Hoo was becoming as tenuous and insubstantial as the sand-stain skeletons for which the original was famous. My Arthur was duck-diving back down to the Lady in the Lake before he'd so much as stuck his head above water. Suddenly I could see it all. The Doctor would get his hands on *Raven-Fish!* and see the clues immediately. With the backing of the powers that be, he'd steam in, walk all over my work, and be there for the big finish. Yes, the Doctor would steal my work, and then to rub it in my face he'd steal my assistant too. I wanted to break something, hit someone, stamp my feet and scream.

'When does James want the book back?' Raz asked opening the desk draw and rummaging through.

'As soon as the snow clears he's sending a courier.' That in itself was odd. Why the sudden rush?

'In that case we shouldn't waste any time,' he said and he stood, triumphant, with a rubber in his raised hand. And before my American readers become too excited or indignant, let me say a rubber to us Brits is what you people call an eraser.

'We'll rub out all the clues before James and the Doctor get their hands on *Raven-Fish!*

For a while, call it a nanosecond, I was aghast. Raz was proposing to alter a document which, in the circumstances, was as good as primary source. Sacrilege! Heresy! Burn the lad at the stake! Pounce him, trounce him, pick him up and bounce him!

After the passing of a nanosecond I'd snatched the rubber from his hand and was flipping through *Raven-Fish!* to clue number one.

'Whoa, Prof! We should photograph the pages first.'

That took us the rest of the afternoon, several megabytes of photo-card and yards of 35mm film; having no faith in technology post-dating the beginning of the last century (typical archaeologist) we went belt and braces with the photography, just as we do on a dig: if the digital failed us we still had a good old roll or two of celluloid.

Erasing the pencilled-in lines and ironing out the indentations was a short job by comparison. I was just commenting on how completely we had obliterated the clues when a motor revved outside and then a car door slammed.

'Surely not in this weather?'

There was a knock at the door.

'I don't believe it,' I said.

Raz took *Raven-Fish!* and flicked through it, one last time. 'Did you photograph the front-piece?'

I hadn't, but that was soon remedied, and the drawing of the tree with all the ravens on the branches was suitably digitized and captured on film for good measure.

The weather was atrocious and Raz invited the courier into the hall.

'How on Earth can you drive in these conditions?' I asked.

The courier, a middle-aged man wrapped up against the cold told me he had special tyres fitted. 'All the way from Russia, they are. Not even sure they're legal over here but they do the job. Now, I'm to collect a book – *Raven-Fish!* – and a manuscript translation of the same.'

'You're out of luck on the translation,' I said, trying to sound convincing. 'We haven't got one prepared. We still have quite a lot of work to do before we can send the translation.'

'No worries, sir, if you'll just sign here to say I only collected the book I'll take it and be on my way.'

And so it was done. We no longer had *Raven-Fish!* in our possession, and short of using police forensic techniques, Dr Smith would just have to see how far he'd get without the pencil-written clues. If on the other hand, he found out what I'd done, and I would take full responsibility, my reputation would be Swiss cheese.

The courier's car moved slowly off the drive and out in to the blizzard.

'It's a bit like losing an old friend,' Raz said.

Having spent so long with our noses in that book, I had to agree. Looking back to that precise moment as we stood in the hall watching the front door, it is hard to imagine that within the next half-hour the whole code would be cracked.

We idled back to the library and as we did I put the digital camera on view and scrolled through the pictures: photo after photo of pages, complete with the pencilled-in clues, and all far too small for me to see properly on the tiny view-screen ... until I came to the one of the front-piece drawing. It looked like a black crack in a tile and nothing like a tree, and the ravens didn't even show up as blobs. But I knew the drawing well enough from memory. The mind works in a strange way, and I wonder if it was because I was using my memory instead of my eyes, that the next piece of the clue suddenly made sense.

'Prof-ess-ooor,' Raz said snapping his fingers an inch from my nose. 'You've got that look again.'

I reminded him of the last clue, the one where Fish had a point and Raven made a dash for it. 'What if the ravens on the branches represent dots and dashes – or rather the ravens are dots and the ravens with fish in their beaks, dashes?'

Raz's eyes widened and in the next instance he was connected the camera to my computer and starting to download the photos. It seemed to take an age, but soon we had the front-piece filling the monitor screen.

'Have you got that Morse Code sheet, Prof? Good! The birds on the branch, top left, there're three of them. First is a raven with a fish in its beak, next two are just plain ravens.'

I scanned down the sheet. 'If our theory is correct that's a dash and two dots ... which is the letter D.'

'Next branch, a little lower and sticking out to the right. Just two fishless ravens.'

'Which makes it an I,' I said. 'Next?'

The next two letters were R and G, and therefore, the word was DIRG.

'DIRG,' Raz said. 'D-I-R-G. Where does that get us? Hey what about those numbers down there under the roots ... 6-3-9-1. Do you think they fit in?'

It was another of those moments of elation followed by the downer of feeling we were not so far forward as we thought. I walked round in a small circle. Raz scratched his head. I sat down at the desk and let my head fall into my hands. Raz went and looked out into the dark night. And then he ran back to the screen.

'Wait a minute! Wait ... just ... one ... minute. Yes! If you read the numbers backwards, you have 1936 – the year *Raven-Fish!* was written as far as we can tell. If you take that as a starting point and continue to read backwards, you get GRID instead of DIRG.

It took us scant moments on the web to find out that the Ordnance Survey grid was introduced in 1936.

'Now we're cooking on gas!' I said. 'All we have to do now is go back to the other clues and find ourselves a grid number, and remember that second from last clue?'

Raz snatched up the clue sheet and read it out loud. 'The south-wall stone bore a graven letter N in the Roman style and the east wall a T. Thereafter the Fish penned upon a piece of scroll these two letters and put down six numbers, which were measure of the hand, the better to find his treasures in some unimaginable hereafter.'

Raz and I were both good map readers – it helps in our line of work – so we knew a standard grid reference comprised two letters followed by six figures. It looked like

Jason Bennett had made a gift of the letters, so we hoped it wouldn't be too hard to work out the numerals.

We brainstormed the answer over the next few minutes. After all those weeks, our minds must have been fine-tuned, for we were as hot as mustard.

'1666 is the key,' I said. 'But in Roman numerals! I think Bennett is trying to tell us that the grid reference we want contains every number, once and in the correct order. Following the pattern of the Roman numerals, I think we're looking for 9-8-7-6-5-4-3-2-1.'

'Too many digits, and if we take the front-piece clue we'll need to reverse it, so that's 1-2-3-4-5-6-7-8-9 … maybe take the first six and use them. The following four, including zero, might make up a ten-figure grid so we can zoom right in.'

Did I mention that my personal library included a full set of Ordnance Survey maps? Soon many of them were spread so that there was more map than floor visible in the library.

We tried numerous variations and most references but our original theory held true. At the grid reference we first cobbled together, there was marked a hill fort. We both knew instinctively, this was it. Not only did it fit the reference we'd discovered, but it was also completely in line with the narrative and sad, bloody ending of *Raven-Fish!* This hill fort held the answer to our great mystery. I've felt it before, but only in short measure, and fleetingly, but in that hour it was a flood of pure joy that surged up from a rarely disturbed well-spring and coloured all my feelings.

'Raz, if you were a girl, and I was thirty years younger, I'd kiss you.'

Raz laughed. 'Just have to make do with a hug, Prof. Come here!'

Oh sweet joy, we had our location. My Sutton Hoo was stirring under the Scottish turf. Arthur was playing hide and seek and peeking out from behind ancient wall-stones. The next problem was to persuade the relevant authority that we had good grounds to conduct a dig. There was also the matter of Raz's employment, or imminent lack of it, and of course, any more obstacles that the Chair or Doc Smith might care to throw our way.

There would be obstacles and problems enough, and we would even find ourselves on the wrong side of the law. But that night we enjoyed our success.

I was so glad Raz had held back a bottle of that Chateau Potensac '79.

After a good sized glass each, and a few moments of silence – we had exhausted discussions of the possibilities of the next few days – we moved into an area we had never covered before.

'It's almost as if we are being guided by some divine influence,' I said. It was a throw-away remark induced by the relaxing effect of the alcohol, and it wasn't meant to lead anywhere.

'God? The only God I recognise is cause and effect.'

'You're a non-believer then, like me?'

'Not at all,' Raz said. 'I am a strong *believer*, for I believe with as much conviction and certainty as the most fervent of those with religious beliefs, that there is no God. Probably more, as I am never troubled by the slightest of doubts, which is a lot more than you can say for the religious.'

My own eye looked up at me, reflected in the deep red of the wine in my glass. Wine-scrying, I like to call it. 'No dark tea-time of the soul for you then?'

Raz appeared to be scrying his own wine. 'My dark times have been and gone and I dare say we must all pass through them. We need the dark times, the crucibles of fire otherwise there could be no gold, and there was a time when mankind needed religion. When we were in our infancy and did not understand, God, the invention of man, comforted us through the night. But now we have grown, it is the time to stand in the light and put childhood behind us.'

Very eloquent, Mr Reeves. Bravo! I could almost see him giving the St Crispin's day speech before leading his men to victory at Agincourt.

208

I had often thought of the authors of the Bible as the speculative fiction writers of their day, and wondered how surprised they would be if they could know that some people in thousands of years to come would take their stories as literal. I chuckled to myself as I imagined a holy book of the future: *The Gospel According to Asimov* or perhaps *Ender's Game: Revelations by Orson Scott Card.*

'So, religion was okay … once … but now it's past its use-by date, is that it?'

'Inasmuch as it gives some people comfort, and a moral framework, I think it's still okay, so long as they see the stories as allegories and not the literal truth.'

Just as the authors intended, I thought.

'Inasmuch as it divides one man from another, or provides evil or deluded men with a flag of respectability to wave over wanton acts, it is more than past its use-by date. It is vile poison!'

Was it the wine or something in his past? Raz was certainly beginning to fire-up. I broached the subject gently, asked him if he had ever suffered as a consequence of religion. He simply flashed me the old Raz smile, apologised for dancing on his soap-box and changed the subject.

We quaffed the last of the wine in a silence that did not need to be filled with words.

Later, just before we parted company for bed, Raz intimated something fantastical about himself, in terms of 'what if'. If there is truth in wine, Raz had past that point, and he really was ready for sleep, for he seemed already to be dreaming.

XIV

~ 793 ~
In which the Fish is bereft of the shoal

The innkeeper's name was Wulf, although his wife and close friends called him Woolfie. His pinched features held in mirth that escaped through smiling eyes and his hair was wayward-curly; light brown where it wasn't flecked with grey. He had a kindly disposition but lest anyone should try to take advantage of his good nature, he wore a keen seax at his belt that matched his warrior's bearing.

Elmo sat cross-legged on the floor by the centrally placed hearth, looking into the flames as he quietly supped ale and took time over the half-loaf the innkeeper's wife had supplied. Finn and Wulf spoke in hushed tones, eyeing Elmo continually lest he should take on the madness that grief sometimes induces.

Elmo let his body relax while waves of grief battered him, but rather than build frail walls against the assault, he let it wash over him. His mother, his brother, his sister-in-law and little Maudie – they were all past the suffering of the world, and for that he tried to be grateful, for of all people, surely they would be admitted to paradise, shriven by life if not a priest.

In all this, Elmo tried to cling on to the smallest of hopes. He had heard the innkeeper say that there was such a glimmer of hope in this sad tale of murder, and at last he could wonder no more. Although what hope could there be amidst such pain?

'Tell me, innkeeper. Where is the hope of which you spoke?'

'Call me Woolfie, young sir, such as my friends do. And as to the hope, it is small enough, and yet it should wait its place in the telling all that befell your family.' Wulf shuffled round from his side of the fire to sit close to Elmo.

'Then please begin, and pray, do not spare me details. I must hear what my loved ones endured and even then my suffering will be but a fraction of theirs.'

And so Wulf began to speak of what had befallen a good family of Annebelle.

'First, sir, came a portly lord dressed in fine armour, polished iron shot through with gilded wire, and with him came his thegns who were armoured so as to be marked as his men, although not as grandly as he.

'The lord, who did not name himself, demanded to know the whereabouts of the residence of the family of the former reeve, Thomas. His tone was rude and he was armed for war, and so nobody would tell him but feigned ignorance. And then came a brother from the island, Sebastian by name, and he told of a raid upon the island by evil, fell men. He called the lord to assist, but he would not.

'And then, learning of the lord's quest, this Brother Sebastian, who knew of the family in question for he had but recently had quarrelsome words with Eric, led the lord to the house of Eric's mother. I believe he thought the sooner the lord completed his business the sooner he may come to aid the brothers on the island.

'The lord's men did not pause to knock at the widow's door but broke it asunder and streamed inside like they were storming a fortress. Nobody remains to say what they did inside, but after a while they set fire to the house, with the widow still inside, and her death-screams brought her family running, and they were seized and made to watch as the house burned and the widow was roasted to death.

'Eric was bound and the family and their slave-boy Ulric, dragged ignominiously to an empty barn where they were kept under guard for some days.

'What befell the family in that rude barn was made known to us by Ulric. For some time, the lord questioned Eric about the whereabouts of his brother Elfgar, but he laid not a finger upon him even though Eric made no answers. Then he had Eric stripped naked, and Ulric believed there would be torture, but instead Eric was bound

211

again and asked the same question though Emma pleaded for her husband's dignity.

'It was only when the lord ordered the woman and little girl stripped that Eric began to call for mercy and said that he would give up his brother so long as his family were left unhurt.

'But the lord would have none of it. Eric told that his brother was a monk who served the Heavenly Lord in the monastery on the island. The lord though would not be deprived of his sport. Ulric was made to strip and was ordered to take Emma but he was afraid, far too afraid for his body to be capable of such an act. He was then threatened with torturous death if he did not ravage the woman and so he performed the actions necessary to quicken himself, and then, through bitter tears of shame, did as he was ordered, while all the time Eric railed against his bindings and screamed for mercy and the lord and his minions mocked and derided like the Hellish devils they be. Through all this and even while Ulric was reluctantly forcing himself upon your brother's wife, Emma told Ulric she forgave him and that it was no evil of his. In all her humiliation and pain Emma's thoughts were not for herself.

'The act done, Ulric was thrown outside, still naked, and mocked by the guards and straight-way ran to Brother Sebastian and there being no priest confessed to the brother instead. But Brother Sebastian would not comfort him and said that he should have died before despoiling his mistress. Though he had not the right, Brother Sebastian called Ulric outlaw whereupon he was immediately seized by the blacksmith and his apprentice and they drowned him in a trough while the brother stood by and mumbled a prayer, and then they threw his body to feed their pig. Thus Ulric atoned for his sin that a priest could have dealt with by a word.

'Eric's wife and little daughter were slain before his eyes – sorry sir, but you said not to spare the detail. Their throats were slit. In this part there is little detail, the only witnesses being the cries through the walls and the spoilt bodies that remained when the lord took his leave.

212

'Not content with all this ...' At last, Wulf failed in the telling. He apologised and took some ale, then apologised again for what he had left to tell.

'Carry on Woolfie. Tell me, what of my brother?' Elmo feared one thing above all and it was that his brother had been thrown onto the midden. Blood dragged down from his heart and left him hollow.

'They put out his eyes and tore out his tongue and then dragged him to the midden where all the townsfolk were ordered to throw filth at him until he be drowned in it and be dead.'

Elmo's head fell and despite his great resolve to bear all and any news with dignity, he let out such a howl that his agony was felt by all who heard and then he sobbed until he felt his heart would stop. 'I saw him there as we came into town, and thought it the body of a felon.'

Wulf put a comforting arm around the distraught young man. 'You saw him not, poor sir, nor did you see a villain. That pitiful sight that can only offend the eyes and the soul was the murdered body of poor Ulric whose only crime was to fear death by torture.'

'Then, my brother ...?'

'Your brother yet lives, though may not for very much longer. Lord Dunstan Chase came through town and saw your brother on the midden. When he heard what had happened, he swore oaths and cussed greatly and then ordered Eric to be taken down and straightway to the physic there to be bathed and to have the wound in his mouth cauterised. Earldorman Chase paid the physic himself and then rode on with the fyrd. "That the fat oaf should want the lad dead makes me resolved he should live," Chase called as he rode away.

'We took poor drowned Ulric from the mess of the pigsty – the pig had shown no interest in his meat as yet – and half-buried him in the mess of folk. He was cast onto the midden for fear the first lord would return and punish us for going against his word. We hoped he might see Ulric and believe him to be Eric, for both were made up much the same in height and girth and figure, and what was different the filth might hide.'

'Take me to my brother,' Elmo said standing and smoothing down his clothes.

'Aye,' Finn said. 'And name this lord whom we might know if we should meet him again, for we saw him ride out to the north some hours past.'

'He did not give his name or rank, but earned obedience by the swords of his thegns. But we know him to be Godwin the King's thegn, for that was the name Ealdorman Chase cursed when he had the description of him.'

Elmo grew impatient. He had heard enough and now wanted nothing more than to be taken to Eric. Wulf called for his pot-boy. He called again after a moment and the boy emerged from a behind a wall of shepherd's plaids hung from a beam to form a screen. A young woman also emerged from the shadow and caught Finn's eye, then cast her looks to the floor and smiled. Both were adjusting their clothes and it appeared to Elmo that they may have recently been intimate, but such thoughts that had not to do with Eric had no hold on him.

Wulf instructed the boy, whose misnomer was Spider, to take the young knights forthwith to his grandmother's house and explained that Elmo was Eric's brother. Spider led the way but Finn said his wound was giving him pain and he felt like to swoon from fatigue.

'Anyway,' Finn said. 'You should meet with your brother alone. I will wait here.'

Elmo saw the way Finn's eyes went to the girl, and he knew at once why Finn had suddenly taken on the uncharacteristic quality of thoughtfulness.

'As you wish,' Elmo said and tried to imbue his countenance with the words he refrained from speaking. *Don't touch her!*

Spider was a lively lad of about fourteen years with hose too short and a worn-out tunic too long. His shoes were out at the toes, the uppers with scant attachment to the soles and he wore a baldric of twine that held a pouch stuffed full with who-knows-what, and a little sheath containing a

214

spoon, a pricker and a knife. His spiky brown hair framed a grubby face and he moved in a noisome fug that indicated a certain reluctance to wash.

They followed the road west out of Annebelle.

'See here, sir, this fine silver coin!'

Elmo took the tiny coin for he felt Spider had offered it for examination in a boyish gesture of trust. 'Fine indeed, but you should be loath to display your wealth, lest a villain takes it from you.' He handed back the coin.

Spider tucked it away in a secret pocket deep inside his clothing. 'They'd better not try, sir, for I earned it by throwing shit at that wicked fat lord, and hit him with it too though it be only upon his foot. I'm not afraid of lords, so why should villains vex me?'

The boy led Elmo further west along the river path. Elmo could think only of his brother, and what state he would find him in, his beautiful eyes put out, his tongue torn from his mouth and the remnant cauterised. Spider jabbered on but Elmo did not hear his words.

They came off the path and into a wood. Elmo forced down the evil images that filled his mind, and made himself think of the here-and-now, even though the horrors to come were minutes away. He had lived in Annebelle until he was past twelve, yet he could not recall any house in this part of the wood. He had no memory of a younger Spider either, and wondered whose boy he was.

'Do you have a name other than Spider?'

Spider frowned, deep in thought, trying to dredge up a memory that was too deep for the grapple. 'I feel sure I did, and sometimes I dream it, but I've always forgotten by cock-crow.'

Spider leapt a tree that had fallen across the path and Elmo climbed over with more decorum.

'Now see here, sir.' Spider stopped and pulled up his tunic and shirt, hitching them high up his back and wincing just a little. He wore no drawers, his hose being suspended by a twine tied about his thin waist.

'I have no desire to see your buttocks, young man. Kindly rearrange your dress at once.'

215

Spider laughed. 'Not my arse, sir. Look higher up my back and see the whipping I took for besmearing that tub of lard who calls himself lord.'

Elmo, who had turned his head away, now looked and saw the many stripes that had cut through the skin of the boy's back. The wounds were livid and wept a little fluid, but were uninfected.

'Put down your tunic and cover yourself lest the wounds corrupt. You are fortunate that they have not already done so.'

'It is not fortune alone,' Spider said pulling down his clothing and smoothing them back in place. 'It is fortune aided by the herb-lore of my gamma. She may not be a physic but she knows of herbs and ointments. See, if she can salve my bloody wounds, she can comfort poor Eric. Hurry now, we'll be there soon.'

Spider lived with his grandmother in rambling house that looked like three roundhouses conjoined, the thatch thin in many places and the woodland encroaching. There were vines reaching out from the dark wood that inveigled the structure of the house; from some angles it looked more forest than dwelling.

Spider entered and called out a merry halloo and Elmo followed expecting to meet a wizened hag but it was not so. Gamma Westwood had white hair pinned neatly into a roll at the back and wore a well laundered white apron over a faded red tunic that almost reached the floor. Over this she wore a brown, hooded cowl, the hood hanging down at the back. But Elmo took none of this in, nor did he pay more than scant attention to the proper greetings and compliments, so intent was he to be at his brother's side. When he heard a soft moan of anguish and pain, he rushed to the room from whence it came without leave.

Eric lay in a makeshift bed of quilts and blankets in a dark room lit by a single lamp. The light fell upon his face and because of the vacant eye sockets and the weakness of the light, the shadows gave it the look of a skull. He was asleep, or unconscious.

'Sir me no more, young Spider. I am Elmo, and please, help me with him.'

When Eric was sitting up, he made a sign with his hands.

'Spider, my brother wants the makings for writing. Does Grandmother Westwood have ink and a pen about the place?'

'Your brother can write?' Spider said, marvelling at the injured young man. He shook off his admiration. 'Gamma can't write no more than me, and sorry sir … Elmo … but we have nothing fit for that purpose, though I might take some soot and … No! Wait a minute, if you would.' Spider flew from the room towards the main door, his shirt flying.

'For pity's sake, put on some drawers before you …'

But it was too late, the door slammed shut and Elmo was left to tend to his brother alone for some time, and so he spoke of the attack on Coquet Island, of his truce with Finn who should be his enemy and of the journey thus far. Spider was gone so long that Elmo went to the door and stepped outside holding up the lamp. He walked a few steps along the path when the slapping of bare feet on stone and a white, ghostlike figure hurrying towards him marked the Spider's return.

'See what I've brought,' Spider said holding out his prizes. 'Slate and chalk. Eric might use these for writing.'

Spider took Elmo's hand and led him back into the house. 'I should have said as I did not, that you must never leave Gamma's house unguided. Her paths are thick-strewn with stray-sods, and anyone stepping upon one will find himself pixie-led and lost in the forest. Nobody can find her house lest she wills it or I lead them.'

Back inside, Eric ceased his whimpering as Elmo and Spider approached, and he was soon propped up, sitting with the rough-hewn slate across his lap. He first wrote that Elmo was in danger from Godwin who would have his head if he knew he still lived. Elmo said what he knew of Godwin, and in their conversation, one side written and one side spoken, Elmo realised it was indeed Godwin they had

'For pity's sake, bind his brow and cover those yawning chasms,' Elmo said with quavering voice. He kneeled down and kissed his brother upon the forehead, and then fell to weeping.

'Now's not the time to bind,' Gamma Westwood said. 'I've packed the voids with pummelled sphagnum wrapped in soft muslin whetted with whole-wine and a salve that heals. Luckily, if you can call it luck, his tongue was couped, not erased, and a clean cut is more like to heal quickly.' The elderly lady called Spider to her by an irritable flap of her hand and had him assist her in kneeling next to Elmo. She rested her hand gently upon his shoulder, and then he turned and buried his head in her bosom and cried like a child while Gamma Westwood comforted like a mother. But he did not cry for long.

'I gave him a draught to make him sleep, for the pain was too much to bear. It is past time when fever should have set in, if it is to come at all, so I believe he may be spared.'

Elmo dried his eyes on his sleeve and reaching out he laid a hand on Eric's chest. 'He is quite cool and but for the ghastly hurts upon him, he looks to be at peace.' He began to lift the blanket over Eric's middle, but let it fall again. He knew the obscene cuts loathsome men such as Godwin liked to make, but could not bear to look.

'He is all complete below his chin, if that's what you were wondering. He's still capable of making babbies if he weds anew.'

'Let's pray for now, only that he lives.'

'Aye, well, if he survives this night and the pain doesn't addle his wits, he is like to become a man again, such as can be called a man who cannot see or talk. There is no magic to bring back his sight or speech, poor lad, not even from the realms of your kin.'

Elmo sought her eyes in the dim shadows and questioned her with his.

'You're First Born,' Gamma said. 'I knew it as soon as you stepped over my threshold.'

Spider gasped and held both hands to his mouth, a gesture that made him appear younger than he was. Although Elmo did not know it, Spider was to be his devoted friend and constant admirer from that moment on.

'Is it the clothes?' Elmo said, his hand falling to a fold of his Frankish tunic.

'I should know you for an elven-lad if you were as naked as the day you were born.'

'Gamma has the sight,' Spider whispered is awe.

Gamma stood, reaching out to hook the lad about the neck and thence to draw him in to a rough hug. She ruffled his hair, planted a wet kiss upon his brow and then pushed him away and told him to go make up another bed.

'You'll want to stay close to your brother?'

'Of course, and thank you.'

'Even though he is no brother at all. Yon ill-done-by lad is no more First Born than I.'

Elmo stiffened. 'There's more to kin than accident of birth. I was taken in by …

'By Wifey Gerefa,' Gamma interrupted. 'She took you in when you was just a babe. Yes, I know. I knew your mam and your father.' She turned to leave and looked over her shoulder. 'I also knew your real father.'

'Did you then perhaps know the deacon, Alcuin of York?'

'Only by reputation, which is exceeding fair, but I never had the honour of meeting him. Now, I'll leave you alone with your brother for a little.'

Elmo knelt again and forced himself to look into the dark voids that dominated Eric's face, wherein his beautiful green eyes, honest and steadfast, had been replaced by Gamma's healing concoctions, and once again he felt tears arising, but he mastered them.

Spider returned with the makings of a bed and put the pallet down so that Elmo could lie close to Eric and watch him through the night. 'Gamma's making us a supper and I have time before the pot boils to run back to the inn and tell your companion that you will stay here the night, and he

should make his own arrangement, for we hav[e] bed.'

'Thank you, Spider. I imagine he has al[l] arrangements.'

Spider grinned. 'You saw how he looked at[her.] Well, he might get an hour or two with her, [not the] whole night. She has coin to earn, as do I.'

Supper was a savoury broth, thick with [something,] three-day-old bread, but good enough for dun[king. Before] he undressed to sleep, Elmo helped Gamma si[t Eric up and] trickle water into his mouth, which Eric swall[owed] semi-conscious. They laid him back gently and [left] them alone. Elmo stripped to his drawers a[nd] settled to sleep, his sword under the blankets w[ith him.]

It was at first light when Eric awoke an[d, rousing] from slumber, whimpers of pain grew to cri[es.] Spider came running from his corner pulling [a tunic] over his head, but Gamma Westwood did [not make an] appearance. Spider explained that she was col[lecting herbs,] some of which had to be gathered by moonlig[ht] to remain efficacious.

Elmo bathed his brother's brow with cool [water and, at] last, his softly spoken words broke through [to Eric] and had a calming effect. Eric made a noise [that sounded] like a question, and Elmo reassured him tha[t he was here] and would remain.

Eric reached out a hand and touched E[lmo,] needing proof that his brother really was wi[th him. Elmo] took the unsteady hand and kissed the tremb[ling fingers] and then Eric wept but they were no longe[r tears of pain] but of relief.

'Do you know how to use your grandmo[ther's brews,] Spider, for I would relieve my brother's suffer[ing.]

Spider shook his head, his face yellow in [the candlelight.] 'We mustn't touch her brews, for to use the[m wrongly] will kill him as surely as a knife between the ri[bs.]

Eric tried to say something, but his v[oice was as] ruined as his eyes.

'I think he wants to sit up, sir.'

seen on the road, and that he was riding hard for Ros's Beacon where Brother Mundwyn lay indisposed.

For a while Elmo was undecided and did not know where his duty laid. Was he to find a horse and ride to the beacon, hopefully to find and rescue Mundwyn, or stay with his brother? Well, in the end he knew it must be too late to come to Mundwyn before Godwin and his men, so he chose the path of common sense and decided he would tend to his brother.

Gamma Westwood came home in the early hours and made a wholesome broth which she fed to Eric following a draught to ease his pain, and a salve to numb the stump of his tongue to facilitate eating. He took small amounts and then with difficulty and he choked and gagged often, but he managed to take down enough sustenance to aid his recovery.

Several days past and each day Eric grew stronger and slowly, a little by a little, his pain diminished. On the sixth day, he rose and dressed in a worn-out suit of clothes that Spider had secured as charity from a kind family at Annebelle. That day Eric ate wincing a little but with no cries of pain, and he sat many hours with Elmo in their exchange or words, written and spoken, and once he even laughed, a clear and happy sound that was not marred by his injury. And when Elmo tired of words, Spider proved himself to be a master of tales and told many stories, some of brave knights and adventure, others of elves and spirits, and those with a hilarious and amusing end to them. On the seventh day Eric washed the dirty pots by feel, while Elmo and Spider saw to the daily chores set them by Gamma Westwood.

Spider had become Elmo's shadow and delighted in his company. His friend Elmo was First Born and therefore linked to the mysteries of the world that Gamma dipped into and from which Spider took joy in this world of pain and toil.

On the evening of the seventh day Spider fetched Finn and he brought with him Mary, the young woman from the inn. Finn was quite changed and clearly enamoured of Mary.

221

Mary for her part appeared equally in love with Finn and somewhat in control of the relationship.

'You were a ravening dog and now you are wide-eyed pup,' Elmo said to Finn when Mary had drawn aside to speak with Gamma.

'I suppose you've had her,' Spider said and quickly ducked the blow that Finn aimed at his head.

'"Had" is a taking word, a word of greed and selfishness and an ugly one I will not have you use of my Mary.'

Elmo and Spider exchanged looks and Spider made his eyes cross and then roll, in imitation of the lovelorn fool.

'What we have shared has been freely given and gratefully received,' Finn said, his face softened by a faraway look. 'It is the like of bards' songs, and such as I have never known before nor even knew existed.'

That night Elmo laid in bed in the dark and heard the soft sounds of lovemaking drift over from Spider's corner of the room which Finn and Mary had made their own. He was quickened by desire and thought that he might have to employ that practice that eases the blood, and that Alcuin had assured him was no sin, despite the edicts of the Church.

'Elmo,' came a sharp whisper from close at hand. It was Spider and he stood shivering in his shirt with stray moonbeams alighting on his skin and giving him the appearance of an emaciated ghost. 'I have been put out of my bed by the lovers and now I freeze. What am I to do?'

Elmo knew a hint when he heard one, and lifted his blankets for Spider to slip under. The boy's skin was like ice as he snuggled close for warmth.

'It must fire the blood to hear your friend at such sport, for I know it does mine,' Spider whispered through chattering teeth. 'I'm that hard I could blunt a knife-edge.' He was silent for a moment, as if waiting for Elmo's reply. 'I can bring you a girl, if you like.'

'And then where should you sleep, young man?'

'Never mind me. I'll find somewhere. So, should I fetch someone?'

'For pity's sake, bind his brow and cover those yawning chasms,' Elmo said with quavering voice. He kneeled down and kissed his brother upon the forehead, and then fell to weeping.

'Now's not the time to bind,' Gamma Westwood said. 'I've packed the voids with pummelled sphagnum wrapped in soft muslin whetted with whole-wine and a salve that heals. Luckily, if you can call it luck, his tongue was couped, not erased, and a clean cut is more like to heal quickly.' The elderly lady called Spider to her by an irritable flap of her hand and had him assist her in kneeling next to Elmo. She rested her hand gently upon his shoulder, and then he turned and buried his head in her bosom and cried like a child while Gamma Westwood comforted like a mother. But he did not cry for long.

'I gave him a draught to make him sleep, for the pain was too much to bear. It is past time when fever should have set in, if it is to come at all, so I believe he may be spared.'

Elmo dried his eyes on his sleeve and reaching out he laid a hand on Eric's chest. 'He is quite cool and but for the ghastly hurts upon him, he looks to be at peace.' He began to lift the blanket over Eric's middle, but let it fall again. He knew the obscene cuts loathsome men such as Godwin liked to make, but could not bear to look.

'He is all complete below his chin, if that's what you were wondering. He's still capable of making babbies if he weds anew.'

'Let's pray for now, only that he lives.'

'Aye, well, if he survives this night and the pain doesn't addle his wits, he is like to become a man again, such as can be called a man who cannot see or talk. There is no magic to bring back his sight or speech, poor lad, not even from the realms of your kin.'

Elmo sought her eyes in the dim shadows and questioned her with his.

'You're First Born,' Gamma said. 'I knew it as soon as you stepped over my threshold.'

Spider gasped and held both hands to his mouth, a gesture that made him appear younger than he was. Although Elmo did not know it, Spider was to be his devoted friend and constant admirer from that moment on.

'Is it the clothes?' Elmo said, his hand falling to a fold of his Frankish tunic.

'I should know you for an elven-lad if you were as naked as the day you were born.'

'Gamma has the sight,' Spider whispered is awe.

Gamma stood, reaching out to hook the lad about the neck and thence to draw him in to a rough hug. She ruffled his hair, planted a wet kiss upon his brow and then pushed him away and told him to go make up another bed.

'You'll want to stay close to your brother?'

'Of course, and thank you.'

'Even though he is no brother at all. Yon ill-done-by lad is no more First Born than I.'

Elmo stiffened. 'There's more to kin than accident of birth. I was taken in by ...

'By Wifey Gerefa,' Gamma interrupted. 'She took you in when you was just a babe. Yes, I know. I knew your mam and your father.' She turned to leave and looked over her shoulder. 'I also knew your real father.'

'Did you then perhaps know the deacon, Alcuin of York?'

'Only by reputation, which is exceeding fair, but I never had the honour of meeting him. Now, I'll leave you alone with your brother for a little.'

Elmo knelt again and forced himself to look into the dark voids that dominated Eric's face, wherein his beautiful green eyes, honest and steadfast, had been replaced by Gamma's healing concoctions, and once again he felt tears arising, but he mastered them.

Spider returned with the makings of a bed and put the pallet down so that Elmo could lie close to Eric and watch him through the night. 'Gamma's making us a supper and I have time before the pot boils to run back to the inn and tell your companion that you will stay here the night, and he should make his own arrangement, for we haven't another bed.'

'Thank you, Spider. I imagine he has already made arrangements.'

Spider grinned. 'You saw how he looked at Mary then? Well, he might get an hour or two with her, but not the whole night. She has coin to earn, as do I.'

Supper was a savoury broth, thick with barley, and three-day-old bread, but good enough for dunking. Before he undressed to sleep, Elmo helped Gamma sit Eric up and trickle water into his mouth, which Eric swallowed, though semi-conscious. They laid him back gently and Gamma left them alone. Elmo stripped to his drawers and shirt and settled to sleep, his sword under the blankets with him.

It was at first light when Eric awoke and as he rose from slumber, whimpers of pain grew to cries of agony. Spider came running from his corner pulling his shirt on over his head, but Gamma Westwood did not make an appearance. Spider explained that she was collecting herbs, some of which had to be gathered by moonlight if they were to remain efficacious.

Elmo bathed his brother's brow with cool water, and at last, his softly spoken words broke through Eric's howling and had a calming effect. Eric made a noise that sounded like a question, and Elmo reassured him that he was here and would remain.

Eric reached out a hand and touched Eric's face as if needing proof that his brother really was with him. Elmo took the unsteady hand and kissed the trembling fingertips, and then Eric wept but they were no longer tears of pain but of relief.

'Do you know how to use your grandmother's potions, Spider, for I would relieve my brother's suffering?'

Spider shook his head, his face yellow in the lamplight. 'We mustn't touch her brews, for to use them without lore will kill him as surely as a knife between the ribs.'

Eric tried to say something, but his words were as ruined as his eyes.

'I think he wants to sit up, sir.'

219

'Sir me no more, young Spider. I am Elmo, and please, help me with him.'

When Eric was sitting up, he made a sign with his hands.

'Spider, my brother wants the makings for writing. Does Grandmother Westwood have ink and a pen about the place?'

'Your brother can write?' Spider said, marvelling at the injured young man. He shook off his admiration. 'Gamma can't write no more than me, and sorry sir … Elmo … but we have nothing fit for that purpose, though I might take some soot and … No! Wait a minute, if you would.' Spider flew from the room towards the main door, his shirt flying.

'For pity's sake, put on some drawers before you …'

But it was too late, the door slammed shut and Elmo was left to tend to his brother alone for some time, and so he spoke of the attack on Coquet Island, of his truce with Finn who should be his enemy and of the journey thus far. Spider was gone so long that Elmo went to the door and stepped outside holding up the lamp. He walked a few steps along the path when the slapping of bare feet on stone and a white, ghostlike figure hurrying towards him marked the Spider's return.

'See what I've brought,' Spider said holding out his prizes. 'Slate and chalk. Eric might use these for writing.'

Spider took Elmo's hand and led him back into the house. 'I should have said as I did not, that you must never leave Gamma's house unguided. Her paths are thick-strewn with stray-sods, and anyone stepping upon one will find himself pixie-led and lost in the forest. Nobody can find her house lest she wills it or I lead them.'

Back inside, Eric ceased his whimpering as Elmo and Spider approached, and he was soon propped up, sitting with the rough-hewn slate across his lap. He first wrote that Elmo was in danger from Godwin who would have his head if he knew he still lived. Elmo said what he knew of Godwin, and in their conversation, one side written and one side spoken, Elmo realised it was indeed Godwin they had seen on the road, and that he was riding hard for Ros's Beacon where Brother Mundwyn lay indisposed.

For a while Elmo was undecided and did not know where his duty laid. Was he to find a horse and ride to the beacon, hopefully to find and rescue Mundwyn, or stay with his brother? Well, in the end he knew it must be too late to come to Mundwyn before Godwin and his men, so he chose the path of common sense and decided he would tend to his brother.

Gamma Westwood came home in the early hours and made a wholesome broth which she fed to Eric following a draught to ease his pain, and a salve to numb the stump of his tongue to facilitate eating. He took small amounts and then with difficulty and he choked and gagged often, but he managed to take down enough sustenance to aid his recovery.

Several days past and each day Eric grew stronger and slowly, a little by a little, his pain diminished. On the sixth day, he rose and dressed in a worn-out suit of clothes that Spider had secured as charity from a kind family at Annebelle. That day Eric ate wincing a little but with no cries of pain, and he sat many hours with Elmo in their exchange or words, written and spoken, and once he even laughed, a clear and happy sound that was not marred by his injury. And when Elmo tired of words, Spider proved himself to be a master of tales and told many stories, some of brave knights and adventure, others of elves and spirits, and those with a hilarious and amusing end to them. On the seventh day Eric washed the dirty pots by feel, while Elmo and Spider saw to the daily chores set them by Gamma Westwood.

Spider had become Elmo's shadow and delighted in his company. His friend Elmo was First Born and therefore linked to the mysteries of the world that Gamma dipped into and from which Spider took joy in this world of pain and toil.

On the evening of the seventh day Spider fetched Finn and he brought with him Mary, the young woman from the inn. Finn was quite changed and clearly enamoured of Mary.

221

Mary for her part appeared equally in love with Finn and somewhat in control of the relationship.

'You were a ravening dog and now you are wide-eyed pup,' Elmo said to Finn when Mary had drawn aside to speak with Gamma.

'I suppose you've had her,' Spider said and quickly ducked the blow that Finn aimed at his head.

'"Had" is a taking word, a word of greed and selfishness and an ugly one I will not have you use of my Mary.'

Elmo and Spider exchanged looks and Spider made his eyes cross and then roll, in imitation of the lovelorn fool.

'What we have shared has been freely given and gratefully received,' Finn said, his face softened by a faraway look. 'It is the like of bards' songs, and such as I have never known before nor even knew existed.'

That night Elmo laid in bed in the dark and heard the soft sounds of lovemaking drift over from Spider's corner of the room which Finn and Mary had made their own. He was quickened by desire and thought that he might have to employ that practice that eases the blood, and that Alcuin had assured him was no sin, despite the edicts of the Church.

'Elmo,' came a sharp whisper from close at hand. It was Spider and he stood shivering in his shirt with stray moonbeams alighting on his skin and giving him the appearance of an emaciated ghost. 'I have been put out of my bed by the lovers and now I freeze. What am I to do?'

Elmo knew a hint when he heard one, and lifted his blankets for Spider to slip under. The boy's skin was like ice as he snuggled close for warmth.

'It must fire the blood to hear your friend at such sport, for I know it does mine,' Spider whispered through chattering teeth. 'I'm that hard I could blunt a knife-edge.' He was silent for a moment, as if waiting for Elmo's reply. 'I can bring you a girl, if you like.'

'And then where should you sleep, young man?'

'Never mind me. I'll find somewhere. So, should I fetch someone?'

222

'Thank you Spider, but I wish only to sleep. So, if you wouldn't mind ...'

Spider was quiet again, but not for very long. Meanwhile the soft moans from the corner of the room spoke of such delights that Elmo would cover his head with a pillow or take a dousing in icy water.

'I am very clean, Elmo,' Spider said, his shiver now abated. 'And bathe sometimes twice a week. I am almost without lice and being a pot-boy I have learnt many skills that men find pleasing. So if it is your way to prefer boys, I would happily give myself freely for all the good you have brought to me and mine.'

Elmo smiled. 'My way is be to master of the urges that seek to rule me, but if it was mine to find pleasure in boys, and it is not, I think there should be none more pleasing than you.' Elmo recalled the last words Alcuin had written to him. 'So, dear Spider, we shall be friends who delight in each other's company for its own sake, and I should like it if you become the kind of pot-boy who does not line himself up with the ale and mead to be had by anybody with a coin who pleases, but save yourself for the woman who one day shall become your wife.'

'I am more glad to be your friend than you can know, and I shall try to wait for my wife, but don't make me promise. In all truth it is far too late for that as I have quite a name with the young ladies of Annebelle. As to lining up with the pots, I must eat and food costs, so where else is the coin to come from, for old Wulf gives me barely enough for bread?'

'Why, tell stories of course, for you are skilled in the art of weaving words.'

Spider looked askance, disbelieving. 'People will pay good money for my words?'

'They will! Especially if you entice them with an adventuresome prologue and then make a charge to have the rest of the story.'

Spider's face lit up. 'I can do that!' And then it dipped again. 'But there are things I would miss. Some of the men are exceeding kind to me, and the pleasure is not all that

223

which is taken. Some give back, and though I may be damned for admitting it, it makes me feel … nice. And wanted.'

'And yet when the day is over and passions spent, you are alone and discarded.'

'Ah! But while it lasts, and for a time thereafter, I am as a prince.' Spider sighed. 'Am I to live on bread alone and always be but one step above slave?'

Elmo did not answer.

'Are you not to take me then, this last time I offer, and make me feel like a prince? I have nothing else to give and from you I should like to receive.' Spider said snuggling close.

How to rebuff such a heartfelt if misplaced offer without giving offence? Elmo considered his answer carefully. 'I shall have your heart and your brotherly love, as you already have mine. If that is not enough, young Spider, then I am sorry.'

In the light of a moonbeam that lanced through the thin thatch and made Spider's white skin glow, Elmo saw the spreading gleam of the boy's teeth as he smiled widely.

'It is enough,' Spider said. 'It is all I could ask and more than I could hope for, but what now of this throbbing dragon betwixt my legs?'

Elmo took one deep breath. 'Attend to it in such a discrete and private way as will tame it but not, I pray, in my bed. Whatever, for pity's sake, let me sleep.'

'Very well, then as it is cold beyond these blankets I am minded to leave it neglected and it must return to its slumber un-sated.'

As shall mine, Elmo thought as the sounds of love-play still drifted from the dark corner.

Despite his faithfulness to chastity, that night Elmo was visited by one of Lillith's sisters who brought him dreams of such torrid couplings that he woke the next morning on the heels of a nocturnal climax: spent, wet and sticky.

As Elmo gathered up the sheets to rinse them in the stream, Spider, who was not noted for his discretion so much as his keen eye, commented that he was sure he had not wrestled with the dragon during the night, so he wondered who had, and this said with such a mischievous grin that Elmo was moved to aim a kick at him.

Spider dodged neatly and sang a mocking little rhyme that seemed to mean nothing: *Hinkey-punk, hinkey-punk, follow his light, the First Born to sunshine all others to night.*

After breakfast Gamma Westwood declared Eric's wounds almost healed. 'The tongue heals quickly and thought the hurt and deprivation are great, the loss of eyes leaves but a tiny wound,' she said.

Eric wrote thank you upon his slate, but Gamma looked at the letters as if they were a kind of magic which bemused her.

'He writes "thank you" Grandmother,' Elmo said, and that set Eric nodding enthusiastically. He even managed a smile. 'Now we should think about moving on, before we draw too heavily on your hospitality and outstay our welcome.

'Yes,' Finn said. 'We have a quest I believe, and though I'd rather not leave my Mary, it is the way of the world that I must. So where to, Elmo?'

'I think it might be safe to return to Ros's Beacon, and see if there is any word of Mundwyn, for without him we do not know our way.'

It was then, as if the mention of his name was a magical summons, that there came a loud knock at the door which swung open to reveal Mundwyn standing on the threshold. He looked older, grizzled and hoarier, his white hair windblown and wayward and somewhat of a beard had grown, and it also was white as if touched by frost. Leaves flew about him as if he were sheathed in a whistling wind and then the air calmed and the leaves fell with the folds of his cloak, which was brown. He no longer wore the garb of a monk.

'How came you to my house unguided,' Gamma Westwood said, her voice tremulous though she tried to make it sound fierce.

225

'The Hidden Paths have many branches,' he replied, bowing low before rising to introduce himself. 'And many are the lamps that light the road between friends.'

Spider looked abashed. 'He didn't spy my light, Gamma. Honest he didn't.'

Gamma brought her hand to rest lightly on Elmo's arm and then approached Mundwyn and looked up into his eyes. 'You are not First Born, but I see you have touched First Born lands, and so for this and that you are a friend of Elmo's, be welcome.'

'Thank you, good lady, but I must not tarry. Water and some bread, if I may be so bold as to ask, and then those of us that can we must leave.'

Elmo stepped forward. 'It's good to see you again, Brother Mundwyn, but I'll not leave without Eric, and he is not yet up to adventure.'

'There are ways,' Mundwyn said gravely. 'And we must take them. The sooner the better, for there are enemies hard on my trail.'

Gamma sniffed the air and cocked her head like a dog that has just heard a sound too hushed for any human to notice. 'There's to be a storm,' she said. 'It will be with us before noon and set in for the day.'

She told Mundwyn that he would have to stay until the morrow, and then began grumbling about here lack of sufficient bedding.

'You, little hinkey-punk,' she called to Spider. 'Keep an eye on the paths and if any travellers come before the storm, light them away so that they be lost. And be back before the gales lift you to the treetops.'

Spider scooted out, his footfalls receding rapidly into the wood.

Elmo helped the others prepare Gamma's house for the storm and was kept too busy to question Mundwyn about the pursuers, or about his adventures since they had left him at Ros's Beacon. It was obvious he had somehow evaded capture by Godwin, and it was also fair to assume that it was Godwin or his men who were in pursuit, but he had to wait for answers until the house was as secure as it could be and anything that wasn't stowed away was tied down.

Spider rushed in from a squall and a sudden downpour and slammed the door behind him.

'Don't be dripping on my clean straw,' Gamma yelled and then skelped him on the back of the head before bending him forward and stripping off his sodden tunic. 'You'll catch your death!'

Spider squealed as she caught his back while removing his shirt and he stood shivering until she threw a blanket at him. She would attend to the wounds, she told him, once the chill was out of him.

'There was that sly-looking monk wandering the paths,' Spider said through chattering teeth as he huddled by the cooking fire. 'The one who'd lick-arsed up to the fat lord, but I led him a fine dance and he'll not find us.'

'Good boy,' Gamma said giving him a rough hug that made him squeal anew.

A sudden gust of fearsome wind lifted out some thatch and rain began to come through the roof. Gamma ran to the spot with a cooking pot and set it to catch the water.

By noon the storm was raging. The trees outside thrashed wildly and Elmo prayed they would all be spared from falling branches. It was a little later when the din had settled sufficiently for conversation to be possible that Elmo found the opportunity to question Mundwyn.

Bray and Amberjill, the beacon keeper and his wife, were in the employ of Lord Godwin. The beacon was not, as Elmo had supposed, to be fired if Bray spied ships out to sea, or fyrds approaching from the north or south, but were there to be lit if there came First Born or rather, those who claimed to be First Born for as Godwin had told them, there were no First Born, nor had there ever been, and to speak otherwise was to be a heretic.

As soon as Elmo and Finn began to descend the hill, Bray had set it to fire, for they had Mundwyn a virtual captive, and the boys could be seized later. They had reckoned without knowledge of Mundwyn's rapid recovery or his ability to walk the Paths, and so when they proudly led Godwin and his thegns to the old monk, he was gone.

'I had slipped to a nearby knoll, for I was quite incapable of covering any great distance. I was close enough to see the beacon keeper's house being torched, and thought perhaps I could just discern the old couple being rough handled. Then there was much commotion – swords drawn, challenges called, horses mounted and a seemingly aimless rushing round of warriors. After a while all was silent and I crept back to Ros's Beacon.

'The beacon had almost burnt out and the blackened, heat-split corpse on top of it was Amberjill. Bray, or what was left of him, lay nearby, and sobbing upon the grass sat a stout fellow of perhaps twenty years, and like a young giant. As I was soon to learn, he was just as devoid of intellect.'

The fellow, Mundwyn explained, was Brom the beacon-keeper's son and once he ceased from weeping he told his story. He was returning home with a brace of conies in time to see Godwin strike his father to the ground and then begin beating his mother. Without hesitation he whipped out his sling, fitted a smooth stone and hurled it with all the might of a triple-twist; the missile struck the side of Godwin's temple where the bone is thin and he immediately fell into a swoon.

'His thegns ran hither and thither like chickens devoid of their heads before settling on improving the comfort of their indisposed lord as the best action.'

Godwin rose and in his pained fury ordered the old couple slain. Still groggy he was taken to Bamburgh.

Mundwyn led the giant of a man, who was not of sufficient wits to care for himself, down to Chatton.

'I thought I would find help for him, but once he told his story, against my specific advice, the reeve, no doubt fearing the consequences of inaction, arrested the hapless Brom and had him hanged before night fell. I was, once again, forced onto the Hidden Path.'

'It's Godwin's men who chase you then?' Elmo said.

'No, it is not. The King, being mightily put out by the assault upon his favourite, has set another of his lords

228

against us. Earldorman Dunstan Chase, aptly named, has been charged with bringing our heads before the King.'

'He doesn't care for the rest of our bodies then,' Finn said and began to laugh.

'No,' Mundwyn said. 'Heads will do.'

There came a wordless mumble and Eric held out his slate upon which he had written, 'Godwin dead?'

'Godwin was the murderer of Eric's family,' Elmo told Mundwyn. 'And the tormentor and torturer of my brother.'

Mundwyn shook his head and pulled his cloak about him. 'Godwin lives, but the crack on his head has left him with pain such as makes him cry out, and he wanders his rooms at Bamburgh in his agony unable to find sleep.' He had that information from the herald who brought news concerning the fugitives from the King to the town of Chatton.

'Serves him right!' Finn said and Mary made a little chuckle of agreement. 'I hope his eyes pop out and blood flows from his ears.'

'It is strange how this all plays out,' Elmo said. 'For it was Dunstan Chase who saved my brother's life, and now he means to have our heads.'

The storm had not blown out by nightfall. Gamma Westwood and her guests were worn out and tired form the constant attack upon their nerves and spirit. A branch fell in through the roof and fully a third of Gamma's home was now unusable. Every gust brought indrawn breaths lest another branch should fall and brain them all.

It was very late when Elmo woke from a light sleep to find the wind had died down to a whisper. Finn and Mary were asleep in Spider's bed and Spider had crawled in with Eric. They too slept. Gamma was either snug in a corner somewhere, or she was out in the dark night. Only Mundwyn was awake, and he sat close to the fire, his old face dancing with shadow. Elmo drew close to him and Mundwyn acknowledged his presence with a smile. They sat in silence for a long time and then Elmo asked when they should proceed with the quest.

'First we must get Eric to a friary I know, where the friars are well-versed in the medical arts.'

'Is it the place of the Blue Friars, your former home?'

Mundwyn nodded and smiled and then fixed his eyes back onto the flames.

'It will be good to meet your friends – your brothers.'

'And yet we may not stay, not even for a night. As soon as Eric is safe, we must make for Skol-Jerrag.'

Elmo looked into the flames too, and tried to imagine what dear Alcuin was doing and whether he still thrived in the court of the great King Charles. 'It would be good to see friends again,' Elmo whispered, but not so softly that Mundwyn's keen ears did not pick up his words.

'Your thoughts are of Alcuin, are they not?'

Elmo nodded for an answer, not trusting his voice to hold true. His eyes began to sting and his nose tingled. He sniffed.

'I shall make a prediction, that I know shall come true,' Mundwyn said. 'And that is, before you go to the realm of the First Born you shall have a friend again, such as Alcuin, and that friend is presently under Grandma Westwood's roof, pray that it remain a roof until morning.'

Elmo heard Finn snoring. He no longer hated him, and if he ignored the boorish manners that were apparently traits of his race, he even quite liked him. In the days ahead, with dangers faced together and adventures shared, perhaps he would come to love him as he loved Alcuin. But somehow, he felt not. His slain brothers would always stand between them.

They set off next afternoon after helping Gamma clear up the storm damage. They had a larger party than they had planned, for Mary would not be left, and nor would Spider.

'A party of six, and three of us hale warriors, will make any brigands think before having at us.' Spider strapped on a rusty seax.

'You, a warrior?' Gamma said. 'A griggling-warrior perhaps.' She hugged him tight and tucked a loaf inside his tunic. 'Now be off with you, and come back with a fortune.'

'Our first stop must be Annebelle,' Mundwyn said. 'And there to make supply.'

'Spider,' Elmo said. 'I should be obliged if you lead my brother.'

Spider grinned widely and Elmo believed, correctly, that should he ask Spider to lie upon flinty ground there to roll a while, he would do so smiling.

~ 2009 ~
Dr Smith Pulls Some Strings

Perhaps it was the wine, but I did not sleep well that night. Raz and I had solved the riddle and we stood on a sturdy stair leading straight up to success, but success was a slippery customer who'd often escaped me before I'd seized a firm hold. What if the board forbade us to continue with our research, or the minister for Historic Scotland withheld scheduled monument consent? Maybe Lord James would lodge an official complaint over our alteration of the book. As I drifted off, all these questions and more buzzed around my skull like a demented swarm of wasps, frequently augmented by acute feelings of failure concerning my marriage and my soon-to-be former wife, not to mention my concerns over the misinterpretations being heaped on my current domestic arrangements.

On one point, at least, I needn't have worried. Despite his imported, spike-laden tyres, the courier did not make it to Lord James's family seat. That information was to come later, and bring its own share of gloom. There had been an accident just outside Hexham, or so we were led to believe, which involved a heavy lorry rear-ending the courier's car and splitting the fuel tank. Nobody was hurt, thank goodness, but as soon as the drivers had got clear the car went up in flames taking the only known copy of *Raven-Fish!* with it. We were not to know that until after a long day of form-filling as required by the laws pertaining to ancient monuments and excavations.

Raz and I spent a second day at home. Once the call came that our attendance was not required, we set-to with the paperwork even though we quite obviously hadn't carried out any preliminary surveys. We figured that permission would take at least a couple of months, and felt we could fit in a sneaky semi-official survey in the meantime, so long as we could get the permission of the land owner.

Some of the questions on the supplementary form for excavations were a bit tricky, such as naming the academic objectives of the proposed dig and detailing the funding, but Raz and I overcame such difficulties by use of lateral thinking. Oh very well, call it deception if you must, but just for a moment, pretend you are the appropriate minister poised with your pen ready to either approve or deny permission and you read that the objective is to unearth a hollow stone containing a work by Alcuin of York that will change our whole perspective on the Dark Ages. Are you going to set your name to the approval of a scheduled monument consent form, or pick up the phone to your colleague in the Health Ministry and nominate a candidate for electric shock treatment?

In all honesty, and I say this without crossed fingers, our deception was only in the omission of the specific objective, for the objectives we listed were generic and somewhat bland. It helped our cause that the hill fort in question hadn't been visited by archaeologists for over thirty years and even then only by way of a light survey.

We were all done by 5pm. I'd volunteered to do dinner but I was tired, so something simple: a *chilli-con-carne* bubbled away in the oven and I was taking out the wine glasses when the phone went. Raz was taking a shower, so I answered.

'Ah, Professor, how are you old chap?'

I wonder if telephone microphones are sensitive enough to pick up the grinding of teeth. 'Dr Smith, I presume? Very well thank you. I take it you wish to speak to Mr Reeves?'

There was a moment's silence. 'Well, I had expected him to answer, but either of you will do.'

Smith then went on to tell me about the disaster concerning the destruction by fire of *Raven-Fish!* I was of course shocked, and part of me felt like an old friend had passed away, but the other part wanted to shriek 'In your face Smith! See how far you can get without the book!'

233

Instead I expressed disappointment and asked him how he had come to learn of the book in the first place.

I should have guessed really. Alerted by the system's administrator who had seen my e-mail to Lord James, Smith had been snooping round the bastle dig, ostensibly to check out our application of the Harris Matrix (which wasn't even applicable to our kind of dig), and Jack Taylor had regaled him with all the information he had given me and no doubt, the doctor had followed the same leads together with those from the system's admin girl and wound up knocking on the palatial front door of Lord James.

I picked a washed-out sweatshirt from the mountain of clean laundry that had accumulated by the fire. It would grow until either Raz or I cracked under the strain and took on the job we both hated. I toyed with the sweatshirt absently while I listened to Old Smarmy twittering on.

Smith then expressed disappointment that I had not immediately declared the presence of the book and included it in my list of finds. I calmly explained that a fantasy novel written in 1936 hardly qualified as an archaeological find. He told me not to be obtuse, and instead of telling him to go roll in broken glass, I remained silent.

'The question is, old boy, will you share your findings to date, concerning anything that might have been in the book – *"Raven-Fish!"* wasn't it?'

Piss off, you slimy bastard! 'Of course I will, Doctor, just as soon as I've written it up in a presentable manner.'

'I was thinking earlier than that, such as straight away. Just e-mail the draft and any notes you might have in document form to my office and that will abrogate the need for me to make anything official *vis-à-vis* your failure to register the find.'

'Piss off, you slimy bastard!' I said, and slammed the receiver down. 'Vis-à-fucking-vis!' I hissed to myself. Well, not quite to myself. Raz was behind me, hair dripping and dressed in those God-awful threadbare boxers. Did he only have one pair, for Christ's sake? He dabbed at his hair with an equally tatty bath towel.

'Now let me guess, apro-fucking-pros nothing,' Raz said while he dabbed his face. 'Doc Smith?'

'The very same.' I outlined his threat while Raz towelled his hair.

'Total load of hot air, Prof.'

I had to smile; Raz was comfortable enough with me to walk round in his shorts, but still couldn't seem to get to grips with my first name.

'He hasn't got any grounds for complaint,' Raz continued. 'Well, not until you gave him a mouthful. He certainly can't make anything of you failing to mention your bedtime reading, because when you come right down to it, there's not a lot more to *Raven-Fish!* I mean, there is, but nothing you can prove now the book's gone up in flames.'

'Me and my big mouth,' I said. 'He's so far up Chair's arse that his heels hardly show. I suppose I can expect a lecture when I get back to the office.'

'How about I give him a call and tell him you've got after-effects from your bash on the head and it's given you a form of Tourette's?'

'How about I tell him the same myself, and spice it up with sufficient bad language to prove the point?' I performed a stage-cough and made it sound like 'arsehole'.

'How about I get dressed and you head back to the kitchen and see to dinner. It smells great but isn't there a hint of 'burnt' about it?' Raz grabbed his jeans from where they were warming in front of the fire and slipped into them. He snagged one foot and fell into the pile of clean washing. 'Who's doing the ironing?' he said ... which I took to be my cue to leave as soon as possible and tend to dinner.

While we were waiting to hear from Historic Scotland, domestic life took on a kind of routine. It was my early morning job to sweep out the ashes of the library fire while Raz worked on the living room. The central heating was mainly kept on tick-over to keep the chill out of the halls and upstairs rooms, but the library and main receptions relied on wood-burning fires for heat. Through a forester friend of Raz's we were kept in good supply of logs, and once the ashes were swept, I'd collect the day's supply from the storage shed outside. I became quite an expert in setting fires.

A set of papers came through from the divorce solicitors and Jenny and I had several telephone conversations which were surprisingly convivial. Even so, the whole situation was depressing and it made our previous life together seem unreal, like reading about a period in history that you had never experienced. Suddenly I realised how little I had ever known Jenny.

Raz worked out his two weeks and unbeknown to me made the very best use of the time he had left. When we needed them most, it transpired that Raz had secured a very useful collection of archaeological tools, including a 'last-season' but still perfectly serviceable set of geophys instrumentation and some useful software. Apparently people found it very difficult to say no when Raz asked for a long-term loan of the equipment. It was all the easier because everyone thought Raz had been badly treated by the board and they were pleased to help where they could.

Dr Smith began to be a persistent pain in the arse rather than a distant unpleasant smell. I got more than a whiff of him as he got Chair in on his plan to secure the transcripts of *Raven-Fish!* It got so bad that I considered writing another story altogether, calling it *Raven-Fish!* and sending it to him, just so that he would shut up.

It was in the first week of March that I was hit with a double whammy. I was called to an extraordinary meeting of the board and advise that I might like to bring a union rep with me. The first thing I thought was 'Bloody Smith!' And then I wondered if I had put Chair's nose out of joint by continuing to sign Raz in as a guest when I needed him at the lab. As far as I could see I hadn't broken any rules at all. As is nearly always the case when you're hit with this kind of thing, the cause is never what you expect.

Chair expressed his disappointment that I had failed, after numerous requests, to supply information that I had obtained through my professional research whilst employed in that capacity by the board. I was depriving the faculty of intellectual information that belonged to them, and that my continual prevarication represented misconduct for which I was to receive a written warning.

If I thought the storm clouds were gathering, the sky was split by lightning on the following Friday. I received a court order demanding that I release the required information or else stand in breach.

What nefarious moves were afoot? Who was behind all this, as if I didn't know? But the real question was, why? Why had Smith brought in the big guns just to secure the transcript of a work of fiction?

Raz and I became a little … no, more than a little nervous. And the nerves led to paranoia, at least in my case. What if, Dan Smith like, there were forces that didn't want us to find Alcuin's book? Maybe Alcuin's book was another *Da Vinci Code,* or rather, a true version.

'Do you think *Raven-Fish!* could be true?' I asked. It was a bright evening in early spring and we'd decided to climb the big hill in the middle of town, through the ornamental gardens.

'Prof, you are funny.'

I acknowledged my eccentricity.

'Of course it's true,' Raz said.

There he was again, fishing for a rise. Always testing my gullibility.

On top of the hill in the tussocky grass we stood in silence for a moment while the sun set and enjoyed the bird's eye view of town. It was up on that hill we decided our next move. They could have the damned transcript. What good would it do them? I was not about to get arrested for breaching a court order. No, they'd have their transcript, but as for the clues, I would deny they had ever existed.

The week was not over. Saturday morning brought an unexpected phone call. It was Gwen McCreedy and she asked if we could meet, somewhere away from campus – away from the city altogether if possible. This was getting very creepy. I invited to over to our place and such was my comfort that I did not feel the need to check with Raz first.

'She's probably going to give me a slap,' Raz said grinning. 'She'll be all "Naughty, naughty Razzy! How dare you spoil my nice DNA sample?" Don't you think?'

It couldn't have been further from the truth. Gwen arrived for afternoon tea. I had already acknowledged the court order and posted off copies of the transcript, as required, to Chair and to Dr Smith and had just got back from the Post Office.

Gwen was maybe five years younger than me, very slender with a short cut for a woman, with a fringe and long at the sides. Her blond hair was flecked with grey, and she wore light-framed spectacles. Always formidable and forthright in the work situation, she appeared rather uncertain of herself and a little shy. I found her quite attractive.

After the preliminary niceties, she asked me what I knew about Blyth Hill Fort.

Raz and I exchanged glances. How on earth had she found out about it?

'I understand you've submitted an application to carry out a dig?'

I could not deny it.

'Well, sorry to say, the application will be turned down. Don't ask! We all have friends and contacts, and I have one who is an archaeologist north of the border.'

'Do you happen to know why it will be turned down?'

'Of course I do. It clashes with another application that has better merits than yours and is backed by a major university.'

I felt my heart sink. Raz was staring into his coffee looking glum.

'Hazarding a remote guess, this university has associations with a certain Dr Smith?'

Gwen pulled a face of mild disgust, dare I hope at the sound of that name which always elicits the same from me. 'As I said, we all have friends and contacts, not excluding Dr Smith. The word is that his application will be passed before the end of the month.'

Bugger that scenario all the way to Hell! It was not that I thought Smith was going to steal my Sutton Hoo. No, it had gone far beyond that. In my mind Smith had assumed the proportions of an anti-Christ. He wanted to find Alcuin's book before I did so he could repress it. If Smith had shown his smirking face at that moment I swear I would have strangled him with my bare hands.

We spent the next hour catching up and the conversation was quite convivial. Gwen seemed to have forgiven Raz for contaminating the DNA sample, and we got to see a side of her that she chose not to bring to work. I must have been a bore because all I could think about was Smith.

'Table for four at Eshott Hall?' Raz said just as I closed the front door, having waved Gwen off. 'Mine's the pheasant in paprika cream.'

'What *are* you talking about?' As if I didn't know.

'You and Gwen, me and Jacquie. After this afternoon I thought we might make a good foursome. Methinks Gwen has designs on the Prof.'

'You told me your arrangement with Jacqueline was based strictly on mutual biological needs.' Raz and Jacqui did not go out together so much as stay in, and even then only about one in every three or four weeks when the scenario played out very much as it had done at Christmas.

'Dinner would be nice too, and I believe eating qualifies as a biological need.'

I think Raz was trying to divert my attention, but all I could think about was Dr Smith and *his* designs on *our* research. I wonder now if I had gone a little insane. I really do. There cannot really be any other explanation. All the frustrations, slights and hurts of the last thirty years were concentrated into the next few moments.

My next plan for action was so against the grain that I really cannot believe I was still in control of myself. Old Prof with his rules; old Prof who did things by the book: I was about to use the rule book for toilet paper and take some unforgivable actions. We had already planned on doing a preliminary survey, but next morning Raz's Land

239

Rover was loaded up with equipment, and we were heading north towards Jedburgh to carry out a completely unsanctioned dig.

Completely illegal and appalling behaviour I know, and all mine. I'll not have it any other way but that Raz was swept up by my actions, sucked into the raging tornado, all resistance futile. When the time comes I shall throw myself upon the mercy of the court. Raz must not suffer for my lamentable folly.

We passed through Jedburgh, Melrose and Galashiels and pressed on deep into Borders country. We had an early pub lunch at an inn that still sported an old water wheel, eating mostly in silence. I was contemplating the enormity of our imminent actions and I guess Raz was doing the same. For hardened criminals and even soft-boiled ones, digging a few illegal holes in the ground might not seem like the crime of the century, but to me ... well, it was if I was about to take a lump-hammer to the body-casts at Pompei. The Rubicon for me was a short stretch of the A701, and I was about to cross it.

We approached the hill fort on foot for there was no road. It was a gentle walk from the east and I tingled with excitement. Raz carried the geophys gizmos and I toted a couple of shovels and carried other tools in my trusty faded khaki webbing gasmask bag.

As hill forts go it was modestly proportioned, a couple of hundred feet across, and the concentric ramparts were clear to the archaeologist's eye. Some showed signs of plough damage but the general layout was not difficult to discern.

I wandered around slowly, taking it all in. Was this really Skol-Jerrag, a home to those illusive people, the Beaker Folk, whom Bennett had given mythical status as the First Born? Not just Bennett, for the grave marker had made reference to the First Born. Raz was fiddling with the GPS device while I soaked up the atmosphere, artificially imbued with the fictions of *Raven-Fish!* My ebullience was further buoyed by the stunningly beautiful views of the surrounding

240

hills and the brilliant sunshine: I knelt to thrust my fingers into the grassy earth. A moment of perfection.

'Hey Prof,' Raz said making me jump. 'It turns out that our grid reference is a little to the south west of the actual fort. To be spot on we have to go down that slope a short way.'

'So be it then.' I stood and winced at the pain in my knees. 'Zero us in and then we can use this ground radar thing you purloined.'

'Borrowed, Prof,' Raz said. 'It's all perfectly above board.'

'It a shame the rest of our venture isn't quite so squeaky clean.'

The slope was hardly precipitous but it was a little too steep to call it a stroll. When we were at the exact centre of the point that showed our grid reference, the gradient eased a little but only just.

Raz began to prepare the instrumentation while I put in some guide lines – string held in place by tent-pegs. 'It's kind of lucky that the grid number fits the clues so well, considering whatever might be under this turf was buried over a thousand years before the grid system was invented.'

I'd wondered about that. 'Maybe Bennett was involved in setting the Ordnance Survey system up and somehow influenced it.'

It has to be said, geophys does not always – or even often – give you what you want or expect. This time it did. Raz surveyed an area fifteen yards across with our grid reference at the centre. When we plugged into the laptop, we saw an image that looked very like a grave, right where we hoped it would be.

We returned to the spot with our shovel and spade and stood there for several moments saying nothing.

'It's now or never,' Raz said. 'And I feel as if I've waited forever already.' He placed the spade to the turf, put his heel on the blade and put all his weight onto it. The blade sank, and the ghostly denizens of Hell did not fly up, filling the sky, while shrieks and wails did not echo around the hillside.

None of those effects were necessary as they were all supplied by my imagination.

We cut the turfs with care and set them aside so that we could replace them, and we made a neat pile of the claggy earth we excavated. At a depth of no more than six inches we came to a slab of stone, saved from the plough only because the plough did not venture onto such inclines. Within an hour we had the top and sides of what could be nothing other than a grave of roughhewn slabs. We knew what to expect from the closing pages of *Raven-Fish!* Inside I knew we would find a skeleton or the trace of one, and below that the stone containing Alcuin's book. I was trembling all over, trying not to anticipate the impossible … and failing miserably. After all these years …

'It'll be nothing but mush by now,' Raz said, proving to me that his thoughts followed the same path as mine. 'A thousand years of damp soil. It couldn't be anything else.'

'And yet,' I said, hoping my words would not jinx the reality. 'And yet in the story Brother Mundwyn sealed the stone shut with molten lead, so there might be a slim chance.'

As we lifted the grave's top-stone I was hit with a wave of emotion. As we lay the stone aside and the facial bones of a skull emerged proud of the surrounding silt, the pricking inside my nose rose to my eyes as tears. I knew who this boy was and how he came to be here, and it was all too much.

My world was here, under this Scottish soil, and nothing else mattered or registered beyond the peripheral. Not the cawing of the crows that circled above, nor the bleating of the distant sheep, and certainly not the approach of many footsteps.

There were five of them: an officer from Historic Scotland; a local archaeologist; a young police constable and a slightly older sergeant. And Dr Smith. My first thought was that I had never before seen policemen wearing Wellington boots.

I can't remember their opening gambit although I'm sure there was one, such as 'What the Hell do you think you're doing? or 'Do you have authority?' … Quite frankly it's all a bit of a blur. My clearest memory is of both the archaeologist and the officer from Historic Scotland dropping to their knees and ogling our find with nothing short of delight. It was Smith that had to remind them that I was in breach of Section 35 of something or other and that I had committed wilful damage. The officer rose somewhat reluctantly, dusted off his knees, and confirmed that I was in breach and the sergeant said he didn't know about that but it was definitely criminal damage. He gave the young constable a meaningful stare whereupon Raz and I were both arrested.

'Don't stop at the skeleton,' I implored of the archaeologist. I'm sure he thought I was a few metatarsals short of a full foot. 'There's something more below.'

The policemen then debated for a moment or two whether we should be taken to Peebles or Hawick Police Station until the sergeant said as it was a bit out from the Bridge it had better be Hawick. It's funny how you remember certain details and completely forget others. For example, I clearly recall the miniature TARDIS-like police call box outside the entrance to the police station, but the inside of the custody suite is all a bit of a blur.

We were treated well and it is fair to say the officer's dealing with us seemed a bit bemused. Not the usual run-of-the-mill hooligans, I would imagine. We were interviewed and bailed to return on a date in April, and when we were released the police retained our shovels and geophys instrumentation as evidence, but let me keep my bag of smaller tools.

While we were inside, a traffic policeman had given Raz's Land Rover the once over and warned him that his windscreen wipers were close to being illegal and that he should change them in the near future.

On the journey home, we covered miles in silence. I felt a heavy sense of loss and a kind of stupefying numbness. We were way south of Jedburgh by the time I had emerged sufficiently from my muddy wallow of self-pity to apologise to Raz.

243

'Prof, I'm not a six-year-old. I went along with you because I wanted to. We're in this together and if you hadn't suggested the dig, I would have.'

Another two miles of contemplative silence. 'I just can't *bear* the thought of that bastard getting hold of Alcuin's book,' I said. 'But if he does I hope he publishes. I'd rather he publishes than suppresses.'

'He's the kind of man who won't be able to resist publishing, and he can't do that without giving you full acknowledgement.'

'Unless, of course, his whole aim is to suppress Alcuin's work. Maybe there are still those who hold dear to the First Born Heresy. And anyway Raz, if there is acknowledgement to be had it is ours, yours and mine, not *just* mine.'

We got home tired and disheartened. I showered and came down to a roaring fire and a large glass of claret. Raz thought we should drink to the boy in the grave near the top of Blyth Hill, faithful guard to Alcuin's book, *The Truth of the First Born*, until beyond the passing of an age.

'I wonder if the dig will reveal any more truths from *Raven-Fish!*' I said.

'An arrow head, perhaps.'

'Or the slash across the jaw.' We drank to the faithful guard and once again I recalled those final sad pages from *Raven-Fish!* 'You know, whatever it says or does not say in *The Truth of the First Born*, Jason Bennett still had to have yet another source for all his information. Perhaps we'll never know.'

A smile spread slowly across Raz's face. 'Or there again, maybe we will.'

A couple of days later I came home early with all my office-based belongings in a cardboard box. I had been suspended pending any possible police prosecution and informed that I should expect dismissal for gross misconduct and bringing the faculty into disrepute if I was convicted of any criminal offence. Even if there was no conviction I should be prepared for a misconduct hearing. Raz was out with his friends from *Granite Harp Strings* and on the TV news, a story was breaking about a mass shooting in Germany. I was at my lowest ebb and I flopped into a chair before the TV and watched the news channel. I hadn't even taken my coat off before I was caste into a geriatric Holden Caulfield moment.

In my wallowing self-pity I knew why that kid had gone ape with daddy's gun. I've known that kind of anger, never felt it more keenly than when I was seventeen. It's all the lies! All the damned lies we're fed. I suppose, when it gets more than you can bear and the switch flips, you take it out on somebody or something ... or in my case, myself. I had a horrible feeling of certainty that I shared something with a boy who would always be remembered with hatred, as a no-hope-loser who tried to murder his way out of the trap.

Isn't it strange that you can know something with certainty in one frame of mind that seems ridiculous in another?

Raz was due home at seven. He phoned to say he'd bring back a takeaway and maybe a couple of his friends from the band. I had met them all and got on with them, but not that night. I didn't think I'd be very good company.

I wonder if Raz read my thoughts. He came home alone, except for the very large bag of fish and chips. It was a night for slumming it. It was a night for comfort food.

'Any news about Doc Smith? Has he announced any finds yet?'

'No Raz, and Gwen's got her ears to the ground. She is aware that something is going on, but the Scottish office is all a bit hush-hush.'

Raz screwed up his empty chip bag and tossed it into the fire where is sizzled briefly. He let out a big sigh. 'Well, I don't know about you, but I could do with some cheering up. It's your birthday Friday after next. We should celebrate.'

What's to celebrate? Another year closer ...

The day before my birthday the summonses arrived. Our bail to return to Hawick Police Station was cancelled. Instead we were to appear at Peebles Sheriff Court on charges relating to our unsanctioned dig. I'd hoped we might get away with a caution.

245

'Don't worry, Raz. I'll take full responsibility.'

'I appreciate the gesture, but we're not going through that again.'

'You don't want a criminal record. It can be extremely restrictive.'

'That's assuming we get convicted. I'm pleading not guilty. We didn't damage anything. In fact we uncovered something rather amazing. I think they'll have trouble making anything stick.'

Friday morning. It was my birthday and another year closer: fifty-six and well past the half-way mark of a very optimistic life span. Career in tatters; facing a criminal hearing and soon to be divorced. Quite possibly the defining moment of my career hijacked by my arch-rival. I don't think it was possible for me to fall any lower. Happy birthday to me.

The plan was I'd meet up with Raz in town where *Granite Harp Strings* were doing a gig. It was good to see them in action and to see how well the crowd received them. Raz played viola and yet it was a modern band, the style being what you might call modern-folk-rock-pop or perhaps Indy, not that I have a clue what that means.

Raz and I went on from there to dinner at a restaurant – his treat – and then it was back home. We kicked off our shoes at the door and hung up our coats.

'Time for your present,' Raz said leading me into the library. He threw a couple of logs onto the fire.

'Present?' I wonder if he'd guessed I'd bought him something too. After all, we were both facing many of the same challenges, and he needed cheering up just as much as I. 'You paid for dinner. I didn't expect a present as well.'

'Well, you're getting one anyway. Catch!'

I caught the little wooden box that sailed through the air and saved it from diving into the flames of the library fire. I was intrigued, and a little embarrassed; the box was embossed *John Greed Design* in gold lettering and hinted of something expensive in the jewellery line.

It was in fact a ring, zirconium I was to learn later. Silver and lustrous graphite in colour, it was engraved with

246

the Roman numerals for 1666. I loved it. Still do. It was a perfect fit for the ring finger of my right hand and like my wedding ring it hasn't come off since it was first put on.

I thanked him and told him it couldn't be better, representing as it did, our adventures together. 1666, the Miraculous Year; we'd had the best part of a miraculous year ourselves. 'I've got something for you too,' I said after naming my new piece of jewellery *Orbis Mirabilis*.

'Why? It's not my birthday until the beginning of June.'

'It won't wait,' I said, chucking him the white carrier bag with the glossy black CK printed on the side. I'd given him a week's supply of designer underwear with absolutely no fear that he would think it odd or misconstrue it. In fact, it is harder for me to write it down than it was to give the gift. I know Raz. I don't know my readers.

Raz peeped into the bag and then threw back his head and laughed. Turning his back he dropped his trousers and changed into a pair of his new underwear, the length of his shirt-tail preserving his modesty, before holding up his old boxers that might once have been navy but were now faded sky blue with a saggy elastic waist band. He then approached the fire with all the ceremony due to such a faithful pair of drawers and gave them a Viking burial – a kind of Marks & Spencer *Up Helly Ar*.

'Get the others,' I said through laughter. 'Kill them all off in one go.'

'What others?' Raz said. 'They were my only pair.'

And he was at it again, trying to fool his old Prof.

It was then that I was struck with a lightning bolt of life-changing clarity. Here was my Arthur. He was flesh and blood, not dusty old bones. And here was my Sutton Hoo, a place where I was accepted: full of warmth, and not a wormy old tomb with skeletons gone to dust. Unbidden, thoughts of Alcuin's lost letter to Elmo came to me, and I knew then that Alcuin and I had a lot in common, as did Elmo and Raz. Despite everything I experience a brief flash of perfection and in that moment life couldn't be better.

That night I stayed up when Raz went to bed, and opened up a word document. *This was not going to be my Sutton Hoo*, I wrote. And, *Where was my Arthur? This wasn't him ...*

It's taken me a few weeks but it's done, and the day after tomorrow I'm due in court. In many ways my life is coming to an end. I don't really care about the outcome very much. I don't really care about anything anymore, at least none of the concerns that used to rule me. At last, I get it. I really *get* it. At least, I think I do.

And now I'm on a threshold. Something old is dying and the new is about to be born. Godot is knocking at the front door, but I can't help wondering if the Fat Lady is about to sing an encore.

Raz has just been in peering over my shoulder.

'You're done then,' he said.

'I'm almost done. I've got to check it for typos.'

'What are you going to do with it?'

'I haven't decided yet, apart from sending Rachel a copy. It's great just to have finished it.'

'That's good, because tomorrow I want to take you somewhere. And if there's anything you truly value and wouldn't want to lose, bring it with you.'

'This,' I said holding up my right hand and wiggling my ring finger.

Raz clucked his tongue and rolled his eyes. 'Something else,' he said.

I opened the desk draw and fumbled around. 'This,' I said holding up the trowel I'd had ever since student days.

'Perfect,' Raz said smiling.

He won't say where we're going. I'll have to wait until tomorrow, and tomorrow is an age away.

Today is now, and now my story ends.

XVI

~ 793 ~
In which the Raven flies and the Fish swims

Earldorman Dunstan Chase sat on a throne-like wooden chair placed in the centre of the roughly constructed dais. That would have been enough to reflect his status and he wished he had not insisted on wearing armour. After sitting in judgement over so many for so long, the weight of the iron-ringed byrnie was beginning to drag on his shoulders. At least the large tent, which served as a field-courthouse, was airy and cool.

They had saved the most interesting case for late in the afternoon. Four men from his fyrd had been charged with raping the womenfolk of the blacksmith's household. It was a simple case for they had been caught in the act, too addled by ale to be furtive in their crime. It was a shame, for when large numbers of men were brought together and fired up for battle, mischief was always inevitable. The trick was to catch early offenders and set an example.

The defendants stood bound in hempen rope and dressed in shirts and drawers, for that's how they were taken by the watch. Two of the men were very young and the other two at, or perhaps a little past, their prime. Chase was not in the least surprised when his thegns pronounced all four guilty.

'Tell me,' Chase said. 'What is known of the prisoners before me?'

Brand Buckley made his report. 'All have served you well as soldiers. Both the older men are married, sir. Finian has a wife and five children living. Rand is bereft of his wife but has four children. The young men, Hugh and Acwel are unwed. Acwel had a brother who was a novice monk on Holy Island. The Northmen drowned the poor lad.'

'Then Acwel, you shall soon be reunited with your brother.'

Acwel's head fell and he began to tremble.

249

Dunstan Chase began to rise from his chair even as he gave out the sentences. He couldn't be away too soon, for he had grown bored with the dispensing of justice.

'The two young men shall hang forthwith. The two older shall be scourged around camp until their backs be bloody and then to have their noses slit, the means to commit a like offence removed and the letter for rapist burned upon their foreheads. Should they survive they may return to support of their families. Let it be done.'

Brand sidled up and spoke quietly. 'Have I heard correct? Hang the young and mark the older? For in a similar case you recently sentenced the older to hang and …'

Chase held up his hand for silence. 'That was last time,' he said. 'This time I choose to be merciful to the young.'

He hopped down from the dais when the reeve called out. There was one more prisoner.

'By Hell's teeth!' Dunstan Chase swore. 'What crime?' he asked as he continued to make for the exit.

'He stole chickens, sir.'

'Is he guilty?'

'Feathers were stuck about his clothing and there was grease upon his chin.'

Chase called the sentence over his shoulder, forgetting the prisoner had not yet been found guilty. 'A scourging then and brand him as a thief.'

With the tent behind him and Brand Buckley in close attendance, Chase felt pleased that he had such a keen and fair sense of justice, but glad that it was all over for another week. His mood was soured somewhat when he noticed one of Godwin's popinjay knights hurrying towards him.

'Sir,' said the splendidly armoured thegn as he bowed low. 'My Lord Godwin has taken a turn for the worse. The physic fears he will not survive the night.'

Chase suppressed the urge to smile. 'And has he regained the use of his tongue?'

'He has not, my Lord. If anything, his speech was more mumbled, before he became unconscious, as if he had taken too much wine.'

'I shall attend to him directly,' Chase said and then dismissed the knight.

'How perfect the world is sometimes,' Chase said to Buckley. 'Godwin's last action was to blind and delinguinate a perfectly innocent and respectable lad, and from a knock on the head by a peasant's stone, darkness slowly falls over his eyes and he loses the power of speech. Now tell me there is no such thing as divine justice, Buckley.'

'It comes, sir, but in my experience not often enough,' Bland said curtly

'Ah! You like it not that the boys will hang?'

'They served you well as rear-guard. They were led astray by the elder men and now they must die while their wicked elders live.'

'If their elders don't die worm-eaten, for few survive such cuts.'

'Nevertheless ...'

The sound of the older men screaming at the biting of whips sliced through the camp. 'Oh very well then, Buckley, I am in a fine mood. If the lads aren't already swinging, intercede and commute my sentence. Have them gelded and then let them be got to a monastery where they will likely learn soon enough what it is to be raped.'

Brand Buckley ran back into camp, the rings of his byrnie jingling, and Chase attended to Godwin, the King's thegn, once so high and now brought low.

Godwin lay in a bed surrounded by candles with the golden cross of the Lord Jesus Christ on the wall at his head. A robed man and two thegns were in attendance.

'My lord, you come too late. It has pleased the Lord to take his good and faithful servant Godwin unto his eternal reward.'

Dunstan Chase sniffed the air. 'And yet the vapours are more of brimstone than sweet unction. Mayhap the Devil has claimed him.'

The physic let out a whimper and stopped his ears, but the thegns exchanged knowing grins.

Dunstan picked up the dead man's dagger and drew the blade, which was broken at the tip. He had been there when

251

Godwin stabbed one of the two young First Born brothers, snapping the tip on one of the boy's bones.

'Bury him now,' Chase ordered. 'And make sure your put this dagger in with him, so that he may be recognised for who he is, and that is the brave slayer of boys.'

'My lord,' began one of the thegns. 'By the King's order we are too give our services to you, now that Godwin has passed, and we are to remind you that as soon as camp is broken, you are to renew your search for Elfgar, son of Elfward, one time King and traitor.'

The hackles rose on Chases back. 'You are the King's voice?'

The thegn bowed low and Chase's ire was soothed. 'No, sir, only his humble messenger, and now yours to command.'

Chase circled the room slowly. 'Where shall we bring the boy when he is found?'

'The King wants only his head, to be brought before him at Bamburgh.'

'Then it shall be done.'

Outside Brand Buckley was waiting. He was smiling so Chase knew he had saved the boys from death, unless their wounds become corrupted and death took them anyway.

Corruption and death. How he missed Frelaf Helton, one day hale and hearty, and four days later dead of an infected tooth.

'Your orders, sir?' Buckley said.

'The Northmen are long gone, so we strike camp. Disperse the fyrd to their wives and families and wish them my luck with the harvest. As for us, no such luxury, for tomorrow we renew our brave and noble quest to find and murder a lad.'

Buckley's face dropped. 'Oh. I had thought with Godwin's death that loathsome task may be forgot.'

'And so thought I, but it was not to be. Never mind Brand, you sensitive soul, when the time comes I shall strike off the boy's head. You don't even have to watch. And I will contrive to take him by surprise so that death precedes any chance of fear.'

Despite his initial enthusiasm, Spider turned back for home a day out from Annebelle. He said Gamma was old and would fare ill without him, and he seemed to diminish the further he strayed from the wood. Elmo was sorry to see him go, for he had grown fond of the lad and his ever cheerful presence.

It took another eight days, riding to the south and west, until Mundwyn was able to lead his small party into Faennas Sandrin, the place where the monks of his Order lived, and they were very thankful that the ponies they had purchased were sound and the little covered wain sturdily put together. They had left the kingdom of Northumbria and come into the land of Mercia where Mundwyn was recognised by a march-ward and welcomed heartily.

Eric had weathered the long journey well and if anything he had grown stronger and more tolerant of his infirmities. He now carried a small slate about his neck on a length of twine, and chalk in his pouch and had learned to draw pictures of his need for those who could not read. The night before they had crossed into Mercia they had come to an inn and he had ordered food for the entire party by such means. It had greatly lifted his spirits.

Mundwyn and his party were given a warm welcome by the brothers of Faennas Sandrin. Also food, ale and wine aplenty. Elmo was hugely relieved when the monks agreed to take Eric in as one of their own and find him useful employ.

That evening when all had eaten their fill and after vespers, Mundwyn took Elmo to a lake that lay within the boundaries of Faennas Sandrin, and at once Elmo discerned an uncanny affinity with the water that reflected the moon and the stars.

'Listen!' Elmo said. Can you hear it ... *feel* it almost?'

'No, for I am not of your kind, but I brought you here so you might know the experience.'

253

'I've known if before, when I was very small. It's a place where I may cross, isn't it?'

'The First Born may cross at many a place, be there water or no, but there must be water if you wish to cross with one who is not of your race.'

'It is almost as if someone calls for me, but not with a voice that touches the ears, more one that ...' Elmo held a hand to his heart. 'It makes me feel happy, and terribly sad at the same time. Is it time for me to cross?'

'Not yet, I think, but one day, near the far end of time, you will come to such a place as this, and then you shall leave behind the cares of this world and join your sisters and brethren ... and it may be that you shall take someone with you.'

Finn? Elmo knelt and dipped his fingers into the water of the lake. It was icy, but there was something else – a tingly feeling that suffused his whole body. He had been with a woman only once and even then long ago, before he took his vows, but he was reminded of intimate pleasures and the warmth that followed lovemaking. He stood and raised his wet hand, letting the water trail down beneath his loose sleeve. The lake was like a deep pool of black in the lighter black of the evening, and all was silence but for the natural sounds of night. There, an owl, and now a vixen calling.

'What is it like, this place to where one day I shall cross?'

Mundwyn touched the water, just as Elmo had a few moments earlier. 'First there are the borders, where I have been and where many First Born tarry. As to its likeness it cannot be explained in words. And then there is a deeper part of the realm from where there is no return, for to be there is to be a part of all there is, and to return to the world of men would be to tear out your heart. It is a place where time has no meaning and distance is not as we know it here. Beyond that, I cannot say.'

Elmo pressed a hand to the middle of elderly brother's back. 'Thank you Mundwyn, for bringing me here. Before I come again, I must fulfil Alcuin's quest.'

'*We* must fulfil it, and I think we should begin tomorrow.'

When the next day came, Elmo, Mundwyn and Finn prepared for the journey to Skol-Jerrag which Mundwyn said was further north than from where they had set off nine days before. Mary wished to stay behind and care for Eric until he had settled in.

'You may lay with Eric,' Finn said to Mary. 'For I have grown to like him, and it has been a long time since his wife was taken from him. But you must think of me as he covers you.' Finn recoiled as Mary aimed a slap at his face, failing to avoid the blow. 'What was that for?'

'Finn, my friend,' Elmo said. 'Let me give you good advice. Before you say anything involving lying with people or any other form of coupling, stop and think and you may save giving offence.'

Finn was still rubbing the sting out of his cheek when Mary stood up on tip-toe and kissed him and told him to behave until his return.

The journey went well and the ponies performed courageously. Now there was room in the wain, Finn sat inside and let his pony trail behind on a long rein.

On the sixth day the party was assailed by brigands who thought to rob them and perhaps slit their throats, but the attackers had numbered their victims as an old man and a youth and thought to outnumber them two-to-one. They had not allowed for Finn in their calculations, hidden as he was under the cover of the wain, and he exploded from it with such ferocity that he was as good as any two lesser warriors.

They rolled the bodies of the brigands into a ditch before they continued on their road. Elmo had never killed a man before and for the first time since he stood by the lake, his mood was soured and the ethereal warmth dispersed. Finn on the other hand was elated that he had slain more enemies.

Two days later with Hexham behind them, they came upon a young man begging for food by the roadside and

255

Mundwyn took pity on him, dishevelled and bloodstained as he was.

'Beg upon the greater road, and you may find more custom,' Elmo said. 'This road probably sees no more than two or three travellers in a day.'

'I fear the great road, for I am a fugitive, accused of a crime I did not commit, and I will be hung if I am taken again.'

Finn began to question him as to his crime but the lad interrupted him.

'Forgive me, but your voice. It has a strange sound to it, and I heard it before. Did we not meet on the Bamburgh road?'

'Why, it's the rear-guard scout who lost his little brother to the marauding Northmen,' Elmo cried. 'How came you to such hard times?'

Acwel told his tale. A wifey had taken a fancy to two older warriors and her daughters had gone to Acwel and his friend, all smiles and fluttering eyelashes. He had lain with a daughter of the blacksmith while his friend lay with her sister and they had taken so much delight in their play that laughter and cries of pleasure brought their father to the house, whereupon one of the girls began to cry rape.

'First I was sentenced to hang, but even as the rope was tightened about my throat a reprieve came and I was to be gelded instead and put away into a monastery.'

'I'm sorry for you loss,' Finn said indicating the bloodstains at the young man's crotch. 'I must say you bear it well.'

'I bear nothing but a small nick low on my belly. The fat thegn who was charged with the task of depriving me took pity and instead dealt the smallest of cuts for appearances sake, so blood would flow from the expected area and fool his less kindly confederates. We were then to be taken under guard to the monastery two days march south, but the guards were lazy and meant to toss us dead into a ditch instead and spend the days drinking in the inn. My friend, who you also met, was killed but I managed to brain one of the guards and make good my escape.'

'What say you lads? Do we have room for another in our quest?' Mundwyn asked.

Neither Elmo nor Finn had any objection, and Acwel was happy to lend his services for bread and ale. And so the little party took on Acwel, and that was to be their downfall.

The following night they fell in with a party of travelling players and they spent a merry time carousing about the fire and telling tall tales and listening to many fine stories from a collection called *The Deeds of the Romans*. When the players asked a story in return, Acwel told his own sorry tale, so thinly disguised that one of the players slipped off in the night sensing there may be reward to be had for one who could lead the watchmen to a fugitive.

Mundwyn sensed the treachery and he rose early to wake his friends, and they made off before the players stirred. They avoided going near towns where they might be known and at all times they chose the lesser road, the small tracks or sometimes the open countryside marked by neither lane nor path. At Chatton they bought cheese and bread and then set off on the last leg of their journey where the hills grew taller and the chances of attack by brigands grew in a like manner.

On the last night before they were hoping to reach Skol-Jerrag, they found refuge at the inn of a small town and there they sat by the fire where they warmed their ale. By and by the conversation turned to the great and the good of the land, and as chance would have it, talk eventually came to Godwin and Acwel told that he had heard word of his death. When Elmo told Acwel about his brother's treatment at the hands of Godwin, he was pleased that the lord had died as he did.

'That such revenge may one day be dealt upon the cowardly Northmen,' Acwel said. And then he went on to curse them and he heaped scorn upon them and likened them to walking middens. Elmo knew that Finn was struggling to hold in any words that might defend his kin, and he tried to steer the conversation to other matters, but time and again Acwel returned to insult the Northmen with ever more filthy and loathsome comparisons. 'See here!' he

257

said drawing forth a trinket that attached around his neck on a thing of leather. 'I had this from the fish-eaten body of one of the scum, washed up onto the beach.'

Elmo recognised it as being very similar to the one Finn wore.

'One of their bawdy-faced gods, so much good it may do them,' Acwel said and launched into a new tirade.

Mundwyn then stepped in and tried to draw Finn outside, but Finn was routed to the spot, fumes almost pouring from his ears, there for all to see except Acwel in his cups.

'Why, if ever I should meet one of the dog turds I'd …' He was cut off as Finn slapped the cup from his hands.

'I stand before you, pip-squeak.' He put his head close to Acwel's ear. 'And I am of the race you so demean.'

Acwel was upon him in an instant and the pair of them rolled onto the floor upending tables and spilling the ale-pots of other revellers. Acwel's nose was smashed by Finn's fist, blood and snot flying, and then Finn found his thumb half-bitten through.

All this took but moments, because in that time Mundwyn had seized Finn and Elmo had Acwel by the collar, and both were dragged out with the help of the innkeeper and his sons.

'Leave off!' Elmo called. 'We needs must be fit and hale for Skol-Jerrag, for our work will be heavy.'

Mundwyn gave Elmo such a look, but it was too late. He had shouted his words, and any number of people had overheard. Something in their faces drew the anger from the combatants and they felt the stupidity of their ways.

'Gather your things,' Mundwyn said. 'We must leave at once and travel through the night.'

It was not a good decision, for they lost their way in the dark and when dawn came they discovered their error. They lost much time finding the right road and eventually came to the river valley below the hill that was once the seat for Skol-Jerrag in the late afternoon of the following day. Only Mundwyn had any idea where they were in relation to the lands they knew. They were hungry and tired, but they had no choice except to climb up to the site of the First Born town.

They approached from the east and the ponies found no hardship in the gentle slope. The walls of the ancient and long gone town stood to waist height in places and here and there remained clues as to its former greatness. Some of the inner walls bore signs of artwork and other's showed a few flakes of gilding.

'Great were the wall-stones, raised by giants,' Mundwyn mused.

'What was that, old man?' Finn asked.

'Oh, just part of a poem I once heard. It speaks of time undoing the work of men, and it feels right for this place.'

'More like the work of giants being pillaged by men for their farmsteads if you ask me,' Finn said. 'Time hasn't played such a big part here.'

'Time has many agents,' Mundwyn said. 'Now, no more time for talk. We must find a place for Alcuin's stone.'

'With the book inside, of course,' Elmo said.

'And a little something I added myself, before I sealed it,' Mundwyn said.

'Our doom is upon us,' cried Acwel as he pointed back down the hill. 'Here come monsters!'

There were five riders in all and there was little doubt they had spotted the party upon the hill, for they approached at a gallop.

Elmo ran for the wain and snatched up his sword. Finn did likewise and took up a shield he had secured for the journey. He threw Mundwyn the sword of Eovan Tucarus and pressed a long seax into Acwel's hand.

'Good odds,' Finn cried with a grin. 'Four of us and only five of them!' He laughed like a drunkard.

The riders moved swiftly and were soon upon them. The band of four stood at guard and the riders reined in forming a half-circle about them.

'Heaven shines upon us, Brand,' said the leader. 'We fly in pursuit of a villain and scoundrel and find the old King's son in his company. And who else do we have here? Name yourselves!'

259

'I am Brother Mundwyn of the Order of Blue Friars. And you sir?'

Earldorman Dunstan Chase introduced himself and said they had no need of the names of his retainers. 'I have no argument with old men or youthful warriors, but I'll have the villain to hang as should have happened in the first place.' He scowled at the portly thegn who lowered his eyes. 'And you sir with your red hair, Elfgar son of Elfward, King Ethelred has a passion for your head, and sorry to say, your head alone, and so I mean to relieve you of it.'

Acwel lost his nerve, turned and fled over the falling wall-stones and towards the south west.

Dunstan Chase gave one of his warriors a brief command. 'Picard here, he has the Parthian's talent of old, and can shoot an arrow while in the saddle. I'll have the felon shot as soon as hung.'

There was a zip as the fletched arrow passed close over Elmo's head, and a sharp cry as it struck Acwel low in the left side of his body. Elmo took his eye off the enemy before him for a brief moment and looked over his shoulder in time to see Acwel disappearing over the brow of the hill, still running with the arrow embedded deep.

Chase appeared bored. 'Go finish him,' he said, and Picard kicked his horse to a canter.

Mundwyn changed his position so that Picard couldn't ride up from the rear unchallenged.

'Five against three then,' Finn said. 'Do your worst pony-boys!'

'Better odds than that,' came a deep, smooth voice close to Elmo's right ear. It was a voice he knew but he could not take his eyes from the enemy, who now started in surprise and struggled to keep their mounts under control. One of the enemy knights reined his horse around sharply and galloped off down the hill as if pursued by a dragon, and then Elmo could restrain himself no longer. He looked, and standing by his side in splendid armour was Eovan Tucarus and two other First Born warriors, all with plumed helmets of polished iron and byrnies rich with polished plate that gave off the colours of oil upon water in the bright sunlight.

Each carried a spear and a shield and Eovan approached Mundwyn and asked if he might have his sword back.

'It's no use in my hands, except for show,' Mundwyn said. 'Take it, and with my gratitude.'

Chase worked to control his horse. 'From where did you three spring, for I but blinked from the sun in my eyes and then there you were where you had not been before?'

'We travel at will between the places that were once ours. Now, lay-on or be gone.' Eovan stood on guard his spear-tip levelled.

'Then we shall do battle,' Dunstan Chase said, whereby his remaining retainers, all but for Brand Buckley, turned tail and galloped off towards the north east, down the gentle slope as fast as their mounts would carry them.

'How quickly the odds change,' Chase said, steadying his horse and assuming a relaxed pose. 'Now just two against six.'

'Then go,' Eovan said putting up his spear. 'I shall not prevent you nor give chase. My argument with you springs forth only when you attempt harm upon my prince.'

Dunstan Chase put up his sword. 'Another day perhaps.' He saluted and Brand Buckley sighed with relief. He began to rein round but stopped and turned back to face the First Born noble. 'I take it you'll have no objection if I tell the King I slew Elfgar?'

'None at all,' Eovan said. 'There is advantage to it if your king ceases to hunt him.'

'Then might I take the villain's head as proof? I will keep it a while and serve it up to the King when corruption has blurred the features.'

'He was no villain, sir,' Elmo said.

'But take the head,' Eovan said quickly. 'It will support the deception.'

Chase began to walk his pony towards the falling slope but Finn stood in his way.

'You stay. I'll take his head and bring it to you.'

When Finn came to the edge of the falling ground, he was not presented with the view he had expected. Picard, the horse-bowman laid dead in the grass, his horse nibbling

261

at the bloody blades nearby and occasionally nuzzling his master's body. Further down, Acwel sat, nursing the arrow shaft that was now broken off in his side.

Elmo watched Finn turn and cry 'Acwel lives!'

Elmo ran to see as Finn disappeared below the brow and before he got to the brow himself he heard a cry and a scream. Horror froze him as he looked down the slope in time to see Finn on his knees, and Acwel strike him a slashing blow across the face.

'His kin killed my brother,' Acwel called up to the party assembled in shock by the crumbling walls of Skol-Jerrag, and then Dunstan Chase kicked his ponies flank and it surged forward.

Acwel saw his doom upon him and he turned to run as fast as he could with an arrow-head in him. He did not see the swinging blow that took off his head.

Elmo had no time left for the dead and he ran down the slope to Finn who was pitched forward upon his front. He turned him over and almost recoiled from the horror of Finn's ruined face. His tunic was blood-soaked and from a cruel gash below his ribs some innards oozed, slick with blood.

One side of Finn's mouth smiled and he tried to talk but he could not form the words with a slashed jaw. He held a hand tight to his cheek and tried again. 'Tonight …' he said, the word just discernible. 'My ancestors.'

Elmo swallowed hard. 'Yes, Finn, you will dine with them.'

Finn breathed deeply and tried to sit up. Mundwyn dropped to his knees and supported him.

'Bury me with the book-stone. Let me guard it through the long ages.'

'We will put it to ground where you lay, Finn son of Bjorn,' Mundwyn said.

Finn let out a ragged groan and then laughed. 'Isn't dying a lot like rutting,' he said, and then his body quivered and his face showed the same mask of pain it had worn when he was in the throes of passion. And life left him, slowly exhaled upon Finn's last breath.

Elmo was numbed and he sat motionless and unaware of his surroundings for many moments, until Mundwyn touched Finn's bloody face, patted it as if comforting a lonely child.

'Until we meet again, brave Finn,' Mundwyn said and then he helped Elmo to his feet. Mundwyn stooped to remove Finn's cloak-pin which he handed to Elmo as a keepsake.

From Finn's bloody face Elmo's gaze fell upon Acwel's severed head as Dunstan Chase lifted it to look into the dead eyes.

'I have my head,' he said. 'If it's all the same to you I'll take the carcase too. We'll dress it in monk's clothes to bolster our lie. Ethelred will know no better than that you, young Elfgar, are as dead as your brothers.'

'Did you kill them too?' Elgar said.

A cloud passed over Dunstan Chase. 'I am ashamed to say I had my part in their fate, but Godwin slew them … eventually. First they were …'

Elmo held up his hand and looked away. 'Spare me the detail.'

They all helped to bury Alcuin's stone-encased book, over which they laid the body of Finn. Elmo reached down and removed Finn's hammer-of-Thor necklace and put it back on so that the eyes looked up to the sky, and then Dunstan Chase dropped in the arrow-head that had pierced Acwel and was still wet with his blood.

They had lined the grave with stones carried from Skol-Jerrag and another they placed over the top, and then filled it with soil and laid over the turfs they had cut.

Mundwyn said a prayer, but it felt wrong to Elmo even though he bowed his head as did the others. This was not a fitting send off for Finn and Elmo wished he knew more of the Northmen's beliefs.

The men, First Born and inheritors, stood about the grave awkwardly, until Elmo felt a little of Finn's spirit stir inside him. He drew his blade, threw back his head and called out as loud as he could.

263

'Raven-Fish!' he cried, and the words were thrown back at him, time and again, now from the left, now the right, as echoes bounced around the hills.

The others all drew their own swords, and Elmo thrust his in the air as a signal, and seven voices raised to the Heavens as one and it was as if the hills were filled with an hundred warriors and all were crying out as heralds so that Finn might be received by the warriors of long ago.

Raven-Fish! Raven-Fish! echoed long into the night. Raven-Fish! trembled the stones and became part of the land's memory.

'I have no grudge against your kind,' Chase said when all was eventually silent. He spoke to Elmo and Eovan Tucarus. 'How can I?' he said touching a finger to the side of his nose, 'For you do not exist. I will wake tomorrow and find this has all been but a dream. You are last night's cold pottage sitting heavy on my stomach.'

'When Rome believes such, our troubles will be over,' Eovan said.

'And yet, your day is over. Of the First Born, how many still live in the world of men?'

'Less than I would like, but more than you think, for in man is the seed of the First Born. And as for our day, it comes to a close whilst it is yet to begin.'

Chase grinned. 'Never let it be said that the First Born speak in riddles. In this world of lies, there is surely room for one more.'

Earldorman Dunstan Chase and Brand Buckley took their leave and rode away leading two spare horses, one carrying the body of Picard the bowman and the other the wrapped bundle that had once been young Acwel.

'Now, Elfgar – who shall be known as Elmo no longer – it is time for us to leave. We have long awaited your presence at the halls of our fathers.' Eovan removed his gauntlet and offered his hand.

'What of Brother Mundwyn?'

'My time here is done. I must travel the Hidden Paths to another place, and speak of our adventures to a man who will set them all down in a book. And then I will join my

264

friend who has waited for me for many long years, and who I have been happy to serve.'

'Friend is a fine word,' Elmo said and he looked briefly to the disturbed earth that was now Finn's bed. 'And perhaps such friendship awaits me, but it must be in this world. I am not ready for the realm of the First-Born.'

There came the sound of many drawn swords, but softer, like the army of the dead preparing for battle, filling the hills with its gentle reverberation and thrilling through Elmo's bones, and when he turned to enquire of the others, whence the sound might have come, he found he was quite alone. Mundwyn had gone, and the First Born knights might never have existed.

Elmo was afraid, until he knelt onto the wet grass by Finn's grave and pressed his fingers to the soil. 'Guard our secrets well, Finn, unto a time when men may listen.'

A cold mist descended all around, and when Elmo tried to return to where the ponies were, within the falling walls of Skol-Jerrag, he could not find his way and he was lost. Trembling with the cold he cast about here and there but it was no good, until he spied a small light, flitting hither and thither like a moth and he thought he heard a song, as faint as breath, so faint in fact that it might have been in his head. *Hinkey-punk, hinkey-punk, follow my light, First Born to sunshine, all others to night.* Elmo followed and with the coming of dawn the mist dispersed and he was in another place, but one which he knew. There was a lake before him set in a green wood and sunlight slanted down through the trees touching his frozen form and warming him.

A young woman collected water in an earthen pitcher and she sang, her voice light and cheerful. A young man sat on the bank nearby with a fishing pole.

'Mary! Is that you?' Elmo called in disbelief.

The young man turned from the lake to reveal bandaged eyes and made a grunt that sounded like 'Elfgar'.

By no known means, Elmo had come to Faennas Sandrin and the reunion with his brother and Mary was sweet, and for a while the sweetness banished all questions. When the greetings were done, Mary told how a warrior had

265

come, in a byrnie of silver rings with plates at the shoulders and a tall helm that shone with all the colours of the rainbow. He told them to expect Elmo, whom he called Elfgar, and that he would come to them by secret paths. Elmo wondered if the First Born knight had told Mary about Finn, but her happiness told him otherwise. There was something in the way she looked at Eric, the lightness of her touch as she guided him. Perhaps she wouldn't take the news as badly as he feared.

'This is such a place as you can hardly imagine,' Eric wrote on his slate as he led his brother in through the great doors of the longhouse.

'Come,' Mary added. 'You must stay and listen to the wonderful tales that are told here.'

Elmo let his muscles truly relax for the first time in many weeks. Yes, he would stay here a while, and hear the tales of other people, before pressing on into the world to forge his own.

'Are there eggs to be had?' Elmo asked. 'For I have a fearful hunger upon me, and a craving for collops.'

'Oh, plenty!' Eric wrote. 'And we don't even have to climb a cliff to find them.'

Afterword

Clare and I have become very good friends. In fact she and her boyfriend are sharing accommodation with Harry and me as I write. We're staying in a delightful holiday cottage for four and we're just half a mile from where Father and Raz … I was about to say *drowned* but I think I'll opt for *were last seen*. After all, their bodies were never found despite the divers and the dredging hooks, and it's not as if it is a terribly large lake.

This morning we all went down to the lake and Clare pointed out the hide and the little square jetty that the fly fishermen use. The area is a little haven of wildlife and beauty, and if you were compelled to choose a place to end your life, you could hardly pick better.

Clare is a keen wildlife photographer and she specialises in birds. That bright April morning she had set up early in the hide – a proper wooden shed-like construction where a twitcher or a photographer might sit with a fair amount of comfort. There was a slight mist on the water and Clare took a beautiful shot of the scenery thinking how lovely it would be to mount and frame for her living room.

At first she had been annoyed when the two strangers intruded into her solitude and she had been on the verge of politely asking them to remove to elsewhere when the younger of the two started to undress. *Scrumptious*, Clare thought. *Cute guy skinny dipping.* He let his shirt fall to the deck and looked up into the brightening sky, exposing his throat. The older man reached out and briefly touched his neck with the back of his fingers.

'I've never noticed it before.' the older man said. 'It's quite diffuse.'

The younger man brought his hand up to cover the mark, which was too distant for Clare to see, but did not reply. After a second or two he continued to undress. By the time he got down to his dazzling white briefs, Clare admitted without a hint of shame, she had her thousand millimetre lens trained on him and somehow she no longer resented the intrusion. Clare described Raz as an utterly stunning specimen of young manhood and contemplated letting the shutter fall. Things took a slight downturn when the older gentleman began to disrobe, but whereas she was a bit put out that the young man kept his underwear firmly in place, she was rather relieved when the senior member of the pair followed suit. She added, no doubt for my benefit, that he actually wasn't half-bad for a middle-aged man: just the slightest hint of a paunch and well-muscled – she would have gone into more detail but I stopped her. Who wants to think of their father in his underwear?

The morning was very still, and although they were at least thirty metres away, when they spoke Clare heard their conversation with clarity.

'Can you feel it?' Father had said.

'Oh yes,' Raz replied. 'Feel it, and hear it to. They're calling.' There was a catch in the young man's voice, and Father comforted him with a brief shoulder squeeze. It was curiously tender and Clare took the pair for father and son.

'Shall we?' Father said.

And then Raz helped Father down (he looked like he had bad knees, Clare said) and he sat on the deck dangling his feet into the water. He shuffled his bottom to the edge and then dropped into the lake, emerging with a sharp intake of breath. A moorhen scooted out from a nearby bed of reeds calling out in alarm. The water must have been freezing. It was then that Clare noticed Dad appeared to be holding a trowel in one hand. She hoped he wasn't planning to dig things up. That would have been an appalling assault on a place of such beauty.

Raz then dived in making hardly a ripple.

A bit cold for swimming, Clare thought, but the young man and the older splashed each other and larked about like a pair of kids for a moment before striking off purposely for the centre of the lake.

A heron was disturbed and flew out from the reeds and Clare tried to get a bead on it with her camera, but it was too fast for her and anyhow, the light was wrong. When she looked back at the lake, the swimmers were no longer there and only the slightest of ripples hinted that they ever had been.

Clare had been so shocked that she ran out to the bank calling for them. Thinking they might have swum underwater for some considerable distance, she ran round the lake calling and calling, an ever increasing feeling of dread closing about her.

Her mobile was useless. There was no signal by the lake, so running the half mile back to the cottage, almost entirely uphill, she arrived at the site office completely out of breath, but managed to convey the seriousness of the situation.

As I have already said, neither Father nor Raz were ever found, despite a prompt response from the emergency services.

Their clothes were on the deck where they had left them, but there was no note, no letter to relatives, nothing to indicate any intention to commit suicide.

In one of Raz's trouser pockets was a small and heavily worn trinket containing a rolled up strip of soft gold. *I am Elfgar, First Born Prince*, it read. He had found three then, in that ancient grave, not two, and was light-fingered enough to hold one back. That's what the faculty intimated. After all, he had nicked a lot of faculty equipment, so why not a little piece of treasure-trove as well?

In Father's shirt pocket was his wedding ring. There was a wallet with the usual array of cards, and that was it.

Well, the press had a field day. One national hinted, in a non-actionable way, that they were star-crossed lovers. Excuse me while I die laughing, what utter bollocks! (Got that from Dad - sorry). Dad might have been ever so slightly homo-romantic, but he certainly wasn't homosexual. (He had quite a thing going for Toyah Wilcox … and Darcy Bussell). Other articles said they were partners in crime who couldn't face the music. Just as ridiculous, if you want my opinion. They'd have ended up with a small fine or a conditional discharge even if they were found guilty. Finally there were stories along the lines that they had ruined their careers and couldn't face a life stacking shelves in a supermarket. Luckily the coroner wasn't swayed by such silly speculation and verdicts of accidental death were returned.

You've read the book, or rather the books, *The Assistant* and *Raven-Fish!* You've seen the parallels. You are possibly wondering do I believe that Father and Raz drowned that morning, or were they somehow whisked into the realm of the First Born? Ask my head and then ask my heart. You'll have two opposite answers. Let's just say my heart recently had some re-enforcements. Two days ago as I was packing to come here, I had a visitor. It was the man Father has consistently called 'Dr Smith', and so I shall call him that too.

He phoned first to see if it would be convenient to call. I was ready to give him a piece of my mind, and I liked the idea of doing it face to face, so I agreed. He was due at three, and the doorbell went at ten seconds past. I opened the door and Dr Smith stood there like some kind of aged suitor with a bunch of cut flowers and an air of embarrassment. The flowers were actually quite lovely and they took the wind out of my sails.

He took his coffee black. He liked my flat and nodded an acknowledgement to Harry who nodded back before disappearing into the kitchenette.

He wondered if I knew that he and my father didn't always see eye to eye.

'Really,' I said. 'I had no idea. He always spoke so highly of you.' I felt there was room to make him squirm.

'We were quite good friends at university,' he said smiling and looking out of the window, perhaps to glimpse a shade of those days long past. 'But we began to move in different directions and had our disagreements.'

'You mean, his book, with all those bad comments on Amazon, and each one-star reviewer recommending your book instead?' I do believe he blushed.

'I could never convince him, but that had nothing to do with me.' His eyes shifted down to the right.

'Oh well, water under the bridge. Dad used to laugh about it so much,' I said lying through my smiling teeth. Dad used to froth at the mouth, more like.

Dr Smith regaled me with a couple of tales of what they used to get up to when they were boys, and then we moved on to the business in hand.

'You're aware no doubt, that your father and Raz uncovered a skeleton close to Blyth Hill Fort? Well, we're pretty certain it was that of a Viking, from a Thor's hammer necklace and the remains of a sword we found among the bones. Curiously the skeleton showed signs of wounds that pretty much matched the description of what befell Finn in the last chapter of *Raven-Fish!* and there was even an arrow head. I take it you read the transcript?'

I affirmed. 'Did you find Alcuin's book?' That was mentioned in *Raven-Fish!* as well. In fact it is pretty much the purpose of the whole story.

Of course they found the book, inside the stone just as it had been written, sealed with melted lead and wrapped in linen and soft leather and then more linen soaked in grease and then the whole lot dipped in wax. The book, once they had extracted in from its many protective layers, was found to be in as near perfect a condition as a thousand-year-old old book buried in the ground can be.

The Truth of the First Born, a compilation of texts removed from the records of the day with a narration by Alcuin of York himself, was the archaeological find of the century and it threw light onto a people for whom the early church had apparently taken a severe dislike.

'Beaker Folk, we call them,' Dr Smith said. 'We have learnt they were known at the time as the First Born, just as *Raven-Fish!* suggests, and there was a lot of airy-faerie superstition surrounding them. All nonsense, of course.'

Of course.

The Doctor told me there would soon be papers written and books published and that he would make it his personal business to fully acknowledge my father's part in the discovery. 'I think we can gloss over the unofficial circumstances of the discovery,' he said. 'But ...'

Here the Doctor failed and he suddenly seemed preoccupied with the shine on his very well polished shoes. There was something else inside the hollow stone,

271

something that was very hard to explain; a veritable conundrum.

Dr Smith opened his briefcase and took out something wrapped in a square of white cloth. He unwrapped it.

'It was this,' he said as he handed me a very ordinary but ancient trowel. It hadn't been quite as well protected as the book. 'You see here, it bears the rune for the letter K. Your father used to carry one very like it when we were students.'

I took the trowel and he emitted a little yelp of anguish as if I were mishandling an ancient relic. 'I guess trowels are trowels. I'm not that surprised they haven't changed their appearance over the centuries,' I said.

He leaned forward and pointed to a barely discernible engraving on the diamond-shaped blade: there were the initials WHS. 'Yes, but as venerable a company as they may be, I don't think *William Hunt & Sons* was big in the eight century.'

'Well, one blade to solve another,' I said. 'By Occam's Razor, unless your suggesting Father found a way to go back in time, the only explanation is that somebody put the trowel in stone fairly recently. You just don't know how yet.'

'I was there when the stone casket was opened.'

I pondered for a second. 'Was *William Hunt & Sons* about in the nineteen-thirties? Because if so it's pretty obvious Jason Bennett is behind all this.'

'I'm certain it's an old company, but that still doesn't explain the rune. You see, I … borrowed it once back in university days and it was by this rune that your father identified it as his.'

'I can hardly imagine he was the only Tolkien fan at university back in the seventies. The place was probably teeming with them, especially in archaeology. There're probably thousands of tools marked with runes.'

'I dare say, but it doesn't help me to understand the incompatible readings I get when I subject the trowel and the material it was touching inside the rock to carbon dating techniques, but as you say …'

If the poor Doctor thought his brain was about to explode wait until he reads *The Assistant*. I'd read it and I was struggling to reconcile known facts with impossible explanations.

It was just after Dr Smith took his leave that I first considered juxtaposing *The Assistant* with *Raven-Fish!* I hope it has provided an interesting diversion for you, at least for a few hours. For me, it helps my heart to overcome my head. In dark days my head rules and I am driven to tears at the thought of my father's deep unhappiness, for why else drown yourself? And Raz, just a few years older than me and so disturbed. But the dark days are few. Most often I go with my heart as I did this morning, standing on that deck that protrudes into the lake, from where my father and Raz slipped into the water. I strained to hear something, and for a moment or two I thought I did.

Harry joined me and slipped his hand into mine. 'Are they out there?' he whispered.

'I don't know where they are Harry, but on days like this I know they are somewhere.'

'What about the other days, when reality and logic creep in?'

'I get through them, because I know there'll be another day, not to far away, when I can dream again.'

Rachel K.
Beacon Hill

THE END

273

Acknowledgements

For their friendly assistance and expert advice: Dr Edward C. Harris, inventor of The Harris Matrix; Paul Morrison, RSPB Manager of Coquet Island; Elizabeth Williams, Historic Environment Record Officer, Northumberland County Council; Eleanor Rideout, Public Service Officer RCAHMS and Heather Pettie, Force Information Officer, Lothian & Borders Police.

For providing the cover image for the First Edition (in this edition as an illustration near the front of the book, with a detail on the back cover): my good friend Zak Thomas (model), and Emma Barrott (photographer).

Other Novels by David Lister

The Last Spellherder

'The Last Spellherder' is the epic tale that introduces 'The Rillton Cycle', a series of stand-alone contemporary fantasy/folklore stories that spring from a mysterious wood near the fictitious Shropshire town of Little Rillton. It is Jason's story, which spans disparate worlds and peoples.

Sex, and constant travel: the only activities that give Jason respite from the insidious Shadows. Either on the run, or on the prowl, his life is spent traversing Britain's motorway networks, trying to keep one step ahead of his nemesis.

There is no escape, only short periods of relief. Jason has always believed that the dark beings are a curse, attributable to an aberration of the mind. But one day he learns they are a threat of a much greater magnitude. They are the eyes of a hunter, and mankind is its prey.

Come Away O Human Child!

Set five years after the 'The Last Spellherder'.

Events draw Chris De'Ath into a world of legends.

If you live in either of the Rilltons or Axenwhit, the Fey Knights, or Young Gentlemen, will almost certainly be part of everyday conversation. But unlike other folk tales, they rarely stray from the valley. Their other unusual quality is that they refuse to behave like good little legends and stay within the pages of books. The legends live, and they prove deadly and terrifying to Chris, who would rather be tackling the universal problems of young manhood than fighting with Fey Knights.

For Chris De'Ath, there is no choice.

Children of Bast

Set a little after 'Come Away O Human Child'.

Just because Wymes Forest is a magnet for all things weird and otherworldly, it doesn't mean it is immune from the more mundane forms of disaster, such as an aeroplane crash. But then, the aircraft itself is otherworldly, and the young pilot even more so.

Cappy Shirakawa, barman at 'The Moiled Bull' in the Shropshire town of Little Rillton, is growing tired of the work-a-day life. He wishes for adventure. He wants to be a hero.

Be careful what you wish for, Cappy. When you are far away in another world, perhaps you will wish for home.

Tallahatchie Timebomb
And Other Stories

The title story, a cold case murder investigation conducted by amateur sleuth and freelance researcher. A take on the story behind the song of a boy who jumped off a bridge.

Non-Fiction by David Lister

Die Hard, Aby!

The true story of Abraham Bevistein, the seventeen-year-old soldier shot in 1916 to encourage the others.